Readers love the Middle of Somewhere series by ROAN PARRISH

In the Middle of Somewhere

"*In the Middle of Somewhere* is a deeply character driven book, which I found at turns to be charming, delightful, fun and poignant. Some of the prose is beautiful and so very apt."

—Dear Author

"…this is a very enjoyable book, beautifully written, with well-drawn characters and just the right mix of angst, emotion and sensuality to make it a beautiful romance."

—Prism Book Alliance

Out of Nowhere

"Redeeming a villain isn't always easy, but Parrish does a great job with that here. I am really a big fan of this series and I am dying for the next book!"

—Joyfully Jay

"This is an absolute *read-this-the-fuck-now* book. I loved everything about it. I loved it as much as I loved the first book and cannot WAIT to read it again."

—Gay Book Reviews

"This book was such an incredible read that I find myself still thinking about. I highly recommend it!"

—Sinfully Gay Romance Book Reviews

By Roan Parrish

MIDDLE OF SOMEWHERE
In the Middle of Somewhere
Out of Nowhere
Where We Left Off

Published by Dreamspinner Press
www.dreamspinnerpress.com

WHERE WE
LEFT OFF

ROAN PARRISH

DREAMSPINNER PRESS

Published by

DREAMSPINNER PRESS

5032 Capital Circle SW, Suite 2, PMB# 279, Tallahassee, FL 32305-7886 USA
www.dreamspinnerpress.com

Where We Left Off
© 2016 Roan Parrish.

Cover Art
© 2016 AngstyG.
http://www.angstyg.com
Cover content is for illustrative purposes only and any person depicted on the cover is a model.

ISBN: 978-1-63477-690-5
Digital ISBN: 978-1-63477-691-2
Library of Congress Control Number: 2016909435
Published September 2016
v. 1.0

Printed in the United States of America
∞
This paper meets the requirements of
ANSI/NISO Z39.48-1992 (Permanence of Paper).

For the new friends who came into my life just when I was starting it over.

Acknowledgments

MY DEEPEST thanks to Anni and Jenny, for being the keenest of readers who always reminded me when I was missing the mark, and for the wicked smart conversations about monogamy, romance, and genre that got me closer to it.

To Liz, whose insight, generosity, and excitement about this book made it a joy to write. (Giving me the soundtrack didn't hurt either.)

To M.M., for solving a problem I didn't even know I had, and for enthusiasm about this story just when it helped the most.

To the other amazing readers who took the time to give me their thoughts on this book at all stages in the process.

To Joe and Alexis, for many thoughts about physics, among other things. (Any inaccuracies are mine alone and were either done on purpose because I wanted them that way or by accident because oops.)

To Layne and Ali, for hours of conspiracy theory realness.

To CMC, for being the best of all possible agents and readers, and for the title.

To my rad yoga teacher, whose approach to connecting the body, the mind, and the world has been an inspiration to me as well as to Leo.

To AngstyG, whose gorgeous covers for this series make me wish my books would be judged by them. Will would absolutely approve.

And to all the readers who told me how much you wanted Will and Leo's story. I hope you enjoy.

Chapter 1

September

IT ONLY took one day in New York City for me to break every single resolution I'd made.

Even after a year of dreaming what it would be like—a year of slogging back and forth between Grayling Community College and my parents' house—I hadn't even come close to anticipating how it would feel to actually leave Holiday, Michigan, much less to arrive in New York.

Nothing in any of the movies I'd seen prepared me for the feeling of watching the city rise like the distant sun of an alien planet miles and miles before the bus would reach it. It was just there, out the windows on both sides, its size an announcement: *you still have time to turn back.* Or: *once you enter you'll never get out again.* Or: *anything you could ever need is waiting for you.*

LATER, AFTER I'd found my way to the dorms, I helped people move in, since I only had two suitcases, a backpack, and my skateboard. They were bringing whole lives with them into their rooms when all I wanted was to leave mine behind.

I exchanged some variation on the themes of *What are you studying, Where are you from,* and *Have you met your roommate yet* about a dozen times in the process.

The first girl I told I was from Holiday wore black jeans, boots, and a short black jacket even though it was in the eighties outside, and she was so amused by the name of the town that afterward I just said Michigan. In fact, all my responses seemed to vaguely amuse people, and I could feel my smile become forced, the muscles in my jaw starting to ache and the skin around my eyes tight.

That was Resolution 1—*Make a good first impression*—scuttled.

I hadn't slept much on the bus, and what with all the changing buses and layovers on the way to New York, it already felt like the world's longest day even though it was still early. The mix of sleep deprivation and overstimulation had made me feel all fluttery and tweaked-out. I finally escaped back to my room, desperate to throw my clothes in drawers and veg with an episode of something on Netflix.

I wanted to rest up before Joseph, my roommate, arrived. Joseph and I had e-mailed all summer, planning to go to the new student orientation together, to scope out campus and the surrounding neighborhood and to locate all our classes before school started so we weren't wandering around like idiots. He'd been nice and funny; safe. And it'd been a relief not to be facing a new school all on my own, to say nothing of a whole new city.

When I opened my computer to find something comforting to watch, though, I found an e-mail from Residential Life instead. Joseph had declined to come to NYU at the last minute and they would be assigning me a different roommate in a few days. My heart started to pound and I closed my eyes. It was a small thing, I told myself. Not a big deal at all. But I guess I didn't believe myself because suddenly I was close to tears, and before I knew it, I'd done what I always did when I felt freaked out or overwhelmed, which had happened a lot this past year: I called Daniel. As friends went, he was pretty much it for me, though I constantly doubted whether he thought of me the same way.

I'd met Daniel two years ago when he'd moved to Holiday from Philadelphia to teach English at Sleeping Bear College in town. Everyone had been talking about him—at least, everyone who was part of the circuit of small business owners around Mr. Zoo's, the jumble-shop-cum-music-store where I worked.

At first, I was just curious. The mythology that had bloomed around him was intriguing, and the fact that one of the rumors was that he was gay made him irresistible. I wanted to see what all the fuss was about. I had begun developing a plan for how I'd choreograph our meeting. It would be casual, of course, subtle. I'd come off as cool and mature, and he wouldn't be able to help wanting to hang out with me. In the end, though, it hadn't gone anything like I'd planned.

Before I could even start phase one of Operation: Nab Daniel, he'd found me, swooping in to rescue me from getting my ass kicked by some jackasses I'd gone to high school with, like the hero of my own personal movie, vanquishing the bad guys with a few well-chosen words and gestures.

He was all messy hair and flashing green eyes and tattoos, his shirtsleeves rolled up after a day of teaching. So, okay, I kind of threw myself at him, but it wasn't just because he was hot. He was like a tornado I wanted to get caught up in—lifted and spun around and deposited in a world more colorful and magical than the black-and-white of Holiday.

Daniel was confirmation that there were other options out there. That there was a world outside of Holiday that didn't just exist in the books I read and the TV and movies I mainlined. I kind of made a fool out of myself making sure that he couldn't ignore me, but somehow I just *knew*. I knew that being friends with him would change my life. I'd been right, too. Because here I was, starting college in a brand-new city because he'd helped me with my applications and my essays, and encouraged me when I wanted to give up on the whole thing.

When Daniel answered the phone, I could tell he was in the middle of something because he was swearing and spluttering when he said hello.

"You okay?"

"What? Shit. Yeah, yeah, just tripped over the damn... thingie. Anyway, hey. You there? You all moved in? Everything okay?"

Just hearing his familiar voice and having someone ask if I'm okay nearly made me lose it. I blinked hard and stared out my window at the endless stream of people cutting through the courtyard.

"Yeah, I'm cool." I tried to sound casual, but it came out shaky, and Daniel knew me too well to be fooled.

"What's up?"

It came out in a sluice, but I knew Daniel would understand because it seemed like he felt kind of the same way when he first moved to Holiday.

"I don't know what I'm doing here, man. I don't even know where to start. My roommate's not coming and I don't know anyone and there's two days before classes but I'm already out of cash. I don't even know how 'cause all I bought was like a coffee and a sandwich. And there's this orientation thing, but I don't want to go do freaking icebreakers with people and talk about my major—I don't have a major. I just got here! Three people have asked me about my major. How do they have majors? I don't understand."

Daniel hummed sympathetically. "Oh Jesus, icebreakers. No. That's no good. Well, you could come here for the weekend if you want. BoltBus is cheap." He paused as his partner Rex said something in the background.

"Ha, yeah. We'll totally put you to work, though. I'm useless because they swapped my class at the last minute and now I have to do all this damn course prep in five minutes."

Just the thought of being around someone familiar calmed me down. The year before, Daniel and Rex had moved into an old industrial space that the owner was happy to rent out cheaply in exchange for Rex's promise that he could build in the interior. Rex had built his house in Michigan and was more than up to the task, in theory, but it had turned out to be a nightmare of zoning permits, arcane city mandates, and the kind of red tape that Rex abhorred, so they were still in the thick of it. Still, I'd gladly clear garbage or sand wood or scrub whatever they wanted if it meant I wasn't by myself here.

"Really? Yeah, man, I could totally help."

"Um," Daniel said, not really into the phone. All I could make out was *orientation* and then Rex's voice in response, pitched too low to hear. "Okaaay," Daniel drawled. "So, good point. Rex says shouldn't you go to orientation so you can meet all the people in your dorm and stuff?" Daniel sounded like it horrified him even more than it did me.

"I don't know." I just wanted someone to tell me what I should do. I could hear Daniel fumbling with the phone and then Rex's voice filled my ear.

When Rex talked I was generally incapable of doing anything but agreeing. Something about his voice just made me melt. Daniel too. I'd seen it happen. He'd start out listening to whatever Rex was saying and then slowly he'd lose the thread because he'd started focusing on the sound of Rex's voice instead of his words. You could tell the exact moment it happened because his eyes would go kind of sleepy and his hands would start to twitch like he was keeping himself from reaching out to touch Rex.

"It seems like a good way to meet people," Rex said. "Nice to know a few before classes start, huh? Might not be the most pleasant experience, but it's better than trying to do it on your own."

"Yeah, maybe."

"You're always welcome, Leo. But why don't you give yourself a chance to make some friends first? Get to know the city a little." He kind of trailed off, and I got the feeling he was talking to himself as much as to me. It was no secret that Rex hadn't been overjoyed to leave Holiday and move to Philly. He didn't like cities and he was shy around new people. Still, he'd wanted to be with Daniel, so he went.

"Yeah, you're probably right. Okay, cool. Well, I guess I'll see you guys. Sometime."

The second I hung up I slumped onto the bed I'd claimed. It was the one next to the window because it seemed nice to be able to glance outside while I sat there and did work, but now I wondered if it'd be too distracting, so I flopped onto the other bed to try it out. From this vantage point, the room seemed completely different. Choosing a bed was choosing between two totally different experiences of the room. Of what the world would look like all year. It was too big a decision for the moment.

In fact, *any* decision felt too big at the moment, so I just grabbed my skateboard and took off. At the street, I closed my eyes for a moment. A blanket of noise lay over everything: traffic, horns, heels hitting pavement, dogs yipping, people talking in every language, music, and, underneath it all, a hum that seemed to rise from the ground itself. It was almost more vibration than sound, as if I were standing on something alive. A great slumbering beast guarding a treasure.

As soon as my feet hit the deck of my board a car nearly sideswiped me in a flurry of honking horns and yelled profanities, and I hit the ground hard, my board skidding against the curb. Within moments fear transmuted into humiliation, and I just hoped no one saw. But, of course, there were people everywhere. The chill of fear gone, it was oppressively hot, the air hanging humid and still, the smells of pizza and smoke, perfume and exhaust suspended.

Shaking off the near miss, I walked around Washington Square Park, and I could hardly believe I was really here. The white stone seemed to glow as it absorbed the sunlight. The soaring arch at the entrance to the park stood out starkly against the blue sky like it could reach the clouds, dwarfing the trees. People passed through like threading a needle, and you could tell the locals from the tourists by who walked by without even sparing it a glance.

I was most assuredly *not* one of the locals, since I was blatantly staring at everything around me, head whipping from sight to sight like I was at a carnival.

That was Resolution 2—*Do not gawk at everything like a total noob*—down the drain, then.

I passed leathery-skinned men and women with their belongings tied up in plastic bags sitting on benches, talking without listening to each other. Some asked for change, some ignored me, and one blew me a kiss. They sat next to men in the nicest suits I'd ever seen, subtle grays, browns, and blues that I could tell, even without knowing anything about fashion, were top quality.

These men sat, resting slices of pizza on paper plates, falafel in foil, and plastic cups of chunked fruit on their elegantly crooked knees, holding newspapers, books, and phones in one hand and eating with the other. The business-y women mostly wore black, and they walked quickly, heels clicking the stones, sipping iced coffees through straws, sunglasses covering half their faces.

There was a set of tables inlaid with chessboards where a surprising collection of people played, some in silence, others bantering with familiarity like they'd been playing together for years.

My favorite pairing was an immaculately dressed African-American man who must've been in his eighties, skin burnished and perfectly manicured fingers clawed inward with arthritis, playing with a white girl who couldn't have been more than ten. She had light brown hair scraped into a raggedy ponytail, and pink wire-framed glasses, behind which she squinted at the board, her small hand with its dirty nails hovering above a piece.

As I walked by, she looked up at her opponent, clearly trying not to smile, and said, "Checkmate." He interlaced his fingers over his stomach and leaned back, assessing the board before nodding once, one side of his mouth lifting. He took off the tidy bowler hat he was wearing and perched it on the girl's messy head, tapping its brim so it slid her glasses down her nose.

Children chased pigeons up and down the park's corridors and parents chased children. Bikers twined around pedestrians lost in their phones and groups of slow-walking tourists taking pictures with selfie sticks or iPads held aloft. Around the perimeter of the fountain, couples sat, hands entwined, or leaning against each other. The sun was directly overhead, sparkling in the droplets of water the fountain kicked up.

I settled in the shade, finally, taking a cue from the less well-dressed, of which I was definitely one. A group of twentysomethings in shredded band T-shirts and cut-off denim sprawled under a tree, heads on each other's stomachs and fingers in each other's hair. Under another tree a family was having a picnic, one of the kids complaining about the heat, the bugs, the food.

I tried to cheer myself up by texting my sister Janie, *In NYC, sucker!* with a picture of the soaring stone arch, and watched for the screen to light up in my hand, but she must've been busy because she didn't write back.

I dozed off for a few minutes, unable to look away from the arch until my eyes closed, curtains coming down on the movie going on around me. A wet nose in the neck woke me, followed by a paw in the stomach. The puppy's owner came running over and apologized, but the golden retriever puppy was adorable, rooting around next to me and throwing itself on the ground. We chatted for a few minutes. The puppy belonged to his boss at the internship he'd just started the week before, and he was terrified of anything happening to it because he was convinced he'd somehow managed to incur his boss' wrath on his first day and didn't want to give the guy any more reasons to hate him.

I found myself telling him about my roommate situation, and he gave me a sweet smile and said, "Well, maybe the new roommate will be even better." I grasped at it desperately—this benediction from a stranger—in an attempt to renew my excitement. He was right! I was here, in New York City, starting over. Starting from scratch. And maybe that included a new roommate I hadn't planned for.

So I didn't know anyone in the city—that was okay. I'd meet people, surely.

Well, I knew one person.

Will Highland. It was Will I hadn't let myself think of on the trip from Michigan. But, honestly? That had just been a stubborn game to prove to myself that I had other reasons for coming to the city.

Will was always lingering in the back of my mind. He was a shadow in my periphery. An unopened gift that might be the thing I had most wished for, or the disappointment of that wish.

There should've been a term for the moments that, when you look back on them, preceded your whole life changing. There probably was one in German—some twisty compound word I didn't know. In a movie, there would've at least been a musical cue. Swooping strings that suddenly gave way to velvet quiet studded with the tinkle of bells as sharp as diamonds. Something that said *Pay attention: this next bit's important.*

But there hadn't even been any kind of bodily early-warning system when I met Will—no skipped heartbeat or light-headedness to indicate that something was about to happen. Nope. I had just fallen off my skateboard when I saw him, like an idiot.

I'd only known him for a few weeks. He had been in Holiday visiting his sister and I'd met him because he was Rex's ex. And, yes, maybe the first thing I'd noticed about him was that he was, hands-down, the most beautiful person I'd ever seen in my life. But it wasn't just that.

He had this… presence. This way of owning every inch of space around him as if he had a right to it. It was the kind of self-possession that can make a tyrant or a prince and Will was a fucking prince. You just got the sense that he knew exactly who he was and he'd never apologize for it. And, okay, I was pretty sure I had no hope of that rubbing off on me. But being around him made me feel like everything was right in my little world. I felt alive in a way I never had. In a colors-look-brighter, food-tastes-better, every-song-is-about-him way.

Though he never would have admitted it, we had… fit together in a way I'd never fit with anyone else. It wasn't that we were similar—we weren't. For every ounce of confidence Will possessed, I had an equal measure of dorkiness. But somehow it just worked. I felt different with him than I had with anyone else. Everything felt different with him.

If Daniel had been a tornado that promised me there was another world out there, Will's arrival in Michigan had been a blizzard—the cold snow and ice that snapped me back to reality, made me take a hard look at my life and what it was likely to become and feel the true terror of it. And if dreamy, distracted Daniel had offered escape, Will had been as sharply present as a pebble in my shoe, making me aware of every moment we spent together.

But that had been almost two years ago. When I'd gotten my letter of acceptance to NYU my heart had begun racing in my chest like a wild thing, as if a part of me was already surging full-speed ahead into the life I could have at an amazing college, in an amazing city.

The life I could have with Will.

I hadn't meant to go there, but my fantasies were traitors, constructing the life we'd have together with such insidious detail that my daydreams seemed almost more real than my actual humdrum life. I'd sit behind the counter at Mr. Zoo's, and my stupid brain would spin tales of swoony romance, corny inside jokes, easy domesticity, and, um, other stuff. Like, okay, fine: sex stuff.

It wasn't just Will, though. It was the promise of a future that was different than anything I'd let myself imagine. Freedom. Possibilities. Hope. When a letter from the financial aid office came a few weeks later, I'd torn it open without a second thought, a rush of pure happiness shooting through me at the purple NYU logo.

The gut punch of despair hit me as soon as I processed the contents of the letter: that they were only giving me enough financial aid to cover about a third of NYU's extremely pricey tuition. My fist tightened unconsciously, along with my stomach. I forced myself to smooth the letter out again and slide it back into the envelope, but every hope I'd let myself have was crumpled as easily as that crisp, watermarked paper.

And talking to Will was a reminder of everything I couldn't have if I didn't want to go into astronomical debt. Because though I felt sure that somehow Will was my destiny, there were some things that even destiny couldn't justify. I'd missed the hell out of talking to him, but it had just been too painful. Instead, I'd thrown myself into classes at the community college, determined to do well enough that the next year I'd get a full financial aid package and could roll up in New York with everything perfect. Just the way it was meant to be.

But now I was here, and every fantasy I'd had of Will being part of my life was stirring again, the slow unfurling of dormant seeds growing up through the ground to meet the light. I thumbed through my contacts to the end of the alphabet, even though he was already one of the five numbers in my Favorites.

Will answered just when I thought the call would go to voice mail, his clear voice electrifying me.

"Hey, kid. Get mugged yet?"

"Ha. How bad would you feel if I actually had gotten mugged?"

"At least a four out of ten."

"So, um, I'm here. Wanna hang out?"

Wow, that sounded like I was about ten. *Can Will come out and play?*

"I'm at work," he said, sounding vaguely amused.

"Oh, right." I had lost all sense of time. My stomach flipped, and I couldn't think of anything to say. It suddenly seemed imperative that I see him.

Voices were audible on Will's end of the conversation for a minute, and I thought I heard Will sigh. "Um, okay, do you want to meet up at my place later? Sixish?"

He gave me directions, but they got immediately jumbled in my relief and excitement about seeing Will in only a few hours. I had already failed at Resolution 3—*Memorize the subway map so you don't get lost and have to ask for directions constantly*—but I had GPS on my phone so whatever.

As I lay back down and stared up at the bright blue sky, I realized I was grinning.

IDEALLY, THE first time I saw Will in New York, I would've breezed through the door looking… I dunno, cute. Like, irresistibly cute. Instead, the back of my hair was flattened from riding with my head against a bus seat for twenty hours, my shirt was stuck to my spine with sweat, and my hands were dirty from sitting in the grass. I was also fairly certain that I'd stepped in something unspeakable on the subway, and I'd gotten dripped on by the air-conditioning units as I approached the building.

God, why hadn't I at least showered before coming here? My hands were so sweaty my thumb nearly slid off the button when I buzzed Will's apartment.

"Stairs are on your right."

Through the crackle, Will's voice was as clear and sharp as always, like even static had no power over him.

Whenever I'd pictured Will living in the city, I'd imagined his apartment building looking like the ones on TV: as modern and shiny and stylish as he was. But the building was… well, ugly. Brown and square and kind of lurking back from the sidewalk like it was embarrassed by its ugliness. And it was bizarre that he lived behind one of these doors, each exactly like the next, when he was completely different from anyone I'd ever met. But when he opened the door, he was so vivid it was like the whole apartment building had been made ordinary to better set him off, like a jewel in a plain setting.

When I'd been around Will for multiple days in succession in Michigan last winter, the effect had worn off a little, like I'd been inoculated. Now, seeing him again, I was so struck by the lines of him that it felt like I was falling. I was staring at him in what was probably a gooberish way, but he was so damn beautiful. Beautiful in an obvious way that everyone would agree on. Beautiful like I couldn't always concentrate on what he was saying because his words got lost somewhere around the curve of his full lower lip that dipped toward his sharp chin.

The lines of his jaw, nose, and cheekbones were clean and defined, his pale skin flawless except for a dark beauty mark over his lip and one next to his eyebrow. His eyes were this grayish-bluish color that could look cold and remote when he was in what Daniel called scornful fashion-model mode, or deep and mischievous when he was more approachable. His hair was longish on top and short at his neck, and this improbably light blond all the way to the roots, like he was limned in frost.

"Are you gonna come in or are you going to stand there gaping? FYI, you might want to lose the whole mouth-hanging-open look before you hit the streets, unless you really do want to get mugged." His teeth were straight, and white, and as sharp as his words, but he was smiling and his eyes sparkled. He was at least a little bit happy to see me.

"Hi," I said and went to hug him. He felt amazing in my arms, and I couldn't help hooking my chin over his shoulder to try and get a whiff of his hair. "Oh, wow, we're the same height now," I noted with my nose in his hair. I thought I heard him sigh a little, and I held on to him a beat after he tensed in my arms. "Sorry. I probably stink." I let him go, missing the feel of him immediately.

"What the hell happened to you?" Will said as he shut the door.

"What? Oh." The knees of my jeans were abraded where I hit the ground to avoid the car hitting me, and there was grass stuck in the creases where the fabric had rucked up above my high-tops. "This car almost hit me, man. It was ridic. Talk about defensive driving."

Will's eyes snapped to my face and then down to my skateboard, and he shook his head. I had almost forgotten how much he could communicate just by the way he looked at things.

"Lesson one," he said, getting me some water and leading me over to sit on the couch. "Everything in New York is designed to kill or maim you and everyone wants something from you. It is basically the Hunger Games. Trust no one. Be ever vigilant."

"Mix your *Hunger Games* and *Harry Potter* streams much? Nah. I met a totally nice guy in the park who I'm pretty sure wasn't trying to kill me. He had a puppy."

Will looked me up and down and winked. "Then he was trying to get in your pants. Puppies are sex bombs. That's not even an advanced technique."

"No! Puppies are *not* sex bombs. God, don't say that. Puppies!"

"True story, sorry. They're like babies. Everyone's already agreed that they know what our reactions to them should be. Have you noticed how pissed parents get if you don't smile at their baby? For real, they look at you like you're the devil."

"Um, I guess I usually smile at them?"

"Of course you do. Try it next time you're walking. Even the sweetest-looking East Village mom straight from baby-and-me yoga will cut a bitch if you don't smile at her baby."

"You just go around glaring at babies?"

"I didn't say I *glared* at them. I just don't smile at them because they don't amuse me. And, seriously, people act like you've broken a basic tenet of human interaction or something."

"And you enjoy this? Terrorizing babies and antagonizing yoga moms?" I teased.

Will's grin was mischievous. He slid down deeper into the couch. It was buttery black leather and, like so much about Will, seemed casually nice but was probably posh and expensive.

"So, did the fam give you a tearful send-off?"

I shook my head. "My mom dropped me off at the bus station in Detroit, but the bus left at like seven in the morning so everyone else was asleep. Besides…." I ran my palm absently over the soft leather of the couch. I was so aware of Will next to me, every shift of his body stirring the air between us. "They probably won't really notice that I'm not there anymore. Not like they cared that much that I was there before."

At Will's sober expression, I immediately felt disloyal to my family.

"I mean, it's not like they're terrible or anything, just… I don't have much in common with them. Like, Eric and my dad have their whole outdoorsy thing going on, and Janie and my mom are all into crafts and tutorials and Pinterest hacks." Will snorted in amusement. "And Eric and Janie are both so… normal, I guess? They just… have friends or whatever. Anyway, they all have stuff they share and I just never did. And especially with the whole college thing…."

"Bad year?" Will asked.

"Oh man. It sucked. It really sucked. The whole thing—" I shook my head.

"What happened?"

I had e-mailed Will when my plans to come to NYU changed. A long and, let's face it, whiny e-mail about how I couldn't justify going into debt for, like, the rest of my life to come to NYU, about how sad I was that I wouldn't get to hang out with him. And his response had been totally nice. That he agreed it wasn't worth it. That he was sure I'd do great at community college. Et cetera, et cetera. But I hadn't wanted him to be nice. I'd wanted him to be as devastated as I was, and he just… wasn't.

It had been Daniel's idea that I could take classes at Grayling rather than have to sit out a whole year, since NYU was the only place I applied to. It's what he had done, transferring to Temple with enough credits under his belt that he only had to pay for a year's tuition. And it was good advice. He'd had a great experience with his classes and his professors. But he'd also been in a city he loved, with friends, and a goal he was working toward.

"It just felt like high school all over again. Half of the people *were* people from high school, actually. And just… it was *depressing*," I admitted. "I didn't want to seem like a snob. I tried to be friendly and keep an open mind and everything. But there was an air of, like… despair. Seriously. It was grim. And my parents—ugh. My mom would be all, 'How was school, honey?' just like she did when I was little."

"God, the unmitigated *gall* of the woman," Will drawled.

"No, I know, it's nice, just—ugh, I'm not explaining it well."

I wasn't sure how to explain it, exactly. What I'd felt was something close to humiliation. I'd never told my family about NYU, so I didn't think they were disappointed in me or anything. Neither of my parents had been to college, so it certainly wasn't something they expected. Eric hadn't gone, and I didn't think Janie was interested. No, it was more like a humiliation born of the distance between what I wanted and the life I was living.

As if I'd somehow tempted fate by thinking I was special enough to get out of Holiday and fate had smacked me down.

"I get it," Will said. "You had an idea of what you wanted from college and that didn't fit it. It's almost worse to have some wack approximation of the thing you want than not to have it at all."

"Yeah, how'd you know?"

Will shrugged and grinned at me.

"Well, now you get your chance."

I nodded but felt the sudden terror that somehow the fantasy of NYU would blow up in my face all over again. That fate would, once again, punish me for dreaming above my station. But Will had successfully gotten out of Holiday and made a go of it here, proof it was possible.

I told Will about my roommate bailing and how big New York seemed. How unfathomable I found the scale of a city where the subway made it so you couldn't see how things were connected. How far it seemed you could go without meeting anyone who knew you.

"At least I have *you*," I said, testing the waters.

Will's eyes were on me, but he didn't say anything, and I started to feel awkward.

"I mean, um, well, and I'll get a new roommate."

"My freshman roommate was a nightmare," Will said. "He'd been homeschooled and he was a total cliché. Awkward as all hell, showered about once a week, and did these relaxation exercises before he went to bed. He'd sit cross-legged and kind of flap his arms and legs around while breathing in through his nose and out through his mouth. Total freak show.

"But, oh man, that was *nothing* compared to this other girl on my hall. She had night terrors, and she'd wake up sometimes convinced that she was part of some kind of army invasion—I think her dad was in the military or something—and bust out her door to forearm crawl down the hallway. Jesus, it was hilarious. And she went to bed early, so she'd wake up this way at like one in the morning and, of course, half the hall was still awake so everyone would see. Ahhh," he sighed, laughing. "Poor Louise. I wonder if her military crawl skills ever came in handy later in life."

I laughed with him, but now he'd gotten me even more nervous about who my roommate was going to be.

"Well, if mine's that bad then I'll just come over and crash on your couch," I said, sliding a little closer to him.

"You'll be fine," he said with a careless smile. "You'll probably forget I'm even here in a week or two. With this grin?" He chucked me under the chin. "You'll make a ton of friends. Besides, you'll have all your classes."

The concept of forgetting about Will was an absurdity of the magnitude of the IC 1101 galaxy. But I was now veering into dangerous territory. Resolution 4 territory.

Resolution 4 was serious. Resolution 4 was essential. Resolution 4 was basically Daniel's voice in my head and it went something like: *Do not stalk Will like a total psycho when you get to New York in order to confess your love for him because you barely know him and haven't seen him in almost two years and also he's a bag of dicks*. The bag of dicks part was definitely Daniel's voice, though the rest of it wasn't exactly untrue.

So, yeeeaaahhh. Did I mention yet that my feelings for Will were pretty… intense? I knew that I didn't *super* know him, but I also knew I wasn't wrong about the connection we had. One half of my brain repeated *Resolution 4, Resolution 4*, while the other half pictured Will and me tucked up together on his couch just like this every night, talking about everything. Getting to know each other the way no one else had ever known me. Going out together so Will could show me the city. We'd hold hands and—

Will was looking at me strangely and my heart started to hammer, an awkward, sick feeling stealing into my stomach. I didn't remember what I'd been saying and became convinced maybe I'd said things about us going out aloud.

Pretend it's casual! I shouted at myself. *Everything's super casual! You're a casual guy!* "Uh, hang out! We can hang out. Right?"

Will's narrowed eyes suggested that I hadn't sounded *quite* as casual as I'd intended.

"Sure," he said, "we can hang out." But the way he said it—like maybe he was just humoring me—scraped at the last nerve I had. And, okay, maybe I slightly overreacted. But I had ridden on buses for what felt like forever, lugged around my hallmates' worldly possessions, been abandoned by my roommate, almost been hit by a car, gotten on the subway going the wrong way twice trying to get here, and now Will was wrenching away the one scrap of comfort I had.

I was trying to keep calm, but my voice had gone all tight with the promise of a subway ride back downtown by myself, each stop putting more and more distance between me and the only person I knew here.

"I don't get it," I said. "We got along so well in Holiday. And now I'm here, and I thought… I mean, I came here so that…." *Abort!* That was definitely not casual. "I just mean that now that I'm here, I thought maybe we might have a chance. Just to try, you know, being together."

I swallowed and I imagined the sound of it echoing through the open window and out into the streets beyond, announcing to the inhabitants of East Harlem that Leo Ware was completely and officially pathetic.

Will was looking at me like he was puzzled by something essential about me. I felt taken apart by his gaze, like he could see things about me I hadn't even figured out yet.

"Leo." He almost never said my name and it cut right through me. "You didn't come here for me. You came here for college. I live here, yeah, but this is a big city. It's a whole world. You'll see."

I opened my mouth to say something, and he pressed a thumb to the swell of my bottom lip, fingers curling around my chin.

"Look, I want to be clear, okay? I'm not looking for a relationship," he said. There was an almost savage cruelty to the gentleness of his tone as his words tore through me. It was a quelling blow from an honored enemy, a poison kiss, an end before things had even started.

"You're... not interested in general, or... with me?" I forced myself to clarify, pressing farther onto the sword.

"In general."

The silence between us stretched. Usually I'd feel compelled to fill such a silence, but I couldn't even find the words.

"So, then, you just...."

Will's eyes went hard with the warning of irritation.

"I sleep with people when I want to, yeah, if that's what you were going to say." His tone dared me to find fault with what he'd said.

I looked at him, but it was as if I were watching myself from outside my own body as the one thing that I had promised myself I wouldn't say fell out of my mouth and landed between us on Will's posh couch like an unwelcome splotch of oatmeal.

"But... you kissed me."

It sounded so inconsequential, so childish; like I was dangling something unsavory and clumsy in front of him and insisting that he take it as proof.

Will's brows drew together, but then he just smiled casually. "Yeah, well, I'm sure I'm not the first to do that. That fucking smirk you throw." He winked and tapped my lip again.

I gaped at him. In fact, he *had* been the first. Well, not counting Christina Marciano at the eighth-grade social that Carter had dragged me to back when we were still best friends. Before he decided that sports were cooler than movie marathons and being popular was more important than me. And she didn't really count because that was spin the bottle, so she kind of had to kiss me. But that wasn't even the point.

Will's smile faded in the silence.

"Okaaay. Um, I shouldn't have done that. I was in a weird place. Being back in Michigan, and stuff with my sister and—"

I couldn't listen. He regretted kissing me—not even regretted: discounted. Basically the best moment of my entire life, and it had been nothing to him. A mistake.

When you're in a weird place you, like, impulse buy dumb trinkets at the gas station or decide that you probably *should* watch *Fifty Shades of Grey* just to see what everyone is talking about. But Will had kissed me. I mean, really kissed me.

Even all these months later I could slide back into the moment like a jacket worn perfectly to fit my shoulders....

Laughing at a snarky joke Will made and looking up to find his eyes locked on my mouth, those honey gold lashes vulnerable where his eyes always flayed me. The sudden heat I felt, like every atom between our bodies was agitated to a singing vibration. The drag of those lashes as his eyes met mine and he inhaled sharply through his nose like he was startled by whatever he saw in me. How slowly he moved—almost imperceptibly—until my eyes crossed trying to track his mouth's approach.

His breath caught moments before we touched, a tiny automatic sound that I thought might be nerves, though Will had never indicated he had any. I closed my eyes at the hint of vulnerability and waited for contact, the whole world—my whole stupid, pathetic life—reduced to our mouths, microns apart, taking each other's breath into our bodies like maybe we could share something.

But when contact came it wasn't Will's lips. It was his hands, one on either side of my face, holding me fiercely still. His eyes were knives again, any hint of uncertainty gone, and he crushed his mouth to mine before I could even register that he'd moved. It startled a sound out of me, a kind of whine in the back of my throat that I try not to think about, and then it was just the taste of him, like warm ocean water on my tongue.

I pushed up on tiptoes to kiss him back, fisting the fabric of his shirt until he yanked me against him and his tongue stroked mine. It was a shock that electrified my whole body. The fucking intimacy of it. Of someone touching my mouth with his. That something of Will was inside me, a part of me—spit and breath and taste and touch. In that instant he owned me.

When I slid my fingers into his hair it even *felt* blond, the strands smooth and heavy, and Will let out a breath into my mouth. We broke apart for a moment and his eyes were narrowed. Had I done something wrong? Made a misstep I didn't even recognize?

Before I could apologize or ask or do anything, really, other than try not to plaster myself back against his body, he covered my mouth with his palm and closed his eyes, shaking his head slightly. I tried to say something, but he pressed his palm tighter against my lips, his fingers a blunt disappointment after the poetry of his mouth. His hand stayed there for a moment before sliding away in a silent benediction as he took a step back, leaving me breathless and shaky and tremblingly hard.

Leaving me totally destroyed for anything but another taste of him.

Since the moment I had gotten my acceptance letter to NYU—no, from the moment it had occurred to me that I could come to New York—I'd had a fantasy of this moment. The one where I saw Will for the first time since our leave-taking in Holiday. I'd played it in my head so often, scripted different versions of it so many times, that it almost felt like it'd already happened. As if this meeting were something I'd already read in a book, years before, its details gone flat and hazy with the familiarity of a scene read a thousand times.

I'd pulled that story around myself like a blanket for so long, and needed it so badly, that I hadn't ever let myself imagine what would happen if Will went off script. After all, I'd written him so many.

There were the ones I'd thought of as realistic, where he smiled and was amused at me and I was awkward and self-deprecating, and we kind of laughed and he said, "Yeah, we'll see," but in a way that left me buoyant with hope. There were the ones that were more porn than romance, where we didn't speak at all, he just stripped me bare and claimed me, as if I had finally come home.

Then there were the swoony ones. The embarrassingly detailed ones that never ended. There was no climax to them because they were just us, always together. Sharing all the small, daily things that people share. They were punctuated by things like Will bringing me my favorite flowers (not that I knew enough about flowers to have one), or buying me a Valentine's Day stuffed animal (not that I could imagine real-life Will ever doing such a thing), or planning an elaborate surprise for our one-year anniversary (this was always hazy, since my only exposure to anniversaries was my parents, who exchanged cards from the grocery store over breakfast on their anniversary like clockwork).

I found myself suddenly furious with Will, not just for not wanting me, but for, with one sentence, wrenching away the fantasies that I'd been playing on a near continuous loop for more than a year. I had needed them just to get through the day sometimes, especially this past year. And now he had burned them to the ground.

I shuffled backward and grabbed my skateboard, determined to get out of there before Will saw me cry. I plastered a smile on my face and nodded.

"Yeah. Yeah, okay. No problem. Cool. Um, thanks for"—I gestured around searchingly—"the water and all. I'll uh, I'll see you around, okay, night!"

I thought he might've said my name as I slammed out the door, but he didn't follow me. I didn't wait for the elevator, just stumbled down the stairs and out onto the street. I wanted to be swallowed up by the noise and the heat and the thick air and everything that didn't care I was crying as I picked a direction blindly and walked, my fantasies joining my well-intentioned resolutions in dissipating around me like smoke in the evening breeze.

Chapter 2

THE NEON plastic cup slipped out of my hand where I sat slumped against the wall of the stairwell and plinked on every step on the way down when someone kicked at my shoe.

"Are you alive?"

With one eye slitted open all I could see were black skinny jeans terminating in expensive-looking black ankle boots. One of those boots nudged my sneaker again.

"Quit it."

Skinny Jeans dropped into a squat one step below me, and I immediately tried to focus because he was wicked hot. He was black, about my height, and everything about his posture said he knew how hot he was, even squatting in a stairwell under fluorescent light. His white T-shirt was almost transparent and it was shredded in places in that artsy way that super expensive stuff sometimes is, so you could see smooth, taut skin through the fabric. He had permanent dimples and a mouth that turned up slightly like he was smirking at everyone.

He crossed his arms, making the deep V-neck of his T-shirt gape even wider and smiled knowingly when my eyes darted to his chest. His smile held no shadows. It was as bright and inviting as a sunrise, and I wished I could return it.

"You're drunk alone in a stairwell, my friend," he said, his voice light and warm and tinged with a New York accent. What I thought was a New York accent, anyway. "It's only day one. You've gotta pace yourself."

He winked at me, and I couldn't find anything to say. I wished I'd had another one of those Jell-O shots. I could still taste the bite of artificial cherry in the back of my throat. But when I tried to stand up to go get one—and get away from the pretty guy who looked as happy as I was miserable—the whole stairwell tilted.

"Whoa, whoa. You're toast," Skinny Jeans said. "Here, sit." My ass hit the step, jarring my whole spine, and I dropped my head to my knees. The guy sat down next to me, every movement graceful.

"Omigod, kill me," I groaned.

"How are you *this* drunk? The party only started an hour ago."

"I don't drink really ever."

He laughed. "Oookay, so, what, you're newly away from home and feeling your freedom and independence or what?"

I squeezed my eyes shut trying not to replay the epic fail end of my hangout with Will in my head. Trying not to relive our first—and what was clearly going to be our only—kiss.

"Uuuggghhh," I groaned, burying my face in my hands.

"What's the problem, sugar?" Somehow Skinny Jeans made that ridiculous endearment sound friendly and casual, and suddenly I was close to tears. "Hey, hey, it's cool," Skinny Jeans crooned. His hands were on my face, and I tried really hard not to map every distinction from the sensation of Will's. "Whoa, boy, what the hell happened to you?" He swiped his thumbs under my eyes and they came away wet. Oh god, I wished the stairs would turn into a slide like in the cartoons and a trapdoor would open up at the bottom of it and swallow me.

Skinny Jeans tried again. "You homesick?"

Was I? I hadn't even thought about it, but when I did, I had to admit to myself that maybe I was just a little bit homesick. Not that I wanted to be back in Holiday, or back in my parents' house. But it was overwhelming, having no clue what the hell my life would be like a month from now. Or a week. Or, really, tomorrow.

It was more than that, though. As long as I was in Holiday, dreaming of being in New York, anything was possible. It was all potential energy, anticipation, promise. Now that I was here, though… fuck, it was all so real it took my breath away.

He put his arms around me, surprisingly strong for how lithe he looked, and pulled me against him, the scent of something warm, like amber, and fresh, like moss, filling my nose. God, he even smelled expensive. And sophisticated. Like he could choose a cologne because he knew who the hell he was and what he was supposed to smell like.

All the things that Will would want in a boyfriend, right? Someone with taste, who knew about clothes and cologne and boots and how to sit in a stairwell and still look classy.

No, I reminded myself. No, Will didn't want a boyfriend at all. Will wasn't interested in a relationship.

I just didn't *get* it. Like, I got wanting to go out and party and screw a different guy every night. The concept of it, anyway, though I was pretty sure it wasn't for me. And I got not wanting to take a relationship further because you didn't like someone enough. And of course I got not being into someone in particular…. But, not *wanting* a relationship? Like, weren't relationships kind of the whole point? The eventual goal?

Having people you connected with, were intimate with, who knew you, understood you… wasn't that sort of… everything?

Snot was streaming out of my nose, so I pulled away because the T-shirt my face was smooshed against probably cost more than anything I'd ever owned in my whole pathetic life.

"Jesus, kid, how many of those Jell-O shots did you have?"

"Don't call me that!" I pushed away from him, missing his smell immediately as the stale air of the stairwell crept back in. He put his hands up in apology. I sagged against the wall. "Three."

"Three Jell-O shots? Good lord." He patted my back and gazed out past the toes of his boots. Next to the scuffed toes of my Vans, they looked aggressively pointy. "Come with me," he said after a minute or two of diplomatically ignoring the sound of me sniffling into the silence. He dragged me up by the hand and kept hold of it, pulling me after him up flights of stairs. Finally, he pushed open a metal door and we were on the roof. He toed a brick between the door and the frame and pulled me to the edge.

"I thought you could use some air."

I took deep breaths, the air thick with the residue of the day's heat, smelling faintly of something metallic, like blood, but mostly of traffic and pavement and the mush of so many warm bodies in proximity.

In the dark that wasn't really dark, the rooftop felt private. I could already tell that this city was a place where you had to make your own privacy. Construct a bubble that you carried with you as you moved through the streets. Something to prevent every little thing from getting to you. Every glance from a stranger, or brush of a shoulder, or startling noise. I'd never been very good at that. Things did get to me. Things that maybe shouldn't have.

Skinny Jeans looked like he belonged on this rooftop. He looked like he could belong anywhere, from a fancy cocktail party to one of the benches in the park I'd seen this morning. Whereas I… didn't.

Looking at all those windows in all those buildings, all of them with lives happening, just made me feel insignificant. Like the more people I could see at once, the easier it was to dismiss them all and myself in the process.

The city spread around me in all directions and, without the guarantee of Will as a touchstone, I was so thoroughly alone I almost couldn't wrap my mind around it. I didn't have even one friend from home close enough to text. When I was still in school I'd hung out with a few people, but mostly not. High school had been small, and I hadn't really fit in any of the groups. I could text Janie, but knowing my sister she was either on a date or recording an episode of her vlog, and either way she wouldn't want to be interrupted. Which left exactly no one.

My stupid brain started trying to quantify it: how many millions of steps in every single direction could I go and not encounter a single person who cared about me? How many miles, how many kilometers, acres, leagues, furlongs, fathoms, hectares, picas.

Then it started making up new units of measurement to quantify my isolation. How many skateboard-lengths away from love was I? How many pineapple-and-bacon pizzas? How many medium lattes, mass-market paperbacks, USB to HDMI cables, park benches? How many Jell-O shots?

"Sometimes it's easier to talk to a stranger," Skinny Jeans said, leaning back against the chest-high wall I was looking over. "You know." He rolled his eyes and gestured expansively, like we both knew he was repeating something common. "Anonymous confession and all that."

"I don't think you're really dressed for the confessional," I told him.

He grinned and turned toward me, his eyes doing that warm smiley thing. "Are you flirting with me?"

"What? No!"

He just smiled and went on.

"Seriously, what the hell is wrong? I get the whole ooh-college-new-city-angst thing, but you don't seem the type to cry alone in a stairwell."

"You don't even know me," I muttered, looking out into the expanse of night.

"Well, shit, I'm trying to! Just give me something."

He was right. How the hell did I think I was going to end up with anyone who knew me if I didn't start somewhere. So I did. I told him about how Daniel showing up in Holiday was about the best thing that had ever happened because for the first time I had someone to talk to who seemed to understand me a little.

I told him about Rex and how I'd watched them fall for each other. How sometimes it was physically painful to be around them because their love was an almost palpable thing in the room, showing me exactly what I wanted and didn't have.

And I told him about Will. By the time I got to the part where Will had kissed me and then left for New York the next day, Skinny Jeans was shaking his head.

"What?"

"Tell me you didn't. Tell me you didn't pull a full-on Felicity and come to school in New York to follow this Will guy."

"Dude, *Felicity*?"

"*Felicity*'s my jam! Whatever, don't judge me. I have an older sister. What the hell's your name, anyway?"

"Leo."

"Ooh, are you one?"

"Um. No. I'm a Pisces, I think? I always forget the dates of it. Wait, what's your name? In my head I've just been calling you Skinny Jeans."

"Oh, weird, that *is* my name."

He bumped me with his shoulder, and I felt this wave of warmth just from some dude palling around with me.

"No, seriously," he went on. "Everyone said to my parents, 'You can't name him that; those aren't even in style yet!' but my folks were all, 'Well, we can't call him Boot Cut, it's not black enough!'"

I started giggling a little, and we both jumped up to sit on the side of the wall.

"It's Milton," he said.

"Whoa. Heavy name."

He grinned at me, then pulled out a flask. It was silver, and not the cheap, plain kind you can get at a gas station. Ornate, with filigreed cuts that shone in the moonlight like it was bejeweled.

"So, you were sad-drinking over whatshisname before. Now you've gotta happy drink with me over being here instead of in whereverthefuck Michigan, and making friends with magnificent me, and all the hot guys who're gonna be psyched to jump the bones of a cute little white-boy skater with serious face."

Whatever was in the flask burned going down but tasted of nothing.

"Just vodka, same as in the Jell-O shots, so you'll be fine," Milton said.

After a few mouthfuls, he pulled me down from the wall. "Just to be safe," he said, and after a few more I was sure that he was going to be the best friend I'd ever had. I was warm in a good way, and the tension seemed to have seeped out of my shoulders.

When I looked out into the night, the lit-up windows twinkled like imperfect stars, waiting for the hand that would extinguish them. Then I was on my back looking up at the real stars, trying to pick out constellations like I had at home, but there was too much light pollution and probably regular pollution, so I couldn't see anything.

Milton was talking about the boyfriend he'd had last year—he'd gone to some school here in the city that he kept calling by name, but I didn't know what it was. Sounded fancy, though. And he talked about all the cute guys he'd already seen.

I guess it was the spirit of confessional that Milton mentioned—or maybe it was the vodka—but I found myself telling him that I'd never really had sex. That Will's kiss hadn't just been the best kiss of my life but also my first. That since then I'd briefly messed around with a guy in my statistics class at Grayling, but it had been... well, awkward would have been an understatement.

"Well, do you want to?" Milton asked, matter-of-factly.

"Ummm, yeah?"

He leaned over and touched his lips to mine softly, his kiss a question. The warmth of him next to me, his smell, the brush of his hand against my face. It didn't feel scary or intense like Will or overwhelming like this city. It just felt comfortable. Welcoming. Like someone actually appreciated me for once. Wanted me. Not out of pity or because I wore them down, but because maybe he actually liked me.

I sought his lips again, pulled him down next to me until we were facing each other. Then he gave me this grin—this bright grin full of joy, and went for it, lips and tongue and hands everywhere. Every time we pulled apart for breath, Milton smiled at me, like he was happy to be there, with me, right then. Until I pushed my hand up the back of his stupid T-shirt and rested it between his shoulder blades, holding him to me. Then his smile turned wolfish, and he tangled our legs together, so we were locked up tight.

I froze when the bulge in his tight jeans ground against my answering hardness. At my stuttering breath, Milton kissed me deeper and rolled his hips into mine. The pulse of pleasure washed through me like a stone dropped into still water and heat crept down the backs of my thighs and up into my stomach.

Milton's groan was unguarded appreciation, and he kissed my neck. I was light-headed with sensation, and I didn't know what I was supposed to do, really, so I just ran my hands over the smooth skin of Milton's back. His kisses canted my head back, and I found myself straining to see the stars like I could at home. It seemed like they should be there, clear and bright, standing witness.

But then Milton went for my zipper and I didn't give a crap about the stars anymore because his hand felt amazing, his grip firm as he started to stroke me. I struggled up to my knees, almost falling on my face because of the tangle Milton had made of my pants, and pulled him up, unzipping him and trying to pull down his jeans. They were so tight I ended up with my face level with his crotch, trying to yank at the fabric.

I was swearing at his pants and kind of laughing, too, because my dick was sort of just bobbing between us. Milton had his lip caught between his teeth, silently cracking up at me.

"Too tight," I complained, and he just laughed harder. Finally he took pity on me and slid his jeans down gracefully, like a snake shedding its skin. We were kneeling, facing each other, and I was appreciating the first hard-on I'd ever seen in, you know, context.

"You want me to shine my flashlight app down there or something, bro?" he asked, and I realized I was basically just staring at his dick in the dark of the rooftop with my junk hanging out like a total fool.

"No, it's okay."

He chuckled and pulled me upright, pressing me against the wall when I lost my balance, my pants still rucked around my ankles, and licked a slow line up my throat. My heart was beating wildly and I grabbed at his shoulders to keep steady.

With his face buried in my neck, he started stroking me, slow and hard, until I was pushing my hips toward him and squirming to encourage him to go faster. His breath against my wet skin was warm, and the smell of his cologne was intoxicating.

I wanted to make him feel as good as he was making me feel, but my hands were shaky and useless. I pulled at his ass, trying to get him closer and, with a groan, he palmed his erection and started stroking us together. He was hard and slick, and we strained together.

I had my eyes squeezed shut so tight I saw starbursts of white before I felt the explosion. Milton's hand took me over the edge, and it was like everything was collapsing. A sky folding in at the edges and buckling like paper crumpled in the hand.

My thighs were trembling and my stomach was clenching and my breath was coming short as I collapsed against the wall, pulling Milton closer. This time when I reached for him, he pressed himself into my hand and both our fists slid over his dick faster, faster, until he swore and came, biting my earlobe hard enough to sting.

He didn't let me feel awkward or weird about being slumped against a total stranger, half-naked, slick with sweat and tacky with come. He just snaked back into those damn jeans and dragged mine up by the belt loops, zipping me back up carefully and kissing me once more on the mouth.

"We're going to be friends," he said and gave me the same warm smile he'd given me before.

I'M LYING in bed with another guy's come all over me, I texted Will once I was back in my room, tipsy with alcohol and overwhelmed by the night, the only light my gently glowing phone screen. Still no sign of my new roommate, and I was glad I'd have a little time by myself. As freaked out as I'd been before, and as lonely, I didn't think I could've stood facing a stranger while trying to strip off come-stuck clothes.

It was a lie. My text. I'd taken a shower as soon as I unstuck myself. But still.

I stared at the screen as it dimmed halfway, any hope of a response fading with it. Fuck, I couldn't believe I actually sent that text. I didn't know what I was hoping for. That it'd make him jealous? Punish him for not wanting me? Both were ridiculous in light of our earlier conversation. God, there should be a function where you can unsend a text for thirty seconds like there is in e-mail.

Just as I buried my head under the pillow, my phone chimed. My breath came quicker as I looked at Will's text.

That's exactly what you should be doing in college. Play safe, kiddo.

I squeezed my eyes shut as if I could unsee the words. Obliterate them. But the hollow feeling gaped in my stomach, and I curled around it, pulling the covers up though it was warm in the room.

The extra-long jersey knit sheets from the bookstore smelled of the plastic package they'd come in. Not comforting at all. No history of sleep or relaxation in their fibers. Just the reminder that they were brand-new, with nothing to make them inviting except time.

Chapter 3

September

I STARTLED awake to the train whistle blowing and wondered for the millionth time why I'd chosen that as my alarm and yet, like always, was too asleep to do anything about it.

Charles was perched on his desk chair, muttering furiously at his computer as usual. For the first week or so that we'd lived together, I'd never seen Charles sleep. I assumed that he just went to bed after me and got up before me, but I legit had a moment once, waking in the middle of the night to find him pacing his side of the room restlessly, where I'd wondered if he had some kind of never-sleeping vampire shit going on.

His trackpad clicks got increasingly more aggressive, and his bony shoulders hunched closer to the screen.

"Are the interwebs hurting you again?"

He wheeled around like he was shocked to see me there, though my alarm had blasted a train whistle through our room not thirty seconds before. He did that a lot: seemed to forget I existed. But it was kind of nice. Like he was so used to me he could forget I was there and just be. I, on the other hand, never forgot about Charles because he practically vibrated this manic energy, and I could feel it from anywhere in the room.

He'd blustered into the dorm room the day after I'd met Milton, a huge lumpy duffel bag strapped to him and four boxes stacked on the seat of a wheeled desk chair that he was pushing like a dolly. He'd stuck out a hand to me, nearly overbalancing the chair and boxes, and introduced himself, explaining that he was supposed to go to MIT but had changed his mind at the last minute—for some reason I've never fully understood—and now he was here, only *yikes*, he didn't have a room and so they'd put him with me.

The whole explanation took place while he was holding my hand, like he'd forgotten we were touching or that hands even existed. He made the kind of eye contact that would've been creepy if he'd seemed douchey, or intimidating if he'd seemed overconfident, but was just intense in the way that everything about Charles was intense.

He was tall and far too thin for his frame, bony shoulders poking at the seams of his T-shirts and knobby spine perpetually bruised from sitting folded into lecture hall seats. His hands and feet looked disproportionately large and his Adam's apple tested the boundaries of his skin when he swallowed. When he gestured, his long arms and bony hands looked skeletal and precarious. But in front of the computer, hunched and intent, he looked completely at home, just as he did walking down the streets in expansive, long-legged steps, his clothes billowing around him like some kind of Arthurian cloak.

His curly brown hair was always frizzy and mussed because he pulled on it, and he had these permanent dark smudges under his eyes, but when he talked he was animated, and I had the suspicion that he might be some kind of secret genius. He'd said he wasn't uncommonly smart, he just went to a good high school, had basic reasoning skills, and didn't allow his personal beliefs to get in the way of reason, which made him seem smarter than most people. But I didn't know. All that seemed pretty uncommon to me.

"Someone on Wikipedia has written, 'the tunnels beneath Paris are almost catacombic,' which number one, is not a word, but even if it were, what would that 'b' be doing exactly—I mean, would it be said like cata-comic? Because that's strangely the opposite. But mostly, they're not catacomb*ic*. They *are* catacombs."

Charles was a near-compulsive Wikipedia editor. His expertise was vast and shallow.

"Would you ever say 'honeycombic'?"

"*I* wouldn't, no." He sounded disgusted.

"Well, how would you… adjectivize it or whatever? Honeycombish? Honeycombesque?"

"They just *are* catacombs. No adjectivizing required."

Sometimes Charles was also super literal.

MILTON PUSHED our door open without knocking, took one look at me, and rolled his eyes, tapping his watch. We had Intro Psych lecture together, and he always came by to collect me because I sometimes fell back asleep after my alarm went off.

Charles ignored Milton in the passive way he mostly ignored everyone—as if they hadn't quite intruded into his headspace yet—and Milton clapped him on the shoulder like he always did, and then left him alone.

Milton was good like that. He didn't take shit personally. Lucky for me, because he was basically the best friend I'd ever had even though I'd acted like a total lunatic after we'd hooked up the first night here.

I had been all, *Oh my god, Milton, that was amazing, but I can't be your boyfriend because my heart belongs to another*, and he'd been all, *Omigod, Leo, I don't want to be your boyfriend, I was just horny as fuck and wanted to jerk off with you on a roof under the stars and now we can be friends because we barely even have chemistry really, okay?*

Well, maybe it hadn't been in those exact words, but that was basically what had happened.

We'd tried an experiment of kissing once more a few weeks later in the library, and both started laughing. I didn't really get it, because that night on the roof, I had been legit into him, and it was super hot, but now… I just didn't think of him that way, I guess. He said that was normal, and I believed him because if I'd learned anything about Milton over the past month, it was that he was like a Sex + Love Genius. He just completely *got* it.

I dragged on yesterday's jeans and a not-too-dirty T-shirt and jammed my feet into my Vans in about fifteen seconds, as Milton looked on, half amused and half silently judging me. He didn't say anything, though, because my total lack of fashion meant we were on time for Psych and even had time to stop in at his preferred coffee shop.

I texted Daniel, like I did almost every time I was in a coffee shop, and told him I was ordering The Daniel, which is what the coffee shop in Holiday christened the drink he always ordered: three shots of espresso in a large coffee. He texted back a string of random letters that culminated in an emoji of a grimacing head making a thumbs-up sign. I suppose that meant he'd finally gotten a smartphone.

I saw the green ellipsis that meant he was trying to write something else, but after it stuttered a few times, it finally went away. I could practically see him, messing with the new phone to try and explain what he meant to type, making more nonsense, and finally giving up in frustration, most likely throwing the phone down on whatever surface was nearest.

He'd probably forget where he tossed it and wander around later looking for it and pulling his hair out. Rex would ask him when he'd used it last, and he'd remember that it was texting with me and that he'd gotten pissed. Rex would go to wherever he was and pull it out of the couch cushions or the stack of books or wherever he'd thrown it and hand it back to him with that soft look he gets only for Daniel. That look that says *I love all these small things about you that are just you but mean something to me.* Maybe he'd slide the phone into Daniel's pocket and kiss him.

Fuck, I missed them.

WE ROLLED into Psych just as Marin, the TA, was setting the professor's notes on the lectern and adjusting the PowerPoint presentation. I was a little bit obsessed with her because she *never* smiled. Professor Ginsberg was pretty amusing and joked around, and Marin was just stone. I mean, maybe she'd heard all the jokes before, but still. Not even a polite, indulgent yes-I-acknowledge-humor quirk of the lips. She was totally nice in discussion section—even cracked jokes herself, so it wasn't like she didn't have a sense of humor. But still, no smiles, even when we laughed. It was like she was playing some kind of secret game and if she smiled it meant she lost.

Thomas waved us over excitedly, having saved us seats. Thomas was always early and liked to sit directly in the middle of the classroom, like it was a movie theater and he wanted the best view. I wasn't sure why he bothered since he drew little comics in his notebook throughout the entire lecture.

"Hey, guys!" Thomas shuffled his stuff aside so we could sit down. "Did you see Marin's shoes?" Everything Thomas said sounded like there was an exclamation point after it.

I squinted to see that stone-faced Marin was rocking some Vans with kitties on them or something.

"Are they cats?" asked Milton, also squinting.

"They're *amaze*!" said Thomas, turning to his notebook where he spent the next fifty minutes drawing a comic about a cat that had wings like Pegasus as Professor Ginsberg talked about Emotions. She said "capital-E emotions" to designate it as a topic. Which cracked me up, because of course I knew emotion was psychology, but the idea that we were studying emotions—going to school to learn about feelings like some alien species studying how to be human—just tickled me.

Not that it'd go amiss for some people.

I'd spent a solid week sulking over Will's rejection. Then I randomly woke up super early one day, as I sometimes had in Holiday, and walked out into the morning. I found myself in Washington Square Park, strolling along the sidewalks as the city woke. I sat on the edge of the fountain, watching as, in the middle of this sprawling city, the water spewed upward, caught the sunlight, and fell down again, recollecting itself only to do it all over again.

I watched, and I started laughing. At myself. Because I was here. *Here.* In New York City. Taking classes at NYU. Sitting smack-dab in the middle of Washington Square Fucking Park. And I was missing it. I was missing the whole damn thing because I was hung up on Will. It was, I told myself, basically the stupidest thing ever.

It felt so good to laugh. I hadn't done much laughing over the last year, what with missing Daniel, feeling abandoned by Will, and any enthusiasm for my classes at Grayling being crushed within a week of the semester starting. And as I sat there, grinning like an idiot, people who walked past me smiled back. I thought about what Will had said about not smiling at babies and their parents getting so offended, and I smiled even bigger.

He'd been right. I'd tried it a few days after he had mentioned it in a twisted attempt to feel closer to him, though I'd broken at the last minute and smiled at the baby anyway. The baby's mom had expected me to smile at her kid, and when I hadn't, it was as if I'd broken some social law.

But, though Will was right, his point wasn't mine. It felt amazing to smile at someone and have them smile back. And I could tell from the way people smiled back at me that morning that they thought so too. After all, things were shitty so much of the time. If you could connect with someone over something as small and easy as a smile, why wouldn't you want to?

In that spirit, I'd texted Will.

It's soooo beautiful here today, I wrote, with three grinning face emojis and a picture of the fountain.

His reply had been almost immediate, though it was barely 8:00 a.m. on a Saturday morning: *Here too*, and a picture of the view from out his living room window, sunlight falling gently on brick and, in the bottom corner, a man buying flowers at the corner bodega.

Since then, Will and I had fallen into the habit of texting each other random silliness. Well. I texted him random stuff that I hoped he'd think was funny, and he texted me back, basically making fun of me. But in a friendly way. A flirty way, I hoped. That was how I chose to take it, anyway.

Last night, for instance, I'd texted him a pic of mud splattered all over my skateboard and my shoes that said *Another driver just tried to kill me. Should I be taking this personally???*

He'd responded: *He probably took your shoes personally and wanted to put them out of their misery. Srsly, they're dead.*

What I hear you saying is that you want to take me shopping! I'd written, though I totally did not have the cash for new anything right now.

He hadn't responded for a while, then wrote, *Well, I'd be doing the entire city a service, I suppose. Saturday afternoon.*

I'd practically run my battery down looking at the text every ten minutes since it came. Every time I did, this warm, kind of *squee*ish happiness burbled up in me. It'd be the first time I'd seen Will since our awkward meeting at his apartment when I first got to town.

Milton bumped me with his shoulder and I nearly dropped my phone.

"What are you all slappy about?"

I hesitated to tell him because Milton has made it really clear that he thinks what he refers to as my obsession with Will is pathetic. Well, misguided, anyway.

"Oh," he said, looking at my phone. "Will?"

"He's taking me shopping on Saturday."

I could see Milton physically stop himself from making whatever comment occurred to him, so to thank him for not harshing my vibe, I told him that he could pick the movies for tonight, even though I knew he'd pick this nine-million-hour-long documentary series about a staircase or something that he'd gotten from the library and had been trying to get me to watch for the last two weeks.

"AND THIS filmmaker was there practically from the very beginning, so you see the direct aftermath of the wife's death, and then it takes you through his whole trial and everything, and each episode is about a different bit of evidence. Oh man, it's so intense—like, in the middle, there's this one—well, okay, no, I won't give it away. But it's so good. Don't look him up online, though, or you'll get totally spoiled."

Milton's movie night pick turned out to be amazing—though at nearly eight hours long we'd stayed up almost all night finishing it—and I'd started telling Will about it right away. Partly because it had been fascinating, and partly in order to keep myself from saying all the things I really wanted to say to him.

Like that the second I'd seen him loping toward me, I'd felt the same way I had when he would walk into a room in Holiday: as if the background receded and he was this pulsing star at the center of things. And how just like then, my face heated up and my stomach went all wobbly.

Nope, definitely didn't need to be saying anything like that. So. Describing an epic documentary about murder it was!

Will said the neighborhood we were in was Chelsea. Brick buildings towered above us, and here and there you could see the ghost of where another building must have rested. The shops all had window displays that looked like art, or like they were trying to look abandoned. He kept pointing things out in displays and asking if I liked them. At first I thought he meant for me, but it quickly became clear he was just curious about what I thought was aesthetically pleasing, because I could never afford any of the stuff he was looking at.

When I told him so, Will ran a finger along the worn neck of my T-shirt and shook his head, making a *tsk*ing sound.

"You know," I told him, "Einstein said 'Once you can accept the universe as matter expanding into nothing that is something, wearing stripes with plaid comes easy.'"

Will snorted. "Yeah? Well, when you're inventing theories of relativity I won't say a word about how you dress like you passed out in a skate park in 1997 and just woke up. Until then, I'm happy both accepting that the universe is matter expanding into nothing and also that the combination of too many design elements in that universe looks like shit."

I elbowed him playfully.

"So, was the guy found guilty?" Will asked.

I gaped at him. "Dude, that's the entire point of the documentary. I'm not going to ruin it. You're supposed to watch and, like, form your own opinion based on the evidence."

"I don't care about spoilers, man—a story's either interesting or it isn't. Besides, I assure you, I don't have any problem forming my own opinion, even in a sea of conflicting ones." He winked at me.

I certainly believed that.

"I can't tell you. No way. If you wanna know, you can google it, but I'm not going to tell you the end. I am firmly in the no spoilers camp. It's a lifestyle."

The look Will gave me was one I liked to think he saved just for me. Like I didn't say what he expected, but he was glad that I didn't, and also irritated with himself for being glad. Will was really not the surprised type. He was more the absolutely-nothing-shocks-me type. In fact, it seemed vital to him that he'd thought of every possible eventuality. So the moments when I did something that bypassed whatever formulas he'd cooked up about how people acted or how the world worked were total wins. Granted, I still couldn't predict what was going to strike him that way. At all. But it was a start.

The thing about walking with Will, I was realizing, was that everybody stared at him. Some people straight up checked him out, but others just… looked at him, like they had every right to. Like he was art, publicly displayed to be publicly appreciated.

At first I thought he was getting a kick out of it. But Will wore his beauty with a kind of scorn that made it even more potent, the way some people in New York seemed to wear expensive clothes with the air that they couldn't care less if they ruined them. Like, *yeah, splatter duck fat on this gazillion-dollar silk shirt, sure.* Or, *what's that? Sit on the dirt in this designer dress and drink champagne? Let's do it.*

After the eight billionth person's head turned to look at him, though, he started to tighten up. It probably just read as good posture to the casual observer, but to me it looked like he was trying to pull into himself. As if by making himself stiller he could escape notice, a gazelle on the plains freezing to elude the chase.

When he shoved his fisted hands into his pockets, though, I pulled him into a little café, seated him facing the wall, and bought him a coffee. And I watched him slowly relax.

He looked tired and still wasn't very talkative, but he seemed happy to listen, so to distract him, I told him about Milton and Charles, and about Gretchen, this awesome girl on my hall, who was the calmest person I'd ever known. Seriously, just being around her made me relax. I'd met Gretchen because we were in a tour group for people who hadn't already visited campus the previous spring. Our tour guide was a sophomore who seemed so jaded that he could hardly raise his voice loud enough to be heard, but clearly took a great deal of pleasure in making us nervous.

When we'd gotten to the lobby in the library, he pointed a languid thumb behind his shoulder and told us that from the fifth or sixth floor looking down, the mosaic tile was laid out to look like spikes rising out of the ground in an attempt to deter students from throwing themselves over. Because before the administration added the cage around the opening, they did that, he told us. *A lot*. He made eye contact with each of us in turn, as if he were making a toast. I let out a nervous laugh.

The girl next to me, tall, with curly hair so blonde it was nearly white and strangely colorless eyes, cocked her head at the mosaic and said, "That's so odd. If people wanted to commit suicide, the promise of spikes would hardly be a deterrent would it?"

"Oh gosh," I said. "You're totally right."

And that, I had quickly learned, was really all it took to make new friends the first week of college.

I told him about classes. How my favorite was this physics class that was blowing my mind. Especially the parts about astrophysics. Physics was like a cheat sheet to the universe. Things that once just *were* suddenly had explanations, a logic all their own—except not all their own because they resonated with other things and forces throughout the universe. I might have gotten pretty excited talking about Newton's second law.

And as long as I was talking and Will was paying attention to me I felt like I could do anything. Like he was a magnifying glass refracting the light of the whole universe onto me in a beam so intense and so warm that every molecule of my being was illuminated and seen. The threat of being burned alive was always in play, but the risk felt totally worth it.

Two girls at the counter lingered over doctoring their coffees, sneaking glances at Will and giggling. Will let out an exasperated breath.

"They stare at you because you're so beautiful," I told him, nudging his coffee with mine.

"Ugh, who fucking cares," he said, flopping backward in his seat and closing his eyes, like if he wasn't able to see people, then they couldn't see him.

I snorted. "Easy to say when you are. I bet everyone wishes they were. Or, most people, anyway," I corrected myself. It drove Daniel batshit when people made generalizations and whenever I did it in front of him I'd get an earful.

"You shouldn't wish for that. You're fine as you are."

"Gee, thanks," I said, but secretly I was a little thrilled even at the faint praise. Will hardly ever gave compliments.

"Whatever, you're fucking adorable. Don't fish."

"I don't get it, though. You like it sometimes, I know. The power it gives you over people. I mean, you use it to, like… meet people, right, so you can't tell me you don't like being so hot—"

"Yeah, at a *bar* or a *club*—when I'm trying to pick someone up. Not at work or buying a fucking newspaper, or"—he nodded to our surroundings—"drinking a damn coffee. Not when I can't control it. You think it's great to look like this? To walk down the street and have everyone stare at you so you can't even trip on the damn sidewalk without an audience. To constantly have people talking to you and smiling and acting all nervous or insecure or like you're better than them?"

He cut himself off with a quick look around, suddenly realizing he'd started ranting.

"Whoa. I guess… I didn't think about that part of it."

"Yeah, nobody ever does."

He took another sip of his coffee and made a face. "Ugh. Overextracted." He was quiet for a while, pushing a finger through the light spill of sugar to leave a trail. "I just…," he said quietly, then shook his head.

"What?"

When Will had things to say, he said them. When he had nothing to say, he didn't make an effort to fill the silence. At first this had made me uncomfortable. It was weird to hang out with someone who might be silent for an hour and then, when something occurred to him, monologue about it. But now it was one of my favorite things about hanging out with Will. Realizing that when he said things they mattered to him.

"I don't *want* to be responsible for other people's feelings, you know? I don't want to know that someone is nervous because they're hot for me and feel like it's my responsibility to be nicer to them to put them at ease or some shit. It's nothing to *do* with me even. They don't like *me*, they don't care about *me*. Hell, they just want to stare at me and have me shut up and smile at them. Like I'm a fucking prop in some fantasy."

His expression was grim, bitter.

"And then, if I don't play along—if I don't smile the way they want, or flirt back, or say thank you to their compliments—it's like I've somehow committed a social foul. I've offended them so they have to get revenge somehow. Like by asserting that I'm an actual fucking person I've invited retribution."

I started to respond, but Will's jaw was tight and he clearly wasn't done.

"And if they aren't turning me into a prop or a fuck toy in their heads, then they just let me do whatever I want because beauty is basically an all-access pass to the world."

"People don't really think that, do they?" But even as I said it, I thought of my own initial reactions to Will's beauty.

Will hit me with a heavy, pitying look.

"Leo, you would not believe the shit I can get away with by looking like this. Seriously. It's sick."

"Like what?"

He sighed, like there were too many to even list.

"The things that I can say to someone and not get called on it.... Like, I was on a date over the summer with this guy and we had nothing in common. He started talking some stupid shit about how stop-and-frisk is the best thing to ever happen to the city. He kept flirting with me and I kept telling him off. Like, he'd say 'Tell me about yourself,' and I'd just dead-eye him and say, 'If you think stop-and-frisk is a good policy, you are a racist.' And he just let me talk all this shit and kind of laughed like I was kidding and never called me on it."

"Well, maybe he was just being polite because you guys were on a date and he was trying to make the best of it since you didn't have anything in common."

"Dude, I called him a racist to his face and he just looked embarrassed and said nothing. Whatever—he's just one example of shit that's happened hundreds of times. I've tried it the other way around too. I've said ignorant, bigoted shit just to see if people will call me on it and they don't. People don't call me on being rude or selfish or ignorant even when the person next to me will get called out for doing the exact same thing. It's like a social experiment at this point. A... screening process for assholes."

The idea of Will wandering through the city feeling like everyone he interacted with was failing him, instead of actually connecting with them, made me incredibly sad.

"They give me credit for something that has nothing to do with me. It's... it's bullshit," Will continued.

"Um, well, I guess it means you get what you want, though?" I was trying to put a positive spin on it, but as someone who had never really felt like I had the license to be rude or selfish or inconsiderate, it didn't seem like the absolute worst thing.

"Yeah, great." Will slumped. Clearly that was the wrong thing to say. "Never knowing if you get something because you deserve it or because someone just likes the way you look is awesome."

"Shit, sorry, I didn't think about it like that."

He threw back the rest of his coffee like a shot and stood abruptly.

"Let's get out of here."

The second we were outside again, Will straightened his spine and set his shoulders. Even his gait changed. The mask slid back into place, like he could filter what went out and what got in. Will was pretty good at that whole making a bubble around yourself thing.

After a few blocks, he pulled me into a store where every single article of clothing was white. Wasn't there supposed to be some kind of rule about white after... some day? I was going to ask Will, but he was distracted, pinching the pressed pleat of a pant leg here, running a fingertip over the crisp collar of shirt there, and caressing the cable of a sweater with the back of his hand as he walked through the store.

"Here, try this on."

Will held up a pair of pants that tied at the waist with a strip of fabric and had built-in suspenders, like in those old Charlie Chaplin films. He handed them to me along with a sleeveless shirt that looked like an undershirt but probably wasn't. It was baby blue and cut low enough that the few chest hairs I had would be on full display.

"Um, why?"

Will's eyes narrowed, like he was seeing me in the outfit he'd chosen, and gestured me toward the dressing rooms.

"Because I want to see. Okay?"

And of course the idea that Will would want to see me in anything was so flattering that I immediately stumbled to the dressing room. Will hooked his thumbs in his belt loops and gave the dressing room attendant a look that said he had this and we didn't need any assistance. She just gave him a bored once-over and raised one painted-on eyebrow, tapping at her phone where it rested on her slender thigh.

I hung the clothes on the back of the door, kicked off my ratty sneakers, and pulled off my jeans and T-shirt, letting them fall in a pile on the floor.

The mirror certainly didn't do me any favors. In the direct lighting, reflected to myself from three angles, there was no avoiding it. I was... not much to look at. Skinny as shit, kind of tan, but it maybe looked more like I was just scruffy. Freckles across my nose and cheeks. Hair on my arms and legs but, for some reason, only a sprinkling of hair on my chest and a few under my belly button.

My shoulders and knees were bony—I mean, I wasn't in Charles' league, but he was about nine feet tall—and my shoulder blades poked out. Once, when he'd had a few drinks, Daniel told me that he thought I would be handsome in a few years. Something about growing into my face. But it had been over a year since he'd said that, and if it was going to happen, it certainly hadn't yet.

My nose still looked like a little kid's, and I had these deep dimples that my grandma used to touch whenever she'd see me and say, "God just took a little stitch." Which was actually terrifying when I thought about it. My mouth was too big for my face. My eyes were... I dunno, they were mine so it was hard to tell. Okay, I guess? Mostly I just thought I looked startled all the time. And my eyebrows kind of didn't go with my face or something. I looked nice, mostly, but my eyebrows were all über serious, like I was concentrating really hard or someone had just hurt my feelings.

Turning my back to concentrate on the pants wasn't much better because even though they were, you know, pants, there was something weird about them, and I couldn't figure out which way around they went. As I was pulling them up, the door opened, nearly pushing me into the mirror, and Will slid in.

"What the hell are you doing in here?" he asked.

He took in my state of half undress with a total lack of concern or interest, and I felt this particular kind of shame that usually comes when you give someone something that really matters to you and they don't even notice.

"These stupid pants are like a puzzle," I said. "I couldn't figure out which—"

Will tossed me the shirt, which I pulled on—couldn't mess up a tank top at least—and the second the fabric touched me he tucked it into the pants, and did something where he tied the fabric and engaged the suspenders in one easy gesture.

"Who could wear white pants anyway?" I muttered. "I'd sit down on a bench or something and be filthy in point five seconds."

He didn't respond, regarding me, leaning against the dressing room door, a hand on his chin like he was considering what he thought of me. And when he smiled it felt emptier than I'd expected, because it was like he was smiling at the clothes and not at me at all. Was this what he was attracted to? People who dressed like this?

Was this what he wanted me to be?

I looked ridiculous. Like I was trying really hard to be someone I wasn't.

"You like this?" I asked Will.

He nodded.

"But, like, for me?"

"Well, you wouldn't wear it, would you?"

His hands went to my shoulders to adjust the suspenders, and I shook my head.

"I don't look like me."

He shrugged like that was nothing.

"You get to decide what you look like. You get to decide who you are."

"You don't get to decide who you are," I said. That was ridiculous. "You just… are who you are."

Will's hands, still hovering at my shoulders, tightened. I took a step toward him so we were almost chest to chest.

"Why did you really want me to try this stuff on? You know I wouldn't wear it."

"Just for fun," he said, but his voice sounded like he was having the opposite of fun.

"I don't believe you." I stepped forward again, putting Will's back against the door. "Seriously. Why?"

I could feel it again. That heat. That pull between us like it was taking more energy to keep our bodies apart than it would to allow their collision. How did that fit with your first law, Newton? We might've been at rest, but everything in us was straining together, like only this skin was keeping us from getting all messed up in each other.

Will's breath came a little short as I stared at him. Somehow, looking at him this close up, his perfect beauty fell apart and reformed into something different. No longer was it about proportion and line and angle. Up close, Will was texture and shadow and something far more human. I could smell him. The familiar, slightly milky smell of the coffee shop. Beneath that, some subtle cologne that smelled like expensive suits and garden parties and maybe just a hint of leather. The slight sour bite of fresh sweat. And then his skin, like dust warmed in a beam of sunlight.

His eyes locked on my mouth and his hands came up like he wanted to put them on my hips but was stopping himself, so they just hovered there.

"See," I said, and it came out as a whisper.

Will shook his head but his eyes didn't leave my mouth. I tugged my bottom lip between my teeth and watched his Adam's apple slide and catch in an audible swallow.

I wanted to press him against the dressing room door and kiss him until he actually talked to me, the way he'd started to do in Holiday. But it was like he'd gotten enough time apart from me for whatever spell Holiday wove to have fallen away. Or maybe it was as simple as he had needed someone to talk to in Holiday and Rex was occupied so it became me by default, and now that he was back in New York I was just… I don't know.

But I could feel this—whatever it was—between us.

"Will."

He was almost glaring at me, like a super turned-up version of The Look. And for some reason it made me ridiculously happy, because with Will, any response other than haughty neutrality was a step in the right direction.

"Hey, kiss me," I said, nudging him, and watched his battle with himself play out over his face.

He stared at me, breathing through his nose, having come, apparently, to no decision whatsoever.

"Okay, I'm going to kiss you now if you don't stop me," I said, which actually sounded a little creepy of me.

But he didn't stop me. And he didn't seem creeped. He just closed his eyes and sighed a little and I didn't know what he was thinking. Now that we were the same height, I just stepped into him and pressed our mouths together.

The second I kissed him he came alive, a sparkler touched by a match. He made a sound in the back of his throat and pulled me against him with a palm at the small of my back, just above those damn pants. His mouth was hot, and I could taste his coffee from earlier, a bitter note that gave way almost immediately to the sweetness of his taste.

I remembered it, even all these months later, and it tasted like home.

Will had his arms around me now, wrapping me up so tight I almost couldn't move. He pushed one hand through my hair to hold my face to his while he—holy shit—while he kissed the hell out of me. One second I was kissing him, and the next he'd flipped me, slammed me against the dressing room door, and was basically eating my face. Only, you know, in a good way. An awesome way.

It felt nothing like my make-out session with Milton. Even when Milton had touched my cock I hadn't felt as electrified as I did from Will's kiss. I scrabbled at his back, trying to… something—to touch skin or trace muscle, but it was really all I could do to keep my feet under me with Will's mouth on mine. Finally, he tickled the roof of my mouth with his tongue, just gently stroked it, and I found myself so close to coming that it shocked me. I let out a groan and tried to grab for his hips, desperate to get some friction.

Then I realized that I was wearing these stupid white pants that I'd probably have to pay like five hundred dollars for if I came in them, and I pulled my hips away, groaning at the loss of his heat.

From outside the door came a very haughty stage cough followed by some heavy-duty throat clearing.

"Fuck," Will snapped and dropped his forehead to my collarbone. "Fuck, Leo. Shit." I could feel the warmth of his skin. He was sweating at his hairline and his back rose and fell with rapid breaths. He stayed like that for a long moment, clutching my hips, each finger palpable even through the pants, before he cleared his throat and told me he'd meet me outside.

And, hell. The idea of Will imprinting himself on the fabric was almost enough to make me want to buy the ridiculous things.

FOR THE next week, I went to sleep with Will's taste on my tongue and woke up to visions of him. I dreamt about him. By Friday night, though, Milton was sick to death of my play-by-play analysis of our dressing room encounter and of watching me (apparently) sigh all through meals in the dining hall, so he said that instead of movie night we were going to go dancing. He spent two hours forcing me to try on clothes from his closet because he said I didn't own anything decent, but I was thinking of Will and our kiss the whole time.

Charles wouldn't come with us—he said dancing was a ludicrous mating ritual, and when Milton said it wasn't about mating, he just looked puzzled and said, "Well, if it isn't at least that, then what possible appeal could it have?"

Thomas came with us, though, as did Gretchen. I hardly recognized Thomas without his Psych notebook, but he seemed bouncy and ready to go. Gretchen shocked me by turning up in a bright green dress and proclaiming her love of dancing. But when we got to the club—some place in Bushwick that Milton said didn't card—I saw that she danced the way she did everything else: with a quiet joy that was just her own. She wasn't there for anyone or anything except dancing. And I kind of got the feeling I could learn something from her on that front.

I sat at the bar with Milton, watching as this mess of people attempted to make connections. Everyone was checking out everyone else. Or they were with their friends and oblivious to anyone else. Or they were with their friends or dates and still looking for someone better or more interesting or flashier to come along. It made me incredibly sad. Like this club was a microcosm of the real world. Except, I guess it actually *was* the real world. And then I was imagining infinitely more bars just like this one, all with people inside them acting the same way.

What blew my mind about physics was how it could account for this whole random set of people. We were all subject to the same forces of the universe. For every action there was an equal and opposite reaction. Like, no matter how illogical an action seemed there was still a sense of predictability in the way the world absorbed it and responded. Maybe that shouldn't have comforted me, but it did. Because it was partly the predictability of those reactions that kept things running smoothly—I mean, that was socialization, right? Take that away and everything was chaotic and terrifying.

The things that *could* happen. Not super dramatic things like getting mugged or killed, even. But, the guy over there in khakis and a polo shirt? He could go and pee in the middle of the dance floor while singing Queen if he chose to. Nothing was stopping him except that he could predict what our reaction would be.

I didn't know why I was thinking about these things when we were there to dance. I think maybe even the two drinks I'd limited myself to had made me pretty tipsy.

Milton delighted me when he drank because he got super loose and brutally honest. And maybe a little bit mean, but in this way that was totally justified because he was such a nice person at base. And because people were idiots. Like, this sleazy guy came up to him and was trying to flirt but kept saying super racist shit in the guise of compliments, and Milton was just like, "Goodness, I am so sorry, but I don't speak English. No, seriously, I have no idea what you're saying to me right now—it all just sounds like nonsense." At which point, Milton slid another drink over to me, and I took it, even though I'd learned at orientation that I was a total lightweight, because I knew he was exasperated and wanted to commiserate.

But then I was definitely tipsy, which meant of course that I fished out my phone and called Will. He didn't answer, and before I could leave a message, Gretchen pulled me off the bar stool to dance. Which was probably for the best, because I didn't know what I would have said to him. Something about forces in the universe and the way he makes me see stars and his mouth and, shit, it was a good thing I didn't leave a message. Well, good for me, not necessarily for the rest of the bar, which had to see me try to dance.

Gretchen's dress was green fire and her light hair floated out around her. It was like she spun without even moving, the pulse of the music carrying her effortlessly. She seemed strong and centered, and I couldn't even imagine what it must feel like, so I tried to match my movements to hers. I was a moon caught in the gravitational pull of her planet, and when I looked up and spun and spun the lights sparkling above were the brightest stars I'd seen since leaving Michigan.

Chapter 4

October

"OMIGOD, THIS is the heaviest thing in the history of things."

"Just keep it level," Will grunted.

Gee. Thanks for that.

Yesterday I'd woken up feeling totally out of it even though Milton assured me I'd only had three drinks. Basically all I did was eat a shitty dining hall bagel and some vanilla soft-serve and sack out in my room. By the time Will called in the afternoon, I'd fallen asleep in the middle of reading Chaucer for my Great Books class. He'd wanted to know if I could help him move some furniture into his apartment from the storage unit in his basement. I hadn't even really listened to what it was for, just agreed that I'd meet him there this afternoon.

He'd been normal when I got here. No mention of how we totally made out in a swanky shop last weekend. Not that I'd been expecting one.

As I inched along Will's endless hallway, some semidetached flap of rubber from the sole of my shoe—I never did get new ones last weekend, since Will was too busy dressing me up and kissing me and not talking about it—nearly tripped me and I caught myself in the doorframe of the apartment before Will's. I guess I kind of thudded against the door to avoid dropping my side of what was clearly the most epically heavy filing cabinet ever made. As I levered myself away from the door, it opened with a squeak and a forty-something dude who looked like he used to be a football player and now just watched a lot of it on TV while downing pizza and beer poked his head out.

"Did you knock?" His tone was primmer than I expected.

"No, Perkins, he didn't knock. He just tripped. Back to your regularly scheduled programming."

The dude—Perkins—just sniffed and looked put out, but he closed his door. We finally got the damn thing into Will's apartment, but he could barely even tell me where to put it because he was too busy muttering ranty things about Perkins.

"What is your problem?"

"That fucking guy," Will snarled.

"He said three words."

"Three asshole words. He's my nemesis. Screw that guy."

"Um, kinda… dying." I indicated the filing cabinet with my chin. My arms were about fifteen seconds from giving out.

We put the filing cabinet in place and lugged a few shelves and a table up from the storage unit too, Will glaring at Perkins' door each time we passed.

"So, why's he your nemesis?" I asked as we set up the shelves and what Will said was a drafting table.

"He's just always around, doing infuriating shit like sticking his head out when I walk past. Or—he straightened my doormat once, the OCD psycho."

I looked around at Will's immaculately organized apartment.

"Um. Isn't that maybe a nice thing to do?"

"No. He's a busybody. Maybe I wanted my mat like that. Maybe I had it that way for a reason. He didn't know. He's just a control freak. You don't go around rearranging other people's stuff."

I couldn't help but smile because he sounded like a pissed-off kid and it was adorable, and when I did Will rolled his eyes and stalked off to the kitchen. He handed me a beer and popped the top off his own.

"Thanks for helping. You're a pal." He clinked his bottle to mine and flopped down on the couch, drinking deeply. I couldn't look away from the movement of his throat as he swallowed. The gold of his weekend stubble faded into the creamy skin of his neck. His lips wrapped around the neck of the bottle.

He drained it, looking at me, and I started to get hard just watching him as he watched me.

"You're—you—gah," I mumbled, my cheeks going hot as Will's gaze traveled down to my crotch and he smirked, but still said nothing. In an attempt to distract myself, I opened my beer, licking quickly at the fizz so it didn't get on the couch, but grimaced at the sour taste. Okay, I guess I now knew I didn't really like beer.

At my expression, Will's smirk turned to a genuine smile, and he held out his hand to me, shaking his head affectionately. My heart beat faster as

I slid my hand into his. He held on for a second, thumb caressing the tender skin on the inside of my wrist.

"I meant gimme the beer," he said.

"Oh, right."

I dropped his hand and passed him the beer, sitting next to him in silence for a few minutes as he flicked through the channels. Finding nothing that suited him, he jammed the power button on the remote and tossed it onto the coffee table with disgust.

"Hey, can I see that cover design?" I asked. Will had been working overtime on the design for some book that his bosses were sure would be huge.

At the console next to the drafting table, Will nudged his mouse to bring the computer to life. He had some kind of black rubber pad where a keyboard would be and a set of black plastic tools lined up next to it. When the screen came to life, his desktop was a blank white background with only one small, unlabeled gray folder in the bottom right corner.

"What happened to your desktop image?"

"Nothing. I just don't like clutter."

"But you're all… artsy. I would've thought you'd want…." I trailed off, realizing how dumb I sounded.

"Number one, don't ever say *artsy* again unless you want to sound like you're eighty-five. And it's visual clutter. I don't want anything competing for my focus on the screen."

I looked around at Will's apartment. I hadn't paid any attention when I'd been here the other night, too nervous and too distracted by Will to notice much about the place. It was stark. All clean lines and well-balanced shapes. Nothing distinguished itself by design, but nothing was exactly plain either. Like the black leather couch, everything seemed very high quality, but nothing screamed money. The furniture didn't seem to belong to any period—not that I'd have recognized such a thing if they were, but it didn't have that aggressively modern, cement-and-steel look, or the bought-the-whole-showroom look, or the I'm-bohemian-and-artsy look. Er, wait, not artsy.

The walls were white, the furniture black or light wood, and the rugs a neutral oatmeal-y color. There were some large framed black-and-white photographs on the wall just inside the door, and I knew I'd seen some kind of art in the bathroom, but there wasn't anything but blank wall near the work area, and the open floor plan left the kitchen no walls at all. The only real color came from the motley spines on the bookcase behind the couch, and a stack of coffee-table books on art and design on the side table. In fact, with the curtains drawn open, the main attraction was the view of the city through the large windows.

Will's clothes were the same as his décor, I realized. Everything fit him perfectly—though that might have been mostly how well-proportioned he was—and they were always sharp, but never flashy. He wore mostly black, white, grays, and neutrals. Sometimes a light gray-blue the color of his eyes, but I didn't think I'd ever seen him in anything else.

"That's it." Will's voice brought me back to the screen between us. "The proofs are at work, but this is the digital version." He leaned in and made a sound of disgust. "The damn—shoot." He pointed. "That has a weird green cast on this screen but it's actually gray."

"Oh, it looks gray to me. Wow."

"It's the first in a trilogy, and when you line the three up, the color will fade down diagonally until it disappears at the bottom right corner of the third book." Will traced a downward arc, finger hovering an inch from a screen totally devoid of fingermarks or dust particles. "Then, here—" He opened a smaller window with a picture of the spine. "See the way the image wraps around here and goes all ghosty? When the three books stand together on the shelves—the hardcovers, anyway—you'll be able to see it's actually part of a larger image."

"It's amazing!"

Will smiled. "The author won't like it. He wanted something flashier. But that's why we don't let authors design their own covers, thank god. I think it'll sell, though. Especially sitting on a shelf next to some of the schlocky garbage that's just the title and the author's name in Arial against a generic stock background."

Then Will was off, talking excitedly about design and marketing, color and balance, pulling up different files on the computer to show me other covers he'd done and images of those he admired. He talked as if I understood what he was saying. As if my knowledge of cover design aesthetic weren't limited to the distinction between, like, a Danielle Steel cover and a Stephen King cover.

I couldn't keep my eyes off him. How his face lit up when he talked about this stuff. How every now and then he'd bump my shoulder with his for emphasis. The way he pushed his hair back absently when he bent closer to the monitor, eyebrows drawing together in concentration as he searched for the next file he wanted to show me. The way his forearm moved when he clicked the mouse, muscle and tendon contracting under pale skin limned with golden hairs.

"So, um, you kissed me. Again." It just kind of popped out, and I felt my face heat in that way that I knew didn't actually look like I was blushing, but made my heart beat fast and my ears buzz with nerves. "In the dressing room," I added stupidly.

His gaze shot to mine, his eyes burning, then slid down to my mouth, and I felt it like a caress. For a moment it seemed like he might respond. Like we might talk things through, instead of continuing this strange dance. But then he blinked and shot me a wink before turning back to the computer.

"You kissed *me*, kiddo."

"So, YOU have no experience working as a barista at all, you can only work on the weekends and when you're not in class, and you've never heard of latte art. *Why* should I hire you when every third person in line to buy a cappuccino is probably more qualified?"

I'd ducked into Mug Shots on a whim when I saw the HIRING sign. I needed a job badly if I was going to have a prayer of being able to do anything in this city besides study, and, well, the state of my shoes was getting pretty dire.

The manager on duty was named Layne. Her dark jeans hung low and her white T-shirt and red-and-brown flannel were spattered with coffee and foam around the edges of a too-long apron. Her brown hair was cut short, her cheeks permanently flushed, and behind thick, nerdy-chic glasses her blue eyes were squinty and shrewd.

She was right. I was woefully unqualified for the job. And yet, it didn't feel like she was shutting me down, exactly. More like she was asking it as a genuine question. And maybe was a little bit amused.

Anyway, she seemed so cheery, despite the chaos going on around her, and the stickers slapped onto her thermos said "Earth First!" and "Queer Rock Camp" and "NYQueer," so I couldn't bring myself to bullshit her.

"Oh gosh, you probably shouldn't, if they're way more qualified," I said. "But—okay, things in favor of hiring me anyway?" I ticked them off on my fingers. "I'm super dependable. Maybe I can only work on specific days, but I'll never call in and leave you searching for someone to take my place. And next semester I could schedule my classes so I'm more flexible. I'm pretty friendly and people usually like me, so I'd be good with, like, grumpy, pre-caffeinated people. What else? Oh, well, I'm smart, I promise. That sounds obnoxious, probably, but I mean that once you show me how to do stuff I'll have it. You won't have to tell me twice. And… well, I really need the money, honestly. So I won't do anything to get me fired."

I leaned in and lowered my voice. "Also, um, I'm gay, if, like, that helps?"

The look she gave me made it immediately clear that this was a miscalculation on my part. But just as she opened her mouth to respond, there was a crash, a splat, and a very inappropriate-for-the-workplace slew of swear words from the front of the line. The customer seemed to have somehow spilled the entire tray of coffee drinks he'd been handed, and half of them ended up on the counter and the girl ringing him up—hence the swearing. She was totally drenched in what smelled like a combination of coffee and hot chocolate, and the counter was swimming in sad islands of melting whipped cream.

Layne narrowed her eyes and sighed.

"What are you doing right now?"

"Nothing," I said.

She nodded once, resigned, but I swear there was a damn sparkle in her eye like she was enjoying this. "Up for a trial by fire?"

"Um, what?"

Which is how I found myself hastily aproned and stationed behind the huge, gleaming machine that loomed like the obelisk in *2001: A Space Odyssey* and would determine my future. After about ten minutes, when it became painfully clear to the other guy stationed at the machine that I had absolutely no clue what the difference was between an Americano, a macchiato, and a latte, to say nothing of how to make them, I was switched to taking orders.

Three hectic hours later, Layne called me over.

"Well," she said matter-of-factly, "you definitely don't know anything about coffee."

"No," I said.

"But you're perky and polite, which shocks people in this industry." She cocked her head, seeming to consider me.

"Look," I said, "sorry about before when I said the thing about being gay. That was like maybe inappropriate? I dunno, I just meant—I was trying to say that—I didn't mean to assume—I just thought you might like me more if—or be more likely to—um, but maybe that's accusing you of some kind of, uh…."

"You're not really helping yourself here."

"Sorry."

She shook her head. "Even if I did happen to be politically committed to providing jobs for queers, some pretty boy cis white dude wouldn't be at the top of my list."

"Oh shit. Good point. Um…."

She looked at me for a while, and I could almost see the questions she wanted to ask running through her head. "How do you feel about puns?" she asked, finally, smiling slightly and narrowing her eyes at me.

Crap! Did she like them and I was supposed to say I loved them? Or did they annoy her and if I said I thought they were cool I wouldn't get hired?

"I-I—well…."

"You're totally trying to figure out what I want to hear right now, aren't you?"

"Yeah."

"Okay, you're hired on a trial basis. Be here tomorrow at three for training."

IT TURNED out to be no coincidence that Milton had known how to get on the roof the night we met. He made it his business to always know an escape route, a side effect of going to a snobby private school, he said, where immediate egress was sometimes the only thing that had stood between him and losing his mind.

We were sitting on the fire escape on the north side of the building where we had Psych. Milton had pulled me out a fire door after lecture unexpectedly, talking loudly about nothing, and then hustled me up two flights before flopping down onto the chilly metal.

"What are you doing? Where are we? Jesus, is this even safe? This doesn't feel safe." The metal was an open grid, so if I looked down, I could see the dumpsters five stories below.

"Oh, just hold on to the railing, we're fine."

"Soooo…."

Milton rubbed his temples. He looked thrown.

"Umm, just this guy. He's a senior and he's like the *best* actor. Seriously, he was on some TV show or something after high school, and he took a few years off to do it and then came back to school because he wanted to learn more about his craft, isn't that cool?"

Milton sounded uncharacteristically swoony.

"And why are we outside on this deathtrap because you have a crush on the next…." I couldn't think of a really famous theater actor, and Milton laughed at me. Then he muttered something.

"What was that?"

"I just saw him coming down the hallway and I panicked is all."

"Oh my gosh, this is great!"

"Not from where I'm sitting."

"Oh, sorry, no, not great for you. Definitely not. For me! Because if you can get all freaked and flustered over a guy, then it means I'm not such a total mess. Jeez, I just thought you were cool all the time, but this is way better."

"Gee, thank you so much, Leo."

"Sorry, sorry, but I mean, obviously this guy will like you. You're so awesome. And you're hot. And a great kisser. I'll testify to it if this guy wants." We could say things like this to one another now, since we'd firmly established that we were not ever going to hook up again. It felt nice. Intimate, in a friends kind of way. "What's his name, anyway?"

"Jason," Milton said, the word practically a sigh.

After a few moments where I thought he'd say more and he stared down at the dumpsters, Milton seemed to shake it off, and he hauled me up by the arm and hustled me back to our dorm saying we were running out of time to eat before movie night.

"Direct all your criticisms to Milton," I told Thomas and Gretchen. "I had absolutely nothing to do with this decision."

When Milton announced that for movie night tonight we'd be starting to watch *Felicity*, I thought he was kidding, until he pulled out a disturbingly pastel box set.

"Are those *DVDs*?" Thomas asked, the way you might ask "Is that a cockroach?" Milton clutched the box set to his chest and glared.

Gretchen narrowed her eyes and looked between me and the box set. "Ah, I get it," she said with what I could've sworn was pity.

"I am not Felicity!"

"Oh, boo," Milton said, shaking his head. "You really haven't ever seen the show, have you?"

MY CULTURAL Foundations paper was due in twenty hours, and Charles was deep into one of his conspiracy theory rants, this one, as far as I could tell, something about the Denver International Airport being secretly designed by the Freemasons.

"—an entire network of subterranean tunnels that they claim were an automated baggage delivery system, but it never worked even though its installation cost millions of dollars," Charles was saying, and I was only half listening, nodding at what seemed to be key phrases, like "bunker" and "shadow government" and "New World Order." Usually, if I just kind of nodded along, Charles would eventually run down his own motor.

It had become my approach ever since the day he'd tried to explain the theories of the second gunman in the JFK assassination, complete with schematics of the grassy knoll, reedited versions of the Zapruder film, and heavily redacted scanned documents from the Warren Commission.

Charles did eventually lose steam, trailing off back into his research. I was exhausted from my first real day of work at Mug Shots, despite my proximity to the espresso machine meaning I could caffeinate at will. Even though I'd taken a shower when I got home, everything still smelled like coffee, to the point where I was convinced that maybe coffee particles were stuck in my nose hairs or something, like bits of pollen on a bee's legs, so that every breath I took was being filtered through coffee. Hell, maybe that's why it was so addictive? I'd have to see if Charles had ever heard of a conspiracy theory about that.

The caffeine had clearly worn off, though, because I was staring at the screen where I'd written some notes for my paper and my brain felt like mush. I wrote a thesis statement and immediately deleted it because it was self-evident. I wrote another that I deleted because I knew I couldn't support it, and another that I deleted because it would be too much work to explain. Ugh.

I closed my laptop and went to see if there was any tea in the hall kitchen. I found a mangled box of jasmine tea that it didn't look like anyone would miss it and put water on to boil, slumping against the counter in the hope that somehow a paper idea would magically fall into my head.

"You gonna get that?"

I jerked up to Gretchen's voice and the sound of the kettle screaming.

"Oh my god, I actually just fell asleep standing up."

"You okay?"

"I have a paper on *Jane Eyre* due tomorrow and everything I think of is idiotic and I'm so tired."

There was something about Gretchen that made me accidentally tell her all my problems.

"Come to yoga with me," she said.

"Oh, no, I don't have time," I said. I thought only hippies and health nuts did yoga.

"Well, you're not getting anything done in the state you're in, are you? Also, you just majorly over-steeped that."

I didn't know you could over-steep tea. I took a sip. It smelled floral and sweet but was intensely bitter. I winced and Gretchen nodded in commiseration.

"Ugh!" I dumped the tea down the drain and slumped. "I can't even make tea, what's wrong with me?"

Apparently she decided this was a rhetorical question because she just nodded and said, "It'll be good, I promise." Then she took me by the elbow and pulled me after her.

The first twenty minutes were ridiculous, the next twenty minutes were torture, and the last twenty minutes were amazing. I was clumsy and not strong and had no idea that I apparently breathe incorrectly. But the instructor was amazing, telling us ways to adjust our bodies to do the poses more safely, more effectively, more beneficially, and every time I followed her instructions, I could *feel* my muscles engage differently, feel my breath deepen, feel myself calm down and my mind clear.

With all my attention focused on breathing in and out through my nose, turning my right hip forward and my left hip back, pulling my navel in, squeezing my shoulder blades together on my back, retracting my chin back so my head was in line with my spine, pulling my feet energetically toward each other, and pushing into the inner edges of my feet, along with a dozen other things I couldn't do, I had no time to feel tired or stressed. I didn't give a single thought to my paper, or to Mug Shots and all the ways I'd managed to humiliate myself in front of my coworkers, mess up people's drinks, or spill things on myself.

I didn't even think of Will. And an activity that managed to take my mind away from him and the fact that he'd kind of blown off my last few invitations to do anything, citing being busy at work? Well, that was worth something.

As we walked back to the dorms, I was alert and energetic, but not bouncing off the walls the way I often felt. I was calm. And how much did I love Gretchen for not asking me how I liked it and saying she told me so.

"I go three times a week" was all she said when we went our separate ways. "Come whenever you want. Good luck with your paper."

THE NEXT month went by in a rush of total chaos, punctuated by the most fun I've ever had. Maybe it's because of how busy and stressful everything was that the moments with my friends felt so intoxicating. Or maybe it was because I'd never really had friends like these before—the kind who knew about my daily life, who I was excited to run into at the library, or slump next to at a table in the dining hall with plates of pizza that managed to be simultaneously dry and greasy.

The kind of friends you told everything to because they were the fixed points in your ever-changing universe and who told you everything because you were the fixed point in theirs.

Milton had a seemingly endless supply of stories about adventures he'd had with his theater friends from high school. Nights they had to stay at school until two in the morning to finish painting the scenery for opening night the next day. Nights they told their parents they were at the theater but actually went out to bars and clubs. Times he snuck away to mess around with guys in the lighting booth or the sound booth or the catwalks (Milton had a bit of a thing for techies).

Milton's roommate, Robbie, seemed to be the one person immune to Milton's charms. He was quiet and kept to himself, leaving the room whenever we were hanging out in there even though Milton always made an effort to include him in the conversation. Milton said at first he'd worried that Robbie was freaked out by having a gay roommate, but he'd realized he was just pretty solitary.

Gretchen's roommate, on the other hand, was the opposite. She was aggressively cheerful and always wanted to talk to anyone that Gretchen brought to their room. She had frizzy red hair that she straightened religiously, but she always missed a spot in the back, like she was waging an epic, unwinnable battle against a part of herself.

Within the first month of school, she had already joined something like ten clubs and was always encouraging Gretchen to come to this meeting or that event with her. Gretchen was basically a saint, but even she couldn't keep her cool with Megan all the time. Thomas started calling her Megan-with-no-H because he said she was like the inverse of Meghan from *Felicity*. Then, so she wouldn't know we were talking about her, we shortened it to No-H.

Sometimes, No-H would launch into cheery, interminable monologues and Gretchen would silently gather up her study materials and slink into the common room. If it was occupied, she'd come to my room, sink to the floor next to my bed—Gretchen loved sitting on the floor and had the kind of excellent posture that made it look like she sat on a throne even when wearing sweats on our dorm carpet—take deep, centering breaths in an attempt to cleanse herself of the static of No-H, and then work in total silence for hours, seemingly undistracted by either my sighs at my work or Charles' clumsy entrances, exits, and muttering at his computer.

After I'd gotten the job at Mug Shots, Gretchen had started coming and doing her work there when No-H was driving her particularly up the wall, and I'd slip her coffees that people sent back or that went unclaimed at the counter.

Gretchen was from just outside Ithaca and was really close with her huge extended family, so she'd had a lot of experience blocking out noise and chaos. That No-H was able to get to her even though that was a true testament to her level of irritation. Gretchen had tons of stories featuring a zillion different cousins, aunts, uncles, and second-somethings-twice-removed that sounded idyllic and chaotic, like scenes from a movie.

Family reunions in parks where picnic tables full of food got eaten by dogs or doused in flash floods. Christmas Eves when all of the siblings and cousins slept jumbled together in living rooms, attics, and basements of various houses and opened metric tons of presents all at once. Birthday parties shared with three other people that sprawled over backyard fields and lasted late into the night.

Thomas' stories were rambling and often featured his twin brother, Andy. They sounded inseparable. Thomas even narrated in the first person plural. They had only gone to different colleges because, after a guidance counselor told their parents she thought they were overly dependent on one another, their parents had said they'd only pay for school if they went along with it. Neither Thomas nor Andy had really spoken to their parents since then. They chatted and texted constantly throughout the day and played video games online together at night with a group of friends they'd been playing with for years.

Charles didn't really tell stories so much as give disquisitions on various topics that sometimes included how he'd learned about them. So, I found out that he knew so much about computers because he built one as part of a school project, taken under the wing of a particularly zealous teacher, scavenging the parts from a computer lab graveyard of tech going back to the seventies in the basement of the school. (This was also the moment when I started to think that maybe when Charles said he went to "a good high school" that he actually meant some kind of super-genius school for science and technology.)

Thomas was irritated by Charles, I knew. He took things Charles said personally and got offended when Charles corrected him. But since Charles was also the only one who No-H seemed flummoxed by talking to, and since Thomas had hated No-H with a passion ever since she'd yammered at him about some study she'd read about how codependent most twin relationships were, Thomas usually suffered him without complaint.

I saw Will a lot, too, and though our hangouts had begun grudgingly, he clearly wasn't just humoring me anymore. We got along in this way that shouldn't have worked but did, like the first time someone tells you that Brie and pear go well together and it seems impossible until the tastes are lingering on your tongue.

Sometimes we just watched Netflix and Will got takeout, never accepting the money I tried to press on him, which was lucky for me since I didn't really have any to spare. With anyone else I would've tried to argue over the bill, but Will rolled his eyes when I tried and made it clear my protests irritated him, so I stopped. Other times we'd talk for hours—meandering conversations that spiked in heated disagreements and equally heated laughter.

Will was the only person who had ever made arguing with him feel safe. He wasn't angry or threatened if I disagreed with him, so I found myself licensed to be more forceful with my opinions than I ever had been. One night, disagreeing over I don't even remember what, I rose onto my knees on the couch and yelled, "That's the dumbest thing you've ever said!" It had sounded ridiculous the moment it was out of my mouth, but Will, after a beat, had grinned and ruffled my hair, pulling me down on top of him as he laughed, clearly pleased with me.

ON HALLOWEEN, Milton, Gretchen, Charles, Thomas, and I went to the Village Parade with a whole group of people from our dorms. In the dining hall before we went, we each came up with lists of things we thought we'd see and then made bingo boards of them, agreeing that the first person to get bingo got to pick the next thing we watched at movie night. Of course, Milton turned out to have a huge advantage because, being from New York, he'd been to the parade before.

The rest of us had no reason to imagine that we should put down things like "a person dropping a puppet head," "someone's hair catching on fire," "a child being terrified of an overly zealous adult in costume and screaming," or "drunk dude running out of the bar and dropping trou to moon the parade." (Although, I did randomly get lucky because I wrote down "a dragon," mostly as a joke, but then there was a sister and brother dressed as Puff the Magic Dragon and Puff's little brother.)

I called Will when I got home, exhilarated and a little tipsy.

"You know we met two years ago, today," I told him.

"I remember," Will said. I could hear the smile in his voice. "You looked hilarious falling off that skateboard."

I got flustered all over again at the memory.

He'd been coordinated and sophisticated, and I—well, I'd fallen off my skateboard, half in actual clumsiness and half to disguise the fact that I got hard under Will's stare, as if his hands were touching me everywhere his gaze landed while he looked me up and down for the first time.

He had been abrupt and aggressive and a little bit rude. He'd pissed off Daniel, made me feel like a loser for having no one to hang out with on Halloween, and had even managed to make Rex roll his eyes. Despite all of it, he had been the most dynamic person I'd ever met. He was honest and uncompromising and didn't seem to second-guess himself. He wasn't awkward or nervous or uncertain about anything, and for some reason that made him seem invincible, superhuman.

He'd driven me home after we'd played Pictionary, and he'd complained about Daniel and what he called his "helpless act." "Of course Rex would go for that," he'd said, shaking his head and muttering something about a hero complex.

"Why do think it's an act?" I asked, since to me Daniel mostly seemed like he tried to cover up the fact that he was sometimes bad at doing things that even I knew were common sense.

Will turned to look at me for the first time since he started driving, as if he'd forgotten I was there, actually listening to his vitriolic monologue. He pursed his lips and let out a long breath. "Ugh, it's probably *not* even an act," he said finally. And then he sulked.

"I don't get it. What's your problem with Daniel? Are you still in love with Rex or something?"

"No," he said, with finality but without force. At first I thought it was because he didn't mean it, but after I knew his habits a little better, I realized it was because Will said what he meant and didn't care if people believed him or not. When he dropped me off at home, just before he drove away, he rolled down the window and said, "Happy Halloween." His voice bordered on mocking, but he had chosen to prolong our conversation, and I decided that had to count for something.

"Watch out for the tricks," I said, trying to wink at him and succeeding only in kind of squeezing my eyes shut emphatically.

"It's the treats you really have to watch out for," he said, and drove away with the window down, like maybe he was hoping to hear more from me. Or maybe he'd just liked the fresh air.

After that, all I'd wanted was for Will to like me. Well, and to be around him all the time. I had always second-guessed myself, always been a little uncertain. I'd been raised to be polite to people and not to make waves. So Will's straightforwardness, even if it *was* a bit abrasive, was intoxicating. The notion that you didn't actually *have* to say what people wanted to hear just to make them feel comfortable—that it was a choice—felt thrilling and transgressive, and I'd become fascinated by watching Will move through the world and interact with people in that way. He wasn't unkind exactly. He just refused to follow what I'd always thought were ironclad rules of social engagement but which, it turned out, were as easily brushed aside as cobweb.

I couldn't believe it had been two years. By comparison, last Halloween didn't even bear thinking about. I'd wandered around Holiday after getting home from a long day of classes, wishing that Daniel and Rex still lived there, wishing that Will were with me, wishing… wishing for there to be *something* that made the day stand out from any of the others.

Now I asked Will, "What did you end up doing tonight?" He'd declined my invitation to come to the parade with us.

"Oh, you know, not much," he said casually, which I was learning was Will code for "I hooked up with someone." Which, of course, I knew he did. But somehow knowing it happened, and knowing it had *just* happened, weren't quite the same, and pain lanced through me at the thought of Will with someone else.

I didn't press him about it, though. I'd made that mistake a few weeks before when I'd shown up to hang out one night, and he was clearly in a bad mood. Even though I took some small pleasure in hearing him complain about what an idiot the guy he'd hooked up with had been, it hadn't outweighed the knowledge that Will would rather mess around with some random guy than try being in a relationship with me. When I'd said as much, Will had fixed me with a pained expression and said, "You're not like those fuckheads."

A million questions had buzzed to the surface with that comment. Like, if they were fuckheads, why did he sleep with them? (Well, fine, that one I could figure out on my own.) Or, if I weren't like them, then wasn't that a *good* thing? Didn't it bode well for our chances?

But before I could start reeling off my questions, Will had patted the couch next to him and rolled his eyes. "I'd rather hang out with you, anyway," he'd said, flicking the TV on. And my breath had caught in my throat so I couldn't have said anything if I'd wanted to.

"So, did you dress up for the parade?" Will asked.

"Yeah, I went as Dream from *The Sandman*. It was pretty awesome." I had borrowed Charles' long black coat and moussed my hair into a gravity-defying mop. No one had known who I was, though, or they'd asked "Are you that dude from The Cure?" To be fair, the hair was rather Robert Smith-esque.

"Ah. Feeling tragic, are we?"

I was, now, kind of.

"What would you do if I was?" I had been going for a flirtatious tone, but it ended up sounding like a genuine question.

"Well, I suppose I'd have to distract you from the utter tragedy of your young life."

That was totally an opening for some kind of racy comment about precisely how he might distract me, but I flubbed it by thinking too hard for something sexy to say, and gave up.

"Midterms are getting so stressful," I said, allowing the legitimate exhaustion I'd been fighting to infuse my voice. "Everyone's totally crazed and everything's loud and I can't concentrate. I have a gazillion things to do, especially this project for my physics class that I really want to do well on." Will was basically a workaholic, so I figured he'd respond well to that.

"I have it on good authority there's a perfectly functional library you could throw yourself out of," he teased.

"Yeah, but *everyone's* at the library this time of year, so it's not even that quiet. Besides, I'm guaranteed to run into someone I know there."

"Aren't you quite the social butterfly."

"And then they'll want to *talk*, and I don't wanna be *rude*...."

"Ugh, the horror." Will sighed. Getting caught in small talk *was* basically his worst nightmare, so I figured that one would get him. I waited, tapping my foot and biting my lip.

"Was there something you wanted to ask me?"

Damn it, I should've known better than to try and float any kind of passive-aggressive shit with Will. He always dismantled it, and then I felt like an idiot for trying.

"Um, maybe I could... come over and do work at your place?"

Will snorted. Clearly he'd known what I was angling for all along.

"Yeah, sure, come over."

"Omigod, thank you *so* much. That's awesome."

THE NEXT evening after I got done with my shift at Mug Shots, I went right to Will's. He was just getting home from work as I turned the corner to his building and we rode the elevator up to his apartment together.

I found myself imagining what it'd be like if we lived together. We'd get home around the same time, both eager to see each other. Maybe some days we'd meet like this on the street, the pleasant surprise of seeing your boyfriend washing over us both. We'd fall into step and hold hands in the elevator. Or maybe we'd get home within a few minutes of each other and chat about our days while Will changed out of his work clothes for the evening. Maybe we'd take a shower together (which would lead to messing around in the shower), or cook dinner together (which would lead to messing around in the kitchen), or order takeout and watch TV together (which would lead to messing around on the couch).

In reality, Will bitched about one of his coworkers in the elevator and shut himself in his room the second we were in his front door. He did not invite me to shower with him or participate in changing his clothes. And he didn't seem to have any plans whatsoever for making dinner, as evidenced by the fact that he grabbed a beer and a box of dry cereal and flopped onto the couch to consume them without speaking to me.

I put my backpack down on the floor next to the desk that sat beside the drafting table I'd helped Will bring up from his storage unit last month. Now it was covered with sketches, graphics, and samples of typography.

I started in on my work, hoping he'd get hungry for real food eventually, because I hadn't eaten since before work and I was starving.

After an hour or so, Will came over and sat at the drafting table, our chairs side by side. He didn't say anything, but he sharpened a pencil and started to work on one of the sketches. I could practically feel his whole vibe change from the moment he came over to when he settled into his work. He relaxed into his chair, and his pencil moved effortlessly over the paper. Even his breathing changed. He seemed the way I feel when I leave yoga.

I'd been going with Gretchen three times a week ever since that first class, and I would never joke about it being just for hippies again. I loved it. I could walk into the room feeling stressed as hell—scattered and anxious, or tired and grouchy—and walk out feeling calmer, more relaxed, and more energized.

I snuck a look at Will while he was concentrating. His full lips were parted, and he was hunched over his drawing, shoulders slumped forward, neck bent. His hair fell in his eyes and his ankles were kind of hooked around the front legs of his chair. It all looked very uncomfortable, but his expression was one of total absorption. His eyes were locked on the pencil lines before him even as he blew the hair out of his face.

I took a chance and rose, moving behind him. In a moment when he'd lifted his pencil from the page, I slid my hands onto his shoulders, pulling gently to straighten his posture the way my yoga teacher moved our shoulder blades together to counteract the posture of living hunched over our computers. I squeezed gently at first, not sure if he'd whirl around in a fury at being interrupted or shrug me off.

Instead, when I began to press into the knots in his muscles with my thumbs, Will softened under my hands and took a deep breath. I let my hands follow the lines of his body, rubbing up his neck and through his hair. I massaged along his spine, feeling his back press closer to me with each breath. When I leaned in and put my weight behind it, Will groaned and the sound sent a bolt of arousal through me. I leaned a little closer and smelled his hair and the scent that was just him.

I slid my hands under his sleeves as I massaged his upper arms, feeling the improbably smooth skin overlying lightly sculpted muscle. I wasn't quite brave enough to ask him to take his shirt off, scared my voice would break the spell, cut short the moment we were suspended in.

He kept making these obscene sounds, and they went straight to my dick.

I slid my hands forward a little, massaging the fronts of his shoulders and along his collarbones. Then I leaned in and kissed his neck. He gasped and tensed for a moment, but though I was sure that he would pull away now, he relaxed when I started massaging again. I squeezed his upper arms and leaned down again, kissing the other side of his neck. This time he didn't tense as much. I rubbed his shoulders and nuzzled his neck, kissed under his ear, along his hairline and down the other side of his neck to where it met his shoulder.

The top of his chair could swivel, and I turned him to face me. His face was impossible to read. He looked relaxed, but it all seemed like it could shatter at any moment. Moving as slowly as I could, I slid in front of him and kept massaging his shoulders from the front. He looked at me, eyelids heavy in relaxation. Then his eyes fluttered shut as I slid my fingers into his hair and massaged the base of his neck. I leaned forward and kissed him softly on the mouth.

He jerked back, startled, and looked at me.

I went back to massaging his shoulders, even though every atom of my being yearned for him. I was stupidly turned-on. I slid my hand around the back of his neck into his hair and leaned in again, kissing him deeper. This time, he kissed me back, the press of his mouth sending my heart racing, and I slid into his lap, twining my arms around his neck.

He tasted like the Honey Nut Cheerios he'd been eating, which I found ridiculously endearing. I could imagine kissing him after he ate breakfast, sending him out the door to work and tasting his cereal on my tongue even after he was gone.

Finally, his pencil clattered on the floor and his arms came around me. He rubbed up and down my back at first, then slid a hand into my hair, holding our faces together as we kissed. It was slow and sweet until Will pulled me closer and I could feel how turned-on he was. The idea that I could turn Will on flushed heat through me and made me strain against him. It was incredible. He was so beautiful. And talented. And... Will-like. I was just... me.

Will groaned into my mouth and pulled back, looking at me with furrowed brows.

"Don't stop," I said quietly.

He framed my face with his hands. "We can't do this."

"Do what?" I asked, smiling, and I leaned back in to try and kiss him again.

He looked at me intently, like he was going to say something serious, but then he just ran his thumb across my eyebrow and down my cheek.

"You're supposed to be studying," he said, finally, and gently eased me back onto my seat. He bent back over his work without another word, the slight tremble in the hand he used to rake his hair back the only indication he was anything but completely relaxed.

Chapter 5

November

BY THE time Charles slouched into our room around eleven the next morning, I was in a full-on panic about my physics project. What was due at the midterm mark was the proposal and a bibliography for what would be my final project. I'd had a frustrating meeting with the teaching assistant who was in charge of my discussion section about it during his office hours last week but had thought we'd worked things out.

Now I was staring at my e-mail in disbelief because he'd just responded to say that I needed to completely reconceive my project.

I barely noticed that Charles was wet until I heard him kind of squelch across the room.

"Is it raining?" I craned to see out the window, but no, it was clear outside.

"I need your help," Charles said. This was just kind of how Charles talked, and there was no point in asking for clarification because then he'd actually explain what he was doing, which would take longer than whatever he needed in the first place.

"Does it have to be right now?"

"Now would be ideal."

"Uh, should I assume I'm going to end up soaking wet?"

"It's a distinct possibility."

I sighed my you're-lucky-I'm-the-best-roommate-in-the-history-of-roommates sigh, which was completely lost on Charles, as I pulled on already dirty clothes and shoved my feet back into my Vans. If nothing else, at least Charles' random excursion would distract me from my physics drama.

"Hey, are you going to Boston for Thanksgiving?" I asked Charles an hour later as we walked back to the dorm. I had not, in fact, ended up getting soaking wet, since apparently the sprinklers Charles had run through earlier were on a timer. He'd never told me exactly *why* he needed to take pictures of me in various locations outside an unmarked building, and I hadn't asked, content that I was serving some greater, mysterious purpose.

"No. Even if I relished the idea of spending time with my family, I can't countenance a celebration of the violent slaughter and subsequent systematic oppression of Native Americans in the service of a massive land grab, followed by sexual violence, cultural negation, and acts of inhumanity perpetrated under the guise of constructing a national identity. Besides, I don't even like turkey. The meat cleaves disturbingly. Are you?"

"What? Oh, no. Can't afford the plane ticket. Besides, Thanksgiving is when my grandparents come over, and they aren't really down with the whole gay thing."

That was an understatement. My dad's father looked at me like I was scum and wouldn't hug me hello, like maybe I was going to try for some action or something. My dad's mom mostly just shot me side-eye and didn't answer me when I talked to her, so I'd stopped trying long ago. On my mom's side, my grandparents acted like they didn't know I was gay.

My grandmother would pat my cheek and say how handsome I was. Then she would ask if I had a girlfriend yet. She always managed the question with such sincerity that I had no clue whether she was legit delusional, being passive-aggressive, or possibly just displaying early-warning signs of Alzheimer's. Except that my grandfather, who was sharp as a tack, did the same thing, making comments about the women we encountered that would've made me uncomfortable even if I had found them attractive.

Like, okay, none of it was The Worst—I knew that people had it way worse with being out to their families. The part that stung the most was that my parents never corrected them, reminded them I was gay, or called them on it when they made derogatory comments about queerness in general.

Sometimes my mom would shoot me apologetic or guilty looks when they said these things. Looks that said, *It's so unfortunate that this is a thing that has to happen.* Like it never even occurred to her that she could intercede. That maybe she should care more about my feelings than about keeping the peace.

Janie and Eric were better. Eric would roll his eyes at them, and Janie'd sometimes say, "He wouldn't have a girlfriend, Nana, he'd have a boyfriend." Of course, she inevitably followed this up with, "if he ever actually spoke to anyone instead of acting like a *freak*," under her breath to me. She meant it affectionately, though. I think.

It had been just this kind of family gloominess that I'd managed to escape when Daniel had invited me to have Thanksgiving with him and Rex the year Will was in Holiday. I'd said yes immediately, even though I'd known that my mom would be upset. She had turned out to be surprisingly understanding, though, and at first I'd wondered if maybe I'd underestimated how bad she felt having to watch me navigate the uncomfortable family conversations.

But another part of me couldn't help but wonder if what I'd actually underestimated was how awkward she felt watching it. How much easier it was if I just wasn't there and she could say, "Oh, Leo's spending the holiday with friends." And I'd wondered if that was how things would be from then on: my absence making things easier for everyone.

"Well, it's fine—the dorms stay open, so it can be just like any other weekend," Charles said.

It was true, and it'd be good to have some quiet time to get a lot of work done before the last push leading up to finals. Still, maybe it made me pathetic, or a terrible person, given the whole slaughter, oppression, inhumanity issue, which I knew was true. But I was still kind of bummed at the idea of having nowhere to go for Thanksgiving.

I shot a quick text off to Daniel asking him what he was doing for Thanksgiving. The idea of spending it in with him and Rex in Philadelphia seemed perfect. Hey, maybe I could even convince Will to come.

Rex is taking me to a cabin, he wrote back, with one of the suspicious-looking crooked mouth emojis that looked laughably like the expression I'd picture him having to accompany that statement in real life. Good to see he'd mastered the smartphone. *In a state park*, he texted, this one accompanied by a straight-line mouth emoji, also eerily accurate. My heart sank.

Omigod, you have total emoji face! I wrote back. And, *Have fun!*

On a whim, I texted Will. *Do you have plans for Thanksgiving?*

Hell no, hate tgiving, he wrote, no emoji. I couldn't even imagine the emoji that could come close to expressing Will levels of scorn.

"Maybe I'll offer to work at Mug Shots on Thanksgiving," I mused. At least I could make some money and maybe even rack up some karma points with Layne by volunteering. I was still trying to come back from the whole telling her I was gay in an attempt to get her to hire me thing.

"Aren't things usually closed on Thanksgiving?" Charles asked absently.

I WAS ready to commit actual bodily harm against my physics TA by the last class before Thanksgiving break. It was infuriating because I loved the lecture so much, the readings were fascinating, and I was actually kind of thinking that being a physics major would be amazing. But this fucking guy made me want to invent new words just to express my loathing for him. I couldn't tell if he had it in for me in particular or if he was this much of a dick to everyone, but it was like he took joy in shooting down my ideas and making everything as difficult as possible by giving me the bare minimum of information in response to any question I asked.

I walked back to my room and fell immediately face-first onto my bed where I lay, backpack still on, until Charles shook me awake a few hours later and asked if I was purposely reenacting what it felt like to be pressed to death. He was writing a paper about the Salem witch trials—I'd had no idea how many theories there were to explain the cause of the girls' mania—and had explained in great detail the week before about pressing as a method of execution.

I woke up long enough to grumble, shrug my backpack off, and pull the covers up before going back to sleep. When I woke up the next morning, I almost panicked when I saw it was after ten until I remembered it was Thanksgiving break and I didn't have anywhere to be until five, when Charles and I were going over to Milton's folks' house for dinner. When they'd heard Milton had friends who were staying in the dorms over Thanksgiving, they'd insisted we come celebrate with them, Charles' critiques of the holiday notwithstanding.

SEND ME a pic of yr outfit, Milton texted me around noon.

Ummmmm, I wrote back. I was just wearing jeans and a hoodie like I always did. *Is Thanksgiving an... outfit occasion?* It never had been in my family. But I guessed I should've known that my parents might not be predictive of the sartorial habits of what I'd gleaned was a pretty stylish New York City family, considering that my mom's idea of fancy was a sweatshirt decorated with white puffy paint lace around the collar and my dad's was his plaid button-down from Lands' End instead of his plaid button-down from Target.

Facepalm, Milton texted. *Never mind. See you at 5.*

"Hey, what are you wearing to dinner?" I asked Charles, who was reading up on the history of Native American cultural appropriation to make sure he could accurately synopsize the various critical positions.

"A navy suit, a light gray shirt, and brown wingtips," he said.

"Right, sure."

Holy shit.

I texted Will: *FASHION EMERGENCY!!! Can I borrow something to wear? P.S. Happy Tgiving.*

"SO YOU seriously aren't doing anything festive for Thanksgiving?"

"I got a turkey sandwich with cranberry compote for lunch. That was festive as hell."

I rolled my eyes at Will and shrugged on the shirt he held out to me.

"Hmm, I wonder if Rex can cook Thanksgiving dinner in the cabin?" I mused. Rex was an amazing cook, and I couldn't imagine him passing up the opportunity.

"Huh? They're going to Michigan?"

"No, no. They went to a cabin in some state park for Thanksgiving. I just figured Rex had told you."

Will snorted. "I never hear from that asshole anymore."

"You don't? Since when?"

He looked at me like I'd said something stupid. "Uh, since he and Daniel shacked up."

"But... why?" I knew Daniel and Will weren't exactly one another's biggest fans, but I couldn't imagine that Daniel would ever ask Rex not to talk to Will.

"Because that's what happens when people get into relationships, kiddo. They don't give a shit about other people anymore." His tone was matter-of-fact.

He slipped the jacket over my shoulders, and we both looked at me in the mirror.

"It doesn't look good on me the way it does on you," I grumbled. The suit was light gray with a dark gray pinstripe, and on him it looked classy, but I looked like I was playing dress-up as a gangster or something.

"It doesn't really go with your coloring. Besides, you're skinny as shit."

I glared at him. "Well, fix it!"

"What, like feed you a calorie-dense meal?"

I slugged him in the shoulder.

He picked through his closet and pulled out a pair of dark gray pants, a thin white shirt, and a thick navy sweater that buttoned with round wooden buttons and looked like it should be worn by a shepherd in Wales or something.

"Ooh, soft." I reached for the clothes.

"Are you wearing boxers?" Will asked, eyeing my ass in a distinctly nonappreciative way.

"Yeah, why?"

"Take them off."

"Um."

He just looked at me.

"Turn around," I said. He rolled his eyes and pulled some underwear out of his drawer, throwing them at me.

"Put those on."

"You want me to wear your underwear?"

"Don't get too excited, kiddo."

He turned back around while I changed. The pants probably weren't supposed to be this baggy, but they didn't look too bad. The shirt was soft and the sweater fit me perfectly in the shoulders, its heavy knit lending me enough bulk that I didn't look so skinny.

"I look like I should be at a fancy ski lodge or something."

Will came and stood behind me, looking at my reflection in the mirror. He nodded, as if satisfied.

"Does it look okay?" I was totally fishing, but I couldn't help it. The sweater smelled like him, and I could smell *him* right there, and his hair gleamed golden in the mirror next to the dark of my own.

Will slid his arms around my waist from behind and rested his chin on my shoulder.

"Yeah," he said. I grinned, and I could feel his lips move against my neck as I saw his smile bloom in the mirror.

MILTON'S PARENTS were nothing like I'd imagined. I'd only ever known people's parents who were… well, parents. Milton's parents were *people*. His mom was in some kind of nonprofit arts administration, and she dressed like the ladies who ran galleries I'd seen in movies about New York: a fitted black skirt that came to midcalf over heeled black boots, a cobalt blue sweater, and a necklace that looked like The Hulk had torn a piece off the side of an airplane and twisted it into a circle and put it over her head. She wore her hair in a riot of natural curls tipped blonde, and her bright pink lipstick would've looked ridiculous on my mom, but on her it was amazing. Even though she was really nice, I'd been ridiculously intimidated by her since the moment she'd first opened the door for Charles and me.

His father was less intimidating because he was less interested in me, clearly wanting to take advantage of his time with Milton and his sister, Clarice, who was in her last year at Parson's studying fashion design. His father did something that I didn't fully understand and taught a class on political economy once a year at The New School. He apparently had a huge Twitter following because he was outspoken about the intersections of race in popular culture and political economy.

The Beales lived in Park Slope and had an amazing view of Prospect Park. I snapped a quick pic and sent it to Will with the caption *Giving thanks that I didn't show up looking like a total scrub! Xoxo.*

Milton's grandparents on his mom's side showed up about an hour after we got there, as did a few of Clarice's friends, all of whom were ridiculously well dressed in this way that I could never pull off even if someone picked my clothes out for me.

I was learning that there was this whole approach to fashion that wasn't about what was most flattering but more about expressing personality. It elevated people-watching all across the city because it gave me even more material to use to try and figure out who people might be. Or, at least, who they wanted the world to think they were.

Some of Milton's parents' friends showed up a little while after that, carrying covered dishes of food and bringing an argument they'd been having in with them. It was about a recent policy change in the mayoral office, and I was embarrassed that I didn't know anything about the local politics of the city yet. I saw the front page of the *New York Times* all over town, strewn across tables in the library or the dorms, and the *Post* and the *Daily News* at the counter of Mug Shots. But I still hadn't absorbed enough of it to be able to remember names and make connections.

"Tommy's a defense attorney and Skya works for the Sylvia Rivera Law Project," Milton told me, eyebrow raised as if I was supposed to know the significance of that. Before I could ask, though, Milton's mom herded us into the dining room where a long table was set with creamy white dishes that were probably the nicest thing I'd ever eaten off. The food was set up on the sideboard against the wall, and we filled our plates, the conversation zinging off in multiple directions.

Mostly I just ate and listened. Charles brought up the origins of Thanksgiving, spitting out his research in a tone with which I was intimately familiar. Milton's dad and Skya, who were sitting closest to him, nodded as he talked about the hypocrisy of celebrating genocide, and I could tell Charles was excited to talk about what he'd learned.

But rather than either dismissing him or praising him, Skya asked Charles what he did to advocate for Native American issues on a daily basis, and told him gently but firmly that while it was all well and good to trot out a critique on a holiday that people have developed a sentimental attachment to for reasons far removed from its origins, it's another entirely to actually do the work to make any kind of difference relating to that critique.

If I'd been Charles, I'd've been mortified, but he just nodded and said that he would look into it. And I was sure he would too. Skya patted his arm affectionately and told him that she could help him with some resources if he wanted.

The food was delicious. There was a turkey, stuffing, and mashed potatoes and gravy, but it was all fancy. The stuffing was made with cornbread and figs, the mashed potatoes were velvety and had a flavor I couldn't place. There were also baked macaroni and cheese with truffle oil, and a shaved brussels sprout salad that managed to make a vegetable my mom usually served boiled to disgustingness taste like fluffy magic. For dessert there was a pecan pie, a blueberry pie, and a chocolate cheesecake with some kind of salted caramel sauce that tasted like liquid gold and that I basically wanted to drink out of a water glass.

After dinner, we sat in the living room having whiskey (the adults) and hot apple cider (the rest of us) and speaking at half speed because we were all too full and relaxed to muster the energy to form complex sentences. I was so satisfied that I was even drifting off a little. If I let my eyes cross slightly, I could make my vision double so that it looked like the Beales' tastefully decorated Christmas tree was also sitting in Prospect Park.

Charles was deep in conversation with Skya about the implications of gender self-determination in the legal system, and Milton was in his element, charming Clarice's friends. I was warm and full and at peace with the world. I nuzzled Will's sweater and replayed the moment when he'd rested his chin on my shoulder.

My phone chirped with a text reply from Will, almost like he'd felt me thinking about him. I grinned. It was a picture of himself, taken in the mirror of a bar. He looked as beautiful as ever. Then I turned my phone over to enlarge the picture and saw that over his shoulder were all men, some of them shirtless. His text said *Gonna be giving thanks pretty soon myself *leer**. My heart instantly plummeted into my stomach and I blinked hard, swallowing, the taste of all that delicious food gone sour in my mouth.

Chapter 6

December

THERE WERE only a few days of classes left before Reading Day and finals period, which was also when my Great Books paper and my dreaded physics final project were due.

Gone was the camaraderie of the week before when, in an attempt to distract myself from the knowledge that Will chose to spend Thanksgiving in a sleazy bar with some other man instead of with me, I'd gone impromptu sledding with Milton and some of his theater friends—including the mysterious Jason, on whom Milton's crush had reached hero-worship levels.

And I kind of understood why. Dude was cool as hell. He was loud and confident and intense, but genuinely nice when you could get him to slow down enough to engage. He liked being the center of attention, but it was natural, not obnoxious. He just had charisma. Everyone, guys and girls alike, seemed to be totally into him. Hell, I couldn't help but stop whatever I was doing to listen when he monologued.

He wasn't handsome exactly—in fact, he was kind of funny looking. His nose was too big for his face and his smile was crooked, and his eyes and hair were a dirty-looking medium brown. But he was compelling. Engaging. All reaction and micro-expression and intense gaze.

We'd taken trays from the dining hall and gone to Prospect Park during the first snowfall that stuck. It wasn't great sledding, but Milton had done it since he was a kid. Besides, I quickly realized that being from Michigan set my expectations of snow much higher than other people's. One girl, a hilarious premed student from Louisiana called Sasha, had only seen snow once before in her life, and she was a riot, reacting to the modest hill we found like it was a black diamond ski slope.

Still, it was some of the most fun I'd had. We all fell over each other like puppies trying to pile onto the trays. There were a few families when we first arrived, but they left soon after dark and we got rowdier, pushing each other down the hill, holding on to each other's hands and trying to slide down in tandem, and generally horsing around like idiots.

One of the guys whose name I never learned made some joke about sledding and *Ethan Frome*, which I didn't get and I made a mental note to ask Daniel about it.

Finally, freezing cold and shaky from exertion, we left the dining hall trays at the top of the hill for anyone else to use, and trooped back toward the subway, stopping for hot chocolates twice at bodegas along the way. My mouth sticky with cheap chocolate and my fingers still numb, I fell asleep that night smiling, imagining someone walking past our trays poised in the snow and jumping on one with a grin, sliding downhill in the quiet darkness of the park.

Now, that night was like a distant memory. I was completely on edge, cursing every moment of leisure I'd ever enjoyed for being one more moment of work I had to do now. Charles was in some kind of intense caffeine and paranoia-fueled frenzy where he didn't sleep, just paced around the room alternately muttering to himself and typing loudly on his computer, which drove me bonkers. He had crudely converted his school-issue side table into a standing desk by stacking it precariously on top of his actual desk and propping up the back edge on books.

Even Milton, who was usually cool as a damn cucumber, wasn't unaffected. His outfits were distinctly uninspired, and he'd canceled the last two movie nights despite *Felicity*—which we had given up trying to pretend we were not full-on watching from start to finish with true gusto and strong contradictory opinions—being his total happy place.

Only Gretchen seemed mostly calm. She had a system that included detailed study and work schedules combined with long periods of rigorous physical exertion and timed psychic relaxation. In fact, I was pretty convinced that the fact that I'd been going to yoga with her regularly was the only thing that kept me from melting into an actual Leo puddle on the horrible carpet of my dorm room. I'd never worked so hard in my life, and things with my physics TA had reached a point where I practically started to freak out anytime his name showed up in my e-mail inbox.

I CAME to Will's in hopes that being around him would calm me down.

He was clearly about to make some snarky comment about my disheveled state, but swallowed it when I rushed in and dropped my backpack on my way to burrow into his couch and have a minor nervous breakdown.

"Ooookay," Will said. "I take it finals are not going well?"

"I'm gonna fail out of college," I groaned into the couch.

"Tell me what you need to do and how long you have to do it, and we'll figure it out."

I held my planner out to him, now a crumpled hank of paper worried into a smeary exclamation-point-riddled mess. He held it between his thumb and forefinger then put it on the coffee table like an undetonated bomb.

"Why don't you take me through it." He patted my back. "One sec."

He came back with a pad of graph paper and a pencil from his drafting table and sat beside me on the couch.

"Okay. Go class by class and tell me what you have left to do and when the deadline is."

I shook my head. "My physics TA is trying to ruin my life. I should just go back to Holiday and rot."

Will snorted. "You gonna work at Mr. Zoo's for the rest of your life?"

"Yes. Someday maybe I'll take it over and rename it Mr. Leo's."

"Great plan, kiddo. Come on, sit up. Tell me what you have to do."

"I can't." I knew I sounded childish and petulant and I just couldn't care. I was too tired, too overwhelmed. "Will," I groaned. "Can't I just drop out and come live here?"

"Christ on toast, Leo, you're fucking depressing me. Sit up." He dragged me up by my sweatshirt hood. "Now tell me what the deal is."

I laid it all out for him. How Clark, my physics TA, hated me. How I'd done everything he asked us to do in terms of the proposal for the final project, but he kept forcing me to redo it because he said it wasn't in compliance with one thing or another. And how, even though I'd asked Professor Ekwensi after class, and she'd mentioned that my project sounded great, Clark still made me revise it again, and when I'd mentioned Ekwensi's approval, Clark had glared at me and gotten all pissy, accusing me of going over his head by talking to her.

"Let me see these e-mails." Will's tone was murderous, and even through my stress and agitation, the warmth of his anger on my behalf settled comfortingly in my stomach.

I showed Will the e-mails, in which Clark had sent comments on the drafts of my proposal where he asked questions that I was really sure most students in an introductory class shouldn't be expected to know the answers to. And I showed him the comments Clark had written where he gave me totally contradictory feedback. I started to get freaked out all over again, and Will squeezed my shoulder as he peered furiously at the screen.

"I'm gonna kill this fucker! This petty, ineffectual little limp-dicked asshole has nothing better to do than lord his power over students like that makes him someone." He devolved into muttering and then flopped back. I smiled at him and kissed the corner of his mouth where his lips turned down in a scowl. To my surprise, he flushed a little and shrugged like his shirt was suddenly too tight.

"Okay. Okay, tell me the rest, and then we'll get back to that fucking guy."

I walked Will through my whole schedule and he wrote it down on the graph paper in that neat all-caps handwriting I associated with architecture schematics. Even rendered in neat rows and tidy handwriting, it was a *lot*.

"I don't think I can—"

"No, no commentary yet. Commentary is the seed of doubt. Doubt is the breeding ground for wasting time."

Will tore off the page and recopied everything on a fresh sheet of paper, every task with a bullet point, every deadline in order of the date it was due, the chaos of my entire finals schedule neatly organized by the calming blue lines of the graph paper as if there weren't a single thing that couldn't be contained, ordered, made achievable. He outlined a box to the left of each task to check off when it had been completed. At the top he wrote *Leo's Guide To Kicking First Semester Finals In the Ass*, which made me crack up to see in his neat handwriting.

It's possible that my laughter was somewhat hysterical because the next thing I knew, Will was squeezing my shoulders and rubbing a hand up and down my back calmingly.

"Okay," he said finally. He pointed to the schedule where he'd put a 1, a 2, and a 3 next to my tasks for the evening. "You start on this stuff."

He pulled me up from the couch, sat me down at the desk, and tacked the schedule to the wall in front of me. While I was still trying to figure out how I'd ended up with a life coach and also wondering how I could make him do this every finals period, Will put a glass of water and a bowl of cashews on the desk.

"Protein. Good for energy. Stay hydrated." Then he squeezed the back of my neck and left me to it.

Later, Will showed me the message he'd drafted to Clark from my e-mail account. It clearly laid out the work I'd already done, the changes he'd requested, and asked for clarification about several points, all of which were numbered. It was written so incisively that I couldn't imagine how anyone could read it and not just agree to everything it said.

"Oh my god, you're a genius."

With Will's eyes on me, I clicked the Send button without changing a word and closed my laptop in relief.

"Thank you." I twined my arms around his neck, holding on tightly. Will's arms tightened around me and he sighed deeply into my hair.

"You can't let people push you around," he said.

"Except for you, right?"

He huffed a breath out against my neck, but didn't disagree.

OVER THE next five days, I only went back to the dorms once, to grab a bag of clothes and the rest of my books. I told Charles I was staying at Will's, and he barely spared me a glance, just muttered something about the role of local politics in the Salem witch trials and nodded at himself as he typed furiously.

When Will went to work, he left me a pot of coffee on the counter and a Post-it note reminder to FOLLOW THE SCHEDULE AND DO NOT PANIC. Even on a Post-it, his handwriting was perfect.

He brought Thai food with him when he came home from work and we ate on the couch. The spicy smells of curry, peanut sauce, and ginger combined with the musky smell of Will's body wash and the clean, bright smell of his shampoo and I wanted to stay here forever.

He was wearing a white T-shirt and gray sweatpants, but they weren't normal—they were some kind of perfectly fitted versions of these staples, just like all his clothes, even the most casual ones, looked like they'd been tailored to fit him. When I asked him about it, he looked at me strangely and said they were just white T-shirts, but it seemed impossible.

Will was inhaling his food at a speed that seemed potentially hazardous for a wild dog, much less an average-sized human, when my phone dinged with an incoming e-mail. I grabbed for it, and when I saw it was from Clark, I almost dropped the phone in my Tom Kha.

"Omigod, he actually answered all the things!" Relief washed through me as I stared at my phone, and the weight that had been hanging around my neck like that damn albatross we read about in Great Books disappeared. I tossed the phone on the couch, and Will put his plate down just before I threw myself into his lap, wrapping my arms around his neck, and hugged him tight.

"Thanks," I said in his ear.

His arms came around me and squeezed me tight, one hand moving up to stroke my hair.

"Sure, babe," he said, and my heart practically stopped from joy.

LATER, I was taking a break, running through some easy yoga sequences. As often happened, after a few minutes of me doing something else, Will started to talk to me.

Initially, I'd thought this tendency was just Will being perverse. Like he was only interested in me when I wasn't interested in him. After it happened a few times, though, I realized it wasn't true. It was that Will felt most comfortable talking about some things when all my attention wasn't on him. So, though my instinct was to pay attention when someone was talking to me, I'd learned it was best to just keep doing whatever I was doing and listen.

So I kept moving, keeping my breaths deep, in through the nose, out through the nose. Move and breathe. He watched me, perching on the arm of the couch so he could look out the window behind me at the same time. Will looked out the window a lot. The view was the main reason he'd taken this apartment, he'd told me once.

"You can't get caught up in that kind of shit like what happened with Clark again," Will was saying, staring past me into the dark city outside. "You're too smart. You shouldn't let people have that kind of power over you."

This was pretty laughable coming from the guy who had such incredible power over me. But I didn't say that. It was best to just let Will say his piece before responding.

"I know he's your TA, so he does technically have actual power over you. But you have to remember: NYU is providing a service, and *you're* the customer. They're there to educate you. To make sure you learn the material. Not to make you feel like shit, or like you're not good enough. Not to try and control what you do with your life."

That gave me pause since Clark had never tried to control anything about my life.

"Did that happen to you?" I asked carefully, pitching my voice softly so it sounded offhand. I moved into downward-facing dog like I was barely listening to the answer.

Will said nothing.

I pressed my thumbs firmly into the carpet, turned my elbows out to protect my shoulder joints, and moved my shoulder blades together on my back, bending into my knees and then pressing my thighs up to straighten my legs. I could practically hear Tonya's voice in my head whispering adjustments.

"What happened?" I asked, and then I just breathed—in through my nose, out through my nose—and waited, not sure if Will would answer or not.

"There was this TA for my Intro to Graphic Design class, second semester freshman year." Will ran a hand through his hair, still looking out the window. "Or, I guess he wasn't technically a TA, since he wasn't a grad student; he was a senior graphic design major, but whatever. He was really talented and really harsh. You could tell he kind of hated doing teaching stuff and thought he was too good for it. But he liked me. Said I had potential. He helped me out a lot—helped me with my designs and with adjusting to school. To the city."

It was strange to be reminded that once Will was just a kid from small-town Michigan who'd never been to the city either. That however far away from me he sometimes seemed now, we'd come from the same place.

"But he was manipulative as hell too. Talked me out of using this one idea I had for a design and then used it himself. And when I called him on it, he told me that I hadn't known what to do with it so it couldn't've worked; that knowing how to use a design is just as important as the design itself."

My arms started to shake, and I moved through a few vinyasas, my attention always on Will.

"Hell, he even manipulated me into thinking that I seduced *him*."

I dropped to my hands and knees, breathing deliberately, like his words hadn't knocked the wind out of me. As I moved into plank pose, out of the corner of my eye I saw him twisting the hem of his shirt between his fingers.

"Anyway, what did I know? I was a baby. If he told me I was good, then I was good, period. I didn't know myself, really. I cared too much what he thought of me so I ran everything through this filter of what he'd think of it before I decided what *I* thought of it. It became automatic. That's the worst part—way worse than him stealing my design, or the rest of it."

Will's voice had gone bitter, cold. Like he was still chastising the version of himself who'd acted that way. And the description was so far from the person he was now that I could almost imagine it as someone else entirely. I wanted to go to him, touch him, but I knew he wouldn't want me to. Not in a mood like this. He shook his head and turned away from the window, hands in his pockets.

"Anyway, whatever. He was a shithead who made me care about him and then fucked my head up and dumped me at the end of the year. I heard he did the same damn thing to someone the next semester. Sociopath creep."

My legs were shaking, my arms were burning, and my stomach was trembling. Tonya said that you should be able to sink into each pose. Hold it and relax and breathe, and that was the challenge: to push your body only so far as it could go without causing agitation for your mind. But now it wasn't the *pose* that was agitating me.

Will took a deep breath and turned to me.

"Look, college is great and everything, just don't make the mistake of thinking those fuckers are magical founts of wisdom or anything, okay? Take everything you can get from it and don't put up with any of the shit that isn't useful."

Okay, that was officially a subject change if I'd ever heard one.

"That sounds like your personal philosophy in a nutshell," I said, collapsing out of plank in a totally un-flowy way. Tonya would not approve.

"I don't have a damn philosophy."

I rocked forward into child's pose to wait him out. Will might be feeling snarky with himself, but he was still the most honest person I'd ever met.

"But okay, fine, if I did, then, yes. People have a terrible habit of not separating things out into their component parts, you know? They think if they accept one part of something, then they're under some obligation to accept it all, as if there's no in-between. As if it's more important to agree than to be accurate."

And there it was again. A reminder of one of the reasons I loved spending time with Will. No one had ever made me feel so comfortable just saying whatever I thought before. I didn't have to worry that disagreeing with Will would hurt his feelings or piss him off. I mean, he might be pissed *because* of my opinion, but not because it was different than his.

I had grown up constantly trying to blend in with people at school so they wouldn't notice I was gay. Constantly trying to find common ground with my family so I could feel like one of them. Always sure that it was because I was weird that I didn't really have many friends in Holiday. To be able to simply speak my mind and know that Will was speaking his... it was a sweet relief.

That didn't mean I didn't still enjoy messing with him a little, though. I flopped onto the couch next to Will.

"You never agree with anything, asshole."

"It doesn't make me an asshole that I actually listen to what people say and address the points where my thoughts diverge instead of ignoring the parts I don't agree with."

"Oh yeah?" I nudged him with my shoulder. "Then what makes you an asshole?"

Will grinned. "A *lot* of other things."

"Well, why focus on the things you disagree with rather than the ones you agree with?"

"I don't focus on them. But if someone says, 'I like peanut butter, cheese, pickles, caramel, and taking it up the ass, don't you?' and I just say *yes*, then they'd assume that I agree on all counts, which is inaccurate. So if I want them to know what is accurate, I'd have to clarify the place where we diverge."

"Um, you don't like…."

He raised his eyebrows at me and smirked.

"Taking it up the ass?" I asked at the same moment he said, "Peanut butter."

"You don't like peanut butter? That's outrageous! Peanut butter's—" Then my brain caught up to the actual content of what he said. "Oh," I said.

AGAINST WHAT felt like all odds, I'd finished everything, Will's blocky letters in their perfectly ordered blue boxes guiding my way through finals.

I was ready to collapse on my bed and sleep for the foreseeable future, but when I got to our room I found Charles packing and ranting because apparently there had been some kind of electrical problem in the dorm designated for the people enrolled in January term classes, and res life had temporarily reassigned them to the rooms on our floor. So now Charles and I, and anyone else on our hall not signed up for January term classes, had to clear our stuff out and store it in basement storage until spring term started.

As Charles explained, gesturing vaguely toward his computer monitor at an e-mail I'd clearly missed in the hustle of finals, total panic set in. Because I realized that I hadn't even thought about what I was doing for January term. Or, I'd thought about it in the vague way that happened when my mom mentioned something about Christmas or people in the dining hall talked about plans for winter break. But I had failed to actually *do* anything about it.

Which is why instead of being facedown on my bed, I found myself knocking on Will's door with my fingers crossed, my heart in my throat, and my duffel bag over my shoulder.

"Did you finish?" he asked, not seeming surprised to see me as he waved me inside.

"Yeah. Um. Haha, about that. Funny story."

I told Will the situation, my panic mounting as I got to the part about how I'd totally fucked up and forgotten to make plans.

Will looked at me skeptically.

"I was just so stressed about all the finals stuff, and stuff with physics. I didn't even notice the e-mail, I swear!"

Suddenly it was less important that I find somewhere to stay for January term. I mean, really, I could go back to Michigan if I needed to. I could take the bus again, or my mom would probably be able to scrape up plane fare for me. It was more that, standing here in Will's apartment after spending the last week so close to him, the idea of leaving him for a month—of not getting to hear him make pronouncements or bitch about things, of not smelling him fresh out of the shower, of not feeling his eyes on me—was unbearable.

"Jesus! Fine, just stay here," he said. "Holy puppy dog eyes, Batman." He shook his head at me and took my duffel bag, putting it next to the couch.

"Wait, really! Oh my god, Will, thank you! You won't regret it, I swear! I'll do the dishes, I'll do… um, you know, other chores. Thank you, thank you, thank you!"

I flung myself into his arms, intensely relieved, and now thrilled to have my life unavoidably intertwined with Will's for the next month.

Will fell backward onto the couch, and I landed half on his lap and half on the floor with an "Oof."

"Ouch, Jesus!"

"Sorry, sorry."

Will dragged me up and kind of wiggled over at the same time, and I ended up lying on top of him. God, he smelled amazing.

"Thanks for letting me stay," I said softly, our mouths an inch apart. His lips were parted, and he was half smiling at me. I wanted him so badly. Wanted to absorb him into my skin and get under his. To feel every inch of him welcome me. I slid my hand to his jaw, leaned in slowly, and kissed him.

His eyelids fluttered shut as his mouth opened to mine. There was the slick heat of his tongue and the rasp of his stubbled chin, and my brain short-circuited in like point five seconds. I could feel his pulse speed up against my fingertips and I pressed against it, the line of his jaw sharp beneath soft skin. Everything about Will was sharp wrapped in soft or vice versa.

He groaned and grabbed me by the biceps. "Saying you could stay was *not* the same as saying we were going to—"

"No, I know that. I know." But I ran my knuckles over his cheekbone and kissed him again, and he didn't stop me.

WE FELL into a rhythm, orbiting around each other like twin satellites. Whether we were cooking, eating, showering, watching TV, or just coexisting, I was always aware of Will. Always attuned.

I learned things about Will by living with him that I'd only seen hints of before. Will could be easygoing and fun, but hated to be scrutinized, so the second I drew too much attention to him, his defenses would snap into place. Sometimes it was sharpness, sometimes silence or irritation. Sometimes it was bravado or flirtation. Sometimes teasing. Whatever the patina, though, it was a cover for the Will that I was getting to know in the times when he wasn't self-conscious. It was like his apartment was his haven, and when I paid too much overt attention, he acted like he did when people stared at him on the streets.

I learned that he was an amazing problem solver, able to look at a complex system and sort it out easily. He was extremely visual, so he solved those problems by writing things down or drawing them out, unraveling things and putting them in an order that was most logical (not to mention aesthetically pleasing) as he'd done with my finals schedule. Every endeavor, no matter how insignificant, was driven by that same logic of optimization. From the way he did laundry to the order of how he gathered the trash, it was a ballet of economy and grace, never a wasted gesture, always the shortest distance between two points.

I'd already known he was passionate about his work, but I hadn't fully grasped how many of his coworkers depended on him to be their second set of eyes. How often they e-mailed him looking for help or a reality check. And, for all that he was brusque and honest with them, they respected him for it. One night he'd gotten an e-mail from his coworker Joanne with a cover design attached that she wanted notes on.

"Christ," he'd muttered, squinting disgustedly at the screen, "that's horrible."

"Oh no, what are you going to tell her?" I asked. That was my worst nightmare, basically—being put in the position of having to lie to someone. No one ever believed me, so it always got awkward.

"Uh, I'm going to tell her it's horrible."

"What? Oh my god, you can't say that; it's so mean!"

Will snorted. "What are you, six? It's not *mean*. This is our job, and Joanne's asking for notes. What good would it do her to tell her it's good when it's not?" He said this like it was just that simple and dialed before I could respond.

"Joanne, hey." He peered at the screen as he talked. "Yeah, I got it. It's… well, it's not working at all, huh?" I gaped at him, but his expression and his voice were totally neutral. "Well, yeah, that's why you sent it to me instead of that ass-kisser, Adamson. So, let's fix it."

And he sat at the computer helping her redesign it for two hours. Before they hung up, he said, "I think it looks great, how about you?" And though I couldn't hear Joanne's response, Will smiled broadly—a sincere, tired, thoroughly satisfied smile—and simply said, "Good. Night," before wandering away to shower. He looked more than just proud; he looked… intoxicated. High on being able to have solved a problem, fixed an error, turned something from bad to good.

I was getting pretty good at reading Will's moods, too, even though I still couldn't predict them. Sometimes he was grouchy and short for no reason that I could tell. Other times he was upbeat, chatting about his coworkers or telling stories about what he'd seen walking home that day. Sometimes he had bouts of being furious with the world, ranting about everything from health care reform to e-mail etiquette. Other times he was quiet, almost meditative, moving through his own apartment like a ghost.

Sometimes he watched me. I'd look up from doing yoga or pouring coffee, feeling his eyes on me. Half the time he'd keep staring until I flushed with self-consciousness or arousal, because when he looked at me like that, it felt like I belonged to him somehow. The rest of the time he'd look away, scowling, irritated at me for catching him, or irritated at himself for looking in the first place, I couldn't tell. At other times it was like he forgot I was even there. He'd come around the corner and look genuinely startled to find me there.

And all the time, between us, the air grew thinner.

I could feel it when we stood close, him pouring coffee and me stirring eggs. The way the hairs on my arms stood up when his sleeve brushed mine. The way the back of my neck tingled when he stretched a casual arm behind me on the couch. Sometimes, it was as if he did everything he could to make sure we didn't make contact. Other times, he'd throw a leg over my knee while we talked like it was nothing, or run his fingers through my hair absently. His touch was electrifying and capricious, and every time it came, the intensity of my reaction startled me.

When I initiated touch with him, I eased into it slowly. I'd pass him his coffee and continue the movement of my hand up to rest on the back of his neck. I'd flip his collar down and keep contact, slowly moving to rest my chin on his shoulder.

One night, when he was standing looking out the window, I tucked my chin into the crook of his neck and he sighed and relaxed into me. I could feel the heat of his body through the fabric of his shirt, smell the scent of his skin and his hair. He reached a hand back and threaded it through my hair, keeping me there. We stood like that for what felt like ages, and just when I was about to blurt the question that felt like it was bursting to get out of me—that I knew he said he didn't want a relationship, but why the hell weren't we together when we so clearly worked?—I caught a glimpse of him in the window.

He looked vulnerable, his light hair a halo against the night sky. His eyes were closed and he was leaning into me like I was the only thing keeping him upright. When I opened my mouth to ask, I felt rather than saw his reaction. His shoulders tightened, and he shifted the balance of his weight away from me, as if preparing to support himself any second. And I couldn't do it. I couldn't shatter the spun-sugar moment, especially as I noticed how tired Will looked.

He had been up late the night before talking on the phone and pacing. So I just nuzzled the side of his neck and snaked my arms around his waist, taking his weight onto myself again.

"Hey, who were you talking to last night?" I kept my voice quiet.

"Hmm? Oh, my nephew." He sighed.

"You talk to him a lot, huh? Something up?"

"Uh, Claire. My sister. Sometimes she… leaves without telling Nathan and Sarah where she's going."

His weight against my shoulder grew heavier.

"She leaves?"

"Yeah." He sighed, and I tightened my arms around him. "She's bipolar—well, she hates that term, thinks it's bullshit, but she was diagnosed just after high school."

"Sorry, I'm not sure I know what that means, exactly."

"Well, it varies a lot. But for Claire... she always had these periods of being really manic. Not sleeping, planning these grand projects or adventures. Her teachers used to send notes home that said she should be checked for ADHD, but my parents never paid attention. When we were younger, she'd do all her school projects for a month in one week, or clean the house from top to bottom. Once, she borrowed a friend's car and drove to Kansas without sleeping because she was obsessed with *The Wizard of Oz*. Then, when she got back, she slept for like forty-eight hours straight and wouldn't come out of her room for the next week. Stuff like that."

"Oh man. That does sound like it'd be really hard for kids." I made sure to keep my voice calm and low so Will wouldn't move out of my arms.

He nodded and sighed. He sounded so tired, and I wondered how many times this had happened before. I kind of couldn't believe he'd never mentioned something so huge.

"Sometimes she'll go to the store and buy hundreds of dollars of groceries and cook for days until she has so much food it won't even fit in the freezer. And sometimes she takes off and doesn't tell Nathan and Sarah where she's going. So, they call me and I call around and try and track her down, but really she just comes back when she's ready. She leaves them food and money. But, you know. They're kids. They get scared."

"Yeah, of course." Nathan was ten and Sarah was only eight. "Can anyone help out? What about Nathan and Sarah's dad?"

"Dads. No. There's no one else."

"Your parents, maybe—"

"No." Will's voice was poisonous and his whole body tensed against me. He'd never even mentioned his parents before. "They couldn't be fucked to take care of their own kids; they certainly don't give a shit about their grandkids. Besides, they're useless. They're worse than children."

I started to ask about his parents, but Will pulled away and went to the kitchen, taking a beer out of the refrigerator. He held it up to me on offer, but I shook my head. I still didn't like the taste.

"Then sometimes... she does other things. Like...." Will bit his lip and sat down on the couch, tucking his knees up. It made him look uncharacteristically young. Uncertain. I sat down, folding my forearms over his knees and resting my chin on them.

"Like she'll drive to Detroit and meet up with these randoms she knows and get wasted in a hotel room for three days. Or she'll bring some guy home and tell Nathan and Sarah that she's in love and she wants them to meet her new boyfriend. I mean, these are guys she's known for like a week. And of course they never stick around. Sometimes they get scared off by the fact that she has kids, or she comes on too strong. And if not that, then she gets bored of them after a few weeks. Or a few days. Not a single one of them has lasted more than two months. And it's fine for her. But Nathan and Sarah…."

I wrapped my arms around his legs, curling around him. He sipped his beer, and his other hand came to rest on my hair.

"Well, I think they know the score by now. But when they were younger they used to call me and say, like, 'we have a new friend,' or, god, the worst, 'we have a new dad.' And when I'd tell Claire to quit introducing these guys to them… depending on her mood, sometimes she'd tell me how this guy was different. He was the one she'd spend her life with. Her soul mate. Or she'd be furious with me. Accuse me of thinking she was a loser who no one would want to stick around for. So there was no point."

Will shook his head, staring out the window into the dark. I took the empty beer bottle from him and slid it onto the coffee table, then I pulled him up toward me. He came into my arms easily, even if he grumbled a bit as he did it.

"It's good that they have you. Nathan and Sarah, I mean. I bet it makes a big difference."

Will nodded. "I guess."

It was a lot to take in all at once, and I felt like I should say something. Reassure him. But platitudes would irritate him and empty assurances enrage him, so I did the only thing I could in comfort.

I ran my fingers through his hair, rubbing his scalp, and he melted against me like a giant cat, content, for the moment, to be petted.

Chapter 7

LAYNE HAD been beside herself with joy when I'd called and said I could work extra hours over break. This guy Travis—who I think might've been in some kind of country band?—had quit, so Mug Shots was suddenly short-staffed. I might've been able to make up for Travis, but Jill, who'd worked there for three years and was a milk frothing wizard, had the flu, and it was total pandemonium in the café.

It was the day before Christmas, so everyone was either attempting to relax with a comforting latte before having to face the stress of a family holiday, desperately caffeinating to finish work before the days off, or trying to show their out-of-town guests an authentic New York coffee shop experience and getting frustrated to find no empty tables and a line that snaked out the door. Then there were the people loading gift cards and buying Mug Shots mugs and whole beans as last-minute Christmas gifts, dithering over whether their secretaries deserved $25 worth of coffee or $30.

We were closing at six, but looking down the barrel of the final two hours of my shift made me slam back another shot of espresso that a customer hadn't wanted.

"Hey, hot stuff," a familiar voice said, and I turned to find Will grinning at me from the other side of the long line.

I waved and grinned back, immediately cheered. Will had the power to render the entire coffee shop happy and homey just with his presence. I passed the drink I'd just made to James so he could ring the customer up, and started in on the next of five empty cups to my left.

I was lost in the rhythm of pulling shots, pouring milk, and measuring syrup when an irate voice said, "Excuse me." I didn't think much of it, since part of the joy of being behind the espresso machine is that you're in the heart of the action but you're behind a wall, only communicating with customers through the boxes ticked on the side of their cups.

"Excuse me," the voice came again. I looked up to find a well-dressed man with immaculately parted and gelled hair waving the coffee drink with "Frank" scrawled on it in my face. "This was supposed to be a flat white." He pushed the coffee toward me across the counter.

"Uh, isn't it?"

I was pretty sure that's what I'd made, though I tended to forget one drink the second I passed it along and started on the next.

"No, it's clearly a latte."

"Oookay, do you want an extra shot in there?" Usually when people said this, they were just angling for more espresso in the drink even when it was made properly.

"No, I don't want you to just *dump* an extra shot in. I want the drink I ordered and paid for."

"Well, it's just that the difference between a flat white and a latte—"

"I don't need a lecture, thank you. Just my drink. It's really not that difficult, you only have *one* job, and it's to add milk to coffee in the proportions people order."

I was pulling the cup toward me and getting ready to remake the drink when Will stepped up.

"Actually," Will said, "he has many jobs every time a new customer comes up in line. Over and over. For hours. For very little money." Will's voice was the lazy drawl he used when he was taking advantage of every bit of force his looks and charisma could exact. He was dressed for work so he looked like he'd stepped out of a *GQ* ad. "*You* have one job, which is to pay someone else to make your coffee for you. So why don't you do that? And then go away."

The man gaped at Will, who never broke eye contact. There was silence in the café for a moment, except for the irritating swing of Christmas music and the steady hum of the milk steamer. Then from the depths of the line someone called, "Preach!" Someone else said, "You're holding up the line," and a third person coughed "douchebag."

AT FIRST I'd thought that Will would let Christmas pass completely unacknowledged. It seemed possible that Christmas fit into the category of things I'd always thought everyone got swept along with but that Will didn't acknowledge. Just in case, I'd been dropping subtle hints for the past week about how much I like Christmas: adding holiday movies to Will's Netflix queue, humming Christmas carols while I was in child's pose on the rug, commenting on the pretty decorations in the shop windows whenever we walked past.

When I came out into the living room after rinsing the film of steamed milk off me from my morning shift at Mug Shots on Christmas Eve, it was to Christmas lights twinkling around the windows and *The Ref* queued up on the TV. On the kitchen counter stood a mini tree, also strung with lights—one of those rosemary trees you can get at the fancy grocery stores, the ones that smell like winter.

"You wanna order food?" Will asked casually from the couch, but he was twisting the waistband of his sweatpants in tight fingers, looking studiedly at the wall behind me.

I threw myself at him on the couch, hugging him and burying my face in his neck. He made a sound like he was annoyed, but his arms came around me, warm and sure, so I stayed put.

"So," Will said once we were ensconced on the couch with Indian food, "you didn't want to go to Michigan for Christmas?"

I shook my head, shoving some naan in my mouth to delay answering. I wasn't sure how to explain it, exactly. Will never talked about his parents and in that avoidance I read that things were probably pretty bad. But I didn't have a sob story. My parents hadn't kicked me out or treated me terribly. They'd never said horrible things, never hit me. But the space between what I wanted a family to be and what mine was gaped like a wound that couldn't heal. And nothing I put into it—not energy or time, patience or distance—could fill it.

"My mom wanted me to," I said finally. "So did Janie." Janie had texted me: *Come for Xmas or itll be toooooo booooooring!!!*

I'd spoken with everyone that afternoon after I got off work. My mom told me a long story involving one of their neighbors and a Christmas-decoration-related power outage. Janie expressed her annoyance that I hadn't come home. Eric described some piece of hiking gear he'd gotten for our dad, and when I told him I'd PayPal him for my share, he seemed to have forgotten that we usually all gave our parents something together. My dad just told me to stay warm, the generic Michigan version of "see ya later" in the winter.

"It's… I dunno, depressing. Last year was…." I shook my head at the memory. "It was just like this pale shadow of what Christmas is supposed to be. There was a tree and presents and carols and some of that eggnog in a carton." I shuddered. "And my mom cooked this... ham thing that she always makes. With pineapple and like cream of mushroom soup or something. But it was just... all wrong. It didn't feel right."

Will had been watching me as he idly mixed saag paneer, chana masala, curried lamb, and chicken tikka masala together in his bowl until it was a brownish slurry. Then he'd dumped in rice and began attacking the whole thing with slabs of naan like I was going to snatch it away from him.

Now he rolled his eyes at me. "You're such a fucking romantic," he said with his mouth full.

"Charming." I handed him a napkin. "It's not... romantic, really. Just, it didn't feel the way you think Christmas is supposed to feel. It never has."

"It didn't feel the way *you* thought Christmas was supposed to feel, which you got from fantasies. Books and movies and Thomas fucking Kinkade paintings and shit."

"My parents have a poster of a Thomas Kinkade painting," I said, grinning at him. "In the living room."

"Case in point," he said, rolling his eyes again and wiping the sides of his bowl with naan. "Growing up under the watchful eye of the Painter of Light, how could you help but turn out to want a Christmas out of a Nicholas Sparks movie? That's what romanticizing something *is*, kiddo. Having the notion that it'll be a certain, perfect way based on something fictional. Something idealized."

"Maybe," I allowed. I *had* kind of liked that Nicholas Sparks movie with the blonde girl from *Dancing With the Stars*. "But the fact remains that it felt shitty to be there. Depressing."

"Fair enough," Will said, reaching over to steal a bite of my chicken. "For you, if something doesn't achieve this level of *Woohoo! Fantasy! Perfect!* then it immediately flips over to being depressing. For me... neutrality seems pretty good."

I thought about that as I finished my food, swatting Will's fork away when I noticed that his stolen bites were making a substantial dent in the tikka masala, which was my favorite. Will had called me a romantic before. Mostly in reference to *actual* romance and relationship stuff. I'd never really thought about what it might mean to be a romantic about other stuff.

"But then what's the difference, really? I mean, I *have* that idea about what I want Christmas to be. What does it matter where it came from?"

"I'm not saying it's an invalid thing to want. Just that it's something you've been fed, like an advertisement. So... okay, the goal of any good book cover, right, is to make someone think that what's inside is going to be awesome. The cover stands in for the content of the book. It has to, because you can't consume the whole book in an instant.

"But it's silly to imagine that the cover is the *same* as what's inside. It's a signal telling you what kind of thing you might get. But not necessarily an accurate signal. It's an advertisement, designed to speak to the audience that might be interested. It's the same thing as your Christmas. Those picture-perfect images of a snowy cabin in the woods, roaring fire, a glowy Christmas tree with perfectly wrapped presents underneath, smiling happy family in sweaters, et cetera. It's a fiction. A romanticization."

I narrowed my eyes at him. "A fiction, huh? Sounds just like Rex's cabin to me. Well, okay, maybe not the perfectly wrapped presents part."

Will barked out a laugh. "Yeah, okay, well, *those* fuckers. Sure. But I mean, they're basically bucking for world's biggest sappy romance, so."

"Why are you so pissed off that they're happy?"

"What? I'm not. I'm glad Rex is happy. Even if it is with the Prince of Poetry." His nostrils flared at the mention of Daniel.

"No, seriously."

"I'm being serious. I am seriously happy that Rex got what he wanted. It obviously wasn't me, so I'm glad he found Mulligan."

"You just sound pretty bitter is all. Is it because you and Rex don't talk as much anymore?"

"Jesus, I'm not *bitter*. I expected that, anyway. It's pretty much what happens. People get into relationships and all they care about is their partner. Same thing happened with my friend Morgan. We used to hang out all the time, then she met her husband and… that was it. Whatever."

"You're not friends anymore?" I'd never even heard him mention a Morgan. "That's so sad."

He shrugged. "People give up pieces of themselves to fit into their relationships. Compromise yourself to fit with another person enough, and pretty soon they're the *only* person you fit with anymore."

"That's the most awful description of relationships I've ever heard!"

"Hey, kiddo, there's only so much that can fit on a postcard."

In the time it took me to come up with a response to that, Will finished the chicken tikka masala in my bowl and began scooping basmati rice out of the container and into his mouth using a piece of naan as a shovel. I gave up the rest of the food for lost and just pushed my bowl toward him so he could sop up the sauce with his rice.

Later, slaphappy and in a food coma from consuming an entire pumpkin pie that Will had pulled out of the freezer with relish and a wink, we put on *Home Alone*, which I hadn't seen since I was a kid.

"This was my fantasy when I was a kid," Will said. "To have the run of a mansion, eat pizza, and play with a shitload of toys."

"Wouldn't you have been lonely by yourself on Christmas?"

"Hell no. Bring it on. I'd rather have been alone instead of just—" He shook his head.

"Lonely?" I guessed.

"Whatever," he murmured. "Move down." And he positioned me where he wanted me, behind him on the couch so he could lean back against me. I was kind of squashed into the back cushions, but it felt perfect.

And so, so easy to almost believe that this was my real life. That Will and I would celebrate next Christmas together just like this, and the one after that.

"Hey, thanks," I murmured into Will's neck a few minutes later, after he'd settled on some old suspense thriller with Sandra Bullock that I'd seen bits and pieces of on TV as a kid. "For Christmas. And for letting me stay."

At first I thought he wasn't going to answer. He did that sometimes. Not to be mean, I had realized. But when he didn't have anything to say. After a minute, though, he turned around to face me, the flicker of the television lighting his face dramatically. The sweep of his eyelashes cast a shadow, and the dip of his upper lip made me long to trace it with my tongue.

Then he kissed me. It wasn't a kiss about lust or whim or chemistry. It was a kiss about Christmas and comfort and the pure joy of being here right now, on this couch with Will's skin warm against mine as the snow blew against the window in a spray of icy crystals.

Will broke the kiss too soon, but didn't turn away.

"So we're basically, like, kissing now, huh?" I asked.

"Shh. We can kiss if we want to," Will said, eyes still closed as if he were asserting a rule in some game that we had made up just for us.

We fell asleep on the couch hours later, and when I woke up in the middle of the night, all I saw was the lights Will had hung twinkling brightly around the windows and the faint answering glow of lights in the windows of the other buildings nearby.

A FEW mornings later, we were eating pancakes and Will was on an epic rant about his coworker Gus.

He'd been really stressed about work the past week, though, and his rant about Gus seemed less like an ad hominem attack and more like him spinning his wheels.

Finally, I couldn't listen anymore.

"Gus is fine, Will. You're the crazy one. You're probably *his* nemesis because he's acting normal and you respond like an insane person. He probably goes home and tells his friends or his wife or whoever about the psycho who hates him for no reason."

Will sulked, shoveling pancakes into his mouth.

"Hey, what's the deal with work, for real? You've been totally stressing about it."

Will made a can't-answer-mouth's-full gesture, and I rolled my eyes at him and waited as he chewed.

He fiddled with his coffee cup and his fork and twisted the hem of his perfect white T-shirt. I leaned into his space and pulled him toward me a little, then I kissed him, licking the syrup from his lips.

Because we were kissing now.

"Well?" I sat back, and Will looked startled. He licked his lips absently.

"Gus asked me to go into business with him. To start our own graphic design company. Be co-owners."

Will loved his job, but one thing he complained about all the time was having to work on other people's schedules and play by other people's rules.

"That sounds great," I told him. "Especially considering that Gus sounds like a totally cool person."

"He's whatever."

"So are you gonna do it?"

Will shrugged, going from rant-tastic to nonverbal in 4.5 seconds. I hadn't seen this mood before, and I mentally labeled it "Petulant Child."

"Oh, I know what you need!" I got up, and Will gestured toward the pancakes on the counter with a totally unnecessary since-you're-up grunt.

I dumped more pancakes on his plate and brought his graph-paper pad and pencil over to the table.

"A pros and cons list."

Will loved lists almost as much as he loved graphs and charts. I waggled the paper in front of him. He pushed it away and concentrated back on the pancakes, drenching them in butter and syrup and chowing down as he stared into space.

Well, a kiss had kind of worked before. I stood up and straddled Will's lap, putting myself between him and the pancakes. I took the dripping fork out of his hand.

"You're gonna make yourself sick," I told him, eating the bite myself. When I kissed him, our lips were sticky-sweet.

Finally, after several more syrupy kisses and a lot of grumbling, I got the truth out of Will. That he valued the prestige of being with a Big Five publisher, which he wouldn't have if he and Gus started over from scratch.

"But you could make the company whatever you wanted," I told him. "You care about the work so much. What would be better than being able to do it the way you think is best?"

He looked surprised at my words and his expression softened.

"Yeah, maybe."

It was the first time I felt like I had been useful to Will for more than just hanging out or doing my share of the dishes. For once, I had helped him instead of the other way around.

I WOKE up in the dark to Will talking on the phone in the bedroom.

"Where did you look already? … Yeah, I can call down there…. Once or twice…. It's okay…. Yeah, let me know…."

Will came out of his room and wandered to the window in the kitchen, staring out at the gyro place, the Mexican restaurant, and the flower shop on the corner.

I slid a hand up his back and felt that every muscle was tensed.

"You okay?"

He kept staring out the window like I wasn't there, but he didn't pull away. When I started to rub his shoulders, though, he shrugged me off.

"Nathan and Sarah?"

Will nodded, but it clearly wasn't an invitation for further discussion. He moved away and I followed him into the kitchen where he started to make coffee automatically, like he did every morning. Halfway through he seemed to notice that it wasn't even 5:00 a.m. and it was Sunday, but he continued doing it anyway.

AFTER FOURTEEN days of living with Will, three things were quite clear.

First, that we were so different I never had a prayer of predicting how he would feel about or react to things.

One morning he came in and made coffee, and I pointed to the bananas I'd gotten at the bodega, saying "There are bananas if you want any."

Will said, "I live here. If I wanted a banana in my own apartment then obviously I would get one."

"I was just telling you they were there," I said.

"I can see they're there. They are a huge bunch of yellow bananas in the middle of my counter, forty microns from where my hand is currently resting. If I couldn't see the bananas there, I would have a major problem, given that I work in a field of visual arts."

"Jesus, sorry, I was just being polite!"

"It's not polite," Will said, rounding on me. "It's not polite to make people respond to inane comments in their own houses at seven in the morning. It's intrusive. I need all my energy to deal with existing in a world filled with idiots and psychopaths. I can't waste any on fucking bananas before I've even had coffee. Next thing I know you'll say *good morning* or ask me how I am and I'll have to kill myself."

"*How are you* and *good morning* are not intrusive, asshole!"

"*How are you* is the root canal of small talk and *good morning* should be shot," he said, and turned on his heel to go get dressed, taking his coffee with him.

Second, and not unrelated, was that Will mostly said whatever he wanted and considered honesty to be far more important than protecting people's feelings.

When I suggested that sometimes a little white lie was more valuable than telling a truth for no reason other than to pat yourself on the back for being truthful, he said that he categorically refused to take other people's feelings on as his responsibility. That if he'd let himself choose his words or his actions based on what might or might not hurt or uplift other people he'd never have made it past high school much less in New York.

It sucked when I was the one on the other end of one of his hard truths, but it was also incredibly reassuring to know where I stood. I knew that if Will paid me a compliment, then he meant it. I knew that if I asked his opinion, I'd get it. Will was aggressively, uncompromisingly himself, and it kind of made me feel like I could be that way with him too.

Third, if I wanted things to progress from the we-kiss-now phase into actual, like, sex stuff—which, uh, I really did—then I was definitely going to have to be the one to make it happen.

Despite the kissing, and the way that more and more often our television watching time turned into a cuddle-fest, Will had remained firm about me sleeping on the couch. He said he liked his privacy.

I was totally respectful of that, of course, but it was honestly torture, lying there and knowing that only about twenty feet and a thin door separated us.

So, since I couldn't hope that maybe one night we'd just… I dunno, like, come together naturally in the middle of the night, I was taking matters into my own hands. I'd decided that tonight would be the night I made my move.

Apparently the universe had other plans, though, because things at Mug Shots went completely batshit. Gretchen, who was in town because she was doing a January term class, had come in to get a coffee and say hi, so I was distracted for a minute while it happened, but some lady drove her scooter into the window of the Starbucks across the street from us, and they had to shut down for the day to clean up the glass. This meant that all the people whose business Starbucks usually drew popped over to us when they found their usual route to caffeine cut off. It was the busiest day I'd ever worked, all of us running around at double-time just to barely keep up with the line. I fell asleep on the subway going back to Will's and missed my stop.

Turned out Will'd had a day from hell too and was already in sweats when I got home, a sure sign he was wrung out.

"You want me to order food?" he asked. "I was thinking of sushi."

I'd never tried sushi, but it seemed like a very New York thing to eat. Besides, if Will wanted it then I wanted to want it, so I nodded.

"Do you mind if I take a shower?"

He waved me into the bathroom absently, like he was totally used to having me here. The bone-deep contentment of being a thing that made sense in Will's well-ordered world filled me, and I practically floated to the shower, my exhaustion evaporating in the steam.

"Oh my god," Will said half an hour later as we sat with the sushi spread between us and I chewed. And chewed. And chewed. "You've never had sushi before have you?"

And, oh shit, I had to spit it out. I just had to. The texture. Oh man. I just couldn't with the texture.

"Gah! Jesus. Sorry."

Will silently pulled my plate toward him and moved most of the sushi onto his own, replacing it with a few things from his and a few from a container to his right, then pushed it back to me where I eyed it suspiciously.

"It's tempura. It's fried. You'll be fine."

I took a cautious bite, but it mostly tasted like sesame-y onion rings, so I munched happily as Will watched me with a mildly amused expression.

After dinner, we flopped onto the couch, and Will put on *Orphan Black*. I fell asleep in about ten minutes, the exhaustion of the day catching up with me, and woke up halfway on top of Will where I must've snuggled him in my sleep. He was asleep too, head thrown back against the couch. The naked curve of his throat in the moonlight was irresistible. I kissed his neck softly.

"Will?"

His nose scrunched at the sound. "Mmphm."

"Do you wanna go to bed?"

He nodded sleepily, but his hand was in my hair, and he was kind of… cuddling me.

My heart started racing. Fully aware that I might be pushing my luck—that I might be gambling for a hundred with a twenty and lose both, I said, "Can I stay with you tonight?"

His eyes tracked from mine down to my mouth, then up again. Then, in a movement so slow I almost thought I was imagining it, he nodded.

I stood up and held out a hand to him, pulling him up. Will moved into my arms like it was natural and we went to his room. I brushed my teeth thoroughly, nervous that I had sushi breath, then made my way to the bed. In the dark, all I could really make out was the light sweep of Will's blond hair.

I'd been so sleepy a minute before, but now I was wide-awake.

And intensely nervous.

I stood there for a minute, trying to figure out how this was going to go. Should I kiss Will? Would he—

"Leo, get in the bed and go to sleep."

"Oh, but I—um, are we—"

"No."

"You don't even know what I was gonna say," I grumbled.

He snorted. "We're not having sex, just come the hell to bed. I'm so tired."

"What time did you leave this morning, anyway?" I slid into bed next to him.

"Like six."

"Is everything okay at work? Why'd you go in so early? You don't usually go that early, do you? No, you don't. I—"

The pillow hit my face and Will pulled the covers up over it, encasing me in a cocoon of Will-smelling warmth. He held the pillow there for a minute. I mean, I could still breathe and everything, he was just making a point. When I relaxed into the bed, he took his pillow back and shoved it under his head, turning onto his stomach.

"What kind of sheets are these?" I asked. "They're *so* comfy."

Will groaned. "Leo!"

"But I'm suddenly not tired anymore," I said.

"Yes, you are. You just forgot about it momentarily because penises don't run on the same clock as the rest of us."

"You mean like a dessert stomach? A cock clock?" I started giggling. Then I laughed some more. Then I turned over to tell Will something terribly important, but I couldn't possibly because I was so very, very asleep.

I FINALLY decided on the direct approach.

"I want us to have sex," I said as we did the dishes the next night. "Okay?"

Honestly, I'd kind of expected surprise at my boldness or… something. But Will just snorted dismissively and said, "You're nineteen. You want to have sex with everything."

"That's not true!" I insisted. "Besides, I'm more mature than you. You're a child basically, only with, like, dicks instead of toys."

"Yeah, you're right about that. I take mine, and I go home as soon as I'm sick of playing." He waggled an eyebrow at me as he dried the final dish, then walked to his desk and starting preparing things for work the next day.

"Will, I'm serious."

He sighed and his shoulders slumped. "Yeah, I know."

Well that was… not encouraging.

"So then… what? Am I really that bad?"

"No, of course not," Will said.

"Then I don't get it. You'll sleep with all those strangers—with guys you don't even like—with guys you kinda hate, but not with me?"

Will cut his eyes to me sharply, though his voice was only a mild warning. "Careful, Leo."

"Sorry, sorry, just…." My stomach turned over. "You must *really* not want me at all, I guess?"

Will opened his mouth and an expression I'd never seen before crossed his face. It was heavy and complicated. I got irritation and curiosity and… maybe fear? I'd never seen Will look afraid before so I couldn't be sure.

"You're sure that's what you want?"

"Well, jeez, don't sound too excited."

Now I just felt stupid, like I was talking him into something he really didn't want. But Will was still looking at me like he expected an answer. Which was ridiculous because I was pretty sure the fact that I wanted Will was up there with "global warming is real" on the list of stuff that is obvious.

"Yeah. Yes, of course I do."

For just a second I imagined that what I saw in Will's expression was… disappointment. Which didn't make any sense, so I must have been wrong. And then whatever it was vanished, the cool mask I recognized from outside the walls of his apartment firmly in place.

"Okay, then," he said, and grabbed my hand, pulling me toward the bedroom.

"Wait, what? Really? Uh, wait, right now?"

At the bed, Will stripped with economy and gestured at me to do the same.

He was perfect, pale velvet skin over long muscles, gleaming with fine golden hairs like he was a marble statue that the sculptor had dusted with gilt. But he looked like he could have been changing in a gym locker room for all the enthusiasm he was showing.

"Umm. This wasn't quite the way I… thought this would go."

"What, you want me to seduce you? You were the one negotiating this like a business transaction not five minutes ago."

"Yeah, but I just thought…."

"You thought it'd be romantic? That you'd stay here for a month and we'd fall in love and be boyfriends and soul mates and get married and artificially inseminate your lesbian BFF and have a kid called Mint? That's not me, Leo. And the sooner you realize that you don't actually want me like that the better."

"But I do want you. I—"

"Look, I'm not saying this to be cute. I'm not doing some 'Oh god, I'm awful, you don't want me, rending my garments in the rain, tortured and riddled with feelings of unworthiness because my little brother drowned while I was supposed to be watching him and I don't deserve love' thing. I'm being honest. You wanna fuck? Let's fuck. But don't have the expectation that then we'll be boyfriends because you'll be disappointed. And if you do it anyway and you get your feelings hurt, I want you to think back to this moment right here, where I'm telling you it's a bad idea, so that you don't blame that shit on me."

I gaped at him, something shaking loose and jangling around inside my chest, my stomach hollow. He had said all this in a tone that was completely sincere. Genuine. Like he could've been giving me advice about someone else.

I wasn't sure how to tell him that, yes, I wanted him. But not the way he thought. Not in the anonymous, impersonal way that he slept with strangers. I didn't know how to say that and not prove him right about what else I wanted from him, though. About all those things he said he didn't want to give.

"Yeah, that's what I thought," Will said before I could find the words, and started pulling his clothes back on.

Something made me say, "Wait." Because part of me didn't believe it could be true. After everything we'd shared, how close we'd gotten, I couldn't quite believe that sex would mean nothing to him. How could it?

Sure, maybe this was all I could get from Will for now. But... after we'd slept together, how could Will not realize how good we could be? Realize how it could be different with me than it was with those other guys?

"I still want to," I said. Will froze, pants half on.

"You do?"

I nodded. He looked uncertain. He had pitched a hardball, fully expecting me to walk away, and I'd taken a swing and hit it squarely. He narrowed his eyes at me.

"I heard you," I said. "And I accept the limitations of your offer. Just sex, we're not boyfriends. I get it. I swear." I sounded at least marginally nonchalant, even if my heart was about to pound out of my chest.

Will crossed his arms. "Okaaaay...."

"Okay."

"Okay. So we're doing this?"

"Yeah, just... um, just know that I've never... exactly... I mean, I *have* done stuff—but I've. Yeah."

"Duly noted," Will said, back in control. He walked over to me and started pulling my clothes off, smirking. "I've got no problem whatsoever telling you exactly how I want you to fuck me."

My knees practically buckled, because, shit, that was hot. "Oh Jesus Okay. You want me to—right, sure, no problem."

"Get on the bed, Leo."

I scrambled to the bed, so distracted by what was about to happen that I almost forgot to store away the image of Will, naked and pale as ice, prowling toward me, thighs tightening and releasing, the perfect cut of muscle at his hips almost ridiculous in its definition.

"Do you have a personal trainer or something?" He just smirked and shook his head, crawling over me in the bed.

"Don't worry," he said. "It won't hurt too much." Then he leered and grabbed my dick.

I already felt ridiculously exposed, and that didn't help.

"Oh my god, can you at least *pretend* that you're taking me a little bit seriously?"

"I take this"—he stroked my erection—"very seriously, Leo."

I groaned, my head falling back. "'Kay, kiss now, please."

Will kissed me and I forgot that he was basically doing me a favor. That this was just sex to him—maybe even pity sex. I forgot everything except that his mouth felt like heaven and his body against mine was intoxicating. I was immediately at about an eight out of ten on the imaginary arousal scale that I'd just created. What would you measure arousal in, anyway? Well, I was at eight out of ten of them, in any case.

"Okay, okay, okay," I chanted, pulling away and praying that Will would see how close I was and ease off just a little.

He reached into the bedside table and pulled out a condom.

"You know how to do this?"

"Yeah, sure," I said, starting to rip it open with my teeth like I'd seen people do in the movies.

"Oh dear god, give me that, I'll do it." He snatched the condom and rolled it over my erection. I bit my lip, and he smirked at me.

"Can I, um."

"Spit it out."

"I want to… can we switch places?"

"Oh, you want to be on top of me?"

I nodded.

"You going to fuck me hard, Leo?" His comment was half flirtatious and half mocking, but somehow I thought he was a little excited at the idea. And my dick definitely was.

"Lie down," I said, and he did. Spread out beneath me, Will looked different. Accessible in one way, but more remote in another. Like he was giving me a part of himself, but if I took it, another part would recede.

Gone was the man I'd made out with over pancakes, or cuddled with on the couch, binge watching *Orphan Black*. Gone was the man I'd listened to as he ranted about typography on book spines, and the one who'd eaten chicken tikka masala off my plate and grinned when he got caught, sauce in his teeth.

The one in his place was sexy, experienced, in control. Distant. But I had said I wanted this and I wasn't sure I'd get another chance to prove to him what we could be.

I thought back on all the porn I'd watched, but couldn't actually remember what happened before the actual fucking part. Maybe they edited that out? Was I supposed to, like....

"It's on the condom already."

"Huh?"

"Lube. If that's what you're waiting for."

"Oh, okay. Um, so should I like... *do* something?"

"Yeah, you might consider fucking me. That or get me something to read in the meantime."

"No, I meant, um, like in terms of preparation or—"

"I know what you meant."

"Okay, then I'll just, uh...."

But my hands were shaking and my knees were shaking and really this did not feel like I wanted it to. And I know Will made fun of me for having these grand romantic notions—"capital-R romantic," Professor Ginsberg would probably say—and maybe he was right, but....

I dropped my chin to my chest.

"Hey, can we not do it like this?" I said, my voice small.

"You're the one who wanted to switch places!"

"No, I mean.... Will, come on. Please. I know it's maybe a joke to you, but I really haven't ever done this before, and you're kind of making me feel like shit."

I opened my eyes a crack and looked at Will. He looked away.

"Like, I want *you* you, not sex you."

"Sex me," he repeated.

"Yeah, with the whole 'I've slept with a ton of people, and this is just one more notch on my bedpost, I'm beautiful and confident and not terrified I'm about to totally fuck it up' thing."

He rolled his eyes. "You're not gonna fuck it up."

"I might," I whispered.

This had been a huge mistake. Will was looking at me like I was a stranger he'd offered a favor to who was now making the favor much more work than he'd anticipated. I'd had warmer, more intimate exchanges checking out library books. This was nothing like what I wanted with him. Nothing at all.

Chapter 8

January

I CLAMBERED off Will and rolled out of the bed in a mortification of clumsiness, running into the living room and tugging on my pants as I went, in a futile attempt to feel less exposed.

God, what the hell just happened?

Images of Will, sublimely beautiful in his nakedness, got all jumbled up with the expression on his face: a neutrality so blank I may as well have been a stranger. A pathetic, overly eager, horny stranger. I dropped my head forward to clunk against the kitchen wall. Fuck my life.

"I didn't quite live up to the fantasy, I guess?" Will's voice was ice.

"Can you… can you please not be mean to me right now?" My voice was muffled by the wall.

"I'm not being *mean* to you. I'm serious. You had a vision of what it'd be like to fuck me, and I didn't fulfill it. Like college, or Christmas."

I turned around, wrapping my arms around myself against the chill. Will's jaw was tensed, his eyebrows drawn together, and the pale skin of his chest mottled with a flush. He'd put his pants on again too.

"Wait, are you… are you *mad* at me?" I asked.

Will gave an uncertain shrug, a gesture so at odds with his usual surety that it distracted me.

"Why are you mad?"

He shook his head in irritation but said nothing, just moved around the kitchen, picking things up and putting them back down again.

"Will." I put a hand on his shoulder, and he shrugged it off. "Will, come on."

"Fine! What do you want me to say, Leo? I thought you were different, okay? I didn't think you saw me that way. The way everyone else does."

Was I imagining it, or did his mouth tremble slightly?

"What do you mean? How does everyone see you?"

Will glared at me. "You know how—you've seen them. Like I'm… like they just care about how I look. They just want to… to fuck me." He spat the word out, making sex sound filthy for the first time since I'd met him.

"Uh, okay, I know what you mean, but the idea that you would lump me in with those people is… it's fucked-up, man."

He set his jaw. "Is it?"

"Will." I put my hand on his arm and this time he didn't shrug me off. "You're totally beautiful. You are." His eyes flew to mine, narrowed, and angry. "Hang on. Jesus. Yeah, you're super hot. But… like, a *lot* of people are. Give me a little credit for not being some mindless… sex zombie or something, would you? I'm not like *totally* powerless in the face of your beauty."

This was *almost* completely true. Will's looks did still take me by surprise sometimes, his beauty rendered something separate from him. A thing he possessed rather than a thing he was. But it definitely wasn't the moment for that shade of distinction to be meaningful to Will.

"Especially not now that I know you."

Will snorted at this though I hadn't actually meant it as an insult. Then he lifted himself up to sit on the counter, leaned back against the cabinet, and stared moodily out the window.

"You seriously think that I just want to… to fuck you because you're pretty and that's all? How could you possibly think that?"

He shook his head, and his expression was confused, like he honestly couldn't quite figure out if I meant what I said.

"I just get tired of not knowing." Will's voice had a darkness to it that was completely different from his pissed-off tone of a minute before. But he shook his head and crossed his arms over his chest. "Never mind."

"What?" I followed him with my body, standing between his knees and putting my hands on his thighs.

"Would you even have liked me when we first met if you hadn't thought I was hot? You totally wouldn't have. I was just some asshole your friend's boyfriend used to date. I made fun of you, gave you shit. Why would you have wanted to spend time with me if you didn't want to fuck me?"

His intonation was flat, like these weren't even questions, but stories he'd told himself for so long he already believed they were true.

And I wasn't sure what to say. Because the truth was that, sure, the first thing I'd noticed about Will was how he looked. And could I honestly separate that from who he was? Not with any certainty.

"Well, okay," I said. "But, attraction's… mysterious, right? At some level that happens whenever people are attracted to each other. Like, someone says something that would one hundred percent annoy you if someone else had said it, but because it's that person it's charming or funny or whatever. And in case you forgot, we *aren't* fucking, and I basically want to hang out with you all the time."

"Yeah, but you want to. Wanted to."

"So… I was supposed to—what?—prove that I was different, that I care about you, by *not* being attracted to you? Now who's being the romantic?" I squeezed his knee to soften my words. "Besides, you wanted to, too, right? At least a little bit?"

He shrugged. And even though I didn't exactly think he meant it, it cut kind of deep.

"Seriously? You have no interest in sleeping with me, but you said okay totally out of pity? Damn, Will, that's kinda cold."

"No, no, fine, yes, I want to, I guess."

"Wow, that's so incredibly flattering."

Will grabbed my chin so I had to look up at him. He looked intense, but he was biting his lip in this maddening way that made him look kind of lost at the same time.

"You're probably my best friend," he said. "And I've been honest with you about not wanting a relationship. So I can't help but wonder."

My brain had short-circuited somewhere back around the words "best friend," and now I was struggling to keep up with Will's logic, which, at its most clear was often inconceivable to me.

"Wonder?"

"If you know that I don't want a relationship, and you wouldn't just be thinking of it as sex, then where does that leave us? Because it kind of seems like it'd leave us someplace where you end up feeling like I've betrayed you, and I end up losing my friend."

"That won't happen, I swear," I said, but my heart was pounding because with a few sentences Will had pretty much blown to smithereens every avenue I'd thought we might walk down together. "I want to—we like each other, right?" Will hesitated but nodded grudgingly. "And we have fun." Another nod. "And you know we have a… like, a *thing*." I ran my hands up his thighs and felt the energy spark between us. Will bit his lip, eyes never leaving my face. "Sooo…." I nudged his knees a little farther apart and stepped closer, leaning in to kiss him.

"You sure?" he murmured, eyelids going heavy.

"Yeah."

And this time when I kissed him it was with the full weight of knowledge behind it that this was really going to happen. This wasn't just *We're kissing now*. It wasn't on an against-all-odds hope that Will might suddenly be taken over by his passion for me and push things further. It was a kiss with intent.

He slid his hands up my arms, squeezing my biceps, holding us together and keeping us apart at the same time, and I pressed myself against him, trying to cast my vote on which way things should go.

"God *damn* it, Leo!" Will bit off, leaning backward. "Are you sure we should do this?" He looked savage, sprawled across his own counter, hair mussed, and pupils dilated.

Lust blasted through me, but his question seemed sincere, and I made it my duty to obliterate every doubt he might have. I threw myself back against him, kissing him with everything I had.

And Will came alive. His hands were in my hair and running up and down my spine. He kissed like a whirlwind. There was nothing tentative about it anymore. He finally kissed me like he meant it. After a few minutes of a make-out session so hot I was trying not to come in my pants, I pulled away long enough to tug Will down off the counter and over to the couch.

Nothing about being with Milton or Terrence, the guy from my statistics class last year, could have prepared me for how things would be with Will. It was like every sensation I'd ever had was amplified, every millimeter of skin sensitized like it had never been touched before. I felt flushed and light-headed with lust as I buried my face in Will's neck and kissed under his jaw.

His pulse raced beneath my mouth, and I licked along his neck, unable to get enough of his skin, his heat, his smell. I traced the shell of his ear with my tongue and licked inside, wanting to taste every inch of him.

"Ah, fuck!"

Will was wild. Not like he was trying to seduce me, but like he was desperate to get at me. I wasn't complaining—hell no—but it was so different from the calm, detached way he'd approached things in the bedroom earlier that it was as if he were a whole different person. Though I don't know why I was surprised that Will's shifting personality would show itself in bed as well as out.

I'd pictured the suave Will who dressed impeccably for work, but I was getting whirlwind Will who stomped around the apartment ranting about weird stuff that I'd never imagined anyone could care about.

And I loved it. Because it was real. I wasn't just another nameless hookup, and this wasn't something that Will could shrug off, deny, sideline.

His pale skin was perfect, just a few of those dark beauty marks clustered near his belly button and one near his left nipple. I kissed it, sucking his nipple into my mouth, and then bit it lightly. Will groaned and let me kiss my way to his other nipple before he lost patience and rolled us so he was on top of me and pulled my pants down to my knees. He tapped my hip bone.

"You're so damn skinny," he muttered.

"Wow, *not* the moment I want to feel self-conscious," I gasped.

Will kissed the spot he'd tapped, his lips a soft apology, and I groaned as his chin hit my crotch. I was ridiculously hard just from kissing him. He pressed his face to my crotch and inhaled my smell.

"Fuck, that's the sexiest thing anyone's ever done to me," I said.

Will let out a scornful breath. "Yeah, *not* the moment to remind me you're basically untouched."

"I'm not untouched! I—" But then he pulled my pants down and swallowed my erection, and suddenly it didn't seem like a point that really needed to be made just at that moment.

His mouth was hot, and he slid a hand between my thighs and started rolling my balls in this way that made me feel like I was going to die.

"Oh my god, oh my god," I said. I twined my fingers in his hair as he sucked me, trying to look down and see myself sliding in and out of his gorgeous mouth, but my brain couldn't do more than two things at once, apparently, and touch Will's hair and have my mind blown were currently occupying those slots.

"Will, fuck, Will," I gasped. I could track the pleasure as it spread across my skin, from my dick and balls up my spine, curling in the pit of my stomach and flushing my chest and throat with heat, tingling down my trembling thighs. Then, in an instant, it all coalesced into a giant heartbeat that throbbed and then exploded, sending shocks of pleasure through me, leaving me light-headed and gasping as the world was swallowed in blackness, my awareness dwindling to my pulsing dick and the halo of Will's hair.

I heard a sound from a long way off. An undignified whimpering sound that I didn't want to believe was coming from me.

"Sorry, sorry, I'm sorry, I meant to warn you," I slurred.

Will raised his eyebrows at me and wiped his mouth. That tore another groan out of me because holy *mother*, Will had just sucked me off, and I could see the evidence of it gleaming on his perfect fucking lips. It was too much.

"Oh god, shit, I just came in like five seconds didn't I?" I put my arm over my eyes as I flushed, this time from embarrassment rather than arousal.

Will snorted and then his mouth was on mine and I could taste the salt of my release on his tongue. The thought of us mingled together like that totally turned me on all over again, and I moaned into his mouth. Will reached down, and I jerked at his touch.

"Jesus," he muttered, but it was fond, appreciative. His kisses were less desperate now, and he positioned us so we were lying on our sides on the couch facing each other.

"Take your pants off too?" I couldn't believe I'd come before he was even naked.

Will shimmied his pants down, and I slung a leg over his hip, pressing our erections together as we kissed slowly.

"Mmmm," Will murmured. I slid a hand down and felt the curve of his ass, pressed him tighter into me, making him shiver. So I did it again, squeezing the round muscle and digging my fingertips in. Will gasped into my mouth and grabbed my ass too. We ground together, the heat building between us, legs tangled together, hips pumping, chests and stomachs sliding together, tongues entwined, every place we touched its own warm point of connection.

I held his face to mine and kissed him, the taste and smell of him gradually taking over my mouth and nose, settling on me like a private atmosphere.

Will pulled my hand between his legs and used both our hands to stroke us off. I came again when he ran a finger over the tip of my cock, gasping as it twitched, spent.

Will smiled wolfishly, his eyes raking over me. He was flushed and panting, his erection throbbing against my hip.

"Ah, youth," he said. And I made a new resolution on the spot. That, inexperience or no, the next time I had the chance I was going to make Will Highland beg me to let him come. I grinned at him and flipped him onto his back, sliding his dick between my thighs, grinding us together even though my sensitive skin protested.

"Oh fuck," he muttered, his breath coming faster. I leaned down and put my lips to his throat. His pulse was racing, artery throbbing with every heartbeat. I nipped at his neck, and he grabbed for my ass, pulling me tighter against him. I bit harder, felt his pulse jump under my tongue. Then I kissed him with everything I had, squeezing his cock with my thighs. I bore down on him, bending my knees so I could squeeze his perfect ass.

Splayed on the couch, his pale skin and blond hair made the black leather look almost sinister. His chest was flushed, his throat bruised from my mouth, and his pupils blown wide. I dragged my fist up and down his erection, tightening my grip until Will moaned and reached for me. I kissed him once more, then set a brutal pace, jerking him off until his eyes rolled back and his mouth fell open.

When Will came, every muscle tightened, and he squeezed his eyes shut. His cry was silent. He looked like he was in pain, his jaw clenched and his mouth in a snarl.

"YOU ARE seriously the worst at choosing produce ever."

As I was unpacking bags from the market, Will was pulling certain things toward him and assembling a pile on the counter.

"These are all bruised. This shit's like misshapen or something. And— are these *all* broken?" He pointed to the chocolate bars. "Do you shop blindfolded? No, even blindfolded you could feel that these are broken!"

I squirmed, putting a box of pasta in the cabinet and cheese and eggs in the refrigerator.

"Seriously, Leo, have you never been grocery shopping before? Oh shit, you haven't, have you?"

"I have," I couldn't resist saying, no matter how many times I'd tried to learn the lesson that if I responded to Will, he'd eventually get any information out of me that he wanted.

He was gaping at me, eyebrows raised expectantly.

"I just… I don't want them to get thrown away… so…."

"What?"

"Well, I just worry that no one else will buy them if they're a little bruised or funny looking. You know. People always buy the most perfect ones. And I feel sorry for the ones that aren't because maybe people won't want them."

"You buy the fucked-up ones on purpose," Will said slowly.

"They're not fucked-up—they're still totally good! They shouldn't have to get thrown away just because they look funny."

Will was shaking his head at me.

"Oh my god, you personify produce."

I started to say something, to defend myself. But he backed me against the counter and slid close, kissing me until my mouth felt as bruised as those rescued apples.

AFTER DINNER a few days later, Will groaned as a text appeared on his phone, and stalked over to the intercom to buzz someone up, muttering.

"Fucking *Gus!*" he said, like his coworker's presence was the most outrageous intrusion he could imagine.

"Did he just show up?"

"No, he told me earlier."

"Jesus, you're so cute," I said. Will's grouchy, shocked at the burden of other people thing really did it for me. It was like, maybe since he let me hang around and didn't seem as horrified by me as he did by others, then I was special.

I don't know what I'd pictured, exactly. But based on what Will had said about Gus I had definitely *not* imagined the totally average-looking white guy in his midforties who walked in the door wearing gray corduroys, a red-and-blue sweater, and a black overcoat. Will had called him arrogant, pushy, obsessive—hell, he'd referred to him as Captain Ahab at some point. This guy looked like… an accountant.

"Gus, Leo. Leo, this is Gus Martelli."

Gus smiled at me and shook my hand. I suddenly felt very weird being here, dressed in sweats and one of Will's perfectly cut white T-shirts (which was totally not perfectly cut for me).

"Um, should I just…." I gestured toward the bedroom, to indicate giving them some privacy, but immediately blushed because that made it seem like I was a fuck toy or something, waiting for Will in bed when he was done with his business meeting.

Will snorted like he could read my mind.

"You're fine here. If you're interested, that is. I'm certainly not sure whether I am or not yet. You want a beer, Martelli?"

"Oh, it's Martelli now, huh?" Gus turned to me. "He only calls me that when he's trying to remind me that we aren't friends." He winked, like we shared a secret about Will.

"I don't know why I'd need to remind you of something so completely self-evident, but whatever. Beer?"

"Sure."

"Want one?" Will asked me, hand on my arm.

"Oh. Um, okay. Thanks." I didn't really, but I wanted to feel like I belonged there with them.

As Will took Gus' coat and got beers, Gus started complaining about things at work. They were things Will had complained to me about before, but he didn't agree with Gus, just let him talk.

"God, do you ever find yourself thinking, 'How the hell did this become my life'?" Gus said finally when he'd tired himself out.

"No," Will said. "The only people who think that are the ones who assume their lives will turn out great from the beginning."

Gus opened his mouth, then shut it again and nodded, like he was evaluating Will's mood and recalibrating.

We sat at the kitchen table because that's where Will put the beers, as if he wanted no confusion that this was a business discussion.

"Okay," Will said, leaning back and crossing his legs, drinking deeply from the beer. "Convince me this isn't idiotic."

I decided I liked Gus when, rather than bristling at Will's challenge or taking it as a criticism, he leaned forward, excited, and started to talk.

"Okay, so," he began. And then he proceeded to lay out what sounded to me, at least, like a pretty compelling list of reasons why he and Will were not only qualified to strike out on their own but would actually benefit from it, both in terms of money and job satisfaction.

Will listened, beer dangling between two casual fingers and eyes slightly narrowed, but I thought he was intrigued at the very least. He wasn't doing the impatient thing he does where his jaw and nostrils are tensed as if stuck in a constant inhale trying to draw breath to interrupt something that bored or irritated him. Little by little he started asking questions, leaned forward slightly, and got another beer for him and for Gus without asking if he wanted one.

When he sat back down at the table, he held his beer out for me. I took a sip and passed it back and he barely looked at me, but he'd known. Known that I wouldn't want another but had wanted me to know he hadn't forgotten about me.

Will herded Gus out when he'd finished his beer, and cleaned up the empties.

"So, what do you think?"

"You want my opinion?" I asked, startled.

Will didn't respond, just wiped down the counters.

"Um. Well, I don't really know much about your business, and... you're way better at reading people than me...."

"I know that. Just, what did you think?"

"It seemed great. Like, I don't get why you wouldn't want to do it, great."

Will sighed. "Yeah."

"So… why wouldn't you?"

Will was staring out the window like maybe the answer was out there. "It's a lot," he said slowly. "To just start over. Start from scratch."

"Yeah, I know, right?"

He looked over, startled, as if he'd forgotten that starting over from scratch was exactly what I'd done when I moved here.

"JESUS GOD," Will muttered. Sweat trickled down his chest, and he clawed at the sheets.

For thirty minutes I'd kept him on the edge, touching, licking, biting, kissing, but not letting him come.

I had a theory that Will was secretly a hedonist, but he disguised it as an insistence that he just had good taste. It was little things that'd made me think so. The way he inhaled from his coffee cup before taking the first sip of the morning. He bought beans from a shop on the corner and ground them himself. He boiled water and poured it over the coffee, taking note of the time so he got the extraction right. With most things he was all about convenience, but he liked his coffee this way, and he liked the ritual of making it.

It was other things too, though. How he'd adjust a flower in an arrangement on a restaurant table to make it more pleasing. How he kept the heat turned a few degrees warmer than was practical so that he could sleep naked in the winter because he liked the feel of the sheets on his skin. The way he leaned into my hand if I touched his hair, like a cat deepening a caress. He loved food, too, even though he ate like an animal, his terrible table manners oddly out of step with the rest of his polished persona.

I knew that Will was way more experienced than me, that he'd been with a ton of men who were probably better than I was in bed. But ever since the other night, I couldn't get this fantasy out of my head. The fantasy where Will came totally undone. Where he dropped his guard and forgot that he was the sexpert and I basically knew jack squat. Where he begged me. Gave himself over to me and showed me something vulnerable. Something real. Something that he didn't show any of the other men he was with.

Because if I could make sex totally satisfying for him then he wouldn't need to go sleep with all those other people. Right?

So in pursuit of my fantasy, I'd decided to test the theory. No way was I going to be able to fuck Will as well as those other men with a ton of experience. Not yet, anyway. So I had to use other means at my disposal to get him so wound up that by the time I did fuck him, he was desperate for it. And so far I thought it was going pretty well.

At first he'd been all, "What are you doing, Leo? Quit it and fuck me." Once he realized that I was committed to driving him out of his mind, though, he'd relaxed a little bit.

Will's skin was like velvet, his hair like silk, and I could've touched him forever, even without the added bonus that it was making him fall apart.

I traced the line of his ribs with my tongue, feeling his heartbeat beneath his flushed skin. Every breath and swallow sank me deeper into the sense that I knew this man whose body I was exploring. I knew him, I saw him, I could touch him however I wanted, and he'd let me. Will, who was usually bossy and impatient and a know-it-all, was lying on the bed, hair clumped with sweat and eyes blazing, completely open to me.

I followed the cut of his abdomen down to the groove of his thigh, hot and salty, and pressed his knees up and apart. I lapped at the base of his cock, holding his hips down when he tried to thrust. He was leaking precome, and I rolled the taste of him around on my tongue. I couldn't take him all the way into my mouth yet, so I licked every inch, the feel of him straining beneath me exhilarating and intimidating.

"Fuck, Leo, I'm gonna—"

I grabbed the base of his dick and shook my head. Will threw his head back and groaned, cursing me again.

I kissed him as he calmed back down a little bit, loving the feel of his full lips on mine, his needy tongue playing against my own. He wrapped his arms around my neck, pressed tight against me. I hadn't realized how intoxicating it would be, the power I had to control Will's pleasure. To watch him made desperate at my hands.

I moved down his body, licking the cut of his stomach muscles, nipping at a hip bone. I scraped my teeth lightly around the base of his erection and smiled as he hissed, thrusting his hips up and clutching my shoulders. I rubbed up and down his thighs, encouraging his legs farther apart for me, then I rolled his balls in my hand and tugged gently, making him cry out. I kissed beneath them, following the thin skin to his ass. I rolled his hips up and tentatively traced his hole with my tongue.

"Oh shit, shit, shit," he groaned, voice gone tight.

"Is that—do you like that?" I asked. It seemed only polite.

"Yes," he said so quickly I almost laughed. But then Will groaned as I increased the pressure and it was anything but funny.

I wasn't exactly sure what I was supposed to do, but I figured being thorough was always a good policy? I pressed into the muscle around his hole with my thumbs, massaging it while I licked and sucked.

"Holy hell, Leo."

I made an inquisitive sound and Will made a confirmatory one, and then I lost track of everything but the slick and give of his skin, the muskiness of his scent here, the muscular clutch of his legs around me, everything in his body clenching and quivering as I worked him open with my tongue.

I loved this. Loved him like this. Loved routing all my attention to the place where I could actually be inside Will, be a part of him. A place where he opened to me. I squeezed his ass and pressed deeper into his hole with my thumbs so I could taste him inside. He relaxed to me and groaned, letting out a shaky laugh.

"That's like full-on merit badge material, kid."

"Gah! Don't call me kid when I'm… erm…."

"When you're what, Leo?" he purred. "What are you doing? Tell me."

"When I'm… you know."

Will chuckled and that was not what I wanted to hear from him right now. I wanted him back in the state where he was so desperate his only words were curses and he barely had breath for them anyway.

"Why don't you tell me what I'm doing to you since you're feeling so chatty, and I'll just keep on doing it," I said, with far more bravado than I felt. "And," I added, "if you stop talking, I'll stop doing it." I thought Will might tell me to piss off, but he gave a shaky moan and started talking.

"You're stretching my hole with your fingers and licking all around—ungh, shit—inside me. Sliding the tip of your tongue in and out of my ass. Licking—fuck…!"

He went on and on, the filthy narration creating a feedback loop of arousal. I did something to Will, Will described it, and it turned me on even more. Which was sort of a problem since the whole point of this was to get *Will* so turned-on that I could maximize my, uh, staying power. So I kissed Will's hole and pulled away, sliding up his body.

I ran a finger up the length of his erection, smearing precome when I got to the tip. He moaned, words gone, and I did it again. I kept the pressure light as a whisper, tracing patterns on his skin until he was panting and his face and throat were flushed, his lips wet. He had one arm flung over his eyes and he was trembling.

"Just a little harder, please," he whispered, but he made no attempt to touch himself. I leaned down and touched my tongue to the tip of his cock, tasting the bead of moisture there, and Will jerked, every muscle tightening, and cried out. I grabbed the root of his cock to make sure he didn't come, and he whimpered.

"Do you want me?" I asked, and he nodded immediately, eyes still covered by his arm. "Tell me." I kissed his mouth.

"I want you."

"Look at me and tell me," I said against his lips.

He moved his arm. His eyelashes were clumped together wetly, his lids half lowered. "I want you," he said, looking at me.

He was the most beautiful thing I'd ever seen. They were the most beautiful words I'd ever heard.

I knelt, just looking at him for a moment. He looked like a debauched angel. Like if a classical painter had ever rendered sex scenes. His flushed skin made him look like he glowed from within. His soft mouth was a daub of glistening paint, his blue eyes heated and bright, blond hair mussed and stuck together with sweat like it had been put in with the hard edge of a palette knife. He looked inhuman. But then he smiled, and he was Will. My Will, who I could taste on my tongue.

"You gonna fuck me finally?" He'd found his attitude again, but his voice was raw.

"Yeah." I nodded.

He flipped the condom at me and lay back, an arm beneath his head like he was sitting on a *chaise longue* around the pool, his grin a challenge now that he knew he was going to get what he wanted.

I leaned forward and licked the powdery pale skin on the inside of his arm, the muscle sliding as he tensed. I had the sudden conviction that I had to kiss every inch of his skin. That somewhere on his body lay a place that I hadn't attended to and that, if I didn't taste it, I would be leaving something important unfinished. Then his mouth was so close that I couldn't help but kiss that too.

I ran my fingertips up and down the tendon at the back of his neck, the skin hot and sweat-damp, and kissed him, wanting to layer every taste of him on my tongue. I handed the condom back to him.

"Put it on me," I murmured into his mouth. "So I can keep kissing you."

I could feel his intake of breath in the kiss, and then felt the slick touch of the condom.

"Yeah, come on," he said against my lips, positioning me where he wanted me, the challenge in his voice replaced by want.

I tilted his hips up, and slid inside him, the clutch of skin and muscle ripping a groan from my mouth. I sank into him, shaking with the sudden buzz of pressure along my cock.

"Fuck, fuck," I muttered into his neck, overcome. With one finger, I traced his opening, felt the place where we were connected. I'd tasted him here. Speared him open with my tongue as he moaned, totally undone.

I was so turned-on I was shaking. Will started to move his hips but I grabbed them and held them down.

"Wait, just wait."

I tried to slow my breathing so the arousal would recede enough for me to actually… do something.

"Leo."

"Hmm?"

"Are you doing yoga breathing right now?"

"Um. Yeah, I'm trying not to come." It wasn't working very well. The creep of arousal wasn't receding. If anything, just the knowledge that I was inside Will's body got me amped up all over again. "This is basically like plank pose, so." I nodded to the way my arms were braced on either side of Will's body.

"You'd better fucking plank *me* right now."

I started laughing, which helped a little.

"Come on, Leo, fuck me." Will was breathless, pressing me deeper inside him.

I did as he said. "You're. So. Fucking. Bossy," I said as I thrust into him.

"You love it," he gasped. And it was true. I loved that I didn't have to guess what Will wanted because he always told me. That I wasn't left wondering if he was faking his reactions to anything because he would never bother. But that all paled in comparison to how much I loved, at this moment, the feeling of fucking him. The cling of his skin and the way he clutched my ass to pull me to him were quickly becoming my favorite things in the world.

Will changed the angle of his hips and started moaning as I slammed into him, tightening his ass around me. I was so turned-on I lost the rhythm completely, almost wincing away from the pleasure skittering up my spine and spreading through my lower belly.

"Lemme just—" Will pulled off me and flipped onto his hands and knees, reaching a hand back to me. I slid back inside him and froze so I wouldn't come at the sound of his groan. He dropped down to his forearms, his gorgeous ass in the air, and I fucked down into him as his ass bounced against my hips, his perfect profile like a cameo against the pillow.

"Will, I'm gonna—"

He made a broken sound and started jerking himself off.

"Oh fuck," I gasped. "That's too hot. Shit."

I closed my eyes and dropped my forehead down to his spine to try and get myself away from the edge, but it was no good. Even with one sense blocked, the rest were saturated with him. The smell and taste of sweat and precome and Will were in my nose and my mouth and the sounds of his moans and his breathing in my ears, and his skin was slick and hot beneath my mouth and my hands.

"Oh god," Will moaned as I thrust into him, holding him at the hip and shoulder. He shook against me, muscles tightening, caught on the edge of his pleasure with his head thrown back and his throat bared.

I pressed even deeper inside him, pulled almost all the way out, and slammed back in. Will let out a sharp cry and came over his hand and his expensive sheets. As he clenched up, pleasure blasted through me, blackening my vision and making me shudder. I let myself fully focus on the feeling of him still clenching around me, his slick heat pulsing around my dick, the gorgeous curve of ass and thigh slick with sweat. I stayed deep inside him, giving short thrusts and feeling every inch of my dick sliding against muscle and skin. The pleasure skittered down my spine, throbbed in my gut, and exploded from me, my orgasm taking me over completely.

I collapsed on top of Will, and he clenched his ass around me, shooting a final spark of pleasure up my dick and through my ass and my thighs and my stomach. I held his hips and inched myself forward, tensing every muscle against the last shudders of pleasure. When I slid from him, I was trembly and spent.

"Mmmmm," he said, reaching a hand back to pat my flank in a listless attaboy gesture. Then he rolled onto his side, avoiding the wet spot by throwing an arm and a leg over me as he stretched luxuriantly.

I kissed him, tasting the metal of salt in his mouth until it faded into the heat of his tongue. We were holding each other's faces as we kissed, inching closer and closer together like the space between us could be obliterated.

In Zeno's paradox, halving the distance between you and what you sought meant that you would go on forever, always moving closer but never actually reaching it. But maybe if you set your sights on a thing beyond what you sought then you would eventually find yourself smack in the middle of it, having tricked the universe into rendering up exactly what you really wanted.

WE HAD fallen asleep tangled up in one another, and I woke during the night to feel fingers in my hair. I made a contented sound and pressed back against Will, but the second he realized I was awake he stopped.

"You okay?"

"Fine," he said. "Go back to sleep." He sounded half-asleep himself. I tilted my chin back, and he pressed a kiss to the side of my neck. I pulled the covers tighter around us, but then he sighed and kissed the back of my neck before rolling away to sit on the side of the bed.

"Hey, what's up?" I slid over to him and rested my head on his thigh, looking up at him.

"Nothing."

"Come on, what's wrong."

He was quiet for a long time, and at first I thought he had fallen asleep sitting up.

"I'm not used to sharing a bed with anyone," he said softly. "That's all."

"You never—with the guys you…."

"Christ, no. Nightmare."

"What about with… that TA?"

"Yeah right, like he would've ever let me spend the night," Will said sharply. I wanted to kill this guy, but I didn't want to say any more about it and make Will feel bad.

"But you must have with Rex, right?"

"Yeah, sometimes. That was a long time ago."

"What was the deal with you and Rex, anyway? How'd you guys end up dating?" I was totally awake now and hoped maybe Will was in a sharing mood.

Will still stared ahead into the dark room, but his hand came down on my head, and he started playing with my hair again, brushing it off my forehead and running his fingers through it.

"Rex is… you know. Rex-like. When I first saw him, I made certain assumptions." He said this slyly, as if I knew what he meant, but I didn't really. "I came on pretty bratty, you know, thinking he'd be into it. When it was clear that wasn't the right tactic, I was just honest. Basically said, 'hey, wanna bonk?' Which he did. It started casual, but you know what a small

town Holiday is. There wasn't anything else to do, so we just kind of kept…
doing each other."

I sat up and stared at him. "You're not seriously expecting me to
believe that you were with Rex for like a year because Holiday is a boring
town. Get real."

"I'd just graduated," he said slowly, and I tugged him back into bed,
pressing him down. "I had no clue what I was doing. I had no money. And
Claire…." He shook his head. "Things weren't… okay for her. Nathan was
five and Sarah was three and she was fucking up bad. Sarah's father was
kind of around, but he was a sociopath. Just completely morally bankrupt,
seriously. And when Claire was with him, she was just as bad. They brought
out the worst in each other, really."

I threw an arm over his waist and put my head on his shoulder, close
enough to his chest that I could feel the reassuring thump of his heart against
my ear.

"I was scared of what she'd do, scared of what would happen to
the kids, scared of what Darren might do to Claire. Just fucking scared of
everything. So I went back to Michigan. And it was a shit show. She didn't
want me there, and then me being there was the only thing that would help.
She wanted my opinion on everything, from what kind of bread to get at
the grocery store to what color she should paint her nails, and then if I tried
to tell her my opinion on something she'd scream at me that I was trying
to control her life. She wanted me to watch the kids twenty-four-seven so
she could go out with Darren or her friends, and then she didn't want me
anywhere near them because she was their parent, not me, and she was
convinced I was going to turn them against her.

"I helped as much as I could when she let me. Or I left her alone when
she asked. Sometimes. Sometimes I couldn't, and then she'd just hate me
for doing what needed to be done. Rex—" He lingered over the name. "Rex
was calm. Predictable. Consistent. He didn't play games, and he didn't fuck
with my head. He didn't stop me from leaving whenever I wanted because
he never expected anything of me in the first place. Around him I was…."
He shrugged like the memory embarrassed him.

"I was shallow and capricious. And I couldn't fucking believe this
good person wanted to spend even one second around me. Couldn't believe
he thought I was funny, or fun. Couldn't believe he just accepted it when I
told him I had to take off and then disappeared for a week without a word,
taking care of stuff at Claire's. And after a little while I got used to him, I

guess. We got along really well. Rex is smart, you know, even if he's not smart like your friend Daniel."

"I know he is," I confirmed, and Will hesitated before nodding, like he'd been prepared for a disagreement.

"You know the way he and Daniel are," Will said, "where they're just kind of… attuned to each other? Like, they aren't close together but if you were standing far enough back to see them both you would see that they were moving in relation to one another?"

"Oh my god, *yes*." I didn't want to admit how often I'd noticed that and wished that I could have something like it. It was basically the most romantic thing I'd ever seen. Like even through space, even separated, their bodies or spirits or whatever it was, could sense each other and move accordingly.

"Rex wasn't like that with me. We weren't like that. And we never would've been. It just wasn't that kind of thing. It was a good fit at the moment. He got a little infusion of fun in his life, and I… was looking for a wall I could keep running into. Anyway, we'd never have actually fit into each other's lives. But I was on pause, and he was kinda locked away. I felt like the girl in that book… what's it? *The Secret Garden*." He looked embarrassed and when he spoke again it was as if he was mocking himself.

"I got to skip into Rex's little garden, and I shook things up for him—he was so damned serious; even worse than he is now, for real—and at the same time I got a place to hide away for a while. A place I could relax, I guess. But yeah." He snorted. "It would never have worked long term. Rex needed a safe space, and I… definitely wasn't. Never would've been for him."

"Wow, and you think of Daniel as a safe space? I more saw Rex as a safe space for him, I guess."

Will bent his head awkwardly to look at me, his stubble catching my hair.

"Everyone's safe space looks different, kiddo. For some people, like messy, messy Daniel, it's someone who takes care of them, sure. But for others it's someone who they can act out certain parts of their personalities with. Or all of their personalities."

Maybe he was half-asleep, but this didn't sound quite like the cynical description of a relationship made of self-annihilating compromise I'd heard from him before.

He rearranged us so his back was to my chest, pulling my arm around his stomach, and smashed his face into the pillow, clearly done with the subject.

I gave him a little squeeze and settled in. Just as I was starting to drift off, though, Will spoke, so softly, and so muffled by the pillow that I almost couldn't make it out.

"It just turns so easily."

"What does?" I said against his neck.

"Love."

"How do you mean?"

He pushed the pillow off his face and stared into the darkness beyond the bed. In the ambient light from the window, I could see that his eyes were open.

"Love and beauty… they look good. On the surface. Perfect. So people think they *are* good. But sometimes they're just… rotten."

I was afraid if I said anything, the spell would break. But I couldn't let it go in case I never got another chance to be sure of what he meant.

"Are you still talking about you and Rex?"

"No, I wasn't talking about me."

"Oh. So, who, then?"

I nuzzled into his soft hair, and he pressed against me just enough that I knew now was one of those moments when he liked me, here, with him.

"My sister. My parents. Whatever."

"What happened with your parents? They just stopped loving each other?"

Will snorted. His voice, when he spoke again, was dark. "No. They were obsessed with each other."

"What do you mean?"

"They met in high school. Sophomore year. And that was it. They just… didn't see anyone else. High school sweethearts." Every word was a dagger.

"Wow, that's romantic," I said automatically, but Will tensed the second it was out of my mouth, and I knew it was the wrong thing to say.

"No. Not romantic. Or sweet." He murdered the word. "All they cared about was each other. Couldn't be bothered with me and Claire. It's not sweet when your parents are making out in the living room when you bring friends over and run off giggling like a couple of kids when you interrupt them. Not romantic when you have to shoplift from the grocery store if you want anything fresh because the only food in the house is canned soup and boxed mac and cheese since they never hesitated to just go out for a date night."

"Fuck."

"I got caught once. Shoplifting. Apples and tomatoes. When my parents came down to the store to get me, my mom smiled this calculated smile. 'Oh, he probably just wanted to make a surprise dinner for us. Isn't that sweet?' And everyone fucking agreed, because in a world of ugliness and divorce and desperation people will do anything to feel like they played some small part in someone's tale of true love. Especially if they don't have one of their own.

"And they were fucking proud of it. Proud I played along. It was this big joke, like they were the romantic leads in some movie and everyone else was just extras. Like they didn't matter. And forget trying to tell anyone that they weren't perfect. That's all anyone saw."

Pieces fell into place as he spoke, and I wanted to ask him a thousand questions, but before I could say anything, Will was on top of me, kissing me fiercely. I opened my mouth to ask if he was okay, but he just slid his tongue against mine, grinding us together hotly. I groaned into his mouth, caught up in his whirlwind, and we moved against each other in the stillness of the night.

Chapter 9

SOMETHING HAD shifted. We teased each other more. We talked more. Touched more.

Will was still Will—he'd tell me that some innocuous thing I did was annoying him, I'd tell him that sometimes you just had to deal with people doing things like eating, brushing their teeth, and breathing in your space, and he'd say, "Not if you live alone, you don't." I'd say, "Well, I'm here too, now, and you're being a dick," and he'd snap, "Yes, I'm an asshole. True facts." And he'd grumble about it and then wander away if he couldn't deal with the sound of me eating, brushing my teeth, or breathing. But I wouldn't become immediately convinced that he hated me and wanted me to leave. Mostly.

We even wandered slowly through MoMA, like we were on a real date (though I made sure not to use the d-word around Will because I knew he'd cancel our plans). I was fascinated by a special exhibit on the fonts and design of the subway maps, and Will kept sneaking away to go stand in front of his favorite piece in the museum, *Christina's World* by Wyeth, hung, strangely, I thought, just outside the elevator.

"What do you think?" he asked. It felt like some kind of test, since he'd said it was his favorite.

"I don't really know much about art," I hedged.

Because I didn't really get it. The colors were ugly and it was kind of boring. But I wanted so badly to see what he saw in it.

"Um, well, it seems peaceful, I guess? Calm. Like she's just hanging out in that field relaxing and looking at her house, but she doesn't *have* to go there...." I trailed off because Will was looking at me strangely.

Suddenly, he leaned forward and kissed me. On the mouth. In public.

I pitched forward in surprise and grabbed his shoulders to keep from falling into the painting.

"What was that for?" I asked when he leaned back, but he didn't say anything. Just shook his head and leaned close enough to the painting that I worried he'd set off some kind of alarm. But there was nothing between him and the canvas at all. He could have reached a hand out and touched it.

He studied it closely, one hand on my wrist. "What do you think that is?" He pointed to a tiny gray splotch between the house and the barn that I hadn't even noticed.

"Um, a bird, I guess?" I said. I had no clue.

Will just looked at me, but when he led me into the next room to look at the Picassos, he didn't let go of my arm right away, just held it like it was natural that we should be connected.

IN HIGH school, the week before winter break was a strange animal. The energy would become more and more frenetic, then explode into temporary cross-clique camaraderie on the last day of the semester, everyone bonding over the one thing we all had in common: excitement about getting the hell out of there.

I felt it too, but whereas it seemed like everyone else had plans for break—ski trips with their families, basketball training, group sledding, shopping trips in Detroit—I... didn't. I liked the time off, of course, but it wasn't really that much different than the rest of my evenings or weekends when school was in session.

When I was younger and Carter and I were still friends, it was our prime time for movie marathons. Rewatching all the series we'd grown up with. *X-Men*, *Harry Potter*, *Underworld*. And without fail, we watched *Lord of the Rings* and our favorite DVD extras. Carter's favorites were always about the sword fighting or hand-to-hand combat in the battle scenes. I loved the ones where they showed how they actually created the Shire—seeding it a year before shooting so that when the actors and crew showed up there was an *actual* world there. (I didn't tell Carter my other favorite extra: when Viggo Mortensen kissed Billy Boyd on the mouth.)

I was captivated by the idea that this epic series had an equally epic parallel story. That they created a world for themselves at the same time they were creating a world for us to view.

Maybe that's why, after Carter had dumped me as a friend, I still spent my winter breaks watching the *Lord of the Rings* extras. Yeah, I probably should've been out trying to make new friends, like my mom and Janie always told me to do. And I tried. Kinda. At first it was mostly just that I had nothing in common with the other kids I went to school with.

Later, once I sort of accidentally outed myself during biology class, it was a combination of people keeping a bit of distance and macho fuckwads deciding that I'd given them an excuse to pick fights.

So I watched DVD extras. Like, all of them. I fell into the world so hard that it started to seem like a movie in its own right. Or a reality TV show where I got to watch these people's lives unfold. I felt like I knew them—knew what they would say or what their reactions would be. Okay, I was a little obsessed. But I didn't have that. Friends, a purpose, a... world of my own.

When I came to college, then, a part of me held that out as the model. I loved getting to know Milton well enough that I could predict which parts of *Felicity* he'd think were funny. Or knowing the sound of Gretchen's breath on the mat beside me in yoga, distinct from anyone else's. Being able to anticipate the way that Thomas would weave bits of what was going on into the comics he drew during class. Knowing that when Charles started to bounce his knee up and down while he looked at the computer, it meant he was reaching the part of whatever he was reading that really convinced him—the part that made him believe there was truth to the conspiracy, no matter how farfetched.

The neighborhood, with campus, the dorms, and the blocks surrounding Washington Square, was our own little Shire, and the city stretching beyond it Middle Earth. I was pretty convinced that the building that housed my Cultural Foundations class was Mordor, but when I told Will my analogy—thinking he'd laugh and call me a geek but instead being pleasantly surprised to find he was a fan too—he said, no, Times Square at peak tourist rush hour in the summer was absolutely the depths of Mordor. "One does not simply walk into Times Square!" he teased the next week when I told him about a harrowingly aggressive incident with a selfie stick outside the TKTS booth when I took an ill-advised shortcut.

For all these reasons, spending winter break with Will was—possibly to a humiliating degree—basically heaven. The awesome sex didn't hurt either. Even though he went back to work while I was still on break, just being in his space felt like I was connected to him. I spent a lot of time reading—Will had similar taste in fantasy, but also a lot of science fiction I hadn't read—and I started writing. Just absently scribbling about New York and my friends. Not for anyone to see, just to remember everything.

I wrote about Will. Things I noticed about him, questions I had. Stuff I wanted to do to him.

I found myself writing a lot about yoga too. I wrote down things Tonya said that resonated with me, feeling ridiculous at first, like I was in some kind of self-help class or something. But I figured if it was a practice that had been around for like five thousand years, they'd probably figured some shit out. And I wrote down the ways that those things changed my perspective. Tonya always said that only ten percent of yoga happens on the mat; the rest of the time you're out in the world, so the trick is to apply the principles more broadly so we get the benefit of them in the world as much as we do on the mat.

Sometimes I'd wander around Will's neighborhood, getting food from La Fonda Boricua or Taqueria Guadalupe and walking through the Vanderbilt Gate and the Conservatory Garden into Central Park to sit by the Untermeyer Fountain or the Burnett Fountain. Sometimes I'd stop at the bodega a few blocks down and get groceries to make simple dinners, so aware always of how different this neighborhood felt than the West Village.

The smell of spilled coffee and the churros for sale on the subway platforms. Tiny old ladies making their way to the bodegas with wheeled carts to do their weekly shopping. How the snow was only shoveled in a thin, perilous strip in the center of the sidewalk so you had to pick your way around people, puddles, and menacing dark patches.

The whole city seemed that way. Each neighborhood—sometimes even just a several block radius—felt unique, and yet there was some essential quality, some… New Yorkness that asserted itself at every turn.

Now it was the last weekend of break and I had talked Will into staying in with me, ordering food, and having a *Lord of the Rings* marathon. We couldn't watch the extras because he didn't own the DVDs. ("I hate clutter," he'd said when I'd asked why. "And DVD packaging is terribly designed. Everything from the shape of the box to the art is an aesthetic abomination.")

We ordered Thai, eating ourselves into a stupor and getting tipsy on Singha beer as we watched. I was coming around to beer. A little.

"You look like Legolas," I told him seriously, knowing it would piss him off because he thought Legolas was prissy and self-satisfied.

"Well, you look like Pippin," he shot back, opening another beer and arranging me on the couch so he could lean into my shoulder, grumbling about how I didn't have enough padding to be comfortable, as usual, but settling in against me nonetheless.

All in all, it was probably one of the best days I've ever had. Of course, when I told Will that, he snarked about how pathetic my life must have been up to this point. He was worse at taking compliments than anyone I'd ever met.

THE NEXT night was my last night at Will's before second semester began, and I was moping around the apartment as I gathered my stuff to go back to the dorms. Finally, I plopped down on the couch next to Will, in a full-on sulk. It was the Sunday night to end all Sunday nights, not just the end of break but the end of my time in the fantasy that Will and I lived here together.

Will had been moody all day, and more irritable than usual, less open to being touched, so I should have known better.

It was the desperate desire to shore up the fantasy that made me stupid enough to say something to Will about it. I wanted some assurance that this month had meant something to him too. That, in the end, it had turned out to be more than just him doing me a favor after I fucked up. That it portended something real.

That things were different now.

We'd had sex the night before, languid and ponderous from our movie marathon, and I'd fallen asleep all tangled up in Will and the covers, his chest against my back, his legs threaded lazily through mine. I must've turned over in my sleep because I woke up facing him, our bent knees touching, our faces close together on the same pillow, my hand on his wrist, resting like twins in the cocoon of blankets as if we'd woken up that way a thousand times.

In that moment, winter sun streaming through the window, the bed warm and smelling of sex and us, the possibility stretched before me, luminous and full of hope, that maybe we'd wake up that way a thousand times more.

That tantalizing hope held before me, as gleaming and as fragile as a soap bubble, made me utter precisely the words that would point a needle at it: "We can still be together, right?" I gestured between us. "Once I go back to the dorms?"

And Will, with more kindness than I might've expected, given his mood, said, "Leo. We're not together. You know that."

Which hurt. Because of course I knew that. But he was choosing to split hairs about my terminology and ignore the feelings it described.

"Okay, sorry, sure, I mean, I know we're not, like, *boyfriends*, but…." I bit my lip and looked up at Will. "But we're… something, right?"

Will didn't say anything.

I looked down at where my hands rested on my thighs. They'd gotten so much stronger since I'd started yoga. Now sometimes I pressed into the muscles as I walked or bent to sit down, feeling the tautness there, feeling the way my own body was pulling itself together to support me.

There were some things that no amount of effort could bring into being. Some poses that no gains of strength or flexibility could realize. But you made the effort anyway.

"I want us to be," I said simply, moving my attention to my hands, looking at each bony knuckle, the folds in the skin that let them bend, the bitten nails with deep white moons.

Will sighed and scrubbed his hands over his face.

"I already told you. I'm not interested in monogamy. I'm not interested in playing house. It's just not how this is gonna go."

"I'm not saying I want to marry you. I just don't understand why we can't… date." Saying it out loud, the word sounded petty and superficial.

"Man, come on! We talked about this." He was pissed, but then his tone changed as he said, "You promised."

And that got me. Because he was right. I had promised. I had made a promise that, if I were totally honest, I really hadn't thought I would have to keep. God, that was terrible. I had promised Will that things were fine the way they were because I'd really believed that he just needed a… like a transition period. An excuse. A low-pressure way to give it a shot.

Wow, I was a complete and total asshole. My stomach turned with guilt and shame, but Will must have read it as hurt.

"Leo, you're in college. You're nineteen years old. It's normal to date a lot of people, sleep with a lot of people—experiment. I know that you think you want me, but there are so many people you're going to like or love or want. So many things you're gonna want to do."

Which was so completely beside that point that I got mad at him all over again.

"Is that what you do? Experiment?" My fingertips dug into the muscles of my thighs in an effort to keep my voice even.

"No, not really. I already know what I like."

At that I totally lost my calm. Lost my pride. Lost even the fiery hook of guilt at secretly, internally breaking my promise. I couldn't help it.

"But if you already know what you like, couldn't I give it to you? I mean, couldn't I be the one to—"

"No!" Will grabbed my forearms and pulled me closer to him on the couch. "No. You do not offer to turn yourself into what someone else wants. Ever. Do you hear me?"

"But I *want* to be with you. I don't understand what you get from them—those men that you—like, the sex stuff…. I can do better. I just haven't had much time, but…."

Will shook his head.

"It's not that I don't like sex with you."

"Then—okay, well, that's good. So then why do you have to—?"

"I don't *have* to. I *choose* to. It's not… pathological, okay, not some manifestation of whateverthefuck. It's my choice to have the option to do whatever I want with whoever I want, whenever."

"Well, something can be a choice, and there are still *reasons* behind it."

"God save me from anyone who just took Intro Psych," Will muttered. "I just told you the reason. Because I fucking want to."

"And you *don't* want me! That's what you're saying!"

Will put his head in his hands like I was the most exasperating thing that had ever happened to him.

"Look, I'm sorry that what I want isn't the same as what you want. Wouldn't it be so convenient if we all agreed about everything and wanted the same things?"

"Don't! Don't make it sound ridiculous that it hurts my fucking feelings to sit here on this couch with you after a month of basically living together and sleeping together and hanging out together and say that I like you and wish it could continue."

"Well then stop acting like I'm deliberately harming you by telling the truth when *you* ask for it. I'm not a monster! I'm not a terrible person or a mean person because I don't want what you want. And I'm not a sad person or a cold person just because I don't *feel* everything that you do!"

I was close enough to him to feel the breath of his exclamation on my face. I didn't think he was a monster. I didn't think he was terrible or mean. I just didn't understand how it was possible to act the way he acted toward me and not have it mean something.

"I didn't say you were deliberately doing anything," I said, choked. "But it still hurts. Sorry."

Will's sigh was huge.

"Man, don't apologize," he said, tugging me a little closer.

I resisted, not wanting to accept comfort from the person who made me need it in the first place. Finally, though, I couldn't resist Will's hands on my shoulders. I slouched down against his chest with a sigh of my own, pathetically aware that I would take whatever he was offering as long as I wasn't being banished from his presence entirely.

"Look." I could feel the vibration of the word through his breastbone. "Leo, you're my…. You're great, okay? But I… the last thing I need is to be responsible for another person's feelings right now. You've got your life, and I've got mine. We'll still see each other, okay? Because we want to. *If you still want to?*"

I bit my lip against the bolt of hurt and frustration that tore through me. I had promised. I nodded. "Course I do."

I knew I wasn't imagining what was between us. That the way we were with each other, the way we touched each other had changed. Where once there was a clear divide between times when we were being sexual and every other moment, now the wall between the categories had eroded.

A hand on my hip as he moved around me in the kitchen to pour his coffee, fingers in my hair when he walked behind me. He touched my freckles sometimes, tracing them across my cheeks and nose with his fingertip. He'd lean his weight against me or drop his chin onto my shoulder to look at what I was doing. And every now and then he'd shove me against the wall and kiss me until I couldn't breathe.

But if we *weren't* dating, if we *weren't* in a relationship, I had no context for understanding what those touches meant. Will didn't seem to need containers for things like that, but I did.

When I'd gathered all my stuff, Will walked me to the door. I felt more like I was leaving home than I had when I left Michigan in the bus' rearview mirror. Every atom in me was agitated toward Will, every muscle tensed to meet his. It was an actual physical wrench to make myself leave.

At the last minute, even though I felt raw and humiliated, I threw my arms around him.

"Thanks for having me," I said.

He ran a hand up and down my back, under my backpack, and squeezed me, almost like he might, just the tiniest bit, miss me too.

"Later," he said when I finally let go.

I turned back to look at his closed door as I waited for the elevator, then turned and took the stairs, bereft of the strength to stop myself from walking toward it again and knocking if it took the elevator more than five seconds to come.

I slouched down the fifteen flights slowly, biting the insides of my cheeks to keep from crying. Shoving my fists into my pockets, I traced the sharp ridges of the key Will had given me when I first arrived a month ago. I hadn't given it back because it felt so final, and now I took a tiny bit of comfort in the fact that, at least, I knew I could come back. The flop of my busted shoes echoed in the stairwell, a reminder that I still needed to get new ones since the soles were coming off.

Chapter 10

February

"You should come out," I told Charles as I tugged on the clothes I'd borrowed from Milton. The tight jeans hugged my legs and the artful layers of shirt, sweater, and jacket were nothing I'd ever have chosen, but I had to admit it all kind of worked. "We're going to see *Into the Woods* at this high school—which, right, sounds like it'd be terrible because high school play, but Milton says it'll be good?"

Milton came in without knocking and tossed a pair of pointy-toed shoes on the bed with a flourish, Thomas trailing in behind him.

"Here. You absolutely cannot wear those scrofulous Vans with my outfit."

I thought about protesting, but the truth was, my shoe situation was actually reaching critical. I'd duct taped the soles back on when they started flapping when I walked, but in the cold the duct tape lost its stickiness and kind of sloughed off, leaving the rubber parts of my shoes gummy so that dirt and hair and dust stuck and crusted in the new layer of duct tape I'd added.

It was pathetic, I knew, but I hadn't bought new ones yet because I'd kind of hoped Will would be so horrified by them that he'd insist on another shopping expedition. The more fool me, since Will was basically immune to manipulation tactics. So I just put on Milton's shoes. They scrunched my toes.

"Wow," said Thomas. "You look really great."

"Thanks," I said, considering my reflection. Was this how Will would want me to dress? Put together and a little bit edgy? I ran a hand through my hair but it just looked sloppy.

"Here, can I…?" Thomas gestured at my hair.

"Yeah, sure."

He and Milton exchanged a look, and Thomas took a small container out of his bag and rubbed a dollop of some product that smelled warm, like a bakery or something, between his hands. He nudged me onto the bed and stood in front of me, touching me tentatively at first and then massaging the stuff into my hair and doing... some kind of arranging. It felt nice, and I leaned into his touch. His hands softened, just touching my scalp.

"Um, o-okay," Thomas said, stepping away.

My hair was still its usual wavy brown mop, but now it looked like I wore it that way on purpose. It made me look older.

"Hey, thanks!"

"You look great," Thomas said, ducking his head and looking at the floor where my poor cast-off Vans sat in a puddle of duct tape and melted slush. "I mean, you always look—I didn't mean, um."

"Ooh, do you mind taking a picture of me?" I asked him, tossing him my phone. "I wanna prove to Will that I'm not always a total wreck."

Thomas didn't say anything as he took the picture.

I texted Will, *Outfit approval? Wish you were coming! xoxox*

"I'll, uh, meet you guys out front," Thomas said, then left.

My phone pinged with a text from Will: *Not bad, cowboy. Bet you *could* make me come if you put your mind to it... ;)*

Heat flushed through me, and I immediately wondered if I should skip the play and go over to Will's instead.

Milton thwacked me with the back of his hand.

"What is wrong with you?!"

"What'd I do?" I looked away from my phone and forced the smile off my face.

"Come *on*, Leo, you cannot be this oblivious. Thomas? Likes you. Obviously."

"No way. Wait, did he tell you that?"

"He didn't have to tell me, you idiot, it's completely obvious. He hangs on every word you say, he stares at you, he invites you to do things." Milton was looking at me with raised eyebrows. "Did you seriously not know?"

I shook my head. I seriously didn't. It hadn't even occurred to me that someone might feel that way about me. I was a radio, and the only station I was tuned to was Will's.

THE PLAY turned out to be great. I'd dragged Charles with us at the last minute after all, and he, Milton, Thomas, Gretchen, and I sat in the very back row, sipping vodka from one of Milton's ever-present flasks mixed with hot chocolate we bought at the concession table.

I was warm and tipsy and full of joy, snuggled in my seat between Milton, who kept up a running stream of funny commentary, and Gretchen, who began adding her own commentary after about half of one of Milton's flasks and enough hot chocolate to send me into a sugar coma. I licked whipped cream off her nose and spent intermission with my head on her shoulder, watching the audience through half-closed eyes.

After the curtain call, we spilled out into the streets with the rest of the audience, everyone talking excitedly, the stress of the parents somewhat dissipated now that the show had finished, people bragging about the lighting effect their son had come up with or the way their daughter had covered for another actor who forgot his lines.

I had one arm linked with Gretchen's and the other with Milton's, and the snap of cold air made us half run and half skip the three blocks to the diner. We ate plates of fries and hummus with olives and pita triangles, and we drank coffee doctored with more vodka from another flask that Milton produced from some mysterious inner pocket that hadn't even disturbed the line of his perfectly cut overcoat, and we talked and laughed in a cloud of fizzy excitement. Charles was explaining the paper he was writing, called "On the Tyranny of Time," to Gretchen, and Milton was telling us his own theatrical greatest hits and misses.

On our way out, I was so tipsy and high on my friends' energy that I tripped going down the narrow, slush-slicked staircase that led to the bathrooms, and Thomas caught my arm to keep me from falling. Did he hold on a little longer than was necessary? I wasn't sure, so I just smiled at him. The smile he gave me back was luminous.

By the time we got back to the dorms, the cold air had sobered me a little, but I was still buzzing, the fluorescent lights in the hallway making my head throb and the texture on the carpet seem hyper-real. Thomas and Gretchen waved good night, and Milton caught my shoulder as I made to follow Charles to our room.

"One sec," he said, suddenly serious. "About Thomas. Just don't fuck with him if you don't mean it, okay?"

"Fuck with him? I don't fuck with him."

Milton hesitated. "Just don't treat him the way Will treats you."

"What!? I don't—"

"Babe, you kind of do. I know you probably don't mean to."

I shook my head, and Milton patted me on the shoulder.

"Okay. Just… you *know* how shitty it feels, so be careful with him."

I nodded, bewildered and nauseated, all the good feelings of the evening rushing out of me like a deflating balloon.

THE STARS rushed past and we zoomed through the planets' atmospheres, space debris suspended in the thick darkness. I was shaky with awe at the scale of the known universe, even rendered in flickering light and color on the ceiling of the planetarium.

The e-mail from my astronomy professor telling us we had to go to the planetarium for class had come while I was FaceTiming with Will, and I told him it'd be more fun if I could go with him. He'd rolled his eyes at me and muttered about "puppy dog eyes," but he'd been smiling when he agreed.

Today was the first time I'd seen him since taking my leave of his apartment after our winter break together. We'd talked and texted over the last couple weeks, but I could tell that Will was skittish about the way we'd left things, and I decided to prove to him that I wasn't some codependent loser by not asking him to hang out every day.

When he'd walked up to where I was waiting in front of the entrance, though, my heart totally leapt. He had come from work, so he was dressed impeccably, and the reminder that he'd left work early to make sure we could catch the last show made me all warm and swoony.

Now, I reached out and twined my fingers through Will's where his hand rested on his thigh. I did it without thinking, seeking some connection in the face of the sublimity of space. Out of the corner of my eye, I could see Will turn to look at me, but I just kept my gaze heavenward and after a minute he squeezed my hand back. My chest was hollow with yearning, my stomach aflutter with affection for Will. For the feel of the hand I held, the leg our hands rested on, the warmth of his shoulder just touching mine.

Love. Not affection. I knew it, really. It had to be love because you didn't feel affection for a hand. You fucking loved it. Right?

I was light-headed, the word zinging around to the tune of the whooshing keyboard and the zinging strings that accompanied our rush through space, my skin tingling as if it were only molecules magnetized toward Will by the force of his pull. I wanted to close my eyes, to shut out a vastness that dwarfed my love, but I couldn't because I wanted both.

I wanted all the solidity of Will's hand on earth, and I wanted to be blasted apart by echoes of it thrumming through space like the afterimage of a supernova.

"MAKES ME feel like we're in *Rebel Without a Cause*," Will was saying as we left the planetarium and walked through Central Park.

"I never saw it."

Will shook his head at me the way he did whenever I hadn't read or seen something he considered essential to being a cultured human in the world. I got the sense he'd worked really hard to catch up on all these things when he left Holiday.

"In class the professor told us this amazing story about Carl Sagan and Ann Druyan," I offered. "Part of the Voyager project was that on board each of the craft were these records where they recorded a bunch of sounds from Earth—like little Earth capsules or something to communicate things about our world and about humanity if they ever made contact with alien life, and Carl Sagan was the one to curate it. Like, jeez, how do you curate the experience of Earth? It's so wild."

My shoulder brushed Will's companionably, but he didn't put any distance between us.

"Ann Druyan was the creative director of the project, and she and Carl Sagan fell in love while they were working on it. So she had the idea that they should include a record where they measure electrical impulses of the brain and the nervous system then translate that into sound, with the idea that possibly if the record were found those sounds could be translated back into thoughts. Which is such a brilliant idea, just in theory.

"So she let them record the sounds while she meditated, and she says that she was thinking about being in love with Carl Sagan, so that really it's like the soundtrack to her feelings of love for him. And, okay, I mean, in meditation you're supposed to *not* really think, but still. Isn't that the most romantic thing you've ever heard? She sent her love into *space* to echo throughout the fucking *cosmos*!"

I hooked my elbow through Will's and squeezed his arm against me, caught up in the story. If only I could transmit to him the feelings that I knew he wouldn't want to hear me say out loud.

Will let me take his arm, but he shook his head.

"I guess, but wasn't Carl Sagan married to someone else, and didn't they have some super dramatic divorce with kids and stuff because he fell in love with Ann Druyan?"

"Oh my *god*, why do you always focus on the part that spoils everything?" I groaned.

"The truth of something doesn't spoil it, kiddo. It's the truth. I'm not saying they weren't in love, I'm just saying—"

"No, but come on. I know you think I'm an über-romantic or whatever, but admit it. You, like, fundamentally *refuse* to believe that something might be romantic."

He swung around and looked at me, eyes narrowed. "No. Things aren't romantic or not romantic. It's not a definitional category. It's individual. And I think it's more accurate to say that a lie is what spoils something. I hate lies."

This I knew. Even the tiny little white lies that most people would consider a part of basic manners weren't safe from Will's scorn.

He started to say something more but stopped when a handsome man in his late-twenties jogged up to us, cheeks flushed and the muscles of his chest defined by sweat.

"Will," the man said, inclining his head.

Will dropped my arm without looking at me, but the man's eyes tracked the movement.

"Hey, Tariq. How's it going?"

Tariq's smile was flirtatious. Filthy. There wasn't a doubt in my mind it was a smile that broadcast *We have had sex*.

"It's going great." His eyes tracked up and down Will's body appreciatively. "You never called," he said flirtatiously.

Will didn't say anything, and Tariq set his jaw and cut his eyes to me.

"I guess your tastes run a little more to the… barely legal? To each his own. You take care."

He gave me a dismissive look, then jogged off, his powerful arms pumping at his sides.

"Asshole. Ignore him," Will muttered before I'd even had time to process what the guy had said.

A part of me had been wondering if an element of Will's reluctance to really give a relationship with me a try was our age difference, but when I took Tariq's comment as an excuse to ask him flat-out, Will dismissed it. "I don't give a shit how old you are," he said.

Still, though we went to dinner and back to his apartment after, he was as distant and unreachable as a star.

LAYNE WAS holding the portafilter in one hand and a bag of beans in the other, and she looked panicked. Probably because she'd finally responded to my laborious sighs and asked if I wanted to talk about it, clearly assuming—and hoping—that I would say no like any polite person. But I was desperate. So I said yes.

"Oh, okay," she said, rallying and putting down the beans.

I gave her a thumbnail sketch of what happened over January break, culminating in me asking Will if we could still be together. I told her about what Tariq said and how Will insisted that he didn't give a shit about my age or about what anyone thought about who he fucked.

How, over the couple of weeks since then, Will had been acting normal, mostly, but how I'd hated it anyway. The idea that Tariq had looked at me and seen not someone that Will cared about, but someone he fucked. The same way I looked at him. Hated that I'd had to encounter him unexpectedly, that he—and god knew how many others going forward—might have to be a part of my life because they'd been a part of Will's.

Or, worse, that I meant just as little to him as they seemed to.

I'd been sulky. At work, in the dorms, at Will's. Sulky the way I'd been sulky as a kid when I asked my parents for a dog over and over despite my dad being allergic. Every birthday, every Christmas, I put it on the list, in between every other thing I wanted, the exclamation points after it cascading down the page and rendering all the other things I wanted afterthoughts to the thing I knew I couldn't have.

But there was nothing to push against, here, no one to hate. Will's transparency made it impossible to rage at him, and since my frustration was that I wanted *more* of him, I was hardly going to alleviate it by avoidance.

When I finally stopped talking, Layne shook her head.

"I'm sorry," she said sincerely. "That fucking sucks."

And then she made like she was going to go back to the beans.

"Wait! What should I do? I mean, do you have any advice? I'd love your opinion."

She sat back down, apparently only comfortable giving advice when directly asked.

Layne blew out a breath. "Well. A couple things. When you asked him if you were together, what did you mean? Because there are a lot of ways to be in someone's life. Being in a monogamous partnership is only one way, and it's not the default mode for everyone. So, if that's the only kind of relationship you're interested and it's not the kind that Will wants, then that's a pretty basic incompatibility. You need to figure out what you want. And why you want it."

"Why I want it?"

"Well, yeah. Like, if monogamy is what you want, do you want it because it's the only thing you've considered, or because it's normal so you assume you want it? Do you want it because monogamy is something you actively desire or value? Do you want it because you're jealous thinking of Will with someone else? Or because you aren't confident about his feelings for you? Et cetera. You know?"

I nodded, wishing I had a pen and paper to write this all down.

"Even if you figure out what you want, though, that doesn't mean that the other person will want the same thing. And it sucks when that happens, but you have to radically recognize the truth before you can hope to either change or accept it."

"What do you mean, radically recognize it?"

"Well, sometimes recognizing the truth requires stripping away what you want to be true, which is hard for a lot of people. You seem, um...."

"What? Just say it."

"You seem like a romantic, I guess. It's not a bad thing, necessarily," she said quickly. "But being a romantic means choosing to see the world as ordered by a central force, or around a central person. And for someone who's romantic, it's maybe harder to acknowledge data that doesn't fit with the fantasy view you have, even if that fantasy's just hope."

I'd never thought of hope as a fantasy before. And, jeez, I couldn't believe Layne, whose only contact with me was at work, had come to the same conclusion about me as Will.

"It's the same in political movement building, really," she went on. This, I knew, was Layne's passion. "There's the romance of the work that you're doing. 'Making the world a better place.'" She made air quotes around the phrase. "But if you're too focused on the romance of it, you forget that someone has to file the paperwork, and get a port-a-potty, and make hundreds of hours of phone calls. And march in the cold and the rain. And you forget that those things aren't supplementary—they're every bit as important and central as making inspiring speeches or seeing that your bill passed in the Senate.

"If you get too caught up in yourself as being a part of that romance you forget that it's not actually about you. That the point isn't for you to feel good about the work you do, but to do the work because it's right and necessary. But that requires you to radically recognize the truth, even when it erases the romance you have or the romance you think you're a part of. I have to recognize that when I go to a Black Lives Matter protest, I'm a white person taking up space, and my very presence there might do harm. That my intentions don't matter, at the most basic material level.

"That's the radical truth: that I might care a whole hell of a lot, but my level of feeling doesn't affect the fact that other people might experience me and the world differently than me, and that no romantic grand narrative I bring into the space, learned from years and years of absorbing the world through headlines and sound bites, is going to change the fact that some people will look at me and feel just the same as if I were some ignorant NYU freshman who jumped on the protest thinking it was a parade I could Instagram."

I gaped at her, never having heard her say more than a casually tossed-off comment here or there about anything but coffee or scheduling or mopping the floors.

She opened her mouth to continue, but paused. I didn't know what my face was doing, but my surprise must've been evident. I gestured that she should continue.

"Practically speaking, thinking about your situation, you need to recognize whatshisname's truth too. Will's. Like, who is he, really? What can you expect? How much is it reasonable to expect someone to change? Is that expectation generous? It means stripping away the romance from them, from your vision of them. It's really hard to see people as they are, sometimes. We have a lot invested in seeing them in relation to ourselves."

"Okay, sorry, but... are you like a licensed therapist or something? A professional philosopher? Sorry, never mind, go on."

Layne shook her head seriously.

"These are all things that I think a lot about," she said. "In my community, among my friends and lovers, nonmonogamy is the norm, so we talk about it a lot, and I have a lot of experience with different ways it can play out. I know some of the questions you need to ask, that's all. And stripping away the narratives—whether of romance or of fear or whatever— that culture has manufactured and perpetuated is at the heart of my political work. You can't have any hope of working toward social justice until you cultivate the ability to see the realities of what you're working with."

JUST AS Charles' philosophy project had taken over his life, he had taken over our room and turned it into something that looked like that dude's office in *A Beautiful Mind*. He restructured his schedule so that each day lasted for thirty-six hours instead of twenty-four. He was still abiding by the whole wake up, eat breakfast, then lunch, then dinner thing. But it was difficult when some of his classes now occurred in the middle of his night. His working with the lights on at all hours of the night—excuse me, of *my* night—hadn't been too bad, but in an attempt to make sure he didn't accidentally sleep at the wrong time, Charles had taken to putting a file cabinet that he found in the basement on top of his bed so that he couldn't go to sleep without wrestling it off his bed—and into the middle of the room, where I inevitably tripped over it or stubbed my toe on it.

But tonight it was our turn to host movie night—which we should just start calling *Felicity* night—so we really needed to move the damn filing cabinet.

Gretchen showed up early with snacks, and I related some of what Layne had told me, because it seemed like stuff Gretchen would be interested in.

I had thought about Layne's words a lot in the last few days. When Will called me a romantic I'd thought of it in contrast to him and his total resistance to romance of all kinds, but to hear it in the context of what Layne said put it in perspective.

She was right that I saw the world as having a kind of meant-to-be. Without many friends or much to see, I started to make a game of seeing things through the lens of the books I read or the movies I watched, imagining drama where there was none, or turning the drama to a different plot.

My parents' dull relationship seemed depressing as a model—certainly nothing to aspire to. Even my sister, who was pretty and popular, mostly seemed dissatisfied with the boys she went out with.

So when Will showed up, looking so much the part of the hero, interesting and cultured and living in New York City… well, I guess I'd cast him as exactly that.

But everything was different now. Now I *knew* him. Knew him, I got the sense, in a way that other people really didn't.

And Layne was right: the truth was that Will didn't want the kind of relationship I was used to seeing. And that wasn't bad, it was just true for him.

"Layne's basically a philosopher," I told Gretchen, Charles' head popping up at the word "philosopher," tuning in for the first time in hours, then immediately turning away again when he realized we were just talking about our actual lives.

"Yeah, she's pretty great," Gretchen said.

Since Gretchen had been hanging out at Mug Shots doing work, she and Layne had spent some time together, I knew, and there was something in Gretchen's voice that sounded strangely….

"Uh, Gretch," I said carefully. "Are you like… *into* my boss?"

She shot me a way-to-make-it-all-about-you look. But then she bit her thumbnail and nodded.

"Kinda. I've seen her a few times. We hit it off, so."

"Whoa. I didn't know you were…." I was going to say I didn't know she was into girls, which was true, but mostly it was that I'd never thought of Gretchen as being into anyone. She never talked about having crushes on anyone or finding people attractive. She never talked about sex or mentioned people she'd dated in the past. I'd kind of assumed she just wasn't particularly interested.

Gretchen shrugged. "I don't know. I just like her." And that was Gretchen, as straightforward about her feelings as she was about everything else.

I smiled at her and she smiled back, seeming to shed any uncertainty. "We'll see how things go. She thinks I'm too young, I think."

"God, what's *up* with that?" I said, thinking back to Tariq's comment in the park.

"I get where she's coming from, though, I guess," Gretchen said, calm logic firmly back in place. "It's not a personal indictment. But we are at different places in our lives. We've had different experiences. We know ourselves differently."

"Ugh, stop being so annoyingly mature and logical. This is feelings stuff! Feelings stuff isn't logical."

"'Annoyingly mature and logical'—can I quote you on that to Layne?"

"I'm sure she already knows. She's annoyingly logical too. Clearly you're meant for each other."

It was a divisive episode, with Milton and Gretchen taking Noel's side and Thomas and me in the Felicity camp. Charles, as usual, was only partly paying attention to the content of the show. Today he was stuck on the conviction that they hadn't shot a scene where it was set because the traffic was going in the wrong direction for that street.

"But don't you admire how she tells him how she really feels? See—" I turned to Gretchen. "—the radical truth, like Layne says."

"I… don't think that's what she means by that," Gretchen said.

"Well, okay, but this is still about telling the truth."

"Mmm, I think there's a big difference between forcing yourself to look at things honestly and blabbing out your personal truth because it makes you feel good," Gretchen said.

"I don't know," Thomas said. "I think it's brave to just put it all out there like that. I could never do that; I'd be too scared of rejection."

"But Felicity doesn't tell the truth because she's brave," said Gretchen. "She tells the truth as a compulsion. She tells the truth because she doesn't want to have to handle her emotions on her own. She makes people complicit in them."

"Well, I think she doesn't know what she wants sometimes too," Milton chimed in, "so she tells the truth hoping that someone will make the decision for her. Take it out of her hands."

"I don't know," I said. "Maybe she just wants genuine connections with people. And she doesn't think you can have that if you don't tell the truth, even when it's hard or it makes someone uncomfortable. And she does know what she wants, it's just different from day to day. Like, she pays attention to how her feelings change. They're still real, even if they're not consistent."

"I like Meghan," asserted Charles from across the room, perched on the filing cabinet to see the schedule he'd tacked high on the wall.

He was taking a one-credit sports medicine class this semester to fulfill some arcane distribution requirement and was developing systems to integrate movement into his daily schedule, which included putting things around the room in configurations that required him to climb over furniture or jump on top of it to access them.

He'd relocated his underwear to the top of my closet and his socks to under his bed so the two things he'd usually reach for at the same time were as geographically distant as you could get in our room—notably smaller than the dorms in *Felicity*—and begun plugging his laptop into the farthest outlet from his desk with a system of extension cords that I was certain would one day kill either me or his computer.

"No surprise there," Milton muttered, looking around. "Your senses of décor are about on par."

I LET myself into Will's apartment with the keys I still had from January, sniffing myself to try and determine just *how* much like milk I smelled. I'd come right from work, figuring Will was just going to pull my clothes off pretty soon after I got there anyway, the way he had the last few times I'd seen him. I had stopped briefly to get a piece of tiramisu, though. Hopefully even if I reeked of coffee shop, the tiramisu would make up for it. It was Will's favorite, and I knew work stuff had been stressing him out the last few weeks.

He'd been staying late and bringing more work home than usual. He still hadn't decided what to do about Gus' offer to go into business for themselves, and he was having a problem with a client whose agent wanted him to produce a cover that would change the face of publishing even though the book she was representing was the third in a pedestrian series.

When I opened the door, I heard a noise from the direction of the bedroom. A low groan. Unmistakably Will. For a moment I held myself suspended in a bubble of fantasy that I was about to walk in on the super hot scene of Will jerking off. He'd be startled to see me at first, but then I'd sit on the edge of the bed and touch him as he pleasured himself. Run my hands over his thighs and between his legs. Suck on his nipples and dip my tongue in his belly button to feel how it changed the way his hand moved on his cock.

Then the bubble burst.

Another groan. This one decidedly not Will.

I should've left. I should have taken the tiramisu and backed out the door like I'd never been here at all.

But I didn't leave. I closed the door behind me carefully and, holding the tiramisu in front of me like a ward, crept toward the bedroom, all the time I'd spent here bent to the purpose of getting there without making a sound so I could see for myself something that Will had insisted upon a hundred times: that he fucked other people.

I pushed the bedroom door open thinking that I knew how I was going to feel because I already felt that way. Gutted. Shredded. Devoured.

But though he had told me a dozen times over the months I'd been here, Will's words were no inoculation. It was so much worse than I'd thought it would be.

Because I'd only thought about how it would feel to see Will with someone else. I hadn't thought about how it would be to see another man with Will. Touching him. Kissing him. Doing all the things to him that I did. Making me totally redundant in Will's life.

The door swung open on a scene so vivid it took me a moment to process the details. Will, on the bed, groaning as a man kissed him, bit his neck, pulled his hair back, hips grinding together, Will in just his underwear, the other man still half dressed. It was both intimate and impersonal, intense physical closeness with purely functional touch.

I must've made some horrible, broken sound because Will craned his head around the guy's shoulder and looked at me. For a moment, I saw something in his eyes that I could read: panic, maybe, or regret. Then his face went blank and shuttered. He struggled underneath the man for a moment before the guy realized he was trying to sit up.

Distantly I heard a wet crunch, and I searched the bed for a detail I'd missed, slowly becoming aware that it was the sound of the tiramisu I'd been holding hitting the ground, its plastic clamshell cracking as it splattered on the floor.

Will shouldered the man to the side and scrambled off the bed, pulling on the same sweatpants that I'd pulled down the other morning when I'd dropped between his knees on the couch and sucked him until he was clutching my hair and cursing at me to let him come, his hands soft afterward, brushing over my cheeks and jaw and settling on my neck as we gazed at each other.

Now when he came over to me, I couldn't stand to look at him, couldn't stand the idea that he'd touch me. I wheeled around and made for the front door. He caught up to me before I opened it and I heard the man swear from the bedroom. I hoped he'd cut his foot open on the tiramisu box.

"Leo, wait," Will said as the man came out of the room, wiping his foot on the rug. He was handsome. Fortyish, with light brown hair and a beard threaded with gray, trim and muscular, and everything I wasn't. He leaned in the doorway, still shirtless, as if they were going to pick up where they'd left off.

"The kid's cute. He can join us if you want," he said, eyes dragging over me. He smiled at me, and I felt a brief flicker of flattery before it was replaced with disgust.

"Can you fuck off now, please," Will told him, never looking away from me.

The man grumbled and went to the bedroom, coming out a minute later fully dressed as Will and I stared at each other. I was cataloging the places I'd seen the man touch him like I was dusting him for fingerprints, each touch standing out, a black spot on his pale skin.

The man crossed between us, patting Will possessively on the ass as he opened the door.

"I left my number on the bed. In case you want to finish what we started." Will didn't even look at him.

"Leo," Will started, his voice unbearably gentle.

I couldn't help it. I burst into tears. It was the final mortification.

"I told you," Will said softly, voice strained. "I told you that I wasn't what you wanted. That you shouldn't expect anything from me."

I shook my head furiously. I knew what he'd said, of course I knew. But so many things he'd done said something so different.

"You like me!" I found myself shouting. "I know you do!"

"I do, Leo. I like you so much. Of *course* I do."

I knew that I sounded foolish. Childish. That Will had been clear on this point. And yet I couldn't help myself. All I could process were the starkest reactions. The most basic hurts.

"Then why? Why would you do this?"

"It has nothing to do with you. I—other people—it's just sex, it doesn't matter."

"If it doesn't matter then stop!" I demanded. I was a hundred yards out of line, I knew, and my voice sounded frenzied.

Will looked down and shook his head.

"That's not…. Leo, I don't want to stop."

"But how? How can you want them if you care about me at all? I would never do that to you. Maybe you're just scared to admit that we could actually work!"

Will frowned and took a deep breath. "I'm trying not to lose my temper because I know you're upset. I never promised you anything. In fact, I stood right here and told you that if we went down this road, it was with the knowledge that if things didn't go the way you wanted then you were choosing it with your eyes open. And you agreed. You agreed that it was okay and that we'd still be friends. You've always known who I was. The fact that you didn't want to admit it to yourself doesn't make me the bad guy. It doesn't mean that I've betrayed you or broken a promise. Just because you wanted something to be true doesn't make it true. You don't get to decide how things go and make them be that way."

"No, *you* always decide! Everything's always on your terms. You decide exactly how close I can get. What I can ask you about and how much I can know you. When I can stay and when I have to go. I'm *always* waiting for you, hoping that you'll—"

"I *get* to decide those things! Everyone gets to set their own terms. That's how being a goddamned adult works. It's my fucking apartment, so of *course* I get to decide when you can stay and when you have to go. And, Jesus, you already know me better than any—"

He broke off, glaring at me.

"And then you just let yourself in here like it's a damned clubhouse or something, and you see something you don't want to see and you call me a fucking whore, like it's not my right to act exactly as I want to in my own house!"

He spun away, grabbing paper towel and squatting down to clean up the tiramisu splattered in the bedroom doorway.

My heart pounded in my throat and my ears rang. I wanted to punch him, kick him, rip at his hair—somehow mar the beauty that mocked me. Make him hurt the way I was hurting right now.

"I think you're doing it on purpose!" I choked out.

"Yeah, Leo, sure," he said tiredly. "I orchestrated bringing some guy back here at exactly the moment you were going to burst in completely unexpected just to prove a point to you that I've been making from the beginning."

"No." I shook my head, eyes squeezed shut. "I think you hurt so much sometimes—hate the world so much—that you think I'll never understand so you're trying to hurt me *so* much that I turn into someone who *can* understand."

Will rocked on his heels, dropping to the floor as if the force of my words had propelled him backward.

"Jesus Christ, no," he said, horrorstruck.

I bit my lip, tears streaming down my face.

"I'm done," I said. "I can't do this anymore. It hurts too much." My voice was ragged, choked. I felt blasted out. Hollow.

Will was still on the floor looking up at me, blond hair mussed, bite marks starting to come out as bruises on his neck, one hand raised as if he could touch me though I was steps away.

"But you knew," he insisted again, clinging to the sentiment the way he clutched the dirty paper towel in his hand. "You knew from the start."

His eyes were bright and his voice quavered slightly.

I bit my lip and nodded, suddenly so exhausted that for once I had nothing to say to him.

"Yeah, okay. I guess I did."

The last thing I saw as the door swung shut was a footprint in tiramisu marring the rug the way the man's bites marred Will's skin.

Chapter 11

THE NEXT month passed in a haze of sleep, forcing myself to eat, going through the motions of attending class, mindlessly making coffee, and, yeah, fine, a lot of crying.

The night I'd walked in on Will with that man, I'd called Daniel sobbing while walking aimlessly. Daniel had gotten freaked out that he couldn't understand me and then, when I'd calmed down enough to explain what had happened, been so furious at Will that he'd threatened to come down and beat the shit out of him, and Rex had taken the phone away.

When I'd hung up with them, Rex having extracted a promise from Daniel that he would not take the early BoltBus to New York and defend my honor, I collapsed in bed, pulled up the covers, and slept for twenty hours. When I woke up, I had the bizarre synchronicity of having inadvertently set myself on Charles' schedule. We went to the dining hall together, and he monologued about how the schedules of modernity enslave us, bending our minds and habits to the patterns enforced by business hours, greeting card designations, and department store sales.

"Fuck time," I'd said. "You think it's moving you forward, moving you closer to something, but it's really just happening without you."

"Yeah, exactly," Charles had said, like I'd finally seen reason.

Milton had found me in the same stairwell where we'd first met at orientation.

"Oh, hon," he'd said when I told him. That's all. He didn't say he told me so, or that he hated Will—though he said both later on, the former to my annoyance and the latter to my vague and petty satisfaction. He'd just held me while I cried and then taken over my life for the next week, making sure that I ate and slept and went to class.

He dragged me bodily from the dorms one night to go to a movie with him and Gretchen that I didn't pay attention to and didn't remember after. I sat between them in the darkness, my friends, and I imagined I was still in the planetarium with Will, and I cried. And then when I got back to my room I YouTubed the planetarium scene from *Rebel Without a Cause* that Will had mentioned, and I thought how James Dean actually looked a little bit like Will—the sharp angle of the jaw and the eyes that shifted from bravado to uncertainty a little too easily.

Two weeks after the night I'd walked in on Will, he called me to ask how I was. I'd left him a drunken message the night before that I only remembered cringingly when I saw his name appear on my phone. I answered but didn't say anything at first. Will talked like things were normal between us. He told me about a client at work (screaming fit when he told her she couldn't have an entirely black cover no matter how edgy her book might be) and about the new Vietnamese place he'd tried in the neighborhood (great bún but bland spring rolls). He told me that he'd been rewatching *Firefly* and wondered if I'd seen it (of course I had; what kind of tasteless moron did he take me for).

And, finally, when he petered out and lapsed into silence, I took a deep breath, sat up straight, and told Will what I'd realized.

My friends had weighed in. Milton was loudest, as usual. *Will is bad for you. He's a drug and you're an addict, and you can't be trusted to make logical, healthy decisions around him, so you should stay the fuck away. But, barring that, just don't make yourself vulnerable to him. Be as remote and untouchable as he is.*

Gretchen was practical and generous: *If he's taking up space in your head, then he's a part of your life, and you owe it to yourself to figure out how you feel about him.* It blended a bit with something that Tonya said in yoga when we were in challenging poses: *Find the place where you're doing work you don't need to do. Soften your jaw, your eyes, your hands. They aren't helping you lunge so you don't need to expend energy on them.*

The truth was that Will was a constantly tensed muscle, using energy even when I wasn't actively engaging with him.

I took a deep breath and told Will, "I guess I kind of thought if I just waited long enough you'd realize that you wanted to be with me." My voice sounded small and pathetic, but I forced myself to go on. "I know you didn't promise me that. I know. We really do want different things, I guess. And I'm just making myself pathetic now, so I need to stop."

Will started to say something, but I didn't let him. I needed to get it out now or I never would.

"The thing is, I can't see you. You take up too much… everything. I don't know how to, I guess, feel things halfway. If you're always there in the back of my mind—if I'm always so invested in you…. See, I *want* to give you what you want. You know? I want you to be happy because I—I care about you so much. But I can't really because giving you what makes you happy makes me so… so fucking miserable." I took a deep breath, trying not to cry and failing.

"So I get that you won't change, but I don't think I can either. I can't stop wanting what I want—so. So I need to stop. I need to like get a fucking *life*, I guess. Of my own. Yeah. I need to get a life."

Silence, but I knew he was still there.

Finally, his voice as small as I'd ever heard it, Will said, "Okay. I understand. Take care of yourself, babe."

He ended the call.

And I broke all over again.

I THREW myself into Project: Get a Life with as much enthusiasm as Charles undertook his Project: 36-Hour Days, and a level of manic desperation that I acknowledged and accepted.

Milton was enthusiastic and got everyone else on board too. He dragged me to campus plays, choir concerts, dance performances, narrating the reviews of each that he'd compose for the Arts column in the school paper that he'd begun writing for.

Thomas took me to Life Drawing with him, at which I produced one ludicrously malformed sketch after another. Thomas being Thomas tried to encourage me, telling me my style was Picassoesque. But a mention of Picasso just made me think of the day Will and I went to MoMA, and I found myself wondering what he'd seen in that painting *Christina's World* that was different enough from what I'd seen that it'd made him kiss me in public.

I wondered what he'd thought the gray thing was between the house and the barn. And, as I sat on the uncomfortable metal stool in the art room while people sketched around me, I had an internal collapse at the realization that I might never know.

Gretchen made sure I went with her to yoga three times a week, pulling me out of my room and throwing sweats at me if I didn't show up in the hallway to meet her at the appropriate time. Of all of it, that was the one activity that felt like it was helping. For those sixty-five minutes, I took myself out of my own hands and placed myself in Tonya's. I followed her instructions with a slavish accuracy, desperate to believe that just showing up in good faith was enough. Desperate to believe what she always said: that *we* were each enough, as we were, and that we could sink into our enoughness and trust it to buoy us.

And if occasionally something she said in class struck my heart or my gut with the precision destruction of a smart bomb—like the day she said, "It's in the moment that you give up that you realize you could have kept going. It's also the moment it's too late."—then no one said anything about the tears that streaked my skin along with sweat.

Gretchen didn't talk much about her personal life, but she and Layne were still seeing each other, and from the brightness of their smiles when Gretchen would show up to Mug Shots, things were going pretty well. I never told Layne how spectacularly I had twisted her advice, but I figured Gretchen had probably given her the basics because, though she never brought it up, I would sometimes catch her looking at me with a kind of sympathy that said she'd been there.

But for all that my friends saved me, week after week, I still wanted something that was just mine. I saw my mistake now. That casting Will in that role—as the thing that was just for me—was paradoxical and had set me off on the wrong foot. No, I wanted something that was mine the way theater was Milton's and art was Thomas', and… you know, toppling the heteropatriarchy was Layne's.

Physics was the thing I'd found that I was constantly interested by, so I talked with my professor, and she let me start working in the physics lab. Just helping out for now, but with the promise that if it was a good fit I could potentially be involved in research projects the next semester. I talked to one of the seniors who told me they sometimes let sophomores assist over the summer in exchange for room and board if they declared a physics major before the end of the semester, so since I was technically a sophomore, credits-wise, that's what I did.

Filing the paperwork made me feel better. As if now that I was affiliated with a department I belonged here somehow. It was the first time I'd felt like I belonged anywhere, really. Even doing scut in the lab was fascinating. Milton always said he didn't get how I—someone he thought of as being creative—could want to be a science major since they were methodical and unimaginative.

But he was so wrong.

Yes, physics was methodical, but the method was part of what the very discipline questioned. It was incredibly creative. These scientists began, sometimes, from whims and questions as personal as any that inspired a play or a song, running those personal investments through the most rigorous of testing, a gorgeous blend of feeling and thought that produced experiments and theories from the atomic level to the heights of philosophical query.

I was particularly fascinated with the crux of astronomy and physics, and when I started looking at the course catalog for fall semester I heard Will's voice in my head for just a moment, saying, "Astrophysics? You're going to study actual rocket science?" I thought he'd be excited by it, actually. One of the things I liked so much about Will was how his creativity and art *were* crossed with a nearly scientific rigor, his designs as much based in layout and market research as they were in aesthetics.

And then I banished his voice from my head like I'd done a thousand times since that night and redoubled my attention to work.

ON VALENTINE'S Day in elementary school, we were instructed to give cards to everyone in the class. We'd made construction paper mailboxes with our names on them and placed them at the front of the room, colorful and open, ready to receive well wishes from anyone who might drop them in.

In fourth grade, I'd followed this instruction as I had every year before, carefully tearing apart the perforated *Batman* cards I'd gotten at Target and writing a classmate's name on the back of each one. I'd saved the best one—Batman standing next to the Bat signal looking out over a moon-drenched Gotham City—for Noah Waldmann, who I thought was the coolest kid in my class. I'd been crushed when I looked through my mailbox to see that I hadn't gotten a card from him. Then embarrassed when I realized that though the girls had given cards to everyone, unlike last year, all the other boys in my class had only given cards to the girls. Something had shifted. An unspoken line had been drawn through our social relations that had been clear to everyone except me.

Aside from that mild humiliation, Valentine's Day was just something that happened, with the bonus that there was usually candy lying around. Sure, maybe I got the slightest bit jealous when I thought about people out with their dates, having attention lavished on them. But I knew it was just a stupid Hallmark holiday, really.

This year, though, it was like every force in the universe seemed hell-bent on shoving Valentine's Day down my throat, up my nose, and into my eyeballs. Every storefront was plastered in a nauseous combination of pinks and purples. Posters for everything from kissing booths to film series appeared on campus bulletin boards, all of them printed on garish pink, purple, and red paper. The dining hall acquired table toppers that left an unsanitary dusting of glitter on the tabletops, which I'd find on my clothes and in my hair throughout the day. Even the radio was in cahoots, rendering songs I usually liked noxious through syrupy dedications of love.

So, though I had never paid the day much mind before, now, at exactly the moment I wanted to avoid thinking about romance, it was everywhere and there was no escape.

When I walked into Mug Shots the week of V-Day, Layne was in the middle of showing George, our newest employee, how best to place red hots just so on the whipped cream that topped our Hearts Afire Hot Chocolate, and where the vat of precrushed candy canes to sprinkle on the Mint Mocha Love Latte was. There was a dish of candy hearts, two of which were to go on every saucer holding a for-here drink. There was white-chocolate syrup dyed red for the Brownie Blitz Cappuccino, pink marshmallows for the Gimme S'Mores, and cinnamon sticks to stir the (Very) Dirty Chai Lattes. It was as if Valentine's Day had exploded. And it was caffeinated.

That whole week I got home from work with red chocolate blood spatter dotting my clothes, shards of candy cane under my nails, and dust and dirt clinging to the marshmallow residue that coated my hands. By the time Gretchen came in to meet me near the end of my shift on Valentine's Day evening, all I wanted was to be stricken with a particular strain of colorblindness that would disable me from seeing any color that contained red pigment. Also if I never heard the phrase, "I guess I'll treat myself since no one else is going to treat me," presaging the order of a drink again it would be too soon.

Somehow, though, all it took was watching calm, practical, totally together Gretchen lean over the counter to kiss Layne, who mumbled and flushed and pushed her glasses up her nose in delight, to make me as melty inside as one of the molten chocolate lava cakes that we served with cinnamon-cardamon marshmallows to dip in their liquid center.

After I'd made us both the most decadent drinks I could concoct (a combination of the Brownie Blitz Cappuccino and the Gimme S'Mores) and poured them into enormous to-go cups, Gretchen and I walked back toward the dorms, cutting through Washington Square Park because we always cut through Washington Square Park.

We sat on the edge of the fountain half sipping our drinks and half scooping them into our mouths with straws because I'd added so many brownie chunks and marshmallows that they were practically solid.

"So, you and Layne are really a thing, huh?"

"Yeah." Gretchen stabbed at brownie chunks with her straw, eating them like shish kebab. "She's pretty great."

"She, um, came around, then? On the you-being-too-young issue?"

"Well, it wasn't that she thought I was too young per se, just that we were in different places in our lives. Which is true. Kind of. But, yeah, she pulled her head out of her ass and realized that if we liked each other, then it was stupid to manufacture reasons not to be together. I mean, it's not necessarily going to be serious or anything. But we… yeah, it's good."

"I'm happy for you." And I really, really was.

Gretchen's grin—complete with brownie in her teeth and whipped cream in the corner of her mouth—lit up her whole face.

BACK AT the dorms, things were underway for what I was informed would be the most epic sugar eating competition I'd ever seen. I informed the boy who told me this (a strange, jockish guy with red hair and eyebrows so blond they were nearly invisible against his ruddy skin) that since I'd never seen any eating competition, it wouldn't take much to impress me.

As it happened, though, even if I'd seen a lot of them, I still would've been amazed and borderline horrified as I watched my peers consume volumes of sugar so great that I actually feared for their lives. Gretchen, uninterested, went to change because she was going over to Layne's later, but I found Milton, Thomas, and Charles standing with some other people from my hall, all of them watching the action with varying levels of bemusement and anticipation. There were six categories of competition, each bizarre and ridiculous in its own way.

"So, like, I heard this premed guy actually went into a sugar coma a couple of years ago," Thomas was saying.

"Should've known better, shouldn't he?" Milton joked. "Never gonna get into medical school with an oversight like that on his record."

"A sugar coma is not a real thing," Charles offered in clarification, and Thomas and Milton rolled their eyes affectionately behind his back.

The first contest was to see who could eat the most marshmallow Peeps in one minute. There were three competitors, all of whom were friends and apparently proposed the contest because they legitimately liked Peeps and wanted to redeem the much-maligned food. The second was a couples' challenge involving truffles and clothing removal that got so messy and scandalous that one of the couples quit. The third challenge almost turned my stomach. It involved the consumption of marshmallow fluff using sex toys as vehicles of delivery in a truly upsetting manner.

The fourth was a team challenge that required each team to construct a house of cards out of chocolate bars and then eat it piece by piece without knocking the rest of the house over, removing the bars of chocolate, Jenga-style. Piles of wrappers mounded underfoot as the constructions grew, nearly tripping one girl and sending her sliding toward the table where she would've knocked over all the houses of chocolate if someone hadn't grabbed her by the back of her shirt at the last minute.

The fifth challenge was really a drinking game, since that hot chocolate was definitely spiked with something stronger than Mug Shots' Hearts Afire cayenne-cinnamon syrup. I knew because they invited audience participation, and Milton pressed a full cup (clearly smuggled out of the dining hall) into my hand with a wink.

But the final challenge was my favorite. Teams of two unrolled yards and yards of licorice around the room in a madcap game of follow-the-leader where they took turns placing and consuming the licorice while crawling under tables, jumping up to tap doorframes, and, once, following the path of licorice that snaked up the leg of a blushing boy's jeans.

By the time Charles and I were heading back to our room, I felt almost cheery, and distinctly more amenable to Valentine's Day. It didn't hurt that I was tipsy from the hot chocolate and that since the event coordinators had given out all the unused candy to the audience at the end of the competition, I was now in possession of enough snacks for a week.

Charles gazed thoughtfully at the pile of candy I put on the dresser, hands in his pockets and a pink lollipop making a comical bulge in his jaw.

"Do you think the Student Activities Board is in cahoots with the parent candy company that owns the brands they just consumed downstairs?" he asked seriously.

THE MORNING of my twentieth birthday, I woke up before my alarm for once, shutting it off before the train whistle could blast through my tender early morning brain. I called my mom to thank her for the birthday card she'd sent with a gift card to Olive Garden in it. "I figured you could take your friends out to a nice dinner after all that dining hall food," she said. It was such a fundamental misunderstanding of my life on every level, but so very like my mom that I was overwhelmed by a sudden and unexpected rush of affection for her.

She told me about how Eric had gotten very into some reality TV show about people who want to be professional wrestlers or something and had started going to the YMCA religiously to lift weights every day.

I talked a little about my classes and satisfied her yen for celebrity sightings by telling her about the time I'd seen Michael Fassbender in Washington Square Park and how I'd served coffee to Michelle Rodriguez. She'd never heard of either one of them but after I'd listed some of their IMDb credits she was excited. She was disappointed to hear that I hadn't been to a Broadway show yet, though, so I told her about going to *Into the Woods*, only I fudged the truth a little and said it was off Broadway. My mom was the only living human who couldn't tell when I was lying, so she just oohed and ahhed over the mention of a play she'd heard of.

That night I really did take everyone to dinner at the Olive Garden in Times Square. It was mobbed with tourists, and we'd had to fight our way through the crowds. *One does not simply walk into Times Square.* But I relished the chaos for once. The bright lights and neon signs and huge television screens and billboards snapping my attention from scene to scene like a music video. People bumping into me and each other in confusion or enthusiasm or distraction, like meteorites colliding in space, or atoms crashing together, trying to get closer or to transform each other.

Inside, Milton, Charles, Thomas, Gretchen, and I laughed at how kitschy the Olive Garden seemed in contrast to the rest of the city. But I think they took as much unexpected comfort in its familiarity as I did, the menu and the décor and the smells the same here in this glittering wonderland as they were anywhere else.

We shared plates of fettuccine Alfredo and gooey cheese ravioli, towering piles of spaghetti with meatballs, and salad and breadsticks that really did seem endless. We drank raspberry lemonades spiked with vodka, courtesy of Milton, and finished with tiramisu, cheesecake, and something called a chocolate caramel lasagna, the flavors somehow so simple and pure that we kept eating them long after we were full, straining, maybe, to keep things recognizable.

I even ate some of the tiramisu, despite its newly negative associations, determined not to let my feelings for Will cast a pall over the evening.

After, we sat in the square for a while, people watching. Milton waltzed with one of the Disney characters, and Gretchen and I planked on the steps outside the TKTS booth. Thomas drew comics with me as the birthday hero, a cape with my initials on it floating out behind me as I rescued a tourist stranded on a billboard. Charles didn't say much—for him the meal had been breakfast—but he took pictures of all the clocks with his phone, muttering notes for his project under his breath until we headed for home.

When we got back to the dorms, giggly and full, Milton invited us all to his room for some birthday *Felicity*, and I went to change into pajamas first.

Outside my door was a gift with my name on it, wrapped in fancy matte paper, gold and purple lines interlocking in a sprawling geometric design. The perfect balance of beauty and organization. My heart stuttered as I scooped it up and went inside, closing the door after me as if the box might contain something clandestine or volatile.

Leo, the card read. *You don't need to change. Not for anyone. But maybe the slightest upgrade won't be unwelcome? Happy birthday.*

Will hadn't signed it. He didn't have to.

Inside the box was a pair of brand-new Vans, identical to the old ones that Will had so scorned.

Chapter 12

March

SOMEHOW THIS semester I had midterms in every class, and they were eating me alive. I barely had time to shower and shove one of the bagels I'd begun stockpiling from the dining hall in the morning into my face while working. I'd even had to switch from Everything to Plain because I couldn't stop typing long enough to eat and the seeds kept getting stuck in my keyboard.

I was a total mess.

Charles' mania had increased as the semester continued. He'd begun setting his alarm to wake him up every ninety minutes because he'd read that based on neurological research, the human brain entered a heightened state of something or other ninety minutes into the sleep cycle and he wanted to harness these periods and maximize his brain activity.

He'd also begun playing these gamma and theta brain wave inducing audio clips on his computer to maximize his creative problem-solving abilities. Of course his alarm startled me awake, too, if I actually managed to get any sleep, and I'd sit straight up in bed in a panic, convinced that I'd missed a deadline or a test. It was no use trying to get him to alter his methods, as I'd learned last semester. Once he'd decided something was advantageous, he stuck to it a hundred percent.

All I could do was console myself with promises of all the fun and relaxation I'd get to have during spring break. I had already planned out the things I'd do in the city that I'd been too busy—or too content spending time at Will's—to do since moving here. I wanted to go to the Cloisters and the Tenement Museum. I wanted to walk across the Brooklyn Bridge. Hell, I even wanted to go see the Statue of Liberty. Maybe one day I'd get one of those hop-on-hop-off bus passes and pretend I was a tourist all day. After all, I still kind of was. For all that I'd been in the city for months, I'd hardly seen any of it.

I also had a full Netflix queue that I'd been adding to all semester. So, it was a plan: I would get my fill of the city during the day, then smuggle dining hall food back to my room and curl up in bed with my computer for as long as I wanted, not speaking to anyone if I didn't want to.

I'd been doubly busy the last few weeks, having volunteered to help a grad student in the lab with some research for her dissertation. Part of her data had gotten mysteriously erased from the university server before she could back it up, and she had to try to re-create six months of work in a week in order to meet a deadline for her dissertation committee and submit her paperwork to the university in time.

It was horrible, and she was, understandably, a wreck, but she also treated me like I was her personal assistant. When I told Gretchen and Milton about it after running into the dining hall, totally frazzled, to explain why I couldn't make it to movie night and why I was currently shoving food into my face faster than I could chew so that I could get back to the lab they'd advised me to blow her off, saying that it was nice of me to help but it was her problem. I couldn't do it, though. Her panic was too real, and I could all too easily see something like that happening to me.

As I ran back to the lab, cramming the piece of pizza I'd carried out with me into my mouth and trying not to indulge in elaborate stories where I tripped at exactly the wrong moment and a ball of chewed bread and cheese lodged in my throat, marking me down in the annals of history as having the most humiliating death on campus, my terrible manners reminded me of Will and I imagined what he would say if he could see me now.

He'd told me more than once that if I always ran to the rescue when someone asked I'd end up living my life in the margins of other people's. That I was a pushover and it wasn't my responsibility to kill myself in order to solve other people's problems. This last had seemed like rather a dramatic pronouncement when he'd initially made it, but now, trying to walk-run and not choke on my pizza, I thought maybe he had a point.

One night I was working late in the lab when a guy I hadn't seen before ambled in looking harassed and confused. There weren't many people around so he came to me right away.

"Hey, have you seen a rock polisher around here anywhere?"

"Um, I don't think so? But to be honest I have no clue what a rock polisher is, so I probably wouldn't've known if I'd seen it."

His name was Russell and he had a halo of frizzy blondish-reddish hair, a brownish-reddish beard, a full mouth, bright white teeth, and the sparkliest blue eyes I'd ever seen. He looked like a handsome, geeky lion and dressed like he was about to go on a hike. He was a geology and physics double major, and he usually worked in the geology lab next door, which was why I hadn't seen him before.

We started talking sometimes when there weren't many people in the lab. He was sweet and smart and funny, and I could tell he liked me. One night, he took me to the commissary for coffee and pie in the middle of the night and used his coffee cup and the pencil that was perpetually stuck behind his ear to explain how, at the molecular level, the pencil could pass through the pottery of the diner mug.

He asked me about my family and told me about his. His older sister was getting married the next month, and he hated the guy she was marrying. I told him about how Janie had a vlog on YouTube where she did makeup and hair tutorials and how funny she was in them. About how my mom had once read a series of mystery novels that featured a duo of New York City detectives, so every time I talked to her on the phone she asked me if I'd been to places that were featured in that series, only it was always things like "the Dunkin' Donuts near the train station" or "the bus stop close to the Brooklyn Bridge" so I was never really sure what she meant.

In the geology lab a few nights later, Russell showed me some of the rock samples he was working with. The lights were dim everywhere else, leaving us in an island of light, like we were the only two people who existed.

"This is a quartz matrix that has rubellite tourmaline crystal in it, and then is scattered with some gold mica. There are even some fluorite crystals." He was totally focused on the rocks. "This one is the prettiest, I think."

He held it out to me, but it didn't honestly look like much. I opened my mouth to say something complimentary anyway.

"Hang on, you can't see the flecks in it unless it's wet," he said absently. He raised the rock to his lips and licked the flat edge of it slowly, tongue coming out as his blue eyes sparkled at me. It was undeniably one of the hottest things I'd ever seen.

When he held the rock out, I could see a riot of colors, from a dark brownish-violet all the way to a pinky-red, some crystals of peach and blue packed together and the whole back of it studded with the gold bits of mica.

Russell's eyes darted down to my mouth and he stepped closer.

I flushed with arousal and the sharp promise of possibility. I liked Russell. He was handsome and nice and smart and maybe… maybe….

"I, um, I just want to say that I…."

I can't kiss you because I'm in love with someone else. I'm a total wreck over someone else, and it isn't fair. But Russell was leaving in a few months, off to grad school in Chicago. He wasn't proposing marriage.

I closed the distance between us, and I kissed him.

His lips were as soft as they looked, and he cupped my elbows firmly as we kissed. He tasted earthy, mineral. It wasn't awkward or strange. It was nice. Comfortable. Sweet. So I kept kissing him. And at some point, I dropped Russell's favorite rock, spit-damp, onto the floor.

I'D SOMEHOW managed to forget about midterms when I'd given Layne my schedule at Mug Shots, and I knew it would make her life harder if I asked her to switch my shifts, so I just kept showing up to work totally harried, downing four shots of espresso and vibrating through my shifts. Then, knowing I'd have to work when I got back to my room, I'd down a few more at the end of my shift, leaving totally strung out with my heart pounding, work intently for a few hours, and then crash hard and have nutso dreams, which made being interrupted by Charles' alarm even more unsettling.

I was tearing my hair out trying to write a paper for my English class—the last thing I had due for midterms, thank god—when my phone rang and Will's name popped up. I'd texted him the day after my birthday to thank him for the shoes, but I had made it clear that we weren't going to start hanging out again.

I still thought about him all the time. Of course I did. But I was neck-deep in "Goblin Market" with no idea what I was writing, and I didn't have the mental energy to hide how hurt I still was while I tried to have a friendly conversation, so I let it go to voice mail. He didn't leave a message and I pushed down my disappointment and got back to writing.

The next morning, having stayed up all night to finish the paper, printing it in dark blue ink because my printer had run out of black and I didn't have time to run to the library and print it there, I sprinted to my class and slammed the paper onto the desk with the rest of them, collapsing in my seat and immediately falling asleep on my *Anthology of Major British Poets* along with about half the class.

At the end of class I dragged myself back to the dorms and fell asleep in point five seconds, relief at not having anything else due (and the fact that Charles and his alarm weren't in the room) letting me sleep for twelve hours straight.

After a shower I felt almost human again, and I met Milton and Gretchen for dinner in the dining hall, where we were mostly silent until we'd eaten. Once we'd satisfied our basic human need for food, though, the giddiness of being off for a week set in and we talked excitedly, lingering over multiple soft serves and more Coke than anyone should really consume, relishing the leisure to drink it.

When I got back to my room, where I'd left my phone charging, I saw that Will had called again, and again left no message.

THE NEXT day while I was at work, I finally had time to think about the calls I'd missed from Will, and I started to worry. If he'd just wanted to ask me a question or say congrats about midterms or something, he would have texted. Besides, he'd totally respected my need for some space. What if something was really wrong? Or what if—just maybe—he'd changed his mind and was ready to take a chance on us? I almost slapped myself at that thought.

But, just like that, any distance that I'd introduced between Will and me was obliterated—a paper folded in half, its opposite edges becoming proximate as instantly and naturally as if they'd always been that way.

The fact was that we had unfinished business. I hadn't been able to let myself think about it during midterms because I was trying too hard just to stay sane, but after I'd slept with Russell, things had… changed. It wasn't about Russell, really, though he was a super nice guy. It was that I thought maybe I finally understood Will a little better. Could finally see past the hurt.

And, given how much he'd hurt me, it was ridiculous how much I still loved him. But none of the hurt touched that core of love.

My feelings for Will were a tender and naked heart beating tentatively in an iron cage, each expansion a risk, each deflation both relief and disappointment.

WILL CALLED for the third time that evening just as I was about to get on the subway to meet Milton at a late movie after work, and this time I scrambled to answer the call. Even after I ran back outside so I could hear him, I just traded no signal for traffic noise and the shouts of a basketball game on the court next to the subway steps.

In the din, Will's voice, apologizing for calling me when I'd told him I didn't want us to talk, sounded small and very, very far away. My heart was pounding in my ears, I was so ridiculously happy to hear from him. I walked around the corner so I could hear him better, phone clamped tight to my ear like I could pull him closer to me through it.

"No, no, it's okay. It's fine. What's up?"

"It's um… I just…."

Something was very wrong. Will didn't stammer. Will didn't trail off. Will didn't sound this uncertain of himself.

"Will, what's wrong?"

"I—you know what, never mind. I'm sorry—I shouldn't've…."

I lost the rest of his sentence to the earsplitting drone of some douchebag revving his motorcycle.

"Sorry, sorry, wait. Let me just—okay." I cut over to a quiet street and perched on a bench outside the door of a nice restaurant. "Okay, sorry, it's quiet now. So, tell me what's going on."

He sighed. "I'm in Holiday," he said. "I got here last night. Claire's in the hospital, and I came out to stay with Nathan and Sarah."

"Oh god. Is she okay?"

"She will be. She went off on one of her jags, disappeared. Nathan and Sarah couldn't find her. I called everyone I could think of, but no one had seen her. They found her yesterday on the merry-go-round in that park at the corner of Willow and Grove. You know?"

"Yeah. Shit. What happened?"

"She'd driven up onto the grass and crashed the car into the swing set. Then she'd fallen asleep on the merry-go-round without a coat. Or maybe passed out. They couldn't tell. I guess she'd been awake for like five days straight, and no one had been able to find her for the last two. She hadn't eaten. She was so dehydrated they had to give her IV fluids. That's why she's still in the hospital, I think. I don't know. They weren't totally clear about it."

Will's voice had gone thin and strained, and I thought I heard him swear under his breath.

"Are you with Nathan and Sarah now?"

"Yeah. They're pretty freaked this time. I guess… she was awake for a couple days before she took off and she got rid of a bunch of her things. She took all the pictures off the walls and destroyed them. Gave away a bunch of clothes. Nathan and Sarah had to lock their doors to keep her from giving away all their stuff. She donated everything that was in the living room and the garage. Their bikes and rollerblades and stuff. Nathan's baseball stuff and Sarah's soccer gear."

I made a sound just so he knew I was listening.

"I guess Claire was saying some pretty weird things to them while she was trying to get their stuff. Like, stuff that just made no sense. I don't know what exactly. They don't like to tattle on her. But… she really scared them this time. I don't know. They know she's not herself when she has these episodes. Or, that's what we've always told them."

"Do you not believe that?"

"Well. It's all part of her, you know? I think it's kind of bullshit the way people treat mental health stuff like it's separate from the person who has it. As if there's some ideal 'normal' person trapped inside that needs to be chiseled out of the marble block, revealed when the 'abnormal' stuff is stripped away. I know it's valid, to a degree—like, people compare it to intoxication and the way people act in ways they wouldn't ordinarily act when sober. But I'm not sure. For me… I love Claire. I accept that it's part of her. I accept that—" His voice was choked. "That I fucking hate her a lot of the time. But they're kids. They shouldn't have to hate her yet."

I could hear that he was doing something while he talked to me, and I imagined him unloading the dishwasher or cleaning up a spill in his sister's house, all alone in the dark while her scared kids were asleep upstairs.

"Do you know how long she'll be in the hospital?"

Will made a sound in the negative, and I could hear his long, shuddery breath. When he spoke again, I could barely hear him, even cupping my hand around the phone and pressing my other ear against my shoulder to block out the noise of the city around me.

"And even when she gets out, there might be problems. I don't know. Anyway, sorry. Oh shit, I forgot—how were midterms?"

"They were fine. Listen, Will, how are *you*?"

If we were in person, Will might blow this question off with an eye roll or go into the kitchen to do something else. Hell, even over the phone, he might ignore me; he might even tell me to fuck off. But he wouldn't lie.

He was quiet for long enough that I thought he was going to ignore me after all.

"Leo. I—fuck, Leo, what if it's always like this? Those poor kids. They're growing up just as fucked as we did."

Will didn't call me by my name that often when we weren't in bed. It was usually "kid" or "kiddo" or, occasionally, if I'd done something idiotic, "fuckhead." It sounded different now. Everything about the way he was talking sounded so un-Will. He sounded scared, vulnerable. Like maybe he needed my help.

"I just, um… I don't suppose you're coming back to Holiday for spring break, huh?"

"Will—"

"Ugh, Jesus, never mind. Don't listen to me. Fuck, I don't know what's wrong with me. It's this *fucking* house. All messed up and creepy with no stuff in it. There are like weird stains and shadows and shit and it's making me go all *Penny Dreadful*, like there are monsters lurking in my periphery or something. Anyway, it'll be fine. Everything's… yeah, it's totally fine."

It was almost painful to listen to him try to reassure himself. Everything in me screamed that I needed to take Will in my arms and reassure him. Or just be there.

"Listen," I began, but before I could say more, there was a voice in the background.

"That's Sarah. She's been having nightmares. Look, I gotta go."

"Okay. Well…." But I couldn't think of a single thing I could say to make any of it the slightest bit better. "Call me whenever," I finished lamely.

Will's whispered "Okay" was lost in the scream of a truck reversing on the next block.

THE SECOND Milton saw me, he knew something was wrong, and I ended up blurting out the whole story and then apologizing profusely when I realized I'd made us miss the movie.

"He's just always so together," I told Milton. "Or, like, I don't know, he says how things will be and the world either falls into line or he rejects it. But he can't really do that with this stuff. Oh shit, maybe I shouldn't have told you about Claire. Fuck. It's… whatever, scary to see him freaked out. I just hate that I'm not there. Maybe I could help. I mean, Milton, he *called* me. He called *me*."

"But you're not together…," Milton said uncertainly.

"No, but…."

But Will's distress was so immediate, his vulnerability so genuine. And the fact that he'd called *me* when he was upset, that even though we weren't sleeping together—fucking, as Will would no doubt put it—I was the one he'd reached out to when things had gone wrong. That *had* to mean something, right?

"Well, it *is* spring break, so I guess you could swing it. Or does he not want you to?" Milton's lip curled as he no doubt remembered all the times Will had turned down my invitations to come with us when we went out.

"Actually… I think he wanted to ask me. Kinda. I dunno, it'd be like the least Will thing of all time to ask for me to be there with him, but I swear he just about did." Milton hit me with this look that said I was being pathetic and also potentially delusional so I swatted at him.

"It doesn't matter anyway, there's no way I can afford a plane ticket and even a train ticket's hella expensive. I looked it up when I got off the phone with him. Besides, it takes forever to get to Detroit and then I'd still have to get up north…."

"You really want to go?"

"It doesn't matter," I said, sighing, sliding into full-on sulk mode. "I hate money. And time. And distance."

Milton laughed. "Well, you're a physics major. I guess you'll have to do something about that. Uh, the time part, anyway. Or the distance part? Whatever. I have no clue what physicists do."

I rolled my eyes at him.

"Listen, I'll give you the money for a plane ticket if you want to go. It's not a big deal."

"No way," I said automatically. "I mean, thanks but—"

"Okay, real talk: I have a credit card. I have a shit-ton of frequent-flier miles. My parents have money. It's seriously *not* an issue. So there's no need to be all weird about it like you always are."

"What? I'm not always weird about it!"

"You so are. You're all pearl-clutchy oh-no-I-couldn't-possibly whenever anyone even pays for a damn coffee. It's kind of charming in, like, a wholesome small-town boy kind of way, but you take it to extremes sometimes."

"Huh." I'd never known I did this at all. "Do I?"

"Dude, you took *us* out to dinner for *your* birthday. You do know it's supposed to be the other way around."

"Um."

"Point is, if this is the part in the movie when you fly across the country and rescue the hero or embrace on the tarmac while your mutual scarves blow in the wind or whatever, then do it. I got you. Mention me on your wedding day. No prob."

I started to dismiss him again, but Milton clapped a hand over my mouth.

"Leo. Pause. Disregard cultural narratives about propriety and capital. Consider. Do you want to go to Michigan? Nod for yes, shake for no."

I rolled my eyes. He left his hand over my mouth. I considered.

I knew Milton was joking about me acting like I was in a rom-com, running to confess my love before the plane could take off or whatever. But it hit a little too close to Will's comments about me being a romantic for comfort. My only relationship experience was from books, movies, and TV, so of *course* I had absorbed that stuff. And maybe when I'd first gotten here my hopes for me and Will had kind of skewed in that direction.

But I was pretty sure that recently I'd—what? Grown out of it? Or, just seen that there were a lot of ways for relationships to go. A lot of ways that romance could look different.

So, did I want to go to Michigan because I had a fantasy of swooping in like the hero to the rescue? I… didn't think so? It didn't feel like it was about playing a role or imagining that I knew what Will needed because I was applying some formula. It felt like I knew what Will needed because I *knew* Will.

I knew how strong he was, how capable of dealing with anything that was thrown his way. I knew how much he cared about his sister and how much he worried about her. I knew he loved Nathan and Sarah and was scared for them. And so I *knew* that when Will called me after he'd promised to give me space, sounding lost and sad and scared, and asked me—even if he said it like a joke—if I was coming to Michigan… that he needed me.

Not someone. Not a blank, generic rescuer. But… me. Just me.

I didn't know where that left us, exactly. I didn't know what it would be like to see him again. But if he needed me, I had to be there for him.

I nodded at Milton.

"Okay," he said. "Will you let me get you a ticket?"

I hesitated, and he rolled his eyes at me. I squeezed my eyes shut and nodded again.

"Glory hallelujah," Milton said, exasperated.

I pushed his hand away from my mouth.

"Thank you," I said, and I hugged him hard as the movie marquis flashed above us.

Chapter 13

WHEN I'D called Will from the airport to tell him I was coming, his reaction had made every moment I'd spent angsting about accepting Milton's frequent miles worth it. "You're really coming?" he'd said, and though he'd tried to play it off like it wasn't necessary, he'd sounded... lighter. When I'd hung up to board the plane, he'd simply said, "thanks." But that one word had been freighted with such relief that I'd grinned all the way to my seat.

I'd clung to it on the flight, too, focusing on how I was going to help Will rather than letting myself sink into the murk of what *precisely* our relationship was, or where *exactly* we stood. I told myself that this didn't necessarily mean something; it just *was*. I congratulated myself because the sentiment seemed to fit with Tonya's yoga teachings about being present and appreciating a thing for itself, and then immediately side-eyed myself because *congratulating* yourself for being present wasn't very... present. Thank god it was a short flight.

The cab dropped me off in a part of Holiday I'd never been to before, which was saying something, given its size. Will's sister's place was a small prefab with a big yard and a mailbox in the shape of a dalmatian.

I could hear the yelling even before I got out of the taxi. One of the voices was definitely Will's and I assumed the other was Claire's. Well, at least she was out of the hospital, anyway.

"Good luck, kid," the driver said to me. "My parents are a nightmare too."

I didn't want to walk into the middle of whatever battle they were having, but it was freezing out, so I knocked tentatively. There was no way they could hear me over the yelling, so I tried the door and, finding it unlocked, went inside. The house was spotless, and there was very little in it. Furniture and basic necessities but no décor, no art, no clutter. Nothing that suggested three people lived here.

I followed the noise and found Will in the kitchen, facing off with one of the most beautiful women I'd ever seen, and now that I'd been in New York for a while, I'd seen a lot. She looked like Will—the clean line of jaw and nose, the high cheekbones and clear brow. But where his beauty could be remote and otherworldly, hers was warm and inviting. She was curvy where he was spare. Her eyes were a darker, brighter blue, and her mouth naturally turned up at the corners. She had dimples and her two front teeth overlapped charmingly, making her seem approachable. Her blonde hair was a shade darker than Will's—a warm honey color that made me want to run my fingers through its smooth thickness.

If Will was the untouchable statue, Claire was vibrant and alive. The girl you were desperate to talk to, desperate to have smile at you. Even like this, her face twisted in anger and her eyes blazing, I immediately wanted her to like me.

When she saw me, she jerked backward, hand to her chest.

"Jesus Christ, you almost gave me a fucking heart attack," she said. Even her voice was attractive, smooth and low.

"Sorry! Sorry, I knocked, but…."

When Will turned to me, I was shocked. He looked utterly exhausted. But when I smiled at him and he smiled back, there was some kind of, like, *light* in his face. And I'd put it there.

"Hey," he said. "Claire, Leo. Leo, Claire."

"Ah," Claire said, her eyes narrowing in a gaze startlingly like Will's. "Skater boy."

"Sis," Will said in a tone I could tell was used between them often.

Wait. She knew who I was. That meant Will had totally talked about me to her! I wondered what he had said, and I was about to ask Claire but bit my tongue since it was clearly not the time.

Before I had a chance to say anything anyway, they were at it again. I didn't have the background to make sense of all the details, but the gist of it seemed to be that Will was insisting that Claire see a certain doctor and Claire was refusing. There were a lot of references to past incidents, and a lot more yelling. Finally, Will grabbed Claire's shoulders and stuck his face in hers.

"You're going, and that's final!"

"You're not fucking in charge of me!"

"I *am*, actually. Or did you forget about that too, the way you forgot about your *kids* for *days*?"

That stopped Claire dead. Her glare turned her face cold, and she and Will could've been twins.

"I really hate you sometimes," she said, low and serious.

I saw her words land, and I saw Will absorb them, taking the hit with a barely perceptible jump in the muscle of his jaw and a clench of his fists where they hung at his sides.

"Yeah," he said, voice thick. "I know. But you're still going."

Claire slumped a bit, her spine softening.

Will clearly saw an opening and took it, grabbing his bag from the kitchen table and shrugging into his coat.

"Okay, we're taking off, then." He hesitated, chin down. "You sure you don't want us to stay here?"

"I told you I was, Willy," Claire said in a singsong voice that sounded almost eerie after her anger of a moment before, like cheery carnival music played over an ominous scene in a scary movie.

"Do not fucking call me that, *Claire Bear*," Will retorted.

She just raised her eyebrows at him mockingly.

"That's Clairevoyant to you, Willful," she said, pinching his cheek. "I'm too tired to even mock you properly right now. Your children are a fucking handful."

Claire's smile faded away. "What, you'd rather they were not seen and not heard the way we were?"

Will stared at his feet. I'd never seen him look like that before. Defeated and ashamed. "No, of course not. Okay, well. I'll see you tomorrow."

Claire walked us to the door and pulled Will down into a fierce hug, twining her arms around his neck and jumping up to wrap her legs around his waist.

"Thanks, little bro. You're always the white hat," she said.

"Your sister's…." I started to say as we got into Will's rental car, but I couldn't think how to finish the sentence so I just let it drop. Will didn't seem much in the mood to make conversation anyway.

He'd been staying at Claire's with Nathan and Sarah while she was in the hospital, but now that she was home we were going to stay at Rex's cabin. Since Rex owned it outright, he and Daniel had decided to keep it in the hopes of visiting there sometimes. That's what Rex said, anyway. I got the sense that Daniel was comforted by the idea of keeping all their options open in case the Temple job didn't work out. Or (unspoken always, but clearly a fear of his) in case they didn't work out.

We drove in silence, the back of Will's right hand resting lazily on his knee so he was steering with two fingers, his left elbow propped against the window. It was how he always drove, all the power and speed of a ton of metal and mechanics controlled by the touch of two fingertips.

We'd driven this route often when he'd been in Holiday, since I couldn't skateboard on the dirt roads strewn with pine needles that led to Rex's cabin. The first time I'd ridden in the car with him, I was so nervous I couldn't stop babbling about nothing, bouncing my knees and running curious fingers along parts of the car's interior just to be doing something, interacting with an extension of Will in some way.

Now, I sat still and silent as the familiar streets of Holiday branched out around us. How could someplace I'd lived my whole life feel so foreign?

How could Will feel the most like home of anything in Holiday?

The cabin revealed itself through the pine boughs, and I felt a rush of longing that Daniel and Rex would be inside when we opened the door, Marilyn trotting up to greet us. Daniel would be sitting at the table, papers strewn out around him, a pained expression on his face and one of Rex's mom's old records playing in the background.

Rex would be in the kitchen making dinner and, every now and then, coming up behind Daniel and squeezing his shoulders or running a hand through his hair. Daniel would lean back, press his head to Rex's stomach, maybe tilt his head back for a kiss. When we'd walk in, Daniel would gesture helplessly at his stack of papers as if one of us could explain why his students tortured him by not writing better essays, and Rex would raise his eyebrows at us slightly, and usher us into the kitchen so we could keep him company as he cooked. He'd cast a glance back at Daniel before following us, affection clear on his face even if Daniel never looked up.

But it was dark and silent, just the bones of the life that was once lived there.

Will made a fire and turned on the heat as I brought our bags inside. Daniel and Rex hadn't gotten around to getting more furniture for the cabin yet, so all that was left in the living room was the plaid couch and a card table, and in the bedroom an uninflated air mattress and linens.

The first time I'd come here it struck me as everything that a home should be. The best combination of comfortable and functional, warm and spare.

Now, though, where I really wanted to be was at Will's apartment Surrounded by Will's drafting table and seemingly unending supply of pencils, his five hundred white T-shirts and coffee-table books that weren' on the coffee table. His sweaters and soft sheets and shampoo that all smelled like him. And the small spaces that I thought of as mine: the desk next to Will's drafting table where I studied, the corner of the counter where I always leaned while he made coffee, the left side of the bed.

Fire made, Will and I stood awkwardly, facing each other.

"Can we…?" He held his arms out tentatively, and I went into them like they were gravity.

If I'd thought his touch would have lost its power I was wrong. I softened against him, and he melted into me too. We kept each other upright, two masses exerting equal force on one another. He held me so close, squeezed me so tight, held on for so long, that when we separated it felt like being torn apart.

I could feel his warmth even when he wasn't touching me, like a slight electrical charge in the places between us.

We ordered pizza and slumped onto the couch, neither of us speaking.

"I can't believe you came here," Will finally muttered. "You didn't have to do that."

He fidgeted for a minute, then grabbed a piece of pizza and shoved it in his mouth like he was trying to keep himself from saying anything else. I studied him, conducting an experiment. Trying to figure out if, after everything, Will still had as much power over me as ever.

Everything about him still called out to me, the distance between us practically painful. But there was a fragility about the moment that stopped me from touching him. What would he do if I closed it? What would it do to me?

I shook my head and took a page out of Will's playbook, snagging a slice of pizza for myself.

"Um, how's your sister?"

Will sighed heavily, clearly exhausted.

"No permanent damage from the dehydration or… anything else she got up to when she was away. She won't say where she was or what she was doing." He shrugged. "So, it could be worse." But he didn't look comforted. He attacked another piece of pizza. Out of habit, he folded it the way he did New York–style pizza, but that just made the fat slice's cheese bunch up and sauce drip out the sides, splatting onto Will's knee.

"Is something else going on? You seem super freaked. I mean, not that you shouldn't be anyway, just, like, extra freaked."

He scraped the sauce off his jeans and kept eating, mindlessly. When he swallowed the last mouthful of crust, he cleared his throat.

"Usually the kids are good about acting normal at school. But I guess, uh, Sarah's teacher noticed that she was real jumpy and called the house to talk to Claire, but she wasn't there so she called CPS."

"Oh shit."

"Yeah. And it's not the first time, which means—well, I'm not sure what will happen, exactly. I'm not sure what… *should* happen."

"Do you want… I mean, do you think it would be better if CPS took Nathan and Sarah away?"

"No. Well, some things might be better, but… you know this town. No way would they get to stay here; Holiday doesn't have the resources or the population. And they'd end up getting split up if they got placed with anyone. It's not ideal. But obviously neither is life with Claire."

"What's going to happen this time, do you think?"

He shook his head again. "I don't know. Most likely? Probably nothing."

"What? How can that be? They must take stuff like this seriously, right? I mean, no offense to your sister who seems super nice and all, but she went off and left her kids alone for days."

"Well, I'm *not* sure. But…. Okay, people look at Claire and they see a beautiful, vibrant woman with cute kids. She's charming and outgoing and everyone she meets likes her. I've seen her talk her way out of every mess she's ever gotten herself into, so the good money's on this time not being any different."

I couldn't believe that they'd really do nothing. Surely an official body like CPS wouldn't care about something as superficial as Claire's charm. As if he could sense my doubt, Will started listing examples.

"When she was twenty, Claire got caught breaking into the middle school and stealing a television set from the media room. The security guard never even called the police because she started talking to him and flirting with him. After an hour, he had her phone number and she walked out. The first time she got busted with drugs she talked her way into a fancy lawyer who took her case pro bono, and she just had to pay a fine. When Nathan was little she'd drive to Kalkaska and have him go into ice-cream places where he'd ask the people who worked there for an ice cream, Claire would look all sad and apologetic and tell him they couldn't afford it, and the people would give Nathan an ice cream for free. And one for Claire.

"And both times someone from CPS looked into things they thought everything seemed fine. The kids obviously weren't dirty or hungry. If they asked about her erratic behavior, Claire would talk sincerely about how hard it was sometimes as a young single mom to maintain a sense of freedom. When it was a female caseworker, she talked about how society tells mothers that they aren't allowed to want things for themselves anymore. When it was a male caseworker she told stories about how aggressively going after her career goals was a good example to set for her kids. Would that shit play in New York? No way. But here? Mostly these are people who are just as desperate for excitement as everyone else. They see Claire, beautiful and having fun, and they see what they wish their lives were like."

Will reached out and took my hand, sliding his fingers through mine without a thought.

"And it's not just CPS," he went on with a sigh. "It's doctors and shrinks and… fuck. I know I probably sound paranoid as hell. But there are pictures that people have in their minds of what mental health issues look like. And Claire is not that picture. I know it's not all about how she looks. It's also about how she presents herself. How fucking sad this town is that they'd rather buy into the romance of Claire's manic shit being her having adventures or living her dreams or whatever than see it for what it is. No one believes she has a problem."

He took a deep breath like he was trying to reset.

"I don't know. Maybe it'll be different this time because she was actually in the hospital. She has to go back for some follow-up blood tests."

"Would they believe you if you told them about how stuff is?"

"And be responsible for Sarah and Nathan maybe getting taken away from their home and their friends and the mom who really fucking loves them and does right by them a hell of a lot more of the time than our parents ever did right by us, and who also, oh yeah, happens to be my sister? Yeah. No."

Will went to run a hand through his hair and noticed for the first time that he was holding mine. I could see the surprise on his face, but I just gave him a small smile to tell him it was okay.

"And there's no one else who could step in when Claire's not… fit? A neighbor or a friend. Or maybe like one of Sarah or Nathan's friends' parents?"

"I… I'm not sure. I wouldn't really trust one of them not to say anything."

"Would you have to explain it all? Maybe Nathan and Sarah could just… know in the backs of their minds or something, like, 'When mom is like this we go to so-and-so's house and sleep over'?"

He hesitated, chewing on his lip. "Maybe. I don't like asking other people to get involved in my shit."

"I know. But sometimes people honestly do want to help."

Will looked at me like this was a thought that had never occurred to him before.

"Like you," he murmured, and it was half question and half acknowledgment of something that I think we'd both known for a while.

I nodded. It was enough for now.

Chapter 14

March

THE NEXT day, while Will took Claire back to the hospital for her tests and got her car fixed, I went to go see my mom and Janie. My dad and Eric were both at work, but they'd be home for dinner.

The first thing my mom said was how much taller I was. I hadn't realized it until Will and I were lying side by side on the air mattress the night before, taking elaborate care not to touch, but I was taller than him now by an inch or two. I'd been so busy lately with school and everything that I hadn't even noticed. And I guess my slouchy jeans had kind of covered it up anyway. Besides, with a roommate as tall as Charles, I always felt short anyway. She also told me how handsome I looked, but she was my mom, so. I stared at myself in the bathroom mirror after she said it. But, no. Same old Leo, my nose too small for my mouth and my straight eyebrows making me look like I took everything too seriously.

We talked about what New York was like, but no matter how much I explained it, she couldn't seem to understand that I didn't live *in* Times Square since it was the foremost picture of New York she had. She was delighted to hear about my new friends, and she seemed really impressed when I told her I had declared a physics major. "I took that class in school," she remarked, meaning at the high school in Holiday. "I think I liked it."

Janie thought it was incredibly cool that I worked at a real-life New York City coffee shop, and when I told her about Layne she said, "Oh, lesbians are so *in* right now," and I didn't even have the energy to ask what that meant.

It was nice to sit there in my mom's kitchen, eating the Girl Scout cookies that she arranged on a plate and sipping the chemically lemon tea she always drank while we talked. Nice, but not like home. It was a sensation I'd had before. Of being a guest in the place that felt like home to the rest of my family.

As the sun started to set, I caught my mom beginning to cast glances at the oven clock. It was time for her to start cooking dinner. I cleared away the cookie crumbs and cold tea bags, and my mom stood up quickly, pulling ingredients out of the refrigerator before I'd even rinsed the dishes. A quick glance at the counter told me just what she'd be cooking. A casserole with chicken, peas, and cream of mushroom soup, and Pillsbury dinner rolls.

I had intended to stay for dinner, but when Eric and my dad got home a few minutes later, it was clear that things wouldn't be different than they'd ever been. They were happy to see me, sure. I asked them each how work was and Eric told me about his new gym routine. I told my dad what classes I was taking when he asked, unsure if he was just trying to make conversation or if my mom really hadn't told him.

But after a few minutes, as always, we ran out of things to say to each other. They weren't interested in hearing about my life. Not really. And they didn't have anything more to tell me about theirs.

Once, early in the year, I told Milton that I kind of wished I'd had some big confrontation with my dad about being gay and how he never really acknowledged it, because that at least would be easier than always tiptoeing around it. Milton had said, "Maybe. But you don't have to tiptoe just because he does. That's his problem." At the time I'd dismissed it because my dad's reluctance to bring it up always felt like such a condemnation. Like I would be embarrassing myself as well as him if I mentioned anything.

Now, though, it just didn't seem worth it. It was so clear, suddenly: my dad had nothing to offer me, really. I guessed that I had always kind of been waiting for him to come around. To decide that really knowing me was worth feeling a little uncomfortable for.

But I was done waiting for people. So I kissed my mom, hugged Janie and Eric, shook my dad's hand, and left with the casserole still in the oven and the rolls unbaked, walking slowly through town and into the woods toward Rex's, knowing that Will would be home soon.

THE FRONT door closed, and Will slumped backward against it, closing his eyes, like everything outside the cabin was a nightmare he was trying to escape.

"What happened?"

Without thinking, I went to him and slid my hands around his back underneath his coat, as if touching him were natural again. It felt natural. Touching him felt like finally letting out a breath I'd taken months ago.

Will transferred his weight from the door to me and let out a rumbling groan of exhaustion and exasperation. I could feel how tense he was in the muscles of his back and shoulders.

"Do you want to take a shower or something?"

Will shook his head and dragged himself upright, dropping his expensive coat in a heap on the floor and coming to the couch.

"Here, one sec."

I brought in the spaghetti I'd made from the kitchen and handed Will a bowl, settling with my own on the other end of the couch, facing him.

He gave me a thankful smile and toed off his shoes before falling on the pasta like a wolf.

"You seriously have the worst table manners I've ever seen. What's up with that?"

He wiped his mouth on the back of his hand and smirked at me, a shadow of his usual attitude in place.

"My parents would leave food for us in the fridge when they went out to dinner, so I'd end up just eating something standing at the counter a lot. Or peanut butter out of the jar with a spoon fast enough that I wouldn't taste it." He made a face.

"That why you don't like it now?" I asked, remembering he'd mentioned that months before. He gave a one-shoulder shrug, then nodded.

"Now, I guess I usually eat while I'm running out the door to work, or at my desk between meetings, or in front of the TV. I don't know, it's probably terrible for me. Whatever."

He went back to his food, finishing the bowl and slouching against the cushions before I was even half-done.

"So how's Claire?"

He closed his eyes and blew out a breath.

"She's fine, physically. I fought with her for, seriously, hours about going back on her medication. Who the hell knows if she'll comply. Nathan came home from school while we were fighting about it, though, so we had to explain. Kind of. Like we told him about how taking medicine made his mom calmer and more... the same every day. And—fuck—he looked right at her and said, 'I always like you, but I guess it would be better if you were more the same every day,' and patted her on the shoulder."

"Oh man."

"So she's crying, and I'm practically crying because, shit, the kid's ten years old. He shouldn't be worrying about this crap. And Nathan goes, 'But don't worry if there are days you can't because Uncle Will takes really good care of us on those days, even if it is over the phone.' And I started actually crying because, damn. And Claire just about gets hysterical because apparently she didn't fucking know that they call me constantly and then I call all over creation looking for her. So, I don't know. Maybe it'll be different this time. Maybe she'll be able to see how much she's hurting everyone by not taking the damn medicine. Like, in the past I've made her. But when I'm not here… I can't really."

"You've *made* her?"

Will's eyes flashed, immediately defensive. "I didn't force it down her throat or anything, Jesus. She always thanked me later, when it had kicked in—said it was the right thing to do. She just couldn't always come to that decision when she wasn't on the medication. That's how it's always been with her. I knew what was the right thing, and I made sure she did it. Even if she hated me for it in the moment—and believe me, there have been plenty of times she's fucking *hated* me. But sometimes, you know, there are things that are more important than someone liking you."

"That's a lot of responsibility to have for someone. A lot of pressure."

"It's just… I know how much she hates it. Admitting there's something… wrong with her." He closed his eyes. "Or, I shouldn't put it that way. Not wrong. Just, we spent so many years swearing we'd never be like them. We'd never be that fucking selfish. For me it was easier, maybe. I knew I'd never have kids. Never be in that situation. Claire. Christ. When she got pregnant with Nathan, she was eighteen. I thought, well, no problem, she'll just get rid of it. But she fucking didn't."

Will's voice wavered, and he bit his thumbnail.

"I don't know why she didn't. And obviously I love Nathan now. But, fuck, Leo. How could she—"

He bit his lip and shook his head and I moved across the couch to him. When he spoke again, it was so quiet I could hardly hear him.

"How could she mess them up this bad when she knows how much it fucking hurts?"

He took a deep breath, and when he spoke again it was like he was forcing himself to tell the other side of the story.

"It's different. I know that. It's completely, totally different. She loves her kids, and our parents didn't love us."

He stood abruptly and cleared our plates, though I wasn't done with mine. The starkness of the sentiment left something stuck in my throat as I followed him into the kitchen, every molecule of my being wanting to make it better. To somehow find the right thing to say or do that could take a stitch in time and act as a balm to the kid who had one day come to the conclusion that he wasn't loved by the people whose job it was to do so.

My own love for him bubbled against my lips, and I gritted my teeth to hold it back. It wasn't the right moment, I knew. Hell, it probably wasn't even the right sentiment.

Being loved by one person didn't cancel out not being loved by another like a math equation.

"Look," he said, his back to me. "Just… just don't say anything, okay?"

It was like he'd plucked the thought right out of my head.

"I just mean… in case you're about to try and convince me that my parents *did* love me, deep down, in some secret chamber of biological necessity or something, just… please don't."

I swallowed hard. "I wasn't going to."

"Good."

He walked back into the living room without looking at me and busied himself with the fire.

"So, um, I think I'm going to do it. Go into business with Gus." It was a clear bid to change the topic, and I was happy to let him.

"Yeah? That's great. What changed your mind?"

"Well. Kinda you, actually. I was thinking about how you said that I cared a lot about my work. It's true, I do. But sometimes I get so hung up on getting ahead in the business, or on one of my bosses approving of what I've done, or on how impressed people get when I tell them where I work and they've heard of it, or they ask what books I've done covers for and they've heard of them. So, really, that's caring more about what other people think than it is actually caring about the work itself. If I do it, then I won't have that recognition. There won't be anyone to approve of the work or disapprove because I'll *be* the boss.

"But I've already achieved all the shit I set out to do when I took that job. So now it's time to do something else. To move forward. Challenge myself. Set new goals. I don't know, seeing college and the city through your eyes—everything new and uncertain—reminded me what it felt like to be that way. To be excited about shit rather than to bend it to someone else's desires."

He looked embarrassed, but it sounded amazing. And the idea that I'd had anything to do with it made me buzz with happiness.

"That's awesome!" I told him, sliding a hand up his arm. "I think you guys are gonna kill it. Besides, it's like you told me about school. Don't believe that the people in charge necessarily know what the hell they're talking about. You know what you're doing. You know when something's good or not. Oh man, I'm so excited for you!"

Will's eyes lit, and he crushed me to him, kissing me hard.

"Sorry," he said, pulling back. "Shit, sorry! Thank you. For being excited for me. I just really missed that."

And fuck, I still wanted him so much.

Wanted to be close to him—intimate. And things had changed. I'd changed. I couldn't fall back into the same situation and expect not to get pulverized all over again. But maybe it didn't have to be the same situation.

"Don't be sorry," I said slowly.

"No. You told me you didn't want this, so."

And wasn't that just about the most absurd thing I'd ever heard. The idea that I didn't want something with Will.

"I've always wanted this. You know that."

"Leo, I—" His voice was choked, and he seemed more worn out than I'd ever seen him.

I thought he couldn't hurt me more than he had the night I'd walked in on him with another man, but, no. This would hurt more. If after calling me and wanting me here with him, he told me that things were the same as they'd ever been.

But then I looked at him, really looked. In the firelight, his eyes were haunted. And I had the sudden horror of something even worse. That he was about to actually give me what I'd wanted for all the wrong reasons. That out of fear and exhaustion and trauma and stress, he was about to tell me what I had been desperate to hear from the moment I met him. And then regret it.

"I slept with someone else." The words exploded between us and I had the momentary satisfaction of watching something like loss break open in Will's expression before he schooled it again. "I was going to tell you."

"Okay," he said. "Um, how was it? Or, not *it* it, I don't mean, but…."

How was it? It was nice. It was hot. Satisfying in the moment. And I had kind of congratulated myself afterward, in an *Oh, well done, you. You had a genuine College Experience* kind of way.

"It was… important," I said. Will clenched his jaw. "Not the guy, exactly. Russell," I added because it seemed wrong to imply that he was nobody. He had been sweet and kind, and he'd definitely wanted to see me again.

"Important because it made me understand something. It made me understand that what you said about having sex with other people not having any bearing on what you felt about me? I... I get it. Like, I can see what you mean now."

That felt strange to say, here, in Rex's cabin where I had fallen in love with the idea of a relationship like Rex and Daniel's.

Will was staring at me intently, but I couldn't quite read his expression.

"It's not for me," I went on. "I just... I don't think I'm the same way, you know?" He nodded. "And, okay, I'm not saying that should be proof for you that I will want to be with you forever or something. Not that I did it so I could have definitive data or anything. But I guess it is good to know that about myself."

"You want to be with me?" Will echoed.

"Yeah, I know you're not into it. We don't have to go through it all again."

Will shook his head. Frustrated? Irritated? I wasn't sure.

"Does that... I mean, does it hurt you, that I slept with someone else?" I asked.

He shook his head. "Not... not exactly." But his hands tightened on my shoulders.

"I kissed him first," I said because it felt important for Will to know that I hadn't just gone along with something. That I'd wanted it. Not the way I wanted him. But that had nothing to do with it.

Will looked at me intently, throat moving as he swallowed. "How did you kiss him? Show me."

I blinked at him, but he just looked at me.

"Um, well."

I moved toward Will and touched my mouth to his. I kissed him as if he were someone I had no physical history with. A kiss that wasn't a promise but an exploration. That carried no past, only a potential future.

When I broke away for air, Will was breathing hard, his eyes intent on mine. "What happened next? Show me."

I took Will by the hand and led him to the bedroom, since unlike the table in the geology lab, there was no furniture here that would take our weight. I unzipped his pants and pulled them off. He started to strip off his shirt, but I stopped him.

"He didn't take his shirt off."

I pushed him down on the air mattress, pulling my own pants off and kneeling between his legs to kiss him. I could smell the unfamiliar shampoo in his hair and the unfamiliar soap on his skin, and a bolt of longing for Will's usual homey smells hit me.

"He kissed my neck," I said, touching the spot where my shoulder met my neck, and Will latched on, kissing me, scraping his teeth over my skin. When he shifted to the other side, I reached into my bag and got lube and a condom, handing them to Will.

Will moved to push the lube away like he often did, but I pressed it on him.

"I don't need that," he said.

"I do."

"Oh. He… okay."

"Okay?"

"Okay."

Will bit his lip and slicked his fingers, never looking away as he reached for me.

"Do you want me to tell you how he—?"

"*No.*" Will pulled me toward him, kissing me hard. He pulled my shirt off, getting lube all over it, then pulled off his own. When he pulled me back toward him, his kiss was desperate, his movements clumsy, his fingers sticky in my hair. I groaned and wrapped my arms around his neck, pressing him back down into the pillow.

Will fumbled with the lube again and then slid slick fingers inside me, his breath catching. I ground against him and held on tight. When I was panting into his mouth and he was hard beneath me, I knelt up.

"The way he—"

"Stop. Please," Will said, squeezing his eyes closed.

"Okay," I said, kissing him softly on the mouth.

Will propped himself up against pillows and rolled on the condom then pulled me into his lap. I braced myself on his shoulders, fingers just touching his neck so I could feel his pulse. I sank down on him slowly, opening to him as he slid inside. I bit my lip, forcing myself to breathe through the strangeness of penetration, waiting for the inevitable shift from invasion to heat.

His hands came to my hips, and his stomach muscles flexed with the effort of keeping still. We looked at each other and moved at the same moment, our mouths meeting desperately as our hands tangled together between us.

I started to move my hips in circles slowly, the feel of him inside me turning to sparks of pleasure as my body adjusted.

"Oh fuck," he said, kissing me again, then putting his feet flat on the floor so I could brace against them. I lifted myself up and slid down, building the rhythm between us, watching the flush spread from Will's face down his throat to feather across his pale chest as his breathing grew ragged. He was watching me intently, his eyes endlessly blue. I rose and fell, then rested my weight down, pressing him deeply inside of me, feeling so full and so light at the same time.

"Touch me?" I said, and Will sat up, grabbing hold of my straining cock and kissing me at the same time, my legs sprawled on either side of his hips, his arms around me, his mouth on mine, and his dick inside me the only things keeping me from falling.

I was sweating, getting tired. I allowed the distant thought that I really needed to add more bridge pose to my yoga practice in case we were going to make this position a regular part of our repertoire, but I let it go when Will swore, frustrated, and dropped back on his forearms, pulsing his hips up, fucking me from below as I moved on him from above.

Heat collected at the base of my spine and each clench of my stomach muscles drew my orgasm closer, my whole body clenching up. As I lost the rhythm hopelessly, Will groaned, grabbed me, and flipped us. His expression was desperate, his focus intense. I landed on my back, and he pulled me toward him by my shoulders, thrusting into me and burying his face in my neck. I spread my legs wide and rolled my hips back, giving him more room, and we rocked together, every movement flooding me with heat.

Will touched my cock and I moaned, pulling him to me and lifting my chin to beg for a kiss. He jerked me off as we kissed, and pleasure seized me, all heat and tension and then a release like a supernova. I exploded between us, dragging Will down on top of me and holding him inside me as the orgasm took me over.

Will was flushed, his teeth gritted and the tendons in his neck standing out with his efforts. I squeezed my legs around him, pulling him closer to me. He circled his hips and let out a whimper, and I kissed him, biting his full lips. He looked like an angel of vengeance, all blond hair and burning blue eyes. He pulled back once more, thrust hard and came, his mouth open on a silent scream, eyes closed, hair dark with sweat.

"Fuck," he muttered, collapsing next to me, chin on my shoulder. He licked a line up my throat, and I shivered, then he kissed salt back to me. We cradled each other's faces as we kissed. Then, exhausted, we just lay there, looking at each other.

I didn't ask and he didn't offer. We just pulled the covers up over us, foreheads nearly touching, sharing each other's breath, and went to sleep.

I WOKE, warm and comfortable, my back pressed to Will's front and his arms around me. My whole body said *Yay!* at being snuggled up with Will and my mind said… well, mushy things about the way Will had opened up to me since I got here.

I couldn't stop thinking about the moment he'd stopped me from playing the game he'd begun. The moment he stopped being able to bear thinking about me with someone else. It made my heart beat fast and my palms sweat. It made the roots of my hair tingle and my teeth itch. It made every surface of my body alive with the effort of holding back my feelings for Will. Of stopping myself from waking him up to ask him what it all meant. Where we stood.

But things weren't about me right now. It was one hundred percent not the moment to pull focus from Will's stuff with his family. So I just brought Will's hand to my lips and kissed it. I got up and took a shower. I sliced bananas into bowls of instant oatmeal because it was the healthiest thing I could think of and that felt like something I could do to show Will how I felt. I made coffee and put it all on the table, and then I sat there waiting for Will to wake up.

When he slouched into the kitchen and flopped down at the table, he stuck his face in his coffee and didn't look at me right away. After the first cup had kicked in, though, he took a bite of oatmeal and made a face, looking up at me like I'd betrayed him.

"There's no brown sugar here," I told him. "But it's good for you."

He pouted and pushed the bowl away, then dropped his head on my shoulder and buried his face in my neck, talking into my sweatshirt.

"What?"

His arms came around my waist and he turned his head slightly.

"I hate stuff that's good for me."

MY FLIGHT left from Detroit at 9:30 a.m., but Will was staying until the next day so he could try to talk to the parent of one of Nathan and Sarah's friends about providing some support if Claire needed it.

Will drove me to the airport in silence, flicking through radio stations and finding nothing he wanted to listen to, then flicking it off again.

We were both exhausted. The easy intimacy of the morning had given way to a day made long by necessities. We'd gone grocery shopping for Claire while she met with a psychologist, then I hung out with Nathan and Sarah while Will took Claire to buy new things for the house.

We hadn't had a moment to talk, but it wasn't as if I'd know what to say anyway. Things felt... different? Will seemed different. But he was also in the middle of a crisis and away from home, so I reminded myself for the umpteenth time that it was definitely not the moment to address it.

"Thank you," Will said as he pulled to a stop at the curb. "For coming here. It never really occurred to me that you would, but... it should have. I—hell, I should've known you that well by now. Anyway, thanks."

And he kissed me, leaning over the cup holders and gearshift. Kissed me like it was a thing we did again. Then he was gone, saying he'd see me back home, leaving me standing at the curb staring after his rental car with my head a total mess and my heart a quivering, hopeful thing.

Chapter 15

March

CHARLES WASN'T back from spring break yet when I got to the dorms. I wasn't used to having the space to myself, but it came in handy because apparently the only thing that I was capable of was pacing. I knew I'd done the right thing by not asking Will a zillion questions about the status of our relationship before I left Michigan. And I wasn't looking for a marriage proposal or anything, but it was disconcerting as hell not to know where we stood.

I forced myself to go down to the dining hall, where I choked down a bowl of cereal and then sat staring at nothing as I used the vanilla soft-serve machine to make Coke float after Coke float. When my knee started bouncing out of control, I realized I had just majorly over-sugared and over-caffeinated myself at nine o'clock at night, and forced myself to go back to my room, pocketing a few cookies for later.

The hum of the fluorescent light drove me to distraction without the incessant tapping of Charles' keyboard and finally I grabbed my phone and sent an SOS, knowing I'd be useless until I made some sense of things.

Can you skype for a sec? I sent to Daniel. *It's about Will so you won't like it but pleaaaase?*

Do I have to kill him again? Daniel wrote back almost immediately. Then, *Yeah, signing on.*

I blew out a deep breath in relief and threw myself onto my bed, flipping open my laptop and opening Skype. Then I waited. Daniel always thought you went online to sign into Skype before he remembered it was an application, so I figured it'd take him a minute.

"Hey," he said before his camera was turned on. "Sorry. I thought I was opening it but I accidentally redownloaded the thingie. Anyway, what's up? What'd Will do now?"

"Click your camera button."

"Huh, oh. Now?"

I nodded as his face appeared on the screen. He was sitting on the floor, leaning back against the couch. His dark hair was mussed, like he'd been running a hand through it, and he squinted at the screen for a moment, then took off his glasses and tossed them on the coffee table, rubbing his eyes.

"Hi." He waved. He always waved on Skype even though he didn't do it in person, and I couldn't help but grin at him despite vibrating with caffeine and feeling like I was about to puke from my guts being tied in knots of uncertainty—although, maybe that was just all the soft-serve.

"You grading?" He only did that particular eye rub after staring at student papers.

"Yes, god help me. Rough drafts. *Why* did I ask to see rough drafts? Seriously, kill me where I stand." He shook his head as if cursing his former self. "Anyway. What's the deal with Dickface?" Then he jerked away from the screen. "Oh shit. I forgot. His sister. Is she okay?"

"Yeah, she's doing better. Will's staying out there another day to help her get some stuff sorted." I wasn't sure how much of Claire's personal info Will would want me to share, especially since he and Daniel weren't exactly buds. "Saw the cabin. I think it misses you guys."

A wistful expression played across Daniel's face. "Yeah. I miss it too. I think…." He looked around. "I think I might take Rex there over the summer. Like, surprise him or whatever."

"Aw, that's so sweet!"

Daniel looked away and got all self-conscious like he did whenever I said anything like that, so I changed the subject quickly.

"So, in Holiday, we… like, I guess, slept together again, but I don't know if that means we're… back on the way we were, or…. It seemed different or something. And I can't talk to Will about it yet because, duh, family crisis and stuff, and also because he'd be about zero percent interested in discussing it, but it's honestly killing me and I won't be able to sleep or work or do really anything until I know more. Just… more. Also, sorry, full disclosure: I've had, like, a *lot* of Coke just now, so. The soda, I mean. And ice cream. Like. A lot."

"Yeah, I thought my picture was shaky, but I guess you're just vibrating."

I filled him in on what had happened between Will and me in Michigan, but I found myself not quite wanting to describe Will's shift in attitude. His vulnerability. The way he seemed to need me. Not just because Will might want to murder me for telling personal details about him to Daniel. But also because I felt protective of this side of Will that only I knew. As if keeping it to myself made me somehow closer to him. It was our secret.

A door slammed on Daniel's side of things and Rex walked behind the couch, arms full of grocery bags. He did a double take at the screen and bent down.

"Hey, Leo."

Daniel smiled as Rex came into the screen and twisted around to him, though the couch was between them. He focused back on me when Rex went to put away the groceries.

"Okay, so, where did you leave things?"

"Well, he drove me to the airport and he thanked me for coming. And he really meant it, I could tell. But I don't know what it means. Like, before the… um, Tiramisu Incident, we were sleeping together but not dating or whatever." I rolled my eyes at the word. "But… Will just seemed different in Holiday. Like he thought of me differently?"

God, that sounded so stupid. But Daniel nodded.

"But Will's made it clear from the beginning that he doesn't want a relationship. Like, *very* clear. Will doesn't really pull punches when it comes to being honest. Or blunt. Or, well, you know. He doesn't actually pull punches, period. So… I guess I don't know why I think things'll be different."

Daniel ran his hand through his hair like he was trying to find a way to say something I wouldn't want to hear.

"Oh, just say it, it's okay," I told him.

"Yeah," he drawled. "You know Will isn't my favorite person, but that's not why I'm saying this. Just, usually if someone tells you they don't want a relationship, then… uh, they don't want one."

"I know." I sighed. "But…." I could see how it sounded. Like Will had told me no and I was looking for excuses not to take him at his word. "Look, the thing is that he… he *acts* like we're in a relationship sometimes. You know? And, in Michigan… fuck, I dunno. You're probably right. Will means what he says; he doesn't, like, play coy or whatever."

The knot in my stomach tightened in a way that had nothing to do with the ice cream.

"I'm sorry, man. I wish shit were different. I mean, *I* don't really get the Will thing, but I get that he's different with you."

My face, in the Skype window, was pathetically miserable, and I made it tiny so I didn't have to look at it.

"He is," I said. "He really is."

Rex appeared onscreen, sliding onto the couch and putting his hands on Daniel's shoulders.

"I couldn't help but overhear," he said, nodding toward the kitchen.

"'S okay. I mean, you probably know Will better than either of us."

Rex's face did this very thoughtful, serious thing and he shook his head tightly.

"I don't think so."

The tiny me onscreen looked like he'd been given a Christmas present. God, Will really hadn't been kidding the times he'd said I was easy to read.

"Can I ask you something?" Rex said.

"God, yes, any thoughts, opinions, questions, and insights are extremely welcome."

"You said that Will means what he says." I nodded. "What does that mean, exactly?"

I opened my mouth, but then forced myself to really think about it. Rex asked these questions sometimes—questions where you thought the answer was obvious but then later realized you had no idea.

"Will's the most honest person I've ever met," I said. "Like, you're really honest, but… you're polite and stuff so sometimes you just don't say things. Like if they'd be rude or offensive or whatever. Will… he's even super blunt about things when it makes people uncomfortable, you know?"

Rex was silent for long enough that I got paranoid the call had dropped, but I could see them moving.

"I know what you mean," he said slowly. "But being blunt isn't the same thing as being honest." His hands tightened on Daniel's shoulders and Daniel leaned back into him. "Just because Will is okay with offending someone or telling someone a hard truth about themselves… that doesn't mean he doesn't get scared. For himself, I mean. It doesn't mean he always volunteers the truth about what he's feeling." He paused again, like he was trying to find the right words. "And sometimes he says things so strong to make it easier for himself."

He shook his head and looked at Daniel.

"I don't know how to say it, exactly."

Daniel bit his lip. "Mmm, like, he asserts things really definitively in order to shut down conversations about topics he doesn't want to think about?"

Rex nodded and said, "Yeah. Yeah, that," and Daniel seemed like he was thinking about it.

"Whoa," I said, also thinking about it.

"Leo," Rex said gently. "Will isn't superhuman. He's just as scared and uncertain as any of us. He just has different ways of dealing with it. And not everyone's so great at talking about that kind of stuff. Sometimes they show you things in other ways."

"Wow, I feel like the biggest idiot in history," I said. Then, when Rex looked guilty: "No, no, you're fine. I just mean, I seriously didn't think about the ways that Will might be… scared about stuff. About relationship stuff."

Which was a pretty major oversight, considering everything he'd told me about his past relationships.

Rex and Daniel were quiet, Daniel's shoulders pressed against Rex's legs, Rex's hands on his shoulders. I wondered what if felt like for them, looking at their image on the screen. Seeing their connectedness reflected back at them.

"I really love him, you guys." My voice was a whisper, and I hadn't meant to tell them that before I'd even told Will. But once I had, I went on. "I know it probably sounds like I think he's perfect or something because of what I just said. And I don't. I just think maybe…." I shook my head. It was too sappy to say out loud.

"Maybe you're perfect for each other," Daniel murmured, like he wasn't even talking to me. Rex's expression turned soft and private, and he touched Daniel's hair, just for a second.

My thoughts were flying at the speed of light, but it was all stuff I should be saying to Will, not to Daniel and Rex. I saw myself nodding onscreen, just a tiny window against the large view of Daniel and Rex, caught up in each other.

"Thanks, you guys. Seriously, thanks a lot. I should go."

Rex gave me a kind smile and Daniel gave me a goofy wave.

"Good luck," he said, and I saw Rex reach for him just before the screen went black.

I THOUGHT a lot about what Daniel and Rex had said. I couldn't sleep because of all the Coke, so I went back to pacing.

Rex was right. Will did sometimes use strong opinions to shut down a conversation he didn't want to have. *Had* I been so distracted by Will's bluntness about small things that I overvalued his honesty about bigger things? Scarier things?

Also—and this was so simple I almost dismissed it the way I had Rex's question earlier—what if Will was just… wrong. Not lying, just… what if he'd spent so long believing he couldn't be in relationships for x, y, and z reasons that he hadn't stopped to reevaluate when a new variable was added to the equation. I actually snorted at myself. Like: NEWSFLASH, it has been suggested that there is the possibility Will Highland is occasionally wrong. Paging everyone everywhere.

So maybe I should just… what? Wait and watch? Look, as Rex had said, for the other ways that Will might express how he felt.

That was that, then. I would watch, keeping in mind my two new laws of Will dynamics: 1. It was possible Will was scared and uncertain, and 2. I had to look at what Will did in addition to what he said. Easy enough, right?

Chapter 16

April

I WATCHED for a month. And all the while, Will's presence glowed like a lantern in the heart of my life, even when he wasn't around.

School was a whirlwind of busy and Will was up to his ears in all the work it took for him and Gus to launch the business, so I didn't see him as much as I'd have liked. But when we did get a chance to see each other I paid attention in a way I never had.

One afternoon when the subway got delayed on my way up to Will's apartment it hit me with a startling clarity. This was the problem with scripting romances in your head. When someone doesn't hit the beats, you expect of them you have no idea what their actual behavior means. Will had tried to tell me. So had Gretchen. Even Layne, in her way, had told me. That this was what being a romantic looked like: paying more attention to your own expectations than to the very real person in front of you.

"Fuck," I muttered.

"I know, right?" replied the guy to my left, looking up from his crossword. "I should just get out and walk. Be faster."

I nodded in sympathy, but he didn't make a move to go anywhere.

THE SEX between us had been intense ever since we got back from Michigan, and tonight I was drawing it out, taking the whirlwind that Will began with and harnessing it, amping us both up, then backing off, keeping Will on the edge as long as I could. At first he threatened to push me away and finish himself off. But he didn't. He looked up at me, and I saw the moment when he accepted that I'd make it good for him if he was patient. He kind of rolled his eyes and groaned, like he was giving in to me, but really I think he was giving in to himself.

More and more, I'd noticed a kind of restlessness in him, a desire to be distracted. He'd wander around the apartment, picking things up and putting them down like he was confused as to what they did. I'd ask him to help me with something, and he'd transfer his attention to it gratefully. Or I'd start something and he'd grab my clothes and my hair as if reminding himself that he could. Because we'd both been so busy lately, usually we'd fall asleep right after sex. It had taken a few times of this happening for me to realize that I was staying over. And Will was letting me.

Tonight, though, after I finally let Will come, I pressed him onto his stomach in his soft bed and rubbed the tension from his shoulders and back, kissing up his spine until I could lay myself down over him. I kissed his neck, his ear, the curve of his jaw, then I buried my face in the crook of his neck. He let out a soft groan and mumbled something into the pillow that I didn't catch.

I rolled him toward me, sliding an arm under his neck.

"What'd you say?"

"I said, are you staying?"

I smiled into his hair.

"'Kay."

He fumbled for the bedside lamp, couldn't reach it, and let his arm drop onto the bed. I leaned over him and flicked it off, lying down on my back next to him.

"Hey, Will?"

He grunted.

There were a hundred things I wanted to say to him. That I loved him and I wanted to be with him and I thought maybe he felt different about me now than he had before Michigan. I wanted to tell him that if he needed to still sleep with other people, I was willing to talk about it if it meant we could… I dunno, have something more.

But the words stuck in my throat. It was too much and not enough.

He'd never asked me to stay before. It felt like a step in the right direction, and I wanted to just let it happen, to enjoy that it was happening right now and not scuttle it by picking it apart or making him self-conscious.

It could wait, I decided. It could all wait until after finals, when we could really talk.

"Nothing," I said. "I just like being here with you."

He reached for my hand in the darkness.

WILL HAD never come to see me on campus, so I was surprised when lying in bed, I looked up from my calculus book a few days later to find him at my door. He looked out of place in the dorm hallway surrounded by scrubby students in sweats and jeans with dirty hair and harried expressions, where he wore black ankle boots, a black-and-white houndstooth shirt tucked casually into gray wool pants, and a black overcoat.

"Hey!" I started to stand up but somehow got all tangled in the sheets and kind of slumped back down. Will smiled and stalked over, pressing me back to the flimsy mattress and kissing me deeply.

"Mmm," he murmured into my mouth. His cheeks and hands were cold, and I tried to pull him down into the bed with me, but he resisted.

"You don't have class until three, right?"

I nodded, ridiculously pleased that he'd remembered my schedule.

"Want to come with me to look at this space Gus wants to set up business from? It's not far from here."

"Okay, sure. Let me put pants on."

Will raised an eyebrow and slid a hand beneath the covers, groping me. He pouted when he realized I was wearing pajama pants, but reached inside the waistband and stroked me gently.

"Gah," I said, hardening for him.

Will "Mmm"ed and leaned in to kiss my neck. There was something ridiculously hot about lying sprawled in my bed in my pajamas with Will looming, fully dressed, having his way with me.

"Oh, oops, sorry" came Milton's voice from the open door. He didn' sound sorry, though. Will, being Will, didn't stand right away, lingering long enough to press one more kiss to my jaw and give me a squeeze beneath the covers that practically made me swallow my tongue.

"This must be Will," Milton said in a voice calculated to express maximal scorn, leaning in the doorframe to show himself off to his best advantage.

"This must be Milton," Will said dismissively, straightening up and squaring his shoulders.

Milton narrowed his eyes, looking Will up and down, and Will faced off, not trying to disguise his once-over of Milton either.

"I basically hate you," Milton said, "for the way you've treated Leo."

"Milton, man, come on," I started, actually managing to get out of bed this time, wanting to at least be standing in case things got ugly.

"I basically like you," Will said evenly, "for being a good friend to Leo and for not dressing like a tsunami has decimated every store selling anything besides track pants and school-affiliated sweatshirts."

"God, *right?*" Milton rolled his eyes toward the hallway where Will was looking. "This is New York, for fuck's sake. Have a little respect."

Will inclined his head approvingly.

"Um, okay, glad you guys've met. I have to get dressed now." I looked at Milton.

"Well, it's nothing I haven't seen before," Milton said, his implication and its challenge to Will clear.

But Will just smiled and said, "Then I'm sure you understand that once Leo's naked, I'm not going to be able to resist being all over that ass. So unless you'd like to watch, you might want to excuse yourself."

Milton's eyes went wide and I flushed hotly, letting out a nervous laugh as he tried to retreat with dignity. Point: Will.

THE PLACE that Gus wanted them to rent was an office in a coworking space near the Tenement Museum on the Lower East Side. He and Will both thought it was important that they have a physical space to work from so they could invest in supplies, have a place to meet with clients, and have an address where things could be delivered. Even if they'd had the money to rent their own space, they didn't want to commit to a long-term lease in case things didn't work out.

It was a converted warehouse space, open on the first floor, with banks of tables full of people typing away on laptops and congregating around screens. In the back were offices for permanent staff, and a shared kitchen, bathroom, and lounge space scattered with smart, modern-looking couches and poured cement tables.

Upstairs were the offices for rent by the month that Will and Gus were interested in. There was a courtyard, and as Will paced out the space, I could see him picturing how he'd set up here. He asked a lot of questions, about Internet speed, tech support, and hourly availability, and took his time looking around.

"What do you think?" he finally asked me.

"Me? Oh, um, yeah, it's really cool." I had no clue what possible insight I could have.

"If you came to meet with a potential collaborator at a place like this, what impression would you have of them?"

"Hm, kind of… edgy, I guess. Like, modern and nontraditional. It's neat, actually. I think I'd be excited to be around so many people working on so many different projects. It'd make me think that the people I was meeting with were on top of, like, trends or popular culture or whatever."

Will had listened to me seriously, and he nodded once, satisfied. "Me too."

"Okay, great," he said to the woman who'd been showing us around. "I think we'll probably go ahead with it. I just need to confirm it with my business partner. Can I let you know later today?"

The woman looked between us and Will offered no explanation.

"Sure, that'll work."

Will shook her hand, and when we walked outside, he was grinning.

"I like that place," he said giddily. "It'll be so different than the office. Want to get a coffee? I want a coffee."

"Yeah, sure." I loved seeing him so happy. So exuberant and light. It didn't happen that often. As we walked, though, and the usual barrage of admirers looked Will up and down, their gazes lingering on him, his mood dimmed. By the time he pulled me into a little café on Houston, he was tapping his fingers against his thighs irritably. There were no empty tables, so we stood at a corner of the counter to drink our coffees, Will glancing around as if he could still feel eyes on him.

My phone chimed with a text from Layne asking if I could come in an hour early for my shift the next day. In the minute it took me to respond, a man sidled up to Will and started talking to him. Will's jaw was tight, teeth gritted.

All the things he'd told me. About being so aware of people's eyes on him that he sometimes felt stripped bare by it. Of the way it gradually wore down his energy and his mood by the end of the day until sometimes he could hardly wait to get home behind closed doors just so he could exist in a space where he wasn't being looked at. They coalesced into a surge of protectiveness like nothing I'd ever felt before.

"Oy," I said to the guy. I slid an arm around Will's waist in a way I had secretly always wanted to but never dared do in public. "Back off my boyfriend, dude." I channeled Daniel, who'd once told me that you had to be totally confident in your superiority over the person you were challenging to make them take you seriously.

The man smirked at me disbelievingly and looked at Will. His look clearly said, *Yeah right. No way did a skinny kid like you manage to land yourself a hottie like that.* I flushed, but stood my ground, fingers curling around Will's hip. I was expecting him to pull away at any minute or tell us both to go fuck ourselves. But he didn't. He narrowed his eyes at the guy and put his arm around me in turn, tugging me closer. Then he kissed me on the cheek, lips lingering long enough for me to smell the vanilla from his latte.

"Oookay," the guy said like he'd just been faced with something too confusing to attempt to puzzle out. "Have a good one." And he walked away.

I felt as triumphant as if I'd been telling the truth about Will and me, the warmth of being able to defend Will suffusing me. I went to drop my arm from his waist before he could call me on the fiction, but he let his arm linger for a minute, so I did too.

"Um, sorry I said you were my boyfriend. I just… I thought you might want a rescue, and that guy seemed like kind of a douchebag."

Will gave me a long assessing look and then smiled. And I couldn't help thinking that maybe he didn't totally hate what I'd done after all.

Chapter 17

April

SPRING HAD sprung with a vengeance and the energy on campus was electric. No matter what time of day I walked through the park, there were groups of students camped out, shirts rolled up to the sun, heads on each other's shoulders, and textbooks lying abandoned in front of them in the new grass.

Those who were staying on campus for the summer were angling for the best rooms, those who were from the city making plans to see each other after the semester ended, and everyone else was grumbling about going home or scheming about how to stay. I didn't know a single person who hadn't fallen in love with New York in some way.

Midway through April, I found out I'd gotten the job working as an assistant in the physics lab and could count myself among the excited ones who would be staying in the city for the summer.

The only problem was that the job was only part-time and wasn't for credit, so I didn't qualify for campus housing.

The next night, we all went to see Milton in his drama class' production of *Pippin*. I'd never heard of it, but Milton assured me it was a classic.

"What… what *is* this?" Charles whispered to me, horrified, about ten minutes in. I had no answer at all. Milton was great, though. He sang, he danced, he had a few lines, and he looked thrilled the whole time. After we'd gathered our bags and the tatters of our sanity, we went backstage and found him in close conversation with a wildly gesticulating, intensely staring Jason, so we just waved and gestured that we'd see him later.

The real surprise of the night came when we got back to the dorm to find Thomas waiting for us. Only it wasn't Thomas because Thomas had been with us.

"Oh wow, they *really* look alike," I said stupidly.

"Identical twins," Charles said, nodding once.

Thomas and his brother hugged like one of them was returning from war. They were all over each other like puppies, with no bubble of personal space. They really did look startlingly alike, but unlike Thomas, Andy was quiet, often looking over at his twin when someone addressed a question to him. I wondered if they had always been this way and, if so, how hard it must've been for Andy, away at school without Thomas there to speak for him.

Andy's school was on a different schedule so he'd taken the train down as soon as the semester ended. I got the sense that he wouldn't mind just hanging out in Thomas' room and playing video games while Thomas studied. I told him he could come by Mug Shots the next day if he wanted a free coffee and a place to hang out, but though he nodded politely, Andy didn't seem to like me. I guessed I couldn't blame him if Thomas had mentioned anything about me not returning his feelings. I wouldn't like me either.

I SAT bolt upright in the dark, confused for a second at when I had finally remembered to change my alarm sound and *why* of all things I'd chosen something that sounded like screaming, until I realized it was the fire alarm. Charles had clearly already been awake, though from the looks of him he'd been about to go to bed, and he was sitting at his desk shaking his head.

"Someone pulled it," he said. "I heard them run away, giggling. But we all have to leave anyway. It's illogical."

"I'll add it to the list of dorm laws: someone always pulls the fire alarm on the one fucking night I was gonna get the doctor's recommended eight hours," I grumbled.

"Or on the night before a big test," Charles said. "Might have to be two different laws."

We trooped into the hall and down the seven flights of stairs, joining the stream of people from our hall. Some were manic, clearly having been awake and studying, some were irate and ranting at being woken up when there was clearly no fire, but the majority were, like me, shambling zombie-like down the hall in an attempt to preserve something of the sleep that had been interrupted.

It was about four in the morning, but outside the city was ticking along like always. In Holiday, one of the things I'd loved was the way there were times of the night and early morning when there was actually no one else around. When I couldn't sleep, sometimes I'd slide out of bed and dress in silence, in the dark, and walk down the streets that would, in a few hours, be full of people, each of them with their own plans and their own desires.

I'd watched them my whole life, like they were a drama playing out before me on the television screen of Holiday, but I'd rarely seen myself as part of it. In the late night and early morning emptiness, the town seemed like a movie set for that drama. And in those moments I would feel a bit sad for it, emptied out and waiting for the people who would make it less lonely.

Here, there was never total emptiness. There was no waiting, no reset where the city breathed in relief for a few hours after the people were gone. There was only a constant readiness. A kind of low-level hum beneath the bones of the city itself, like the cranking, coiled machinery of a roller coaster being pulled uphill.

A true perpetual-motion machine is an impossibility, we learned in physics, since it violates the laws of thermodynamics. "Even the sun, as a source of energy, will eventually burn out," Professor Ekwensi had said, matter-of-factly and as if that weren't basically the most terrifying sentence ever to be uttered in a college classroom. Still, if there was ever something that felt like it came close, this city was it.

I had been tearing my hair out over my final project for physics. The assignment was as irritatingly vague as it was intriguing: measure something. I'd changed my topic three times since midterms and was still searching for the right thing.

Coming home from Will's the other morning, I'd gotten off at 33rd Street and walked over to the High Line, hoping a coffee and some fresh air would clear my head, that some bolt of inspiration would strike since I was getting down to the wire.

It was a sunny morning, with a chill still in the air, and I was in a well-fucked, under-caffeinated trance, my eye catching on the smallest details. The way tiny ruffs of new plants were pushing their way through the spaces between the metal slats. How at that exact moment the scaffolding on a nearby building cast a shadow at a perfect perpendicular to the pink edge of the mural I was walking past.

A bench where, from my angle of approach it looked like a man sat alone. When I walked five steps closer, though, I saw that the breadth of his body had completely hidden the woman sitting with him. They were looking at each other with a kind of absorption that made me soften my steps because it felt intrusive to even stir the air around them, to cause vibrations from my footfalls that would reach them. As I walked by, though, they both glanced up at me and smiled. Like the joy they shared was large enough to include me, and the plants, and the shadows, and everything around them.

I smiled back and lifted my coffee in a toast, not just to them but to the High Line and the river and the traffic, and the whole goddamned beautiful city around us. I was so giddy with it that for a moment, grin wrinkling my whole face, I made the kind of sound that's completely embarrassing outside of, like, a movie musical or an episode of *Glee*.

It was a perfect moment. So perfect that I found myself almost frantically trying to catalog it. To break it down to its component parts so I could re-create it. But as I tried to measure it—to make it reducible to some kind of system or law—it slipped away.

And that was my problem. *Measure something.* All the things that truly mattered were immeasurable. Using any system of quantification currently in existence, anyway. And I wanted to do something meaningful, otherwise, what was the point?

I'd tried to think of ways to measure everything important in my life. And god knew Milton had given me enough shit about it, singing that damn song from *Rent* about measuring a life until I actually wondered if the professor had ever needed to ban its lyrics from being the titles of final projects.

In an admittedly sappy moment—though I consoled myself that sappiness and science were *not* necessarily opposed by thinking of Carl Sagan and Anne Druyan—I'd even tried to think through how I would measure love.

I'd been in the physics lab scribbling ideas in my notebook when Max, one of the grad students came in. Max had intimidated me when I first started at the lab. He was tall and muscular, and I heard someone say he was ex-military. He narrowed his eyes when he listened closely, which made it look like he doubted what you were saying, and though he was taller than everyone in the lab, he never inclined his head when he spoke to people, which gave him the impression of being even taller. But he was wicked good at physics and clearly loved it.

So when he asked what I was working on, I posed the question, though I imagined he'd probably laugh in my face.

"Do you think it's possible to… measure love?"

He cocked his head, eyes sharp. "Didn't they do that in that Christopher Nolan movie? *Interstellar?*"

"Oh, I dunno, I didn't see it."

He squinted at me and then leaned over the lab table, tapping my notebook.

"Well, you can't measure something unless we can agree on what it actually *is*, which is a problem, since love is abstract… but, okay, let's see. Maybe we can't measure it directly, but we could measure its effects, like with entropy. Love… people do some crazy-ass shit for love," he mused, gaze fixed on the wall above my head.

I knew Max had a wife and a baby daughter—he'd shown me their picture on his phone one day, with soft eyes and a private smile. I wondered if he was thinking about them. I wondered what kind of crazy-ass shit he'd done for love.

"Does the degree of crazy imply a greater degree of love?" he mused. "A higher intensity, or larger… amount. Are there different flavors of love like there are flavors of quarks?—heh, yeah. Up love and down love, charm love and strange love, top love and bottom love. I like that."

He lapsed into silence, like he'd forgotten I was there. When he remembered me, he stabbed a thick finger at my notebook. "Yeah, I'd try and formulate a hypothesis that measured the effects of love *on* something." Then he nodded once, signaling that he'd said all he had to say on the matter, and bent back over his own work.

My mind went immediately to the way Will had writhed beneath me days before as I worshiped his cock with my mouth. It had been love for me—love that made me want to shake him apart with pleasure, to transmit my adoration. I blinked until I cleared the images of Will from my mind, but when I thanked Max for his help, he just raised an eyebrow as he wished me good luck. And I had the sense that he didn't just mean with my physics project.

So, yeah, I'd tried to explain wanting to do my project on something meaningful to Will the night before. Will, practical as ever, had cut rather to the chase.

"You don't need to make your major contribution to the discipline in the last three weeks of your first year at NYU, Leo," he'd said. "Just pick something—it doesn't matter what—and do a good job with it. If you have grand ambitions to create the…" He searched for an incisive example and came up adorably short. His physics knowledge was basically nil. "… to create *whatever*, then write your ideas down in that damn raggedy-ass notebook you're always hauling around and get back to them when you write your dissertation or whatever. You're wasting time you could just be doing it. And honestly, you're driving me fucking nuts trying to turn my can openers and shit into your physics project."

I knew he was right. That this was just one project for one class, and as far as that went, it didn't technically *matter* what I did.

"Ooh, okay, I know," Will said when it was clear I was still sulking about it. "You could measure how fast Superman would have had to fly around the world backward to actually reverse time. Cartoon physics, get it?" He winked at me.

I smiled at him. "I think there's a book about that, actually. That explains all the physics of comic books and superheroes and stuff. Pretty cool."

"Soooo geeky." But I could tell he thought it was cool too. Then he was off, listing what seemed to be an experiment I could do from every sci-fi show or movie we'd watched together.

"Oh! You could do like an *Orphan Black* thing, and—"

"Cloning is biology, not physics," I said, and I kissed him to shut him up.

He narrowed his eyes at me like I was spoiling all his fun, then brightened and shoved down his pants.

"I've got it," he said with a wicked grin. "You can measure my dick with your mouth." He waggled his eyebrows and tilted his hips toward me as I cracked up.

NOW, STANDING with my hallmates in the middle of the night, the stars splashed high above us through the clouds, I imagined Will asleep five miles away, the same moonlight sneaking through the window to alight on his hair, pillow-mussed, or the soft curve of his shoulder, or the groove of his spine. And I liked that, at the level of starlight and moonlight, something connected us even when we weren't together. Will would give me immense shit if I said something like that out loud, but it was maybe why my project *did* matter to me. Because the laws that governed Will's can opener *were* the laws that governed the moon, that governed both of us, even miles apart.

Gretchen came to stand beside me. "I know what we have to do." Her voice was low and calm as always, but she grabbed my arm with uncharacteristic excitement.

"Uh… go back to bed?" I asked hopefully.

"Sunrise. Yoga."

Sunrise yoga was more myth than reality. I knew it existed since Tonya always announced it. I knew there were true devotees who showed up every morning, ready to welcome the sunrise with yoga. But though I had sometimes randomly woken up early in Holiday because I couldn't sleep, I was *not* a morning person. And now that I routinely didn't get enough sleep, I was certainly never up before I had to be.

"Absolutely not."

"Oh, come *on*, Leo, when will we have another chance?"

"Like… every morning that isn't today."

"Yes, but we *won't*. We're already up! And the class starts at five. That means we have an hour to change, get breakfast, and get to the gym. Besides, the year's almost over and we've been saying we were going to go since September."

This wasn't strictly true. Gretchen had been saying she wanted to go since September and I had routinely smiled and nodded, assuming she was aware that this meant I had no interest whatsoever.

I opened my mouth to tell her absolutely not. That I had too much work the next day. That I was tired. That the idea of doing yoga in the dark before dawn sounded like a total suckfest. But she was holding my arm, her white-blonde hair escaping its nighttime braid in frizzy puffs and curls, like the plants on the High Line, and her strangely colorless eyes looked like twin moons, yellow-gray and luminous, and I started to smile.

"Okay, sure. Why not."

"Yes!" Gretchen's excitement was reward enough. She squeezed my arm in triumph and tipped her chin up to the night sky.

AS WE walked down 14th Street in our yoga clothes, sipping coffee and eating cinnamon bagels, Gretchen said, "It's strange to see the city this early in the morning. It's so empty, it's like everything's still asleep." And I nodded at her, but was struck by the intensely dislocating feeling that hit me whenever I was reminded how staggeringly different people's impressions of the same thing could be.

If Tonya was surprised to see us, she didn't show it, just nodded warmly and smiled. There were only three other people there, clearly regulars by the way they greeted each other silently and settled onto their mats with none of the chatter of our usual classes.

The yoga studio had windows on one side, and Tonya had us positioned so that we were facing them. Her voice was serene, almost lulling, where usually she had more energy.

"In the Yoga Sutras, we find the principles of *Abhyasa* and *Vairagya*. Practice and nonattachment. Practice means always showing up to do the work. Putting forth effort. Nonattachment means letting go of the outcome of that work. Letting go of the things that prevent us from seeing ourselves clearly—fear or pain, expectation or pleasure. We observe those things, and then we let them pass us by.

"Together, we can express *Abhyasa* and *Vairagya* as 'Never give up and always surrender.' Always keep striving in the direction of what you want to bring into being. But recognize when you've done all you can and have reached the moment to surrender to the outcomes of that work. The moment when doing more becomes detrimental to your efforts.

"In practical terms this might look like riding your bike up a hill: you have to pedal hard, hard, hard enough to get the bike to the top of the hill. But then, when you start to crest the hill, you can stop pedaling. Stop exerting effort and surrender to the way gravity will carry you down the other side. Recognize that in fact the attempt to keep pedaling when your wheels are moving so fast is dangerous and won't serve you.

"This is the balance. Never giving up in working to achieve what you desire. Always remembering that sometimes the outcome of your work can look different than you expected. And sometimes it might give you things you couldn't have anticipated. Let's practice with that in mind today."

I'd been thinking about my physics project so single-mindedly that physics was where my brain went naturally. Though I'd heard Tonya use the phrase "never give up and always surrender" before, the bike metaphor somehow made it stunningly clear. Because that was just physics. But as I moved through sun salutations—which definitely felt a bit more salutatory in advance of the actual sun—I kept thinking of her words in terms of Will.

How I'd done the work. *So* much damn work, if I was being honest. And it hadn't gotten me what I'd wanted. It hadn't gotten me Will. Not an acknowledged monogamous relationship with Will, anyway.

But the part about surrendering to the unexpected things that the work can bring about stuck with me. Will telling me that I was his best friend.

Telling me that I was the first one he called when shit went down with
Claire. That I was the one he wanted to tell when good things happened
Showing me that he trusted me more than he trusted other people, let me in
farther than he let in others. That he cared about me.

I wondered how many more things like that I'd dismissed or
undervalued, too distracted by the fact that I wasn't getting the results I'd
set my sights on. How often important, meaningful, *real* things had slipped
away from me, unacknowledged, as I measured only their distance from
what I'd wanted.

They were unrecoverable losses. But maybe things could be different
going forward.

I could be different.

We moved from Standing Split to Warrior III and finally settled in
Warrior II, sinking deeper and deeper into the pose as the sun began to peek
up over the buildings, spilling its rays down on the waking city below.

At the end of the class, the sun had fully risen, appearing to rest in my
hands like a child's ball, as if we'd dragged it from the very depths of the
cosmos with our outstretched arms, all laws of physics shattered in the wake
of sheer perception and will.

Chapter 18

April

IT WAS finals week again, but this time everything was different.

This time, I knew to load up empty containers with D-Hall food at breakfast so I'd have snacks all day. This time, I knew to make a schedule so I spaced out everything that was due to make it more manageable. This time, I knew to take the week off from Mug Shots so I didn't lose my mind with stress and explode my heart with caffeine.

And this time I was studying at Will's in the evenings because I spent most evenings there anyway.

"Okay," I said, dropping my backpack on the couch and throwing myself over Will's lap exhaustedly, needing just a little bit of a cuddle before starting in on the last push of writing and studying before this year was over.

Will ran his hand through my hair, and I nuzzled his hip.

"Hmm?"

"We've figured it out. Milton and Charles are getting a place, and probably Thomas, if he can convince his brother to stay in the city, which he thinks he can. And if I go in on it with them, then my rent'll be affordable. Ish. I can get a bunch of hours at Mug Shots after my physics lab hours, and it'll be totally fine. I won't have to go back to Holiday."

I said this last mostly to myself, since I didn't think I'd even mentioned the possibility of it to Will.

Will's hand had stilled in my hair, resting along the curve of my scalp, and I pressed into his palm, hoping he'd start rubbing my head again.

"Isn't Thomas the one who's in love with you?" Will asked.

I started to explain that, no, it had just been a crush and I was sure he was past it now. But instead I pitched my voice softly near his ear. "Jealous?" Then I kissed him on the cheek before he could answer, and eased away to do my work.

THE NEXT evening, I was working on my Cultural Foundations II paper, but I was hopelessly distracted. Everything in the apartment seemed more interesting than Dante, especially Will, working at the drafting table next to me. I could smell him every now and then when he'd reach his arms up to stretch his shoulders or recross his legs. The sinews of his forearm tensed as he drew, and his hair seemed perfectly arranged to torment me with the shadow it cast beneath his cheekbone.

"Eyes on your own paper, young Leo," he said without looking up, and I realized I was staring at the curve of his biceps that his white T-shirt revealed. I looked down at my work with a little shiver; Will's half-amused, half-scolding voice just did things to me.

A few minutes later, Will pressed his hand to my thigh, just above my knee, and I became aware that I'd been bouncing it.

"You're shaking the whole floor, babe." He rapped my thigh with the pencil he still held and turned back to his work.

"Sorry," I muttered. I leaned back in my chair, the front two legs coming off the ground, and closed my eyes for just a minute, letting the sounds from outside—traffic and birds and a song in Spanish—filter in.

Hands on my shoulders pushed the chair back onto all four legs, and Will said, "Would you do your damn work? I can feel how distracted you are from two feet away." I made a pathetic groaning complaint and tried to rest my head back on his chest for some sympathy, but he just tapped the desk in front of me with that damn pencil, his breath ghosting the back of my neck. I shifted in my chair.

"Ummm, this should probably not turn me on, but I love it when you're so fucking bossy," I muttered, shaking my head.

"Is that right?" Will drawled, his voice taking on an edge. "What do you love about it?"

"Uh…." Was he serious?

I craned my neck to look behind me. He let go of my shoulders and sat down, looking at me.

"Tell me why it turns you on when I'm bossy, Leo."

My face and neck got hot. I wasn't sure why exactly, only that it somehow felt like when Will made decisions for me that he was exerting some kind of ownership over me. Like by deciding that I was his to order around, he was decided that I was just… his.

Then there was the way his eyes burned when I told him no. How he liked to push my buttons, liked to see how far he could go before I'd stop him. How much I would give him. But my mouth didn't currently seem to be connected to my brain, so when I opened it all that came out was an inarticulate noise from the back of my throat.

"Do you like when people tell you what to do, Leo?" His voice was filthy. "You got a little hot-for-teacher action going on?"

"I… I like it when you tell me what you want," I finally stammered out. "I like giving it to you." Will's expression softened for a moment, then his mouth curled into a smirk.

"Well, then." He leaned in close to me, expression stern. "I *want* you to write for ten minutes." He tapped the desk. "With no distractions." He tapped my cheek.

"Can I—?"

"Work time is not talking time, Leo." He turned back to his own paper.

"Whoa."

I looked back at my computer, not even sure what was going on. All the blood had left my head and rushed… elsewhere, and when I looked at the words on the screen, they all blended together. I was too aware of Will next to me. The heat of his body, his smell. The drag of his pencil along paper hit me like a caress up my spine and raised goose bumps on my arms. I reached down to adjust my erection and felt Will's eyes on me.

Will slid a hand to the inside of my thigh. Just that touch sent warmth rushing through my legs, made me want to press into his hand to feel his strength against mine. "I'm going to need to see a bit more dedication to your work."

I swallowed hard and found myself nodding.

I wrote a few sentences, but I couldn't have said what they were about to save my life. My heart was beating faster and faster and every hair on my body was raised. Will kept drafting like he didn't notice the state I was in at all.

"How close are you?" he asked without looking up, and I practically swallowed my own tongue as my dick pulsed. Will rolled his eyes. "To finishing your paper."

"Uh, like one more page."

"Write it."

"I'm trying," I grumbled.

Will stood up and looked down at my work, resting his hand casually on my shoulder. He leaned just close enough that my skin buzzed with proximity, my hands itching to grab fistfuls of that perfect white T-shirt and pull him down into my lap. Kiss him until he forgot about what I was supposed to be doing and just begged me to fuck him. I groaned at the picture.

"Are you having trouble concentrating?" Will said in my ear. I let out a nervous laugh. "Maybe you need an incentive. Beyond, of course, the reward of a job well done." I groaned as his voice dropped lower on the last three words and nodded so quickly I almost gave myself whiplash.

Will moved behind me and put his hands on my shoulders, pressing me closer to the desk. "Start writing," he murmured and then proceeded to do something to my neck that "kiss" was far too tame a word for. He *feasted* on me—licking and sucking at the place where my neck met my shoulder, biting gently at the muscle there, scraping his teeth over tendons and breathing on my damp skin.

He kissed the back of my neck softly, nose in my hair, on his way to the other side, and did the whole thing all over again. I was writhing in the desk chair, hard as rock and gasping at the sudden attack that had amped up my arousal so quickly I was almost light-headed with it.

By the time I coordinated my brain and my limbs to reach back and touch Will, he had pulled away with one final, hair-raising kiss to the back of my neck. Then he sat down at the drafting table, and the *scritch* of his pencil tip tore through me.

"Fuuuuck."

"Do your work," he said softly, his voice rough. I groaned and dropped my forehead to the desk. His hand settled warm and heavy on the back of my neck and squeezed.

"Fuck!" I said again, and he chuckled, leaning close.

"Leo. Your first job is to finish your paper, and your second job is to fuck me over this desk." He rested his palm on the desk near my face. "Each are worth fifty percent of your grade," he said, voice teasing, and then sat back in his chair.

"Oh my god, seriously, why is this turning me on so much?" I shook my head at myself.

"Who cares why? Do your first job so you can *do* your second job, would you?"

"Mmhmm." It came out as kind of a whine.

I wrote the end of my paper, the words coming from somewhere and who the hell knew what they were, but I told myself I would fix it in the morning before I turned it in. I hit Command+S and slammed my laptop shut, looking to Will immediately.

He raised an eyebrow. "Finished."

"Yeah."

"How did it turn out?"

"Uh-huh," I said, taking in the angle of his jaw, the line of his neck, and then moving down to the strong planes of his chest. "Wait, what?"

He was up in a flash, straddling my thighs and attacking my mouth. I groaned as his tongue slid against mine and clutched him tight, grabbing his ass in both hands and dragging him onto my erection. He grabbed the back of the chair with one hand and wrapped the other around my neck.

We kissed with all the pent-up heat of the last hour. I was desperate for him. For the taste of his hot mouth and the feel of his weight on my lap, the sensation of his arms around me and the muscular thrusts of his hips flexing to stay on my lap, struggling to get us at the right angle.

When we found it, we ground together, groaning. I leaned back a little so he could balance and he folded against me, his weight pressing our dicks together. He made a tiny gasping sound in my ear, and I was wild with need for him. I started pulling at his clothes, just needing skin on skin contact. His chest was flushed and I pinched his nipple, loving his hiss in response, the feel of his nails digging into my shoulders. Then he found my mouth again, latching on and kissing me until we were both breathless and sweating.

I pressed him back against the desk, pushing the chair away so I could get his pants off. My movements wild, I kind of squashed him backward, and he grabbed for my laptop, catching it before it toppled off the desk. We both froze for a moment, and he laid it gently on his drafting table, on top of the drawing he'd been working on.

"Top marks for enthusiasm, but I'd hate you to have to explain to your professor how you couldn't turn in your paper due to busting your laptop in a freak desk-sex accident." I didn't even know how he could say "desk sex," which was a real tongue twister, when I could barely think in more than grunts, so I just nodded and went back to kissing the shit out of him. It was, after all, my job.

I bore him back onto the desk, and we ground into each other, arms clutching, hands everywhere, mouths meeting so heatedly my lips buzzed, and I could feel them bruising. And I loved it. I loved any evidence of Will's passion that I could keep with me on my body. Whenever he left marks on my skin, I'd track their progress as they lingered on me, feeling bereft when they faded, like without them my skin was too uncomplicated.

I couldn't get enough of him. I dropped to my knees before him and kissed his belly, exalting in the way his hands fell immediately to my shoulders to keep in contact. I cupped his hips and dipped my head lower nuzzling into the crease of his groin, kissing the insides of his thighs until they trembled. I buried my face in his crotch, mad with the need to touch him, smell him, taste him everywhere.

"Ah fuck," Will groaned as I sucked the base of his cock, pressing my thumb behind his balls. He canted his hips forward, and I slid my mouth over his erection, the taste of him exploding on my tongue, all heat and salt and sweet sweat. Will's legs softened as he gave himself over to my mouth.

I worked him slowly at first, then lapped at the tip of his cock to make him shudder and pull away, only to press closer again. The sounds that were coming from above me sent bolts of arousal through me that gathered in the pit of my stomach and made my ass clench.

I stroked Will's balls until he whined. I pulled off him and rested my forehead against his stomach, trying to calm down a bit. Will ran sweaty fingers through my hair and held me to him.

"One sec," he said and pulled me up, twisting away. He tore open the condom and rolled it on me, and I bit my lip at his touch. I couldn' look away from him. He was sweaty and flushed with arousal, his hair a mess and his lips swollen. His jaw and around his mouth were pinked from the stubble I hadn't bothered to shave the last few days, and his eye were wild.

I wanted to tell him how beautiful he was, how absolutely stunning, but I was afraid he'd hear only the emptiness of the words he'd heard so many others say to him in the past.

Someday I would find a way to tell him that his beauty wasn't separate from him for me. That it was animated by the real him he let me see— made complicated and imperfect and specific because of his Will-ness. And I thought maybe he saw some of it on my face, because he softened for a moment, his eyebrows drawing together slightly and his eyelashes fluttering as he leaned in to kiss me, just a sweet press of his mouth to mine as we stood together.

"I want you so much" was all I said.

"I want you too," he whispered against my lips.

I took his shoulder and turned him onto the desk, chest down and ass up. I kissed down his back to the perfect curve of his ass and bit lightly at one cheek, patting the other.

"This is a whole new level of ass-kissing to try and get a higher grade, Leo. You know, you already—nnggh!" He groaned brokenly when I licked his hole, holding him open for me.

He swore wildly, and I huffed out a laugh against his skin. "Okay, okay, do your job, please," he said finally, breathing heavily.

"Wow, was that a please I just got?" I stood up and leaned over Will's back to kiss his neck.

"It's all you're gonna get unless you get on with it right fucking now."

"Always something to say, huh?" I spread his legs wider, felt his opening relax to my cock as I pressed against him.

"You love it," he retorted.

"Yeah. I do," I said, and I thrust inside him, pleasure shooting up my spine and down the backs of my thighs as I joined us together. We both groaned, and I stilled inside him, enjoying the closeness, the heat, the fucking delicious pressure of his body around mine. I could feel his heartbeat and smell his sweat, and I pulled out slowly to feel the drag of his ass, then slammed back inside him, groaning as pleasure tore through me.

We went fast and hard, and I bent my knees to get the angle right, governing my body by Will's every reaction.

"Oh fuck, yes, harder," he demanded when I changed position slightly, and I did as he said, the desk slamming into the wall. "Oh my god, if you break my apartment, I will kill you," he groaned, then, "Fuck, don't stop!"

I laughed into his neck as I tried to fuck him harder and not break his apartment at the same time. Finally, I just grabbed his hip and his shoulder and pulled him back against me as I pounded him as hard as I could.

I felt him come apart in my hands, his back bowing, his head thrown back, his hands scrabbling at the wood of the desk. I bit the side of his neck and used every muscle I'd developed in yoga over the past year to maintain enough of a crouch that I could thrust upward at just the right angle.

He went wild around me and then froze, letting out a broken cry as he came all over the desk. He grabbed his dick, stroking hard and groaning as he kept coming.

"Oh god." I slammed into him in a rush of hot pleasure, my hips moving even after my orgasm had wrung me dry, body seeking each shivery tendril of sensation. I collapsed over Will's back, and he whimpered. Then the whimper dissolved into a laugh and I looked down to see that he'd come all over my notebook.

"Omigod," I said into his neck.

"Good thing I moved your laptop."

"Thanks," I murmured absently, kissing up his neck and jaw to his ear. He shivered a little, so I did it again. After a minute, I eased out of him, biting my lip at the loss of his heat. I turned him around and pulled him to me, kissing his mouth. Then I wrapped my arms around him and just hugged him. He always tensed at first, and then he always softened. I waited for it, and when it came, I squeezed him even tighter.

"So, what'd I get?" I asked.

"Hmm?"

"Well, you said this was fifty percent of my grade. That's a lot, especially during finals."

Will grabbed my ass and squeezed. "An A," he said softly. "Definitely an A."

His voice was gentler than I expected, and there was no tease in it at all. He didn't let go but kept holding on to me, wrapping his arms around my waist.

It felt… heavy somehow. But good. Right.

"What?" I teased, just a little, so he didn't get self-conscious the way he sometimes did. "Not an A plus?"

Will squeezed me, and I could feel his smile against my collarbone.

"NYU doesn't give A-pluses, silly. You know that."

TWO DAYS, many bagels and coffees, and not enough hours of sleep later, my last paper was turned in and my final final taken. I thought my physics project had turned out well, despite changing it *again* at the last minute.

After Gretchen and I left sunrise yoga, I'd been floaty, almost drunk on the morning, but for all that I'd considered grand notions like measuring love and every yoga-related physics experiment I could think of, the image I couldn't get out of my head was of standing with my friends and hallmates in the middle of the night, during finals of my first year in a brand-new city, and picturing Will bathed in the light of the same moon.

It was sappy and personal, and no one would know that it had anything to do with Will except me, but I couldn't help it. I measured the gravitational force of the moon.

At first I wanted to measure its effects on me and then on Will, so I could have actual data that would show how much of it we shared. But when I sat down to actually design the experiment, I realized I'd have to measure the fluctuations in weight over a twenty-four-hour period, during which we'd have to basically stay totally still in the same spot. And, like, not eat or pee or sweat or anything, so that wasn't really feasible. So I just measured its effects on a glass of water instead. After all, we were seventy percent water, so whatever effects the moon had on water it had on us, right? Plus, you know, it was a way easier experiment.

Anyway, call it a love letter sent in the form of a final project—that was as romantic as sending the sounds of your love into space, right? Even if Will would never know about it.

It had been hard to leave Will's the other night. After we had sex, he was in a mood I didn't recognize. Like he had something to say but was holding back. Everything in me wanted to stay and pry it out of him, but I reminded myself of Tonya's words and I made myself let go. My work now was to finish finals. I knew I had to have a major conversation with Will, but that wasn't the moment.

Our dorm room looked like a whirlwind had hit it. An FBI-profiling, serial-killer-tracking genius whirlwind. The filing cabinet seemed to have taken up permanent residence on Charles' bed, and I didn't even think he was paying attention to where he was in any schedule, thirty-six-hour days or otherwise, because he had, as far as I could tell, been up for two days straight, finishing the write-up of his behavioral psychology project. I couldn't really bring myself to care much, though, and, since the filing cabinet wasn't on *my* bed, I dropped onto the messy covers and was asleep before I could even think the words *filing cabinet*.

Later, I'd just gotten out of a much-needed shower and was feeling shockingly not dead when I got a text from Will telling me to come over whenever I was done and we could watch the *Lord of the Rings* extras in celebration.

When I'd been at my parents' house in Holiday, I'd grabbed the DVDs out of my bedroom. I had been teasing him ever since about how in love I was with Viggo Mortensen and how Will would have to sword fight him to compete for my affection. And I'd extracted the promise from him that when I was finally done for the year, he'd watch them with me. All of them. I couldn't fucking wait. I also couldn't wait to tease him about looking like Legolas, who he always referred to as "that elf douche."

As I stepped out of the elevator on Will's floor, Mrs. Gemelli was leaving her apartment, flowered silk scarf wrapped around her hair, pink lipstick bleeding into the wrinkles around her lips. We had bonded over fabric softener in the laundry room when I stayed here over January term.

"Hi, Mrs. Gemelli."

"Hiya, DaVinci. What's cooking?"

"Just finished up with finals, so I'm free!"

She clapped her hands in front of her, pink press-ons clacking together. "How's Toadstool?"

"Oh, the little shit started taking a wee in my shower. It was too much. I put him on Prozac, so that should help. Damn cat's out of his mind." She shook her head.

"Wow, I didn't know they even made Prozac for cats."

"Honey, this is the twenty-first century. They make Prozac for everyone." She winked at me and walked slowly to the elevator, her hand resting on my shoulder for just a moment as she passed, light as a leaf, leaving a whisper of violets behind her in the hall.

It was quickly overpowered the second I opened Will's door, though, the smell of Thai food making my stomach lurch with hunger.

"Did you know they made Prozac for *cats*?" I asked as Will came over to me.

He kissed me hard. "Uh-huh," he said, then he kissed me again.

I gave him the highlights while we ate, the most significant of which was that Milton's roommate had had some kind of breakdown and they'd had to call his parents in the middle of the night. It was horrible and Milton felt awful because he was convinced he should have said something earlier when he noticed that Robbie was staying in the room more—honestly, though, Milton was almost never in their room and they weren't friends, so I thought he was being too hard on himself.

Will didn't want to admit it, but he was *so* into the extras. It was a cool, breezy night and we had the window open, the sounds of the city drifting in to mix with the sounds of the New Zealand-created Middle Earth. Will kept saying "Whoa"—as the timeline for creating the Shire was revealed, as horses galloped over the plain, as huge blocks of foam were carved into the exterior of castle walls. I think he was even kind of developing a crush on Orlando Bloom (out of costume, that was), much to his horror. "He kind of reminds me of you, actually," Will said. "He's all… twitchy and soft."

"It's strange watching these now," I said when we'd finished one branch of the extras tree. I hadn't seen them in a few years and the first time I saw them I'd been a kid. "The way they make all new friends and they're far from home and everything—it's like college." I ducked my head, embarrassed to admit it. "I actually hoped it was what college would be like." Will raised an eyebrow. "That sense of becoming part of a group, mostly. Of making a place feel like home because of the people there. Well, and, you know, I hoped it would be like the Shire."

"And does it?"

"New York, not quite yet. But, school? Yeah. And here." I gestured around his apartment.

He smiled. "You gotta give New York at least another year. Takes that long for the shock to wear off."

I had been waiting for the right moment—a good opening or the perfect segue, but this wasn't an essay for school and it was bound to be a hard conversation whenever we had it, so I let the idea of the right moment go. I slid closer to Will and took his hands in mine, the haunting menu screen music hiccoughing momentarily, then the loop restarting.

"Listen," I said. "I have things. To say."

Will was immediately on guard, and I squeezed his hands and moved closer.

"No, no, I don't want to fight, just talk, okay? We've kind of been… you know, doing our thing, but we've both been so busy we haven't really talked about what it is."

"How about we just make out instead?" he offered, but I could tell he knew it wouldn't work.

"I need to explain something," I said. "I'm not quite sure how to say it and I don't want you to get mad, so just listen, okay? Because it sounds wrong if I can't say the whole thing."

Will gave me a *whatever* eyebrow raise and waved me ahead.

I cleared my throat nervously, still unsure how to say everything I wanted to say even though I'd rehearsed it on the subway coming here.

"Okay, so. This thing happened where I was at sunrise yoga—'
Will snorted. "No, yeah, I know, anyway, and it was kind of part of my
physics project because I was realizing that I could try and measure
effects instead of the thing itself, and so I had to convert it to entropy
and like what *is* the flavor of love and then when I was looking at you
the other day it was like your... your whole... gorgeousness became
this other *thing*, and I realized what you'd been saying about *its* effects
and then that made me think about the laws themselves, and that to
be laws they have to be applicable for always, but in this scale that's
so massive that it almost doesn't matter anymore, like *the sun* kind of
massive, and really that's not the level of constancy that any relationship
demands, you know? Or any person. And you've been *right* to say that
I don't know for always, but then the *point* is that always isn't the scale
that makes any sense to use given where we are right now. So Tonya
was right too about it being about the present moment and things are
always shifting and changing and there's *no* law because the second you
learn something you're changed forever, and then everything's different
anyway, you know?"

Will was silent for a beat and then he nodded. "Yeah, totally."

"Yeah?" I let out a breath of pure relief.

"No! I have no fucking clue what you're talking about! Key terms
heard: sunrise yoga, which I really want to refer to a cocktail; flavor of love
which I think was a reality show on VH1; entropy, which I know is a band
and changed forever, which is what I *hope* this topic is about to be."

I giggled nervously. That did not go well.

"Can I get like even a Jeopardy category idea of what this conversation
is about?"

About fifteen cute, cheesy, romantic answers popped into my head
that I knew I could use to change the subject or alleviate the awkwardness.
A hundred ways I could give up. And then we could go back to watching
the extras, cuddling on Will's couch, which was pretty perfect just the way
it was. But I didn't.

"The Jeopardy category is 'Our Relationship.'"

"Ugh, is there anything *less* than a $100?"

I shook my head. "They're all Daily Doubles." I pushed the blanket
aside and kind of clambered into his lap. "Will, kiss me."

He kissed me tentatively, like maybe there was a catch.

"Okay, now lemme try again."

Will's sigh was long-suffering but he ran his fingers through my hair. I hadn't cut it all year and it had gotten pretty long.

"Babe…."

"No, let me. Okay. You tease me about being a romantic. And you're right. I like to imagine that things make sense. That everything isn't just chaos and meaninglessness. That things are predictable, or knowable."

"Like physics."

"Yeah, like physics. Where there are laws that govern things. Only, the thing about physics laws is that what makes them laws is that they're *so* enormous and universal that, yeah, they explain things, but they're also too big for those explanations to be super useful in the particular. Like, okay, sure, *gravity*, but, like, if my question is why did I fall down, then yeah, I know it was gravity in the universal sense, but what I *mean* is what the hell did I just trip over and who the hell left it there."

Will nodded, fingers still in my hair. Good, he was listening.

"So I've been thinking about it. The way being a romantic or whatever is kind of like saying that the universal laws, like gravity, are more important than the particular details, like who left the thing there. When really, it's a lot more like yoga than like physics. Where it's all about how things are in the present. Not because the future doesn't exist or because there's nothing bigger, but because every day we change just by being in the world and learning about ourselves."

Will's expression softened a little.

"And it's bigger than just you and me, actually. It's not how I want to *be*. Thinking that I know some right way to do things that ignores all the other ways. Not leaving room for, like, surprises and new possibilities, and changing my mind. And I definitely don't want to make someone else feel that way. Anyone else. It's scary. Not feeling like you know how things should be. But… a good scary, maybe? A necessary scary. It is for me, anyway," I said when Will jutted his jaw out in a yeah-right-nothing-scares-me expression.

"Okay, so anyway, I'm just gonna say this, and it's what *I* want. I'm not saying you have to agree, or even respond right away if you want to think about things or whatever. So. Here goes."

My heart felt like a candle flame guttering in the wind, and my stomach felt like someone had reached in and scooped it hollow. I squeezed my eyes shut the way I used to when Janie and I would ride the wooden roller coaster at Michigan's Adventure. Just at the apex of the hill, hovering in the air before we slid over the other side and hurtled downward, I would close my eyes and try to identify the exact tipping point when gravity acted on the combined weight of human and machine and dragged us down, screaming.

My voice was a whisper. "I… I love you. I want to be with you. I want to try. I want to figure out a way that we can both get what we want. And I guess I just want to know what it would take for you to want that too."

My heart was still pounding as my eyes fluttered open and the wave of adrenaline that had carried me through the last few seconds drained away, leaving me shaky and with a weird ringing in my ears. I ventured a quick look at Will. He was frowning.

"Will, did you hear me?"

"I don't understand," Will said slowly. And, wow, that was really not the response I wanted.

"Maybe I'm not explaining it well…." I swallowed hard.

"No." He shook his head frustratedly. "I thought… I…." He sounded confused in a deep way. Like, fundamentally confused. "I guess I thought we… were. After Holiday—after we—" He narrowed his eyes at me. "You said you understood. After you… fucked the geologist or whatever," he spat out. "You said you understood that I wasn't trying to hurt you. That night." He winced. "You… I thought you forgave me for that night."

Wait, what?

"Forgave you? For the Tiramisu Incident? There was nothing to forgive, Will. I mean, it was awful and I was upset and, okay, fucking heartbroken. But like you said at the time, you didn't break any promises to me. You had told me what the reality was and I was the one who was out of touch with it."

Will stood up suddenly, looming over me with his hands on his hips and his eyes fixed on mine.

"But you fucking left!"

"Well, yeah. I was sad as hell and embarrassed and it was too much, thinking of you with another guy. But that doesn't mean you were wrong."

"No." He spun away from me, hands fisted at his sides. "You left *me*! You… you fucking *left* me, Leo." His voice broke. I tried to pull him to face me but he wouldn't, so I stood up and walked in front of him. All I could see as he stared at the floor was the fall of blond hair and the tip of his nose.

"Hey."

I tried to tilt his chin up so I could see his face, but he shook me off.

"It was just sex with him."

"Yeah, I know, Will. You don't have to—"

Will's head snapped up and his eyes were a blaze of blue.

"It was just sex. It was *nothing*. You were my best friend. You were my best fucking friend and I'd told you the truth and you just *left* me. No more hanging out, no more talking or texts. No more… anything. That one moment meant more to you than every fucking thing we'd shared. That sex meant more to you than it ever could have to me. Because then you were just gone."

Oh Jesus.

Before the Tiramisu Incident, Will and I had been hanging out all the time, cooking, watching TV shows together, going all over the city together, having a lot of (I thought) hot sex. And all those things meant a *ton* to me. Had made me deliriously happy, which Will no doubt knew since it's not like I was super subtle about it. And during that, I had always known Will slept with other people, though I hadn't let myself think about it. But seeing it in the flesh *had* in some ways overpowered all the rest of what we'd shared.

And I had left him.

"I—you never said…."

"You told me not to! You told me you didn't want anything to do with me, Leo. And I understand, right: you were looking out for yourself. You were taking what you needed. And fuck if that isn't exactly what you should've done. It's what I'd been telling you to do all along. It just…." He jutted his chin out like he was preparing to take a punch and clenched his jaw.

"It hurt you."

He gave a shrug, absorbing it. It was like everything had polarized. *I* had hurt Will. I had hurt him with my absence. I had hurt him when I lied and said I could handle things the way they'd been when I knew that I couldn't. I'd hurt him and he hadn't said a thing. He'd respected my wishes and left me alone until… what? Until he absolutely couldn't anymore. And then I was the one he'd called. The first one. The only one.

"I'm so sorry, Will. Fuck, I'm so, so sorry I hurt you." I grabbed his arms and turned him so he was facing me. He sighed, still silent, but his muscles unclenched a little under my palms. I stayed that way until he finally looked at me.

"The thing is, though? When you told me you didn't want to be around me anymore."

"Couldn't. I *couldn't*. Not didn't want to." It was essential that he understood the difference.

"Okay," he conceded, "couldn't. That was the first time I believed that maybe I was wrong about what being in a relationship meant." He shook his head at himself.

"How do you mean?"

"I always saw them as the Borg, where the two of you just kind of sloshed into one being. Or that you had to sacrifice all the pieces of yourself that didn't fit with the other person. But you... didn't. You were totally yourself. Even though you wanted us to be in a relationship. Even though you knew getting upset about it wasn't what I would want. I don't know, maybe that makes me a total dick. But it made me kind of hope that it was possible. Autonomy *and* a relationship."

"Wow," I said.

"What, you think it does make me a total dick?"

"No. Well, when you put it like that, I guess it kind of makes you a total dick that you realized it *when* we broke up. Or—sorry, I mean, not broke up. Stopped being whatever we were being. But, no, I was gonna say, wow, Rex was right."

"Huh? Rex. About what?"

"Oh, um, well...." I gave a nervous laugh. "I kinda... asked Daniel for advice. About you. Us, I mean. And Rex was there because, duh, he lives there, and he overheard and, yeah. It was the night I got home from Holiday. You were still there and I didn't want to bug you about like, What Does It All Mean, because you were handling everything with Claire and the kids.

"But I was dying, seriously. Like, chugged five Cokes and couldn't sit still dying over not knowing where we stood. Point is, Rex told me that just because you seem fearless about being blunt to people doesn't mean you don't get scared and resist saying stuff about yourself. Anyway...."

Will was glaring.

"Fuckin' Rex," he muttered, shaking his head.

I stepped closer to him and slid my arms around his neck, wanting the closeness, the feel of him. "It's just... I want... I *want* you to tell me that stuff."

"I *do*," Will insisted. "I do tell you stuff. I called you about Claire even though you'd told me you basically never wanted to see me again!"

"You're right." I bit my lip, trying to figure out how to explain what I meant. "I just… I want…. Okay, you know how you tell me what you want when we're, uh, you know—"

"Having sex?"

"Yeah."

"Yes," Will said, and he wrapped the word around his tongue like a caress, like maybe he thought he was about to distract me from this discussion.

"Right, well, I love when you do that. When you tell me what you want, what you like. Even if I don't… give it to you right away, I always want to know it. I like knowing where we stand. I feel—I don't know, *free* when I don't have to wonder. I don't have to worry about whether I'm pleasing you or question where we stand. I'd rather fight with you than not know what you think."

Will looked uncertain. "But you *do* know me, that's what I'm saying. You know me better than… anyone. I mean, hell, you're a scientist, you collect data. You're great at figuring it all out."

"I don't want to *have* to conduct a science experiment to know how you feel! Do you know how shitty it is to say that to me? Like it's one hundred percent my responsibility to… *study* you? That I'm supposed to look at everything you do and draw my own conclusions and act based on them with no confirmation? Why? Why would you want it to be like that?"

And it hit me with a twist of nausea that this was how Will thought things *had* to be. That he'd grown up watching for signs of what things might mean. Clues. Were his parents going to be distracted enough with each other that he could take money from them to go buy whatever he wanted at the grocery store? Was Claire in a mood where he needed to tell her this thing or that one in order to handle a situation? Was someone giving him something because of how he looked or on his merit?

Will had become so adept at reading the signs that it never occurred to him to say something if he thought he'd already communicated it in another way. With a gesture or an eye roll, a pattern or a habit. Words were just a redundancy to him. Like the time I pointed out that there were bananas and he got pissy because he could see them.

And maybe there Rex was right again. If I took away what Will had never said as well as what he had, I was left with someone who hung out with me, had sex with me, hugged me, joked with me, ate with me, slept with me, and told me about his day. I was left with… someone who acted like we were together.

I took his hands and pulled him back down on the couch.

"Okay, so, it's not about me being dumb or oblivious. It's not that I don't notice things about you." I rolled my eyes at myself. "I basically notice every stupid little thing about you, so. But sometimes things are complicated and they mean different things to different people, and I don't want to assume that I know something about you just because I think I do, you know? Because sometimes I'll get it wrong. Sometimes you're not as obvious as you think you are, or sometimes my perception of stuff is more about me than about you, honestly. Like, if I'm feeling shitty about stuff, I might read something you did differently than if I'm feeling great, you know?"

"Yes, I understand. I'm not a sociopath. Even though you're basically making me feel like Patrick Bateman over here."

"Okay, good! See? Great example of how sometimes people feel things differently." He glared at me. "I just mean, I wasn't trying to say you were a sociopathic serial killer—although actually that scene with the business cards I can totally see—"

He snorted a laugh.

"But that's what I'm *saying*, Will. I wasn't trying to be patronizing. I was trying to explain how there is no, like, *truth* that we both share on anything. There are just so many ways it can go wrong to assume that we know what each other are thinking."

"God, did you read Nietzsche this semester or something?"

"Um. No? Okay, but so the point is that even when you think you're communicating something, I might not get it. Also, though, I just…." I twined our fingers together. "I want to hear you say things. Like, I know I'm a dork or whatever, and I'm skinny and clumsy and you think I'm all overenthusiastic or not cool enough and stuff. So maybe sometimes when there's something about me that you *do* like, you could… I dunno, tell me. Just to balance things out a little bit. Maybe."

I looked down at our hands, Will's beautifully proportioned and nimble, with neat, clean nails, and mine, long fingers interrupted by knobby knuckles and various nicks and smudges from being clumsy, fingernails bitten down roughly.

"Leo." Will said my name in that way he had that felt like a whole conversation in one word. And, shit, how had I not noticed how eloquent he sometimes was without saying anything at all.

He pulled me toward him, and I kind of draped my legs over his until we were sitting the way I'd sat as a child on the swings with Janie, each of us facing in opposite directions, one of us always moving backward while the other moved forward.

Will looked at me with soft eyes. "I like a lot of things about you," he said. "I'd be saying things an awful lot if I always commented on them."

"Yeah?" I grinned at him, and he rolled his eyes at me. I couldn't help myself. "Okay, will you tell me just one?"

Will searched my face and ran a finger over my eyebrow as he started to say something.

"Wait, wait, but make it a really good one," I interrupted. "I mean, if it's just gonna be one."

"I was about to say some flattering romantic shit to you, and you interrupt me to tell me how to do it?"

"Well we've already established you don't know how to do it right." I grinned at him.

"Oh yeah, good thing you told me because I guess what I was going to say wasn't actually *that* good."

"Aw, no, wait, but now you have to tell me."

Will pursed his lips and shook his head. "Nah, you clearly didn't want to hear."

I pouted at him, and he smiled, but his finger went back to my eyebrow again.

"Your eyebrows do this thing," he said, slowly pressing his fingertip to the inside of my eyebrow, "when you feel something really intensely. And sometimes all I have to do when you're talking, or when you're looking at something, or when I'm touching you, is look right here—" He tapped the spot. "—and I can tell if you're kidding, or if you're upset, or if you're about to come. The whole rest of your face can lie sometimes. But this never does.

"And the night that you came over and I was with that guy?"

I bit my lip and Will smoothed my eyebrow.

"All I had to do was look right here, and I knew I'd fucked up in this major way I couldn't take back. Not because I did anything wrong," he said quickly when I started to protest that again. "But because I'd hurt you in this deep way that I never intended."

Will gritted his teeth. His eyes were a little wild, and he squeezed my hands.

"Look, you have to understand, okay. I don't discount the effects my behavior has. I'm not… I'm not oblivious either. And I'm not my sister. I can control what I do. I'm just so *fucking* scared that if I do this—if we do this… I have to know that we're both being honest about what's okay. Not like before."

Shame washed over me for how much I'd hurt Will by trying to give him what I thought he'd wanted. I nodded silently.

"I can try not sleeping with other people," he went on, "but I don't know if I can promise it forever. I don't know what will happen in the future. And I can't fucking take it if you leave me again because you were making us something in your head that we aren't."

"Are you serious?"

"Yeah, I'm fucking serious. I wasn't okay when you told me to fuck off. I was…." He sighed. "I wasn't good. At all."

I had actually meant was he serious that he'd try not sleeping with other people, but I'd be damned if I was going to make him regret admitting he'd been a mess without me.

"And you'd… you'd want to try. With me? With just me? For now?"

"Yeah, I'll try." Then a strange look came over his face. "I didn't mean it like that. I didn't mean it would be a hardship to only have sex with you. That's—that's not what I meant. It's not about sex between us at all. It's… it's separate, you know. It's about me. I… we're great at sex."

"We are?"

He rolled his eyes. "Quit fishing, I just said so, didn't I?"

"'Kay." I smiled at him and he smiled grudgingly back.

"I *still* don't think that I'm the only person *you'll* ever want to sleep with," he said, like he couldn't stand to let us just be happy for a minute.

"I think we've already covered the we're-not-sure-what-the-future-holds bit."

"Fine," he said.

"Fine." I glared down at Will, whose face was set in a defiant sneer. It was the arms-crossed-over-the-chest of facial expressions, and I did the only thing I could think to do with that stupid sneer. I kissed it. Just a peck in the corner of his stupid mouth, but his arms came around me, and as always, the taste of him drew me in.

"Soooo," I said a minute later, pulling away. "What does this mean?"

"This—" He pressed his hips up so his hard cock ground against mine. "—means shut the hell up and fuck me."

"'Kay, in a minute, but seriously."

Will groaned. "Seriously, what? What more do you want me to say?"

My first thought was that I knew exactly what I wanted him to say. The three words that I'd let loose like hellhounds a few minutes before and that Will had barely even seemed to register. But if I thought about it— really thought about it....

"I want you to say whatever you're thinking. For real, though."

I pushed myself off Will, and he winced when I accidentally elbowed him in the ribs. He ran a hand through his hair and threw his head back, addressing his words to the ceiling.

"Look, I don't have a lot of answers here, okay? I am very aware that I'm not the easiest person to be around sometimes, and you're... well, you're not exactly a paragon of experience yourself. And I reserve the right to find other people desirable. And to, like, renegotiate shit down the line."

"Okay, great, fine, and I reserve the right to maybe want only you and for you to not act like that's me lying to myself."

Will nodded, though I could tell this part made him uncomfortable. That he couldn't believe someone could want only him.

"Okaaaay," I said, "so we've established that neither of us knows what we're doing, so we both just have to trust that we know what we want right now and that what we want might change?"

"I... guess so?"

"So are we... together?"

Will rolled his eyes so hard I was surprised he didn't have an aneurysm. "What, you want to update your Facebook status?"

"I don't even have Facebook, you fucker." I shoved at Will's shoulder. "But like... just *say* I did, what would I be updating my status to?"

"It's complicated," Will mocked in a singsongy voice. I elbowed him. "How about 'Leo is now in a relationship with Thai Food'?"

"Huh, you totally have Facebook, don't you?"

"Whatever, Claire set it up for me a hundred years ago."

"Wiiiiill," I whined.

"Leooooo," he whined back.

I climbed on top of him again, snaking my hand down his pants. "Well, you should be happy, anyway. This was, like, the absolute *least* romantic getting-together moment of all time. I should just go offer myself to Viggo

Mortensen," I told him, kissing his jaw. "He'd totally update his Facebook profile to include me."

Will groaned like maybe the thought of me with Viggo Mortensen was kind of doing it for him, and arched up underneath me. I leaned down slowly, loving the way he tilted his chin up so our mouths met, like his lips were just waiting for mine. I put a hand on either side of his face, holding him still. His golden lashes fluttered open, and his brows drew together.

"Why did you do it?" I asked him slowly. His brow wrinkled in confusion. "In Holiday. Why did you really kiss me?"

Will pushed me off so he could sit up.

"I shouldn't have," he said so softly I could barely hear him.

I sighed.

"I didn't say I didn't want to," he muttered.

I pulled him to look at me, willing him to give me something.

"Look, I don't have a good answer for you, Leo."

"Just tell me the truth."

"You were honest and sweet and infuriatingly hot, and I wanted you to want me. It seemed like if someone like you could like me, then maybe it would mean I was worth liking."

I gaped at him.

"That morning, I was packing my stuff up at Claire's and she was upset that I was leaving, even though I'd been telling her for days, and I was too tired to get into it with her. She said, 'You make it so easy for people to hate you. It's the only thing you never fight about.' I just… I wanted you be different. I wanted you to like me, okay? And that was the only way I could think to do it. And then when I kissed you—" He shook his head sharply. "I knew I'd made a big mistake."

My stomach sank a little at that, even after all these months and everything that had happened between us since then. When he spoke again, his voice was rough.

"Because I was the one who ended up wanting you."

He looked down, and I couldn't quite catch my breath.

"You promised," he said, still looking down. I bit my lip as guilt washed through me again. "You promised that when you found out I wasn't the… the fantasy you wanted that I wouldn't lose my best friend. But I did. The thing is… I knew I would. I knew it would all go to shit and I would lose you and I would miss you and it would suck, and I did it fucking anyway. Because I wanted you. I didn't know how exactly, but I just… I wanted you, Leo. I always wanted you."

He bit his lip and took my face in his hands like he had that first time. He leaned in slowly and we kissed and kissed and kissed.

Chapter 19

May

"OH JESUS, no. No. No fucking way," Milton said. "Hard limit. Just no."

We were standing in the kitchen of an apartment where Melissa, one of the seniors in Milton's acting class, lived. She was leaving for the summer going on tour with some Disney cruise or something, and was offering to let us rent it cheap. We'd dragged our asses out of bed at seven in the morning on the day after finals to look at the place because she had to go to a 9:00 a.m. training on the particulars of how to comport oneself while in Disney costume on the ship or something.

"It's not a big deal," Melissa said. "You just stomp when you come into the kitchen and they totally scatter. Little fuckers." She kicked at a roach that was skittering down the side of the cabinet. "They mostly stay in the kitchen, anyway. And the bathroom," she said upon consideration. "Well, and sometimes—"

"Dude," Thomas said to Milton. "I know you don't want to, like, be dependent on your folks anymore or whatever, but…."

Milton sighed.

"Roaches are fascinating," Charles said, peering at one that was poised at the corner of the doorframe. "Did you know some of the largest ones fly? Strange. They seem so grounded. Armored. But I suppose so are planes."

Andy and Thomas conversed in glances, Andy's saying, "Yo, your friend is weird as hell," and Thomas' answering, "Yeah, but he's not so bad once you get used to it."

"Maybe we should just check Craigslist," I offered.

We had really left looking for a place until it was too late, none of us quite making it from thought to action, even though we'd been talking about living together for the better part of a month.

We trudged back to the dorms in low spirits, deciding we needed sustenance in order to sort out the whole mess. We only had two more days before we needed to vacate our rooms, so whatever we were going to find, it had to be quick.

"Hey, how was it?" Gretchen asked, finishing her oatmeal as we dropped down at our usual table in the corner of the dining hall.

"Remember the *Felicity* where she and Ben move in together and she rents the place with all the roaches?"

Gretchen nodded, wrinkling her nose.

"Well it was like that," Milton said. "Only worse because no Ben."

"Yikes. Well, good luck, guys. I'm going to meet Layne. She's taking me on a picnic in Central Park." Gretchen grinned and scuffed her toe.

"Aww," Thomas and Milton chorused.

"But we're on for tomorrow night, right?"

We were going to smuggle all the food out of the dining hall that we could and then hole up in our room (Charles had returned the filing cabinet to the hallway and largely deconstructed the FBI profiler wall above his desk since finals had ended). We had the second half of the final season of *Felicity* to watch, and we were going to marathon it as our farewell to the year. Milton had seen it before, of course, but the rest of us had all laid bets on how things would end.

"You guys," Milton had said repeatedly. "You guys, you have *no* idea how intense shit's about to get."

"I Wikipediaed it," Charles said, shrugging, "and I don't understand why—" Milton practically flew across the table to clap his hand over Charles' mouth.

"Say not one single word," Milton hissed.

"We are absolutely on," I said to Gretchen, and she gathered her dishes and walked off toward the door, hair almost white in the bright sun that streamed through the windows.

We spent the next hour combing through Craigslist properties. It was becoming increasingly clear that the things Milton had told us about our real estate options were inaccurate and likely gleaned from overhearing conversations among people with a lot more money than us.

A few hours later, I was officially exhausted and completely demoralized. We'd traipsed to four apartments, each one more horrible than the last. There was one place we all loved, but when we tried to sign the lease, it turned out that the Craigslist poster had transposed the first two numbers of the rent on the announcement. He apologized profusely and said that explained why he'd gotten so many calls about the place, but the fact remained that it was now about a thousand dollars out of our price range.

As I walked past Washington Square Park, the white arch against blue sky funneled me in. My phone rang as I dropped down under a tree and when I swiped to answer, Daniel's face was looking at me, shocked.

"Holy... what did you... how are you on my phone?" he said, shaking it.

"Dude, you FaceTimed me."

"What the shit is a face time?"

"You video called me instead of regular calling me. Like Skype."

"Shit, that's a thing?"

I nodded as he paced around the room. "Um, you're kind of giving me vertigo. Can you either sit still or just regular call me."

"Oh, sorry." He threw himself down on the couch. "Where are you?" He cocked his head, squinting at the phone.

"Washington Square Park." I tilted the phone so he could see the arch and then the fountain.

"Oh, nice."

We chatted for a bit and swapped finals horror stories. One of his students had asked for an extension on a paper because his roommate accidentally took mushrooms and then dropped his computer out their window on the tenth floor.

"How do you *accidentally* take mushrooms?"

"I don't think he *took* them accidentally," Daniel said. "I think he probably just misestimated their efficacy."

"Did you give him the extension?"

"Yeah. I mean, Jesus. Living with people sounds like utter hell."

Since Daniel had never lived in the dorms while he was in college, he had been fascinated all year to hear my stories of the bizarre goings-on there.

"Well you *do* live with someone, you know."

"Oh, well, but Rex isn't someone." I could see the softness that always crept into Daniel's voice when he mentioned Rex in his eyes too. "He redid all the cabinets this weekend." He pointed the phone into the kitchen where I could see exactly nothing because he wasn't holding his hand still or angling the screen right.

"You'll have to give me the grand tour in person."

"Oh, right, right, that's why I called. So, do you want to come next weekend or the weekend after? Either is fine, but Rex is doing this workshop at the queer youth group where Colin volunteers next Saturday, so he just wouldn't be around for some of it."

"Oh man, how's stuff going with you and Colin?"

"The same, really. It's good, but kinda awkward. He never comes here because he says he can tell that Rex still hates him. Basically true. But Rafe and Rex actually get along really well—they're ridiculous together. Like, Rafe will talk super seriously about something and explain the whole thing and then ask Rex what he thinks, and Rex will say like five words, but of course they're so perfectly true, and Rafe actually gets him, so he'll just sit there and be like, 'Huh. Yes. That's true.' And then they'll both sit there and think about shit together."

"Can I meet them when I visit?"

"Yeah, sure. You'll think they're weird. Rafe has like zero sense of humor, and Colin will probably do magic tricks for you."

"Um. Yeah, that is weird. Okay, so weekend after next sounds good. Hopefully I won't be homeless by then."

I filled Daniel in on our fruitless search for an apartment.

"Ugh, what a shit show. You should go to res life. They usually have a list of buildings around campus that do deals with students who are staying in the summer."

"Seriously? Oh god, thank you, you're a life saver."

At the far end of the park a camera crew was setting up, clearing an area for a group of women in colorful saris who began to dance, their movements made magical by the spray of the fountain.

"Hey, so, listen," I said just before we hung up. "Um. What if I could convince Will to come to Philly with me? Would that be cool? I mean, I don't know if I'll be able to, but. Just in case."

"So… does that mean you guys are like…. What does that mean?"

"We're gonna try being… a thing or whatever." My grin was so huge it was kind of hurting my face.

Daniel got this almost sappy expression on his face.

"Aw, man. That's great. I know it's what you wanted. Also, PS, if that fucker does anything to you, I'll—"

"Yeah, yeah, I know. Thanks. Really, thanks."

He nodded, but then his expression soured.

"Ugh, so I guess that means we'll have to try and get along better." His mouth was in a resentful pout. "So, okay, yeah, sure, bring Mini-Skarsgård, whatever."

"You know he calls you the Prince of Poetry."

Daniel scowled and muttered something that sounded like "pretty boy model asshole bullshit," but I couldn't be sure.

HAVING DONE all the laundry I'd been hoarding during the last month, I was idly packing my clothes while Charles and I listened to *Serial*, pausing it every few minutes to argue about what was going on.

I'd texted Milton to go to res life since he had already packed, and he'd gotten leads on three really good options for apartments. We were going to go see them the next morning.

I couldn't believe the year was over. It was kind of how I felt when I sank into watching a really immersive TV show—like I couldn't imagine the characters and settings not being parts of my life—and then it was over. Only, unlike a show, there was no real climax.

I was glad we had a concrete activity tonight to celebrate the end of the year. Besides, I was actually dying to see how *Felicity* turned out. Will could say whatever he wanted about how it was unrealistic to expect life to be like fiction, but I was pretty sure most people would agree it feels better to have some kind of closure. Some way of marking a momentous occasion.

WILL TEXTED while I was in the middle of packing, a strangely elliptical text asking me to meet him at the planetarium at five. When I wrote back to ask why, he just said, *Duh, what do you think you do at a planetarium.*

When I got there, he took my arm and led me inside. He seemed tense and kind of irritable, which wasn't that unusual, but he didn't generally invite me to do stuff when he was irritable.

"I watched that scene in *Rebel Without a Cause*," I told him as the lights dimmed.

"Just the scene? Oy vey, the younger generation." But he slid his hand onto my thigh and settled into his seat as the show started. I leaned my head against Will's shoulder and breathed in his smell, and his hand tightened on my thigh. The stars were as interesting as ever, but Will was clearly distracted, which made me unsure why he'd invited me.

After the show let out, we lingered in the park, Will still seeming fidgety even though we were outside. He kept fiddling with his phone and didn't seem to hear me when I asked if he wanted to get food.

Finally, assuming he was just in a mood, I said, "Okay, well thanks for taking me to the show," and leaned in to kiss his cheek, ready to go back to the dorms and leave him to his brooding. When I went for a peck, though, he grabbed my hand almost painfully. I raised my eyebrows at him as if to say *What is your problem today?* Finally, he jerked a folded piece of paper out of his back pocket and thrust it at me.

"Here," he said, holding on for a second after I'd taken it so I had to tug it from his fingers. He made a sound like *Ugh* and a waving me off gesture, then stuck his hands in his pockets and half turned away.

I opened the paper, feeling the residual heat from Will's body. It was a color print-off from a website. At first glance it looked like a star chart and I thought it had something to do with the show we'd just seen, but when I looked closer….

"Oh. My. God."

"Oh, just shut up about it, okay? I just thought you'd like it."

"Oh my *god*, you bought me a *star*?"

The paper was a certificate printed out from a website called StarRegistry, declaring me to be the proud owner of a star called The Shire.

"*Wiiiiiiill*," I whined, grabbing his arm and bouncing up and down on my toes. "You made a romantic gesture!"

Will looked like he was about to vomit.

"Okay," he said, "whatever, the point is that you should just stay with me this summer. It's stupid to waste your money on an apartment with those guys. Besides, you'll be so busy with two jobs that you won't have time to do anything else, and it's supposed to be your summer vacation, so whatever. It's cheaper if you just stay with me."

I couldn't believe what I was hearing. Little bubbles of joy started to rise in my stomach and chest like champagne. I couldn't stop bouncing, and the moment stretched out as vast as a galaxy. There was me, standing there, my arms tethering me to Will, and there was Will, holding something out to me that was as delicate as starlight and as ineffable.

Where once I would have grabbed at it, only to watch my hands slide through nothing, now I just watched it, appreciating everything it illuminated.

Will was eyeing me suspiciously, lower lip caught in his teeth. I shook my head, forcing myself to stop bouncing.

"Gonna need a little more than 'it's cheaper,'" I told him with a smirk, still holding on to his arm. Star or no star, I wasn't about to impose myself on Will for three months if he was just letting me stay out of pity or because he was jealous I might live with someone who had a crush on me.

I mean, okay, I was mostly just giving him shit. Obviously, I wanted to stay with him. I just wanted him to say it nicely.

Clearly I had underestimated either Will's level of irritation at having done anything that could be construed as romantic or Will's level of nervousness about asking me to live with him, though, because he was *no* amused by my teasing at all.

"Oh my god," he said, throwing up his arms and breaking my hold on him in the process. "Haven't we been through this?! What do you want me to say to you? That you're my sun, my moon, my starlit sky, and without you I dwell in darkness?"

That took a moment to register, especially since stars were kind of on topic, but then….

"Are you… are you quoting *Willow* to me right now?!"

Will rolled his eyes. "I mean!" And he gestured at the star, like he'd bought himself a certain amount of leeway with it. Which is probably exactly what he'd been trying to do. To, as usual, let a gesture stand in for having to say how he felt.

"Will," I said, trying not to laugh at how upset he was. "Is it really so hard to say those things? I mean, not *those* things, obviously. But… is it really so hard for you to just tell me why you want me to stay with you?"

Will purposely ignored the last part of my comment. "You actually want someone to say shit to you just because it sounds like a line from some romance?"

"No! I think we've established that I don't need you to be… is it Val Kilmer? Jesus, you know that movie's from before I was even born, right? Anyway, I just… come on. Can't you just tell me how you feel?"

Again, Will gestured wildly between himself and me and the paper I held clutched in my hand. He was angry for real now. I could tell the difference.

But this time I wasn't backing down. It was too important. I wasn't going to let there be one more thing between us that lingered unsaid, guessed at, talked around. So I just stood there and waited. Will glared at me, clearly expecting that I would fill the silence like I usually did, but I raised my eyebrows at him. Will's elegant nostrils flared, and he narrowed his eyes at me.

"You *know* how I feel. I don't believe for one *second* that you don't!"

Now I was getting pissed too. Pissed that he would deny me a simple explanation, pissed that he thought I was still enough of a pushover to let him get away with it, and pissed that he'd clearly planned the planetarium trip as an emotional shortcut—using the romantic gestures I'd once wanted to soften me up so I wouldn't force him to express the feelings behind them

"Then why can't you just say it, Will? Just tell me why, and don't you dare say money!"

"Christ! Do you want me to arrange a fucking flash mob for you too?" Will spat. "Or—oh!—get us on the kiss cam at Madison Square Garden! How about that?"

His face was flushed as he leaned toward me, hands on his hips, and yelled.

"Exactly *how* much audience participation would you like there to be when I tell you that I fucking want you with me, huh? Tell me! Give me a number of exactly how many fucking people you need to witness me tell you that I *want* you to come live with me this summer! That I'll miss the shit out of you if I don't get to see you because you're too busy working two jobs! That I want to come home from work in the evenings and get to fucking hang out with you and watch those—god *damn*—those *stupid* fucking DVD extras? Just a ballpark fucking figure of how many goddamn people you need to hear me tell you that I fucking love you, Leo!"

Will fell silent, fists clenched, as people around us stared. After a moment, he narrowed his eyes in mortification and looked up slowly, cheeks burning, at the crowd that had gathered around us. One man walking a dog started to clap. He was quickly joined by a lady jogging, and soon everyone who had overheard was clapping and whistling.

"Oh my fucking god," Will whispered.

My heart was pounding, and my skin felt like it couldn't contain me. My breath came fast and my head felt light, like at the very end of a long yoga class when every worry I'd carried in with me had been purged in sweat.

I looked at Will, his cheeks flushed, his hair mussed, and his expression mortified. And none of it mattered. Because there, in the twist of his mouth and the corners of his eyes, I saw it. The truth. That I *was* his sun and his moon and his damn starlit sky. That, without me, maybe he did dwell in a little bit more darkness than with me. He might never say it. But, goddamn, his version of it was way, way better.

Then I looked around us and started giggling.

"Um, maybe like… I'd say about fifteen would probably do it. No, definitely more like twenty." I gave a little nod and grin at the people who had gathered around us.

One guy had a phone out and was filming us—from behind Will, thankfully, because the last thing I needed right now was for Will to go ballistic and get arrested for assaulting some tourist.

"Oh my god, just kill me please," Will said, the applause making it hard for me to hear him.

I closed the distance between us in one step, the Vans he got me for my birthday touching the toes of his designer sneakers, our shadows overlapping on the ground as I reached for him, creating a shadow deeper than either of them on their own.

"Sometimes I want to," I said. "And then you buy me stars and declare your love for me in public and ask me to move in with you, because you're *so* romantic."

I could see the glare start to form in Will's eyes, the edge of the snarl on his lips as he prepared to fight. So before he could, I pulled him to me, held him at the waist, and dipped him backward so he had to grab my shoulders to keep from falling.

And then—like an iconic photograph, a movie musical, the swooniest of swoony romance novel covers—I kissed the hell out of Will Highland in front of a crowd, on a spring afternoon in Central Park, as the city came alive around us.

ROAN PARRISH is currently wandering between Philadelphia and New Orleans. When not writing, she can usually be found cutting her friends' hair, meandering through whatever city she's in while listening to torch songs and melodic death metal, or cooking overly elaborate meals. She loves bonfires, winter beaches, minor chord harmonies, and self-tattooing. One time she may or may not have baked a six-layer chocolate cake and then thrown it out the window in a fit of pique.

Website: www.roanparrish.com
Twitter: @RoanParrish
E-mail: roanparrish@gmail.com
Facebook: www.facebook.com/roanparrish
Pinterest: www.pinterest.com/ARoanParrish
Instagram: www.instagram.com/roanparrish
Newsletter signup: eepurl.com/bmJUbr

IN THE MIDDLE OF
SOMEWHERE

Roan Parrish

Middle of Somewhere: Book One

Daniel Mulligan is tough, snarky, and tattooed, hiding his self-consciousness behind sarcasm. Daniel has never fit in—not at home in Philadelphia with his auto mechanic father and brothers, and not at school where his Ivy League classmates looked down on him. Now, Daniel's relieved to have a job at a small college in Holiday, Northern Michigan, but he's a city boy through and through, and it's clear that this small town is one more place he won't fit in.

Rex Vale clings to routine to keep loneliness at bay: honing his muscular body, perfecting his recipes, and making custom furniture. Rex has lived in Holiday for years, but his shyness and imposing size have kept him from connecting with people.

When the two men meet, their chemistry is explosive, but Rex fears Daniel will be another in a long line of people to leave him, and Daniel has learned that letting anyone in can be a fatal weakness. Just as they begin to break down the walls keeping them apart, Daniel is called home to Philadelphia, where he discovers a secret that changes the way he understands everything.

www.dreamspinnerpress.com

OUT OF NOWHERE

ROAN PARRISH

Middle of Somewhere: Book Two

The only thing in Colin Mulligan's life that makes sense is taking cars apart and putting them back together. In the auto shop where he works with his father and brothers, he tries to get through the day without having a panic attack or flying into a rage. Drinking helps. So does running and lifting weights until he can hardly stand. But none of it can change the fact that he's gay, a secret he has kept from everyone.

Rafael Guerrera has found ways to live with the past he's ashamed of. He's dedicated his life to social justice work and to helping youth who, like him, had very little growing up. He has no time for love. Hell, he barely has time for himself. Somehow, everything about miserable, self-destructive Colin cries out to him. But down that path lie the troubles Rafe has worked so hard to leave behind. And as their relationship intensifies, Rafe and Colin are forced to dredge up secrets that both men would prefer stay buried.

www.dreamspinnerpress.com